Z-ROD

Part 3: Fire-Bearers

A Celtic saga of warriors and saints

The greater your destiny, the greater the price
Celtic proverb

Martin C. Haworth

To Alastair,
Enjoy the finale!
Best Wishes
Martin

malcolm down

PUBLISHING

First published 2023 by Malcolm Down Publishing Ltd
www.malcolmdown.co.uk

British Library Cataloguing in Publication Data
A catalogue record for this book is available from the British Library.

ISBN 978-1-915046-52-9

Cover design and Celtic geometrical designs by Meg Daniels
www.bergamotbrown.com

The maps and Pictish images are drawn by the author.

Art direction by Sarah Grace

Printed in the UK

Commendations

With *Fire-Bearers* Martin C. Haworth's Z-Rod trilogy reaches a climax. This vivid imagining of war and peace in 6th century Scotland immerses us in the landscape of Pict and Gael, and in the ideological conflict between the old beliefs centred on the Bulàch and her druidic priesthood and the new spirituality brought by the High King's servants, the monks.

It's a story of prophets and prophecies, signs and visions, conflict with darkness, a quest for a new (and yet ancient) wisdom. As we turn the pages, we are there with our ancestors, observing as beliefs shape lives, and then are tested in action.

There's a lengthy, sure-footed description of a Pictish fort under siege from the vicious king Brude. A gripping description of a monk's perilous voyage in a coracle as death seems inevitable. Then the climactic drama of the one who was to bring 'fire to the north' standing at the entrance to a chambered cairn as the winter solstice sun pierces its very heart, recognizing that his time has come.

We read on eagerly to see how characters cope under pressure, how crises are resolved. Can the many obstacles to love be removed for the characters who briefly held hands at the very beginning of the trilogy? Does King Brude come to acknowledge a greater King? Can a treacherous cousin ever be forgiven? And what of the prophecy that the humble hero will 'return east with great peace'?

This novel is informed by Martin C. Haworth's painstaking research and familiarity with the terrain where *Fire-Bearers* is set. And he is able to enter into the state of mind both of those whose life is shaped by obedience to the Bulàch and those who have responded to the High King's Presence.

Fire-Bearers is an absorbing story from remote history which nevertheless has profound implications for readers today. This book has the potential to change lives.

Dr John Dempster, Highland News columnist

This is a TRUE story, in that attitudes and actions can have consequences. Time and again we are faced with events we are powerless to prepare for. People are more complicated than they themselves have recognised. There are different ways to be strong.

'Z-Rod' is timeless, but feels very *now*. Its detail keeps the happenings vivid and unexpected. Leaders prioritise their personal ambition. But when do dreams and decisions become destiny? Are old prophecies sometimes a curse? or promises to keep? This final volume will not disappoint.

Andy Raine, Northumbria Community

Contents

Characters featured in the story

(arranged in alphabetical order)

Adda – male refugee.

Aleine Brona – crippled girl on Inis Kayru.

Alpia – Conchen's great niece and Oengus's wife.

Aniel – hermit near Dindurn.

Brendan – missionary saint famous for navigating to far distant lands.

Broichan – druid in Brude's court.

Brude – warlord of the Fortriu and overlord of the northern Picts.

Caltram – Oengus's son.

Carvorst – the ferryman.

Coblaith and Elpin – Ce peasants who provided refuge for Taran.

Colmcille – (known as Columba in Latin) – missionary saint at Iona.

Conall – king of Dal Riata after Gabran.

Conchen – great aunt to Alpia and Oengus.

Cynbel – warlord of the Circinn.

Derile – Oengus's sister and widow of Cynbel, the Circinn warlord.

Domech – warlord of the Fotla with seat of power at Dindurn.

Domelch – Taran's mother.

Drostan – Taran's pseudonym, later adopted as his new name.

Drust – Oengus's deputy commander.

Drustan – Alpia's first son.

Drusticc – Oengus's mother.

Eithni – Oengus's first wife.

Fillan – abbot of Dindurn.

Fotel – druid at Meini Heyon y Pentir.

Gabran – king of Dal Riata.

Garn – formerly Taran's pet dog, cross bred with a wolf.

Gest – Maelchon's druid assistant.

Kessog – Fillan's martyred mentor.

Maelchon – chief druid at Rhynie.

Maevis – chief priestess of the Bulàch.

Mongfind – matriarch of the Ce.

Munait (Maon) – son of Elpin and Coblaith.

Nechtan – Taran's father.

Nola – midwife in Rhynie.

Oengus – warlord of the Ce.

Ossian – ex-itinerant bard now turned hermit.

Rowena – Alpia's daughter.

Taran – exiled prince and pilgrim, also known as Drostan.

Talorc – Taran's rebel brother.

Talorgen – former warlord of the Ce.

Map of 'Scotland' in the 6ᵗʰ century AD

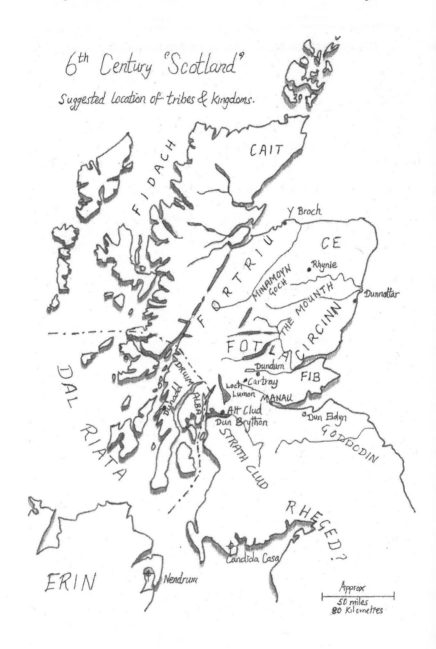

6ᵗʰ Century 'Scotland'

Suggested location of tribes & kingdoms.

CAIT

FIDACH

Y Broch

CE

FORTRIU

MINAMOYN GOCH

Rhynie

THE MOUNTH

Dunnottar

FOTLA

CIRCINN

Dundurn

FIB

Loch Cartray

Lumon

MANAU

DAL

Donald DRUIM ALBA

Alt Clud

Dun Brython

Dun Eidyn

GODDODIN

RIATA

STRATH CLUD

RHEGED?

ERIN

Nendrum

Candida Casa

Approx
50 miles
80 Kilometres

Taran's Travels

1. Inis Gemaich.
2. Meini Heyon y Pentir.
3. The Ring of Brodgar.

Acknowledgements

Again, a heartfelt thanks to Andy Raine and Dr John Dempster for their endorsement of the Z-Rod Series, valuing as always, their commendation, and for Andy's guidance on the Celtic expression of faith. A special gratitude to Malcolm Duff for assisting with an initial edit of this volume, and to Meg Daniels for another iconic illustration concluding this series of covers. I am grateful to those whose enthusiasm for the first two parts of this trilogy also encouraged me to conclude this project.

Dedication

To my wife, Alexandra, for her keenness to see the trilogy completed and published when it seemed pursuing publication was an egotistical undertaking given the obscurity of these books out in the world. I am indebted to her belief and her patience over the many months spent bringing this project to a conclusion.

Also, to our beautiful collie, Spartikades Keristophanes (Sparkie), whose last day started by my side on the day I completed this book in which references are made on the significance of his companionship.

Synopsis of Books 1 & 2:
Chosen Wanderers &
Heirs of Promise

This is the third and concluding part of the Z-Rod Series. The first book, *Chosen Wanderers*, tells how cousins Taran and Oengus are driven apart by the marking of the Z-rod on Taran's back, a mysterious Pictish power symbol, reserved exclusively for the warlord. After the loss of lives in an ambush, a council is convened at which Oengus's dying father names Taran as a traitor. The chief druid leads the main characters to his mentor's crannog to determine a dire remedy. Sensing that he is to be sacrificed, Taran makes good his escape despite his cousin's efforts to kill him.

Running parallel to the main drama, Fillan's story begins with his leaving Erin (Ireland) with an older monk, Kessog, and of their establishing a muintir – a Christian monastic community – on Loch Lumon on the borders of the Pictish world. Their island fastness acts as a springboard for forays into the territory of the Fotla Picts, one of which is detailed as they confront the powers of pagandom and Domech, the unpredictable warlord of the Fotla. After a contest of spiritual knowledge and strength, Fillan is invited to establish a muintir at the seat of the warlord's power at Dindurn.

With Taran out of the way, Oengus is frustrated in his plans to reform his tribe by his revitalised great-uncle, the existing warlord, Talorgen. The mounting tension between the two ends with Talorgen's mysterious death, and Oengus sweeps to power unopposed. His headstrong ways are typified by rejecting Eithni, who is carrying his child, but is checked by the outspoken and powerful chief priestess of the Bulàch, the mother-earth goddess. Increasing alienation and lack of popularity lead Oengus to follow the advice of his aunt Conchen, a fount of homely wisdom, resulting in him bringing Eithni back to their community as his wife. Overshadowing his rule is the unknown whereabouts of his missing cousin and the hostility of Taran's family and Taran's former girlfriend, Alpia.

Nurtured by a peasant couple in an obscure place in the mountains, Taran begins to recall the prophecies surrounding the Z-rod in a bid to take revenge on his cousin, reclaim his right to become warlord and be reunited with Alpia. His onward adventure leads to a surprise meeting under the Stone of Refuge with Ossian, the bard who had uttered prophetic words determining Taran's mysterious destiny. At Ossian's injunction, Taran goes south to Dindurn to find sanctuary in Fillan's muintir. The abbot prophetically reveals how Taran could move beyond his fallen status and remake himself as a warrior-saint by acquiring nine graces through undertaking a series of quests to enable him in the ultimate challenge of *bearing fire to the north.*

The second book, *Heirs of Promise*, propels Taran on a *white martyrdom* as an exile from the muintir, after Abbot Fillan foresees the treachery of the local warlord intending to sell Taran to his enemies. Fleeing for his life, a precarious adventure ensues up Scotland's west coast in a flimsy coracle, seeking a particular mountain Fillan has detailed from a word of knowledge he has received. After taking faith to pray for a crippled girl, this initial quest fulfils part of Ossian's prophecy concerning Taran's *transformation in the isles of the west*. His transformation, and a growing love for the girl, leads to conflict and an onward pursuit of the nine graces as outlined in Fillan's prophetic prayer.

Concurrent with Taran's rise as a warrior of Christ is his cousin's consolidation as the warlord of the Ce, aspiring to be a force to rival the neighbouring tribes. The drama details the various stages of Oengus's ascent as he gathers the support of his druids, warriors and tribal neighbours in realising his grand ambition of building a new community inspired by the fierce and wily character of the boar he deliberately emulates.

After losing his wife in childbirth, Oengus's son is brought up by Alpia. This is a relationship of tension, since Alpia is repelled by Oengus's rash and uncouth ways, and by her often-subconscious loyalty towards Taran. This seemingly impossible situation is sustained by the calming and wise presence of Aunt Conchen – in whose home the child is raised – an aunt who Alpia and Oengus mutually respect and love. Her steady counsel steers Alpia to recognise Oengus's qualities as a leader and a visionary, and suggests Alpia has a role to influence. With the intervention of the prophetic, the couple are eventually married. At the zenith of his career, one brooding cloud darkens Oengus's horizon – Brude, his nemesis and overlord.

The scene is set for this concluding drama as the Gaels of Dal Riata bristle themselves for war against their northern Pictish neighbours – an event that threatens to engulf both cousins in its onslaught. Taran is recalled by Fillan, who pleased by his protégé's acquisition of five of the nine graces, sends him south to Erin to be further educated in *the way*. Taran rebels, knowing that Ossian's prophecy directs him to the north, but has to acquiesce.

The Ossian Prophecy

Make great haste when you leave. Be cunning, be brave, be humble. Your surrender will be in the south; your transformation in the isles of the west; your fulfilment coincides with the anticipation of the learned ones far to the north, before you return east with great peace.

Before that peace blossoms, there will come much strife, like a blight threatening to consume. Heartache and anguish lie before you. Many a journey awaits, full of ordeals that you consider will be your undoing, though these are in truth, rites of passage for your own preparation. You will be the doer of mighty deeds and the acts will be the making of the man. Take heart, my son, through one you will overcome the world.

Fillan's prophetic prayer

*The nine graces for a warrior saint to withstand
the powers of this world.*

*May these be acquired:
mercy to confound the foe,
and to bind up the injured;
humility and perseverance as characteristics
to be known by and be outstanding in.
Render your sword in surrender
so that obedience to the King will be complete
and thereby, to be rid of all pride so as to love totally.
May valour, to champion the oppressed, be for your renown;
and peace abundant when considering apparent failure;
hope to prove firm in the face of despair;
and faithfulness to lead to the very ends of the earth.
Where there is loss, may gain be known;
with ill-repute, the High King's approval;
where there is disgust, the favour of the Almighty;
and when in poverty to perceive the riches of the
Everlasting's glory.*

Chapter One

The Call

AD 559 Rhynie and the Great Glen

"We cannot go without our supply train!" remarked Drust.

Oengus knew his commander spoke wisely. He had been optimistic of embarking at dawn, executing what he had promised at the close of his rousing speech to his warriors, of advancing with proud long shadows before them with the rising sun at their backs. The long waiting made him feel powerless to expedite procedures, and the tension could only be eased by giving the order to march, but that release continued to elude. It was late morning when they eventually moved down the brae, heading northwards out of the hill country before turning westward. The hoped-for long shadows of men on horseback riding valiantly before them had long since passed. The squat shadows cast beneath them, trodden by horses' hooves, struck him as a reprimand, and possibly an ill-omen.

The discouragement of the appallingly slow start was heavy to shift, making him wonder what other things loomed for which they were ill-prepared. Ultimately, he did not wish to come to Brude too soon, but they had to be seen to have acted promptly, to prove they had responded in earnest to meet the overlord's need. It was a delicate timing, one which he wished to control and not to have imposed upon him due to inefficiency.

They forded the Deveron, glad that the river was not in spate, and riding all afternoon, they arrived at the Spey as the shadows were lengthening. There, they decided to camp on the border of their own territory to enjoy the hospitality of friends who would not give begrudgingly. The following day, they crossed the river at dawn, passed the junction of the road that went to the coast at Y Broch, and after a day's good ride, reached Craig Padrig at the head of the Great Glen. A small retinue remained at the hillfort and their commander received them civilly enough, dining them whilst the main force of the Ce warriors encamped outside the fortress on the high slopes overlooking the estuary that tapered out towards the sea.

Assigned a local guide to lead down the Great Glen, they spent the following day threading their way between loch and hill the entire long length of Loch Rihoh, camping at its southern end beside the river that fed the loch. Progress had been hampered by the swollen streams crossed and the mud churned by the horses into a quagmire that frequently bogged down the supply carts.

"It is only another day's ride before we will join the Lord Brude's army," declared the guide. "My lord is encamped at the far end of the Great Glen, before the sea that brings the over ambitious Gaels."

Feeling the unease rise from his bowels as he anticipated the considerable clash of forces with all the uncertainty of its outcome, Oengus said nothing in reply.

As they journeyed southward on the following morning, the mountains flanking the glen on each side rose ominously higher, initially casting vast shadows over them until the sun rose high enough to shorten the gloom in the glen.

The steep hills, still crested with snow, looked inhospitable presenting a barrier on both sides, ushering them onwards towards their uncertain fate in the impending battle. The air was damp and the wind funnelling this unsettled atmosphere into their faces reminded Oengus that he was in alien territory, far from home. He wondered how many of his men would fall in this foreign land, and whether he too would lie with them.

Moving towards them rode a man on a horse-drawn cart. At first, Oengus presumed him to be a farmer, but as they approached it became apparent he was a wealthy merchant, judging by his well-fed form and the pile of wares stacked behind him. The merchant stared with a sense of disbelief at the sight of their army.

"The Gaels boldly sailed up the sea loch yesterday," the merchant reported. "They appeared in a vast fleet, making the blue sea grey with their mass of boats. When they neared the beach at the head of the loch, the Lord Brude and his men intercepted them and cut them down."

It was not the outcome Oengus had wanted to hear. At least we have been spared a fight, he thought, and I have met our obligation to bring three hundred men. Now it only remains to present ourselves to Brude to prove we responded to his call.

On reaching the sea loch, the local inhabitants were a-buzz with excitement, celebrating their lord's success. "Even before the Gaels could get out of their boats, we had cut them down. Our brave men waded into the shallows where the boats of the Gaels seemed to have slowed and had become entangled together."

"The Dal Riatans had sailed into the bay with the wind in their sails," took up an elderly man with just one tooth showing in his mouth. "Just at the critical point, the wind suddenly turned and stopped their swift advance. We caught them confused in the shallows and slaughtered them till the tide ran red!"

"Our druids caused the wind to change direction," declared another local. "Mighty is the Bulàch over the god of the Gaels!"

The timing had appeared to have been impeccable, thought Oengus. The gods seemed to smile down upon his overlord. Oengus led his men to the head of the loch where a cluster of men were digging a long pit overseen by another group. It became clear that those digging were captured Gaels preparing a burial for their fallen comrades under the gaze and insults of their Pictish victors.

"Look!" said a Pictish warrior, pointing over at a tree. "There is King Gabran's torso lashed to an oak."

Oengus looked on the gruesome sight. The torso was impressively broad and tall, like the man he had met the previous year when he had visited Dunadd, but it was hard to ascertain the identity of the slain since his head had been removed.

"Our Lord Brude has taken his head as a trophy and sailed to Dunadd to throw it down at the gates of their fort."

"When did they leave?" Oengus asked.

"Yesterday. They went in the currachs seized from the Gaels as well as in our own." He added with admiration, "Their currachs are large and swift."

"Are there any more boats left?" enquired Oengus, wondering whether they should follow.

"No, they are all gone, packed full of men."

"Maybe we can march along the coast!?" suggested Oengus to their Craig Padrig guide, keen to give the impression of their willingness to assist.

"No," their guide shook his head. "This coast is indented with lochs that go deep inland. There is one, not that far to the south, that to round would take a hard day's march. In a boat, you would cross the mouth of that loch in no time for the distance is little more than an arrow's flight!"

"Our lord's arm is valiant and mighty," boasted one of the soldiers looking somewhat disdainfully at their late arrival. Raising a blood-stained sword in the air, he cried, "Hail King Brude!"

"King?" Oengus found himself involuntarily questioning.

"The mighty Brude has slain King Gabran with his own hands, therefore the title of king is rightfully his."

Oengus went down to the bay where bodies were still being recovered from the sea by morose Gaels under the watchful eye of the Fortriu. Many of the bodies were naked from the waist upwards, stripped of armour, weaponry and adornment.

"How odd that not a single man bears a tattoo!" remarked Drust to Oengus.

"They do not see the need to protect their bodies!" remarked Gest, shaking his head at their assumed arrogance to shun the gods.

"They are Christian," responded Oengus, "who do not share our beliefs in the protection of our symbols, nor the never-ending swirls of our tattoos that confound the onlooker!"

"So much for the supposed superiority of their Christ!" spat Drust with disdain. "Truly, they over-reached themselves and underestimated the power of us Picts."

"What are we to do now?" Gest asked in an undertone looking to Oengus.

Partly raising his hand, Oengus turned to Drust. "Send word to pitch camp." Reverting his attention to his druid, he answered, "We need to wait for Brude's return."

A leaden mass of cloud, moving up the sea loch towards them, accelerated the erection of awnings. Soon a heavy squall of rain deluged the beach. The huge bulk of a mountain rising to the east, darkened and then disappeared in a dark turmoil. When it briefly cleared later, fresh snow made its summit dome brilliant. The rising tide was restless, driven by the prevailing wind that blew from where the Dal Riatans had sailed, and seemed to mourn the loss of their best men. Oengus felt unsettled.

Over the next days, Oengus prepared himself for meeting with his nemesis, knowing he would have to feign delight over his victory. "This will have strengthened his arm immeasurably," he remarked.

"Undoubtedly," agreed Drust, "as if his acclaim was not already considerable! To have defeated a king and his army will vault his reputation."

"It is impetuous, though, of Brude to strike at Dunadd without pause!" observed Gest.

"He is buoyed up by his victory, driven on by the momentum," remarked Drust almost admiringly.

"What if he meets resistance at Dunadd?" Oengus commented wistfully. "He might yet fall foul of the gods' favour."

"Do you really believe he has gone all the way to Dunadd?" Drust queried as he scratched behind an ear.

"Who knows." Oengus paused. "It would sound good to say that he did!"

They were quiet for a while before Gest broke the silence. "We now have our answer to what the falling star conveyed!"

The other two nodded. Oengus was relieved that the heavenly omen had not concerned his own demise.

When the victors returned up the loch, Oengus assembled his men on the firm ground above the beach bearing banners in tribute to Brude's victory. Oengus went forward to congratulate the hero flanked by two of his captains. "We hail you as king!" began Oengus bowing before his overlord.

King Brude returned his salute with a stony stare. Finally, he brought himself to remark, "You took your time coming!"

"Lord, we arrived the very day after your victory and have since been waiting here," Oengus said in defence.

"How many days did it take you to come from Rhynie?" the king pursued.

"Only four days, my lord!"

"You should have done it in three! We were expecting you to join our ranks." His tone changed as he uttered rather dismissively, "As it was, we did not need your help."

"With better conditions we might have reached here in three days. But ask your own guide — he will affirm how swollen were the rivers, and how boggy the trail, so that our carts were constantly in need of being freed from the mire!"

"Huh!" Brude grunted, looking at the long rows of the Ce warriors. "How many men have you brought?" His tone had lost some of its critical edge as he craned his neck, taking in the mass of Oengus's men neatly arrayed with shields daubed in bold blue depicting the boar's head.

"Three hundred, my lord, just as your messenger had stated we were to bring."

Brude took a couple of paces towards the Ce warriors, nodding his head slowly with what looked like approval. Turning back, he said to Oengus, "Let me inspect them."

Oengus and Drust joined Brude, walking along the lengthy line of men which was four deep.

"You have a well-turned-out force," conceded Brude, "I will give you that. And properly equipped. They are impressive to behold."

Oengus felt a swell of pride in having his achievements noted, and by so formidable a commander.

"I did not imagine you could field three hundred men, certainly not of this stature!" On reaching the end of the line, he chose to walk back by inspecting the next line. "These men are equally as good as those you had positioned at the front! I had imagined that your best men were only at the front!"

Oengus hoped that Brude would not continue to the rear rank where the younger and less trained guard were positioned. How fortunate it was that he had not carried through with his initial plan of bringing largely untrained men.

On coming to the end of the second line, Brude remarked, "It is a shame that I could not have seen your men in action!"

Drust spoke up for the first time, "My lord, it was not for lack of trying!"

"I am sure there will be another occasion," returned Brude ominously.

"You will find us ready, at your disposal," returned Oengus, hoping that the inferred blame was dissolving. Deciding to move their conversation along, he asked, "Tell me – what happened at Dunadd?"

Brude broke into a smile, apparently glad of the opportunity to swagger. "We astounded Dunadd by arriving in their own boats. Anticipating seeing their own men, they were appalled when confronted by us Picts bearing Gabran's severed head. Their citadel was largely unguarded, for Gabran must have been confident of victory, not feeling the need to guard their homes." He paused to stroke his bent nose and run his hand through a head of brown curls that fell beyond his shoulders. He struck Oengus as the man of strength, bold, keen-eyed, shrewd, irrepressible.

"Gabran was nothing but a hot-head, an ambitious young upstart who grossly underestimated us. When I sported his head from the tip of a spear, the people looked on in horror." He stopped to laugh spitefully, smug to have marched unopposed to their stronghold. "The king's family fled. I could have lingered to flush them out and have them put to the sword. Instead, I showed clemency. After all, I had proved our supremacy by coming to the heart of Dal Riata. They have learned a lesson not to meddle with the Fortriu. I told their officials to halt their advances up our coastlines or else I shall return and slaughter them all to a child and burn down their fortress."

"We congratulate you!" said Oengus, genuinely impressed by Brude's supremacy. His own achievements seemed paltry in comparison to this demonstration of strength. He felt humbled, conscious of his need to show extreme respect and pay his tribute dues to the full and without delay. The longed-for new order would have to be put on hold.

Chapter Two

Saintly Preparation

AD 559-563 Clonard and Candida Casa

The Clonard community had substantially grown following the plague of AD 547 that had so devastated the land. Both high and low were reminded of the transience of life and the plague's indiscrimination in exacting a considerable toll, including the community's founder, Finnian. Yet his celebrated brilliance had left its mark, and this combined with the heavenly concerns of a generation, drew three thousand souls to commit to the ways of the muintir. One of these was Taran himself.

"Would you say your knowledge of the scriptures is expanding here?" asked Findlay, an older monk assigned to be Taran's anam cara.

Taran considered the question, in no hurry to respond. "Teachings that sound familiar from my time at Dindurn are now imbued with new meaning. They no longer appear . . ." he waved his hand, willing the words to come, "– shadowy but are now illuminated by the testimony of personal experience and the desire to understand more."

"I see," replied Findlay with a tone that struck Taran as sounding ambiguous. Taran watched the elder rest his elbows on the edge of the table and, placing the tips of his fingers together, drew his hands to his mouth in a thoughtful gesture. Findlay observed him closely without speaking.

Finding the silence uncomfortable, Taran took the initiative, "Why is our diet so meagre?"

"Self-denial makes the soul keener," Findlay replied in a monotone that matched the grey pallor of his face.

"But it is bordering on starvation!" Taran challenged, with some indignation.

His anam cara responded with a sickly smile. "Only through discipline can you discern the High King. We must do battle with the flesh to better know Christ."

Feeling that the reply sounded hollow – more taught than entirely owned – he persisted in making known his point of view. "I know that desire for purity – but is starving really the way?"

"Our bellies remind us of our carnal appetites, prompting us to pray!" Findlay returned rather dryly.

"And who said that?" he pursued, curious to fathom the source of these beliefs.

"It probably originates from Finnian." Findlay sat more upright. "It is the pathway to seek God with all our souls."

"Is this not somewhat contrived?" Taran felt impatient with what he considered the dull acceptance of practices passed down without due examination. "I have experienced want, enduring it as part of a white martyrdom, but I did not deliberately half-starve myself! Hunger was often a consequence, not the pursuit of my quest."

Findlay soon brought their brief session to a close, unprepared to discuss the matter further. Their exchange later preyed on Taran's mind, for he recognised his own proud spirit rebelling against perceived indoctrination. However, he still felt the duty to be candid, determined to be transparent about his struggles in surrendering to the ascetic life, and disliking the sham that paraded their ability in conquering carnal appetites.

"It is important, as brothers, that we remain genuine with one another," Taran challenged his anam cara, "for warriors do not fight on their own – their strength is in the comradeship fostered between them. Therefore, let us be real so that trust can be built to achieve the strength of a unit."

After Finnian's passing, a new luminary was on the rise in Erin. Whilst visiting Clonard, Colmcille called Taran to a private audience. A good fifteen years Taran's senior, Colmcille exuded a confidence derived from his upbringing as a significant prince, enhanced by a force of character, keen intellect and reputation – qualities which had helped him to establish several muintirs around Erin.

"Tell me, Taran, about your people," the churchman's lively grey eyes fixed him with great intensity. "I sense the exile of the white martyrdom is to be my way if I am to bring light to dark places, for Erin is full of muintirs."

"Where to begin!" remarked Taran, genuinely confounded.

"Are your people united as a single people? Or are you divided by tribal loyalties?"

Again, Taran felt the piercing look from those grey eyes searching him. "We are divided. There are always petty skirmishes – the lifting of cattle followed by reprisals. We are a proud warrior people, celebrated for withstanding the might of the Romans." He expanded at length on what he had been taught by his foster father concerning the Pictish resistance to the Romans and concluded, "Our defence was so great that the Romans withdrew to build two walls from coast to coast – even those did not contain us!"

"Spoken like one of noble blood," observed Colmcille holding his head erect with the faintest of smiles.

Taran modestly lowered his head.

"But you were raised to lead, were you not?"

"I was, but it was not to be by the sword."

"That is true of myself too!" remarked the older man. "I had both the right, and the desire at one time, to rule my people, but the High King made it clear that I was to be a soldier of his cause." He swept a hand to one side and, looking at him as though sizing him up, continued, "You are not the first Pict to be in a muintir over here, nor the first noble born either. One called Nechtan, who once ruled in the north of your land, studied here in Erin after being ousted by his brother. Later, as was prophesied, he returned to his people as their leader."

"Nechtan ruled over the Fortriu when I was a boy . . . I did not know he was a pilgrim! Brude rules now with a different persuasion – a true Pict, mighty in battle. His reputation will have reached you even here when he defeated your kinsfolk in Dal Riata and slaughtered King Gabran."

"How the mighty have fallen!" His expression registered the catastrophe of Gabran's ambition that had led to his early death. "I wonder what shall become of Brude?" He seemed to consider his own question which he dismissed with a vague smile. "But who are warlords to withstand the might of our King?"

Finding Colmcille's intense look unsettling, Taran changed the subject. "Thanks to Fillan, I found the true way. Do you know Fillan?"

Colmcille shook his head.

"Kessog was Fillan's anam cara . . ."

"Kessog I knew – a former prince of Cashel."

"So I believe. Kessog embraced the red martyrdom. I once thought it defeat but, thanks to Fillan, I now view things differently."

Colmcille questioned him at length about place names he had heard of among the Picts, elaborating where pilgrims from Erin had established colonies of heaven. "...Boethius went to a place called Migdele."

"Migdele!" Taran pronounced with a hint of disdain. "That is in the heart of the Circinn – they are our neighbours!"

"Neighbours, I take from your expression, with whom you do not get on?"

Taran nodded, slightly bothered to allow old enmities to still rankle him. "All these places you mention are to the south of the great mountainous divide that we call the Mounth. North of that range, no pilgrim has ventured, except for Nechtan apparently, a lone light which the darkness has since consumed."

"Then that is where I should go!" Colmcille rose vigorously to his feet. "It is my desire to establish a colony of heaven, which will spread its influence throughout the land. What about you, Taran? What do you sense is the High King's call?"

Roused by this kindred spirit, Taran declared, "To take *fire to the north*! I have received prophecies concerning this very thing." He glowed with pleasure being on such terms with an illustrious companion, divulging his hopes and dreams.

"Then, our calling is the same!" announced Colmcille with evident delight. He slowly paced the cell. "May the Lord speed your return home, and if he be willing, may our paths cross again. May the power of the everlasting kingdom be revealed, even in the courts of the mighty

Brude." He halted in the middle of the room. "I would not be surprised if we shall have a part in this together! Mark my words, Taran – these are not idle fantasies!"

Taran averted his eyes from the older man's imposing stare, declaring, "May the Lord help you to establish a light in the north."

"Before we part, I have been meaning to tell you that I came across another Pict – one who is older than you and studies at Clonmacnoise. His name is Maon, at least that is the name that has been given him, which I believe is close in sound to his Pictish name. Brought here as a slave, he was made free when his master became a pilgrim." Colmcille paused thoughtfully, "If I were you, I should pay him a visit. Clonmacnoise is not far. Maon has the same heart to bring the light to the north."

These parting words made Taran mindful of Maon. As his time neared its conclusion at Clonard, he learned about the intentions of one of his fellow monks to travel to Clonmacnoise, and remembering Maon, he decided to pay him a visit.

When introduced to Maon, he saw someone who looked hauntingly familiar.

"I have been Maon these past twenty years or more, ever since I was brought to Erin," the man smiled briefly.

"What was your former name?"

"Munait – but my master, saying how strange it seemed to the ear of the Gael, chose a name that sounded similar. I suppose it also expressed his ownership over me for I was his slave until four years ago."

"Can you still remember how to speak our language? It has been a long time since I have been able to speak to anyone in Pictish . . . but as for you, it will have been many more years."

"Well, let us try," laughed Munait, speaking Pictish hesitantly. "How strange to be speaking it again! I used to speak Pictish to myself, but as the years passed, I used it less, especially when becoming accustomed to Gaelic. When I became a follower of *the way*, along with my master's household, I was trained to read and write as I studied the ... what would you call them ... the 'writings'?"

"*Writings* sounds good. Was your master good to you?"

"Aye, as slave masters go. He was fair and never abusive, even before he became a pilgrim. On Sundays, we worked only a half-day, and were relieved from our farming duties for the afternoon. He welcomed us to his family home for lunch, and after we ate, he had a monk read the gospel aloud, who then explained its meaning and answered our questions. His wife taught us spiritual songs and we prayed together. Our shared faith took away some of the great division between us."

Munait fell silent with a far-away look in his eyes. Sensing that he was deep in a particular thought, Taran waited.

"You know, my life has followed the pattern of Patrick somewhat, for he was a slave like me," continued Munait, "brought here against his will, and in his abject poverty, he discerned the Presence."

"Patrick is one of my heroes!" declared Taran, enthusiastically.

"Mine too! I admire his daring to light the pascal fire on the Hill of Slane in defiance of the chief druid who was preparing to strike a flint on the Hill of Tara."

"I know! 'Unless that fire is put out,' the chief druid had declared, 'it will spread a fire throughout the land that cannot be extinguished.'"

Munait smiled. "It stirs the heart that these things took place. Imagine the bravery it took for Patrick and his followers to defy the chief druid and the high king of Erin; and then the consequences when soldiers were despatched to put out the fire on the Hill of Slane and, no doubt, to slaughter Patrick and his people!"

"That episode teaches much about how God protects his people! Did they not pass the soldiers unnoticed?"

"Indeed! The soldiers reported to the high king that they only saw a herd of deer pass them by! Do you think we shall experience such things ourselves?"

"No doubt about it!" returned Taran with conviction, and he shared something of the testimonies of Kessog and Fillan at Cartray and Dindurn, followed by his own experience of Aleine Brona's healing. Keen to move on from talking about himself, Taran asked, "But tell me, how is it that you are studying here?"

"My master declared that I could gain my freedom if I prepared myself to share God's love with our own people. But first, I had to study here." Munait sat quietly, with his hands folded in his lap, striking Taran as a man who was intent on fulfilling his destiny.

"Am I right in thinking that you hail from the Ce, for your accent is like mine?"

"I am! I come from a very obscure place."

"Where exactly? I know our country quite well."

"Upstream on the River Dee, near the borderlands with the Circinn."

"Truly! I spent a summer and a winter there on a remote farmstead. It was a good walk into the hills from the Dee itself."

"Really? Who do you know in those parts? Maybe we know people in common."

"Probably not. It was a very remote place. I stayed with an old couple called Elpin and Coblaith. They . . ."

Munait interrupted him with a loud exclamation. "They are my parents!" Recovering from the shock, he asked, "How are they?"

"They are your parents?" His mind reeled over this disclosure. "While I was with them, your father died."

There was a silence.

"But he would have been of an age," Munait began, recovering himself. "It is what is to be expected. Truth be told, I expected them to have both died a long time ago. So, my mother is alive?"

"When I left, she was strong." Taran spoke with feeling, "Munait, your mother was like a mother to me. Without her help, I doubt that I would be alive now — truly! Your parents mistrusted me at first — as well they might — but later, they nurtured me back to full health." Elaborating on events, Taran concluded with a smile, visualising a collage of images that came to mind. Coming round, he remarked, "Your mother is a fine shot with a bow!"

Munait perceptibly smiled.

Taran described her humble circumstances. "After we buried your father, I delayed my plans to leave that autumn, and even cultivated some virgin ground and repaired the hut." Taran paused. "It was not easy leaving your mother! You know, she spoke of you, always sorrowful to have lost you, wondering whether you were still alive. I should also tell you that at Samhainn, after your father had passed away, your mother spoke with him in the otherworld. He told her that he had been searching for you among the dead but had not found you. Understanding that you had been taken across the water, he even conveyed a message that I was to look out for you! I must confess to have forgotten about that."

"My dear father!" Munait smiled in recollection. "Even though he did not know it in life, at least he found out in death that I am still alive."

They sat for some moments in silence, lost in their own recollections. Taran broke the quiet. "Your father was a fine singer. He taught me most of the songs of home I know!"

"Yes, he could be very lively. When did you leave my mother?"

"Oh, it would be about six years ago now. She sent me away with all kinds of provisions to preserve me through the Minamoyn Goch. Why, this knife I have here is one of her gifts." He removed it, admiringly, from its sheaf. "With it fastened to a shaft, I caught fish, fought off a bear and withstood an assault from a wolf pack."

"It sounds a legendary weapon!"

"She also insisted I took her dog, Garn – did you know him?"

"No."

"He was descended from a wolf."

"Really? Where is he now?"

"He was meaninglessly slain by a crazed man," Taran replied with renewed remorse. "Garn was a faithful companion who saved my life from a bear! If I spoke of Garn's exploits, we would be up for half the night! I miss him at times. Even to this day, I mourn his loss."

"Life is brutal at times!" said Munait, shaking his head. "Twenty years I have been separated from my people. I wonder if my mother is still alive? I must see her. How providential that you should be here now! My parents must have been devastated when I disappeared, for I was their only child. The Circinn set upon me when I was down at the Dee, carried me away, then sold me to others, who, in turn, sold me at Alt Clud from where I was shipped off to Erin. A man's life can change in an instant. A moment's lack of vigilance and I end up sold to herd the cattle of foreigners across the seas."

"Truly, these things are in God's hands!" spoke Taran, shaking his head.

"In some respect, I should be grateful; for had it not been for my master, I should never have heard of the High King."

They spoke a good deal more until there was not a detail remaining that Taran had not disclosed.

"Anyway, what brings you here?" Munait asked.

"Colmcille told me about a fellow Pict studying here – I just had to come!"

"Colmcille!" he exclaimed with evident surprise.

"Aye."

"Judging from your lack of surprise, it seems that you have not heard!" Munait replied curiously.

"Heard what?"

"Whilst staying at Movilla Abbey, Colmcille had apparently copied a psalter brought from Rome belonging to the abbot. The abbot had insisted that the copy should remain at the abbey, but as maker of the book, Colmcille refused." Munait paused reflectively. "Can you imagine such a thing?"

Taran shook his head confused.

"But the matter did not end there. The dispute was referred to the high king of Erin, who decreed, *to every cow her calf, to every book its copy.* Allegedly, Colmcille did not respect the king's injunction. It was said that he could not even abide the king's person on account of something that had happened years back. Apparently, a certain youth, granted sanctuary by Colmcille, had been slain by the king. Given that background, matters were bound to grow heated over this disputed psalter. But no one could have imagined what happened next!"

As Munait paused for effect, it caused Taran to ask, "And so, what did happen?"

"Colmcille's people took up arms against the high king! They defeated him, leaving three thousand slain on the field!"

"We heard report of a battle and the many slain, but heard no mention of Colmcille being mixed up in it all!" Taran went silent, confused by this astonishing course of events. Had things come so tragically to an end for this soldier of Christ? With his reputation in tatters, those noble aims to establish a muintir in the north, seemed impossible. His warrior spirit is too fervent, he thought, trying to make sense of events. But am I not hot-headed too? He recalled his fight with Domech's son who had stolen the kid goat. But I, although a monk, was not regenerate at that time. How tragic that a man of Colmcille's eminence could cause so many deaths.

"A synod was convened to determine what should be done with this warrior monk," continued Munait. "They decreed that Colmcille should lead as many into the light as the number he had consigned to darkness."

"Then what happened?"

"Before the dust had settled, Colmcille set sail for Dal Riata with twelve companions who he labelled 'apostles'."

Taran's thoughts were turbulent. After so great a descent, could there be a recovery? He considered some of the heroes of the faith who were no strangers to failure. Could a sovereign God still not use human fallibility and tragedy to serve his bigger purpose? The synod might have appeared to have exiled Colmcille, but had not reaching the Picts been his vision all along? Their decision had only accelerated his purpose.

Munait cleared his throat. "When I finish my studies in a few weeks' time, I will make straight for home and see whether my mother still lives."

"Aye, do that. Share my peace with her and tell her I am hugely indebted to her."

"I shall . . . should she still live!"

Taran described the way to reach the River Dee without having to pass through Circinnian territory.

"Thank you for bothering to come to find me here – it is quite providential that you should have arrived shortly before I am to leave, bringing news of my family. It is so extraordinary a thing!"

"I feel that we shall meet again," Taran said, rising to his feet to bid him farewell.

"That, I am sure of – for we are both of one mind in reaching our people. I intend to find Colmcille, for I choose to believe that he will be a trail-blazer, like Patrick, despite what has passed here in Erin. Rather, I feel – because of what has taken place here – Colmcille will be keen to offset those many deaths by bringing life to our people!"

When Taran's own time came to depart from Erin, he met with his abbot, to whom he declared, "I believe that my destiny is wrapped up with Colmcille and the twelve who went to Dal Riata."

"Why is that?" the abbot asked dubiously. "I thought you wished to return to the Picts."

"When I met with Colmcille, he shared his concern for the Picts, desiring to establish a muintir to achieve that purpose. He mentioned his hope that one day we would work together."

"I am not sure it is wise to work with Colmcille." The abbot grimaced. Clearing his throat, he said with an officious tone, "You are to go to Candida Casa to complete your studies."

Taran was much taken aback. "But I have completed my studies here and have already studied longer than others, for I was also instructed by Fillan of Dindurn for two years."

Ignoring his remark, the abbot continued, "Our revered founder, Finnian, once studied at Candida Casa, so you are following an excellent example. Besides, studying there will broaden your understanding of the traditions of the Britons."

"But, sir, I do believe I am called to my own people and have received prophecies . . ."

"Prophecies!" He puffed out his cheeks and slowly exhaled. "They can wait. If they are true, they shall be fulfilled in God's good time." Pulling his cloak about him and stretching out his feet, he remarked, *"It is not a delay to stop and sharpen the scythe."*

By the time Taran had left for Candida Casa, he was down-hearted to not have received fresh revelation since standing at the base of the giant waterfall four years previously. This hiatus had been a time of so much learning that he had had enough. Was his destiny not *to bear fire to the north*? Ever since leaving Carvorst's home, he had travelled in the opposite direction, settling in the south. Candida Casa was still south of where he believed his north to lie.

Had not the shining one said there were seven preparatory quests to fulfil before he could achieve his ultimate mission? Only three had been attained and all within one winter. How would he become aware of the fourth quest? The shining one had only given specific direction as far as the waterfall. Had it been a mistake to come to Erin? Another year of study felt like a delay.

Candida Casa was a foreign place and although intelligible, their dialect taxed him at first. However, he did warm to the abbot, who, being half-blind, had the tendency to peer with intensity under a head of snow-white hair that was unusually cropped short. He found the abbot's knowledge of history particularly engaging, due to his ability to pass on the lessons gleaned from former times, with enthusiasm.

"Never neglect the vision and passion to see godly aims through," the abbot often repeated with a gravity that never dulled. "Ninian endured abuse and ridicule from the pagan rulers; nevertheless, he laboured hard to establish this muintir."

That seems true for anyone who pioneers, thought Taran.

"Never tire," the old abbot continued. "When one task is complete, as Ninian achieved in the construction of this white church, the salvation of the Picts became his all-consuming aim. The High King protected him on forays north, enabling him to sow the seed, not that it took root! But it is not always for us to see the fruit, is it? We are only called to be faithful."

He speaks wisely, thought Taran, and treasured these wise comments.

Chapter Three

The Bull Advances

AD 560 Rhynie

One morning, Oengus had an unexpected visitor. He was conducting some business in the hall when a woman, with a wild look in her eyes, boldly approached. He recognised her instantly. No other woman he knew wore her hair with a short, high fringe. He gave Maevis his immediate attention.

"Warriors are on the move – hundreds of them! Their feet and their many wagons raise a cloud of dust."

"You have seen them?" questioned Oengus.

"Aye, last night! From afar," she spoke in her strange, detached way.

"Not as you would normally see!" clarified Gest. "Who are they?"

"I cannot tell!"

Not doubting her ability, Oengus was keen to extract as much information as he could. "Where are they coming from? Did you see the emblems upon their shields?"

"No, I saw no emblems. But, I saw a great fortress raised upon sea cliffs with a series of high walls flanking it on the landward side. From these walls marched the men."

"That will be Y Broch!" stated Oengus.

"Or Dinottar?" countered Drust.

"That is unhelpful!" observed Oengus, "for one fort belongs to the Fortriu, the other to the Circinn!" Turning again to Maevis, he asked, "Was the land flat beyond the walls and lower than the fort?"

"It was," she confirmed.

"Then it is Y Broch of the Fortriu," ascertained Oengus. "Do you know in which direction they marched?" He gestured her to be seated.

Refusing the seat, she shook her head slowly, and although she looked him in the eye it was as though she was gazing beyond. "I thought you should know, especially if it is a neighbour who is on the move."

"Quite right. Are you able to tell us anything else? I mean, are they already on the move or is this a premonition of something yet to happen?"

Alpia rose and, coming round the table, tried to encourage Maevis to be seated. Again, the seer refused, looking uncomfortable in these surroundings. Alpia put a cup of herbal infusion in her hands from which Maevis took a couple of sips. In no hurry to answer, Oengus was on the point of repeating the question.

When she spoke, now more in a monotone, it seemed to him that she was absent in spirit. "The bull paws the ground and flicks the dust." She clumsily placed the cup down, spilling some of the contents on the table. "His nostrils flare, and he snorts. When he bellows, all the cows lift their heads and take note. When he lowers his horns, the earth trembles as though under the stampede of a thousand cattle, and when he raises those horns, they run with blood and the earth is stunned into silence." With that, she turned and left the hall, clutching her plaid with tight fists as though someone was about to seize it. She walked like a child, half-asleep, falteringly and vulnerable. When she reached the hall's doorway, she looked back to cast an anxious glance, looking as though she might say something more. Turning, she walked pensively away. Although still a young woman, she looked, at that moment, emaciated and frail, like one three times her age.

Gest rose to follow Maevis, and upon reaching the door, he turned and said, "Heed Maevis's words."

"And do you think we will not?" Oengus looked at him reproachfully, annoyed that his friend should state the obvious, especially after he had paid all due attention.

"I am just adding emphasis to her words lest they be overlooked," Gest remarked, before disappearing.

"It is anyone's guess who he will fight!" Drust uttered a curse under his breath.

Oengus shuddered. "The bull also confirms that it is Brude! Ever since calling himself king, that man has been spoiling for another fight."

"His victory over Dal Riata has gone to his head!"

Alpia interjected impatiently, "Never mind airing opinions about Brude — have you paid the tribute?"

"Yes, yes!" Oengus returned impatiently. "After his official's visit, I would not be so stupid as to delay, or to yield less than what was asked."

"Then why is he threatening us?" She looked anxious as she placed a hand on her belly swollen with child.

"Sit down, and do not distress yourself!" Oengus rose, leading her back to the seat she had occupied beside him. It struck him that she was reluctant. "We will take this threat seriously, for what Maevis sees always proves true."

"Are we to move to the hillfort?" Drust asked, seemingly keen to ascertain the level of their response.

"Yes, we must." Oengus turned to Alpia. She looked overwhelmed by the news, which was so unlike her usual calm demeanour. It must be due to her being with child, he thought. "Go and prepare our things and help Aunt Conchen."

Alpia rose slowly, perceptibly shaking her head, and spoke like one awakening from a deep sleep. "I feel so weary and a little sick! I will leave military matters to you men. These tidings bode ill!"

"Do not worry – Drust and I will arrange everything. Maevis has ensured that we will not be taken by surprise."

"It is well that the Bulàch has forewarned us," agreed Maelchon with surprising brightness. He rose with Alpia and placed a hand caringly upon her shoulder. "This provides us time to make intercessions to the Bulàch." Then turning to Oengus, he continued, "If you will excuse me, I will find Gest and Maevis – we have preparations to do."

After their departure, Oengus noted that his commander looked as agitated as he felt.

Drust was the one who spoke. "I suppose it was for this purpose that we rebuilt the hillfort two years back."

"Yes, it is well that we have a proper defence to withstand a siege. Did you notice that Maelchon, of all people, sounded optimistic!" Oengus remarked reflectively and, for once, he thought well of the high priestess of the Bulàch and his chief druid.

Left on their own, Drust and Oengus wasted no time in devising plans that concerned domestic arrangements for the community as well as military considerations. Their orders sent several men urgently departing. Word spread like wildfire, rousing the entire community like never before.

Previously persuaded by Alpia to make Nechtan commander of the fort when the main fighting force of the Ce had gone to fight the Gaels, Oengus decided to appoint his long-seasoned campaigner of an uncle to oversee the exodus from Rhynie. Oengus had buried the hatchet, able to lay aside their antagonism concerning Nechtan's son Taran. Once again, they were cooperating, brought together by facing a common enemy. Having a most capable commander at his side, highly respected by the men, comforted him.

The older residents of Rhynie, requiring help to climb the steep slopes, made a pitiful sight as Oengus looked on. He consciously shook off feelings of vulnerability by reverting his attention to the plans laid with Drust. By midday, not a single resident remained in Rhynie.

On reaching the summit of the Pap, Oengus found it a hive of activity, astir with everyone settling in and cooking food. The cattle were lowing and sheep were bleating in their new surroundings, expressing the unease of the human settlers.

Oengus and Drust returned to Rhynie's citadel and overnighted there with half a contingent of fighting men. Sleep was difficult, with both men rising early to make further planning in the hall. When the sun was already high, they were interrupted by a flustered man, striding briskly up to their table.

"Lord! Grave news!" the messenger breathed heavily. "Brude has crossed the Spey with a huge army!"

"How many would you say?"

"I am not sure, but no one has ever seen an army this size before. Maybe five or six hundred!"

Oengus said to one of his guards, "Take three men with you and go immediately to the Lord Cynbel. Tell him to send the agreed number of men . . ." He elaborated on the message.

"We are not taken unawares," he uttered defiantly, "and thanks to Maevis, we have had a whole day to make good all these preparations."

Drust spoke reflectively. "It will be three days minimum for the Circinnian force to reach us if Cynbel sends the men immediately on the day our messenger arrives. As that is unlikely to happen so quickly, we should reckon on four, or even five days."

Oengus shrugged his shoulders. "There is nothing we can do to speed things up with the Circinn, but we can slow down Brude with the things we have already discussed. Let me see – Brude could arrive as early as this evening, but he will not anticipate us being so well-prepared."

His commander looked brighter. "Our families are all installed upon the hilltop along with half of our force and enough provisions for months!"

Maelchon and Gest arrived and joined the commanders at the table at the head of the hall.

"I will not speak of the falling star," began Maelchon, "except to say that the Bulàch is not taken by surprise by these events. Taking refuge upon her sacred hill is no small thing for we entrust ourselves to her. If she has forewarned us, then she probably favours us."

Oengus looked at his chief druid, who although appearing resolute, looked decidedly old, his complexion greyer than usual. "If there is any sorcery you can conjure, now is the time!" Oengus spoke in semi-jest, trying to alleviate the heavy mood.

"I am no sorcerer!" replied Maelchon seriously, appearing slightly affronted by the suggestion. "I trust in the Bulàch for she is greater than a hundred sorcerers! Is she not the queen of sorcerers?"

"This advance does not surprise us," Oengus shared his thoughts aloud. "Flushed with his victory last year over Dal Riata, Brude believes himself invincible." Turning to Drust, he elaborated, "Could you not tell, after Brude returned from Dunadd, that he was surprised by the number of our warriors lining the shores, and how able we were turned out for combat? He means to cut us down to size!"

"We should cull the cattle, so our enemy does not benefit from anything that we have," spoke Maelchon gravely.

"No need to," Oengus replied. "We have already deliberated upon such matters. The hillfort is provisioned with everything we need for a lengthy siege and Drust's force will have their share of provisions too."

"The surplus is already being driven towards the Dee," expanded Drust. "Nothing will be left in Rhynie, or in this neighbourhood to sustain our enemy."

"This will not be a quick fight," Oengus expanded. "The siege will be determined by resources like an adequate number of missiles, not just by food and water."

"Do you think we should burn Rhynie, so we do not provide quarters for Brude and his men?" suggested Maelchon gravely.

"We have considered that too," Drust replied, "but decided against it. We will lure them into a place of false security and then deprive them of it. That should dishearten them!"

"We might even dispatch some of Brude's men in the process. At the very least, we shall shake their morale and not give them the upper hand."

Maelchon nodded with approval and Oengus welcomed it.

"Good!" Maelchon pronounced. "Gest and I will make a sacrifice and offer up the entreaties of the entire community." He rose from the table and departed.

"We, too, should depart," Oengus said rising. Drust joined him and they walked out of the hall into a day made cool by a fresh wind. They clasped one another's wrists.

"May the gods be kind that we may greet one another again in this place when this ordeal is over!" said Drust.

"May it be so!" Oengus embraced him.

"This is quite a day!" Oengus detected his commander's voice tremble with a touch of emotion. "I cannot help but think on what the outcome could be!"

"Have we not discussed our strategy and agreed our signals to counter Brude's attack? We have come far to reach where we are now," Oengus raised a smile. "We may be fewer in number than Brude's men, but our men are highly trained and strike-and-run tactics are proven to be a thorn in the side of even the largest of armies. Did our forebears not send the Romans south by such a strategy? Besides, we fight on home soil where we know every hill and wood – that will be to our advantage. We also hold the fort and as the ones who stand to lose the most, we will fight the harder."

Drust smiled and clapped him on the back a final time. Oengus walked with him to the citadel's portal where Drust's contingent of warriors were waiting. Oengus watched him mount his horse and lead the men southwest. Would either of them survive what was to come? Drust had seemed particularly plagued by such thoughts. Brude was coming with the success of having crushed the Dal Riatans – a force reckoned greater than that of the Fortriu. But those had been different circumstances involving boats, where fickle winds had played havoc with the invaders at a crucial moment. Refusing to give in to fear, he took heart from Maelchon's remark about how the goddess would protect them on the Pap of the Bulàch. Did they not have a fighting chance to withstand the might of the Fortriu?

"Where is Drust?" Alpia asked once Oengus had reached the hillfort.

"He has taken half of the fighting force to a camp concealed in the thick of the forests." He could feel a satisfied smile play on his lips. "We have sentries posted on a hilltop within line of sight of us and their camp, and have a whole series of signals devised to communicate between us."

Alpia looked unimpressed.

"Drust's force will ensure that we will not always be the ones on the defence. Then, once the Circinnian forces arrive, the odds will be made more even."

She turned away and busied herself folding some laundered clothes. Hard as he tried to keep focused on their good strategy and remind himself of the approval of his druids, it was only natural that the tension unsettled him when so much was at stake. After awhile, growing anxious, he rejoined his sentries on the ramparts, this time with Caltram at his side holding his hand.

The sun had set, leaving a sky quite starless with a chill breeze blowing upon their heights.

"Daddy! Will we always be sleeping here?"

"No. It is just for a few nights. It is quite the adventure, eh?" He tried to sound bright, especially within earshot of his men.

He peered through the darkness, scanning for any movement to suggest the enemy's approach. The breeze blew in fresh gusts, whispering eerily upon the rough stonework of the fort. Becoming accustomed to the dark, his eyes could now differentiate not only woods from fields, but could also make out the trail sinewing north along which Brude and his men were anticipated. He reminded himself that Brude could possibly come by the north-westerly route; a more arduous way for an army with its baggage train to traverse broken ground. It would not matter which, for Drust and his men had that route covered from their hill position. Turning to the south, he indicated with an outstretched arm, a distinctive summit with a pointed top showing clearly against the sky.

"That is the Buck of Cabrach!" he informed Caltram.

"What is that?"

"That is what the hill is called. There are rocky crags at the top, a little like this hillfort, but not built by man."

"Who made the forts there?"

"The gods." He glanced down at his son, noting how Caltram looked enthralled, unable to stop peering in that direction.

They waited, and when they had grown cold, they walked along the ramparts. Nothing untoward was heard or seen.

"Time to sleep," Oengus said, leading Caltram resolutely by the hand back to their new home. He noted that Alpia looked more settled now, calmed by the company of their aunt. Oengus found sleep fitful and twice he returned to the ramparts, learning there was nothing to report.

The next day at around noon, Brude's men marched in from the north, forming a lengthy column along the road.

"Look at the dogs moving into Rhynie!" Oengus said to Gest, feeling the rising indignation of their affront. He spat over the wall in their direction.

"They are far greater in number than our combined forces," surmised Gest. "But we hold the high ground, and it is no small thing that this is a sacred hill. Surely, the Bulàch will defend us."

"Are you sure about that?" Oengus looked at him dubiously. "You and Maelchon forever point out how fickle and unpredictable she can be!"

"Oengus! All due reverence has been paid."

"I declared my loyalty to her at Mabon last year. But still, I prefer to trust in our military strategy. Is that wrong of me?"

"It is natural." Gest shrugged a shoulder. "You know, though, how things operate together between man and the gods. It was like that with the Z-rod. Initially, it did not look well for you, as Taran appeared the favoured one, seemingly chosen by the Bulàch to become the warlord. But look at how it worked out! Man still has influence to shape events – and you might argue that the Bulàch contrived things to have Taran for herself."

Oengus cast him a searching look. "We could do with the fortune of the gods. Outcomes are so unpredictable in matters of war! Look at what happened to King Gabran who strutted north like a cockerel, sure of victory."

Later that afternoon, they watched scouts from the Fortriu camp ride up the hill, no doubt to verify their position. They returned to Rhynie, which had become their camp just as Oengus had predicted.

"Our messengers will have reached Migdele," Oengus remarked, feeling a sense of optimism about Brude's slow progress.

"When do you think Drust will strike at Brude?" enquired Gest.

"Oh, tonight. Expect fire and commotion, my friend!" he smiled. "Just when they thought they had a ready-made camp. We can watch, like the gods, from up here."

Later that night, Oengus returned to the wall to find Maelchon talking with Gest. Maelchon was wearing his rabbit-skin cap for the weather had turned colder under a cloudless sky. They could clearly see Rhynie in the distance.

"Bad times!" remarked Maelchon in his usual laconic manner.

Oengus chose to ignore his comment.

"Nothing like this happened during Talorgen's time," Maelchon ventured further.

"We did not choose this fight," Oengus raised his voice. "Brude would have done this if Talorgen were alive. He calls himself king now, stating clearly his intent to dominate all Picts."

"I am not criticising!" Maelchon tried to sound conciliatory. "I was merely observing the upheaval of the times . . ."

"And what can you tell me about the outcome?" he interrogated his chief druid impatiently.

"Poof!" the druid uttered with dismay.

"Is Maevis with us?" Oengus asked. "Maybe she could tell us of outcomes."

"No, she is not. She went home," Gest informed.

Oengus felt disappointed. Despite the bite he had endured from her unbridled tongue, Maevis did have ability in her craft. "Do you think we could send for her?"

"She would only come if she felt there was a good reason," Gest observed.

That is typical of the woman, thought Oengus. She is a law unto herself and has no fear of, nor respect for, her warlord.

Later that night Drust attacked. They could not see from the hill how it all unfolded, but Rhynie was on fire. It was not a gradual spreading of fire, for flaming arrows must have been fired in a concentrated volley, catching the thatch of the roofs to create such a sudden burst of flames. There would have been chaos, but they were too far away to either see or hear. And yet he could sense the consternation, because the very air seemed to vibrate with the commotion.

Oengus smiled, but then found it unsettling taking pleasure in seeing the fortress he had expanded going up in flames. The stakes are extremely high, he rationalised, fighting for the preservation of life and tribe, so the burning of our tribal home is a necessary sacrifice. They had seized the initiative and had ruffled Brude, ensuring that he did not have it all his own way. Brude will have had his guard out and, despite that, Drust had broken through with lightning speed, striking the first blow.

"We are not to be trifled with!" he remarked gleefully. His druids returned the grin, even Maelchon. They parted company. He tried to sleep. Although he thought he had been awake he must have dozed off, for he was suddenly awakened by a guard.

"My lord, riders are approaching."

It was still dark.

He felt tense, thinking Brude had perhaps rallied a swift counterattack. "How many?"

"Five, my lord."

"Let us see if they come from Brude, or from Drust."

Wrapping his plaid about him, he followed the sentry onto the walls. The five riders were just arriving at the fort.

"Greetings! We come from Drust to report on what took place earlier."

"Open the gates," commanded Oengus.

The riders entered and the gates closed behind them. Oengus watched a young man descend from the saddle.

The torch lights revealed an animated face and fair hair falling away in curls from below his helmet.

"We took Brude totally by surprise," the messenger began with a confident smile. "He had stationed a ring of men beyond Rhynie's palisade, but we struck with lightning speed, galloping over the brow of the hill. We were upon them before they could properly muster themselves, the larger part of our group cutting them down whilst the remainder fired a volley of flaming arrows over the walls without hinderance. You would surely have seen the effect from up here?"

"Oh yes, we did! It was a fine sight!" he returned approvingly.

"We rode once around Rhynie, obliterating his external guard before intercepting the first of their men emerging from Rhynie's gates. We cut them down with swords and took others out with spears and arrows, before disappearing into the night."

"Well done!" Oengus congratulated him.

"Thanks be to the Bulàch!" Maelchon muttered almost cheerfully.

"Drust says to tell you that attacks will be made on Brude's supply train and upon any groups who forage away from their camp. We will isolate them in their position."

"Good work. You have started well. Tell Drust that we all congratulate him."

"Drust also informs you that he has a guard all the way over at the Dee crossing, ready to gallop back with news of the Circinnian approach."

"Be sure to sound the three low blasts on the carnyx to signal their coming."

The fair-haired warrior bowed his head and re-mounted his horse.

The new day dawned, and they could see that Rhynie had been burnt out and the tents of the Fortriu had sprouted over the surrounding open ground. Later that morning, a small delegation of the Fortriu came riding up to the fort. Oengus joined his guard looking down upon them from the battlements.

"I am the Lord Oengus whom you seek. State your business?"

"That you surrender and yield all your weapons."

"And why should we do that?" he returned confidently.

"So that it would preserve your people and spare you from the wrath of the mighty King Brude."

"He was not so mighty last night!"

"That! You think a pinprick would have us return to Y Broch? If you do not surrender, you will experience a real attack. Unless you yield, King Brude assures you there will be great bloodshed . . ."

Oengus interrupted him. "Aye! Your blood dripping from our swords. You do not trifle with the boar without rousing his anger! You will regret straying into his lair."

The guard looked nonplussed and steadied his agitated horse. "What is a common boar from the hill country compared to the mighty bull?"

"The Bulàch will shower retribution upon every head of the Fortriu from this her sacred hill," interjected Maelchon with druidic authority.

The Fortriu spokesman looked unimpressed. "The bull snorts in your direction and salivates as he is constrained. As you will not heed this warning, steady yourselves to feel the ground quake beneath your feet. The bull will charge with murderous intent to toss what he despises from these heights!" With that, the rider turned his horse and cantered off with his companions.

Later that afternoon, the bull assembled his army on the flattening ridge to the east of the hilltop, a good distance from the extended ramparts.

"Sound the carnyx," Oengus ordered.

The man raised the long horn to an arm-span's height above his head. As the man blew, Oengus watched the jaws of the boar, decorated at the end of the horn, move in response to the player's skill. He could just make out the wooden tongue within the carnyx's head, vibrate, lending a hoarse, rasping note to its disturbing sound. The boar's head was embellished with two red garnets for its eyes which looked luridly upon their foe. With another puff, the instrument emitted a low drone that bellowed like a monster disturbed, threatening reprisal for any audacious advance. The sound reverberated out across the valley to the hills to the south where Drust and his men would understand its message. Three times it sent this deep booming roar through the air, each one indicating that the beast had been truly aroused. To conclude, sounding like the worst of insults, the player made a final rasping noise followed by a high shrill gesticulation in the direction of the Fortriu forming below.

Oengus instructed Nechtan, "Tell all men to hold fire until the Fortriu are within easy range so that our arrows find their target and none are wasted."

Nechtan passed the word on to runners who conveyed the message swiftly along the line of battlements.

The Fortriu were the first to fire. Three successive volleys of arrows came whistling down upon them. The Ce took cover beneath their raised shields. Many of the arrows bounced off the walls, others flew overhead and a few hit shields. A child shrieked. Oengus observed a young boy with an arrow in his leg being picked up by his mother.

Through a gap in the wooden palisade raised on top of the stonework Oengus peered at Brude's men now mounting a charge, with their archers covering them from the rear.

Holding his nerve until Brude's men were within easy range, Oengus could feel his heart pounding but resisted the urge to retaliate too soon. Once he could see the faces of the Fortriu he shouted the command, "Fire!" and felt the pent-up tension suddenly released.

The Ce rose from their squatting position and returned a volley of arrows, troubling the advance of the Fortriu. Undeterred by the fallen, the attackers came in a swarm whilst the Ce continued their bombardment. No longer sheltered behind their shields, the Ce took several casualties, but far fewer than those imposed upon the Fortriu. In fear of taking out their own men, the enemy barrage ceased once the Fortriu reached the base of the outer ramparts. Now it was a battle of spears with the advantage held by the Ce, hurling spears and rocks down from their height. Oengus looked on, proud of his men who kept their heads and only fired when the enemy was at close quarters. Repelled, the attackers scattered back to their lines with several more taken down by arrows.

"Some bull was that!" remarked Gest. "It seems they have underestimated us."

"It is not over." Oengus spoke, studying the Fortriu as they regrouped beyond range of the Ce archers. "Brude will have been assessing our fire power and our spirit for a fight. We should expect a greater number at their next assault. He has a far greater advantage in numbers, and he will now know it!"

Nechtan approached. "There is a detachment coming round the hill to attack from the north!"

"Ensure we have every wall manned equally and hold position until the command is given before any man moves." Oengus bit his lower lip, anticipating Brude's tactics, and breathed deeply. "Be ready with the rocks when the Fortriu are at the base of our walls and let every man keep a spear for close combat."

Nechtan withdrew, passing the command on to three other orderlies who moved along the outer defences.

The warriors of the Fortriu came in two charging columns, far more numerous than the previous strike. Those coming from the east running across easier ground were approaching the fort faster than the other contingent, which Oengus regarded as a miscalculation on Brude's part. The Ce waited crouched again behind raised shields, each looking to Oengus and Nechtan for their raised arms to fall, to signal fire. The enemy were so many that Oengus's heart was pounding. Still, he resisted the urge to retaliate too soon. With the sheer volume of the attackers, he gave the order to fire sooner than before, figuring that many arrows would find a target amongst the serried lines of the advancing Fortriu. Every Ce warrior rose with a coordination that impressed and rained down several volleys. He watched a succession of warriors fall leaving a thickening trail of injured and dead behind the advancing horde.

With the Fortriu sprinting, they reached the eastern wall in a mass and hurled grappling irons onto the tops of the ramparts whilst others brought ladders with a rope attached near the top end. As soon as a ladder touched the palisade it was held in position by a man holding the rope on the ground, allowing his comrade to scamper up the runners. The Ce were able to push some ladders away, but others, better secured, had to be pushed over at an angle to frustrate the assault. However, other ladders held firm, especially where the defenders fell to the rain of arrows and spears. For a moment it looked like the Fortriu had breached the hillfort's defences until a barrage of rocks and stones were flung down, taking off many an assailant. Oengus ensured reinforcements took the place of the fallen and for a while the attackers were held at bay.

Meanwhile, the other advancing flank of the Fortriu had reached the top of the battlements of the northern wall. Still vulnerable without a palisade to protect them, they pushed forwards through sheer force of numbers, swinging axes and swords to take a section of wall.

Oengus could see Nechtan in the thick of it, slashing at two Fortriu attackers, bringing down one with a well-aimed blow. The other assailant looking like he would get the better of his uncle, was brought down by another defender. Before long, Oengus found himself in the thick of the battle as their eastern flank came under pressure as many Fortriu breached the wall.

How much longer could they repel them? Oengus thought, as he signalled for reinforcements to come from the southern and western walls. He wondered what the outcome would be, should those held in reserve by Brude be sent into the fray. Not fighting for their own preservation alone, but for the lives of their women folk and children, the Ce began to fight back with renewed determination, and with their better discipline, started to gain an advantage. Ladders were pushed off and the Fortriu remaining upon the battlements were cut down and those at the base of the walls fled in a rabble.

Heaving a sigh of relief, Oengus gave the order to regroup and clear the battlements of corpses and to deal with their own wounded. Looking over to the east, he saw the sickening sight of another column of Fortriu advancing, and those who had just fled now joining the new attack. Fearing what the outcome would be, he tried to take heart that they still held position and had lost far fewer men than the Fortriu. Brude must have seen that the Fortriu were gaining a foothold, and had he sent the reserves in earlier, he would have gained the advantage. Again, Oengus was surprised by the poor tactics of his celebrated adversary.

Oengus gave the order to open fire upon the new onslaught. Although some of the attackers fell prey to the Ce arrows, the Fortriu were too many for their advance to be halted. How would the Ce hold their position? he wondered. He thought of Alpia and Caltram and felt an inner fury rise within. A carnyx then sounded, blowing a long-sustained blast and he was confused for it was not a signal agreed with Drust. The lengthy blast was followed by another and came from Brude's position, causing the advancing horde to hastily retreat. The Ce pushed home their advantage by firing arrows, with a good many finding their mark.

With the Fortriu evaporating from the ridge, Nechtan joined him and asked, "Why do you suppose Brude sounded the retreat?"

"I do not know – and just after deploying his reserves too!"

"Quite extraordinary," Nechtan pondered as he removed his helmet to wipe his brow.

"You are injured!" Oengus observed a gash down his uncle's forearm.

"Caught on a lance, but I felled the man before he mounted the ramparts," he returned with some satisfaction.

"You should get it attended to," Oengus remarked and turned to look at Brude's men descend from the ridge. The

Fortriu retreat was not an orderly one, for the advance guard running down the slopes in the direction of Rhynie were being overtaken by horsemen. The steepness of the slope forced them to check their speed to what must have seemed a frustrating pace. Why were they running back to base just when they were consolidating their attack? he thought.

"Send a party out beyond our walls to gather up every weapon," he ordered, "and ensure that no Fortriu is left living upon this ridge."

A carnyx sounded from Drust's position. Gest joined Oengus as he listened carefully to its twice repeated signal.

"Drust has mounted a counterattack!" Oengus informed his druid friend.

"Where?"

"Signals cannot be so detailed. All we know is that Drust has made an attack, causing Brude to call off his own attack."

"Where do you suppose he struck?"

Oengus thought for a moment. "If I were Drust, I would have struck at Brude's base back in Rhynie. There would be few men there for I am sure Brude had brought almost all his warriors up here, thinking that we are all contained within the fort."

As they peered towards far-off Rhynie, Oengus could detect smoke suggesting a successful strike had been made to waste the enemy camp. He thought for a moment before announcing, "I must go and speak with Nechtan. Come and join me."

They found Nechtan being treated for his wound and informed him about the new development.

"Drust has saved the day!" Nechtan responded with relief.

"Brude will now know about our second division operating remotely from us."

"It is a distraction, giving us respite," Nechtan said through gritted teeth as his wound was being bound up with a rag.

"It will also tell Brude that we are only half the force," Oengus thought aloud. "Anyway, those who retreated from our battlements will have told him that much. Brude could push home his advantage, knowing that if his reserves had only reached us earlier, they could have overwhelmed us."

"We should send runners through to Drust to ask for reinforcements."

Oengus considered this proposal. "We need to find a way to stall this campaign as best we can until the Circinn arrive."

"The Circinn!" Nechtan said with evident disdain.

"But are they not another day away at the earliest?" questioned Gest.

"I do not see us being able to hold this position if we are attacked again like today," his uncle reflected. "Even with Drust's reinforcements, the Fortriu have such vast numbers!"

"But Brude has lost more than we have for sure," countered Gest.

"Aye," Oengus exclaimed, "he is not finding us a push-over, is he!"

He noted his uncle's expression grow thoughtful. "Some of our women are fighters, able to wield the sword and thrust with the spear. We should equip them, so our numbers are increased."

"That is a good plan!" agreed Oengus. "I am thinking, though, to get through to Drust. The day is almost over, and darkness will give us cover through to his position."

Nechtan frowned. "That would be risky. Morale will be affected if you are not with us!"

"It would only be brief, and I will be returning before daybreak."

"Why not just send a runner?"

"Because I need to coordinate our next move with Drust. All has gone to plan so far, but things are developing quickly, beyond what we had initially anticipated."

He could see his uncle compress his lips before speaking. "You are right about seizing the initiative! If we just sit tight here, Brude will overwhelm us."

"I am thinking that if we can attack Rhynie at dawn," Oengus began, "with a feigned retreat into the forest to lure them into an ambush, then we could draw them away from this hill. If we do nothing, I fear he will hold this fort by the end of tomorrow."

"Aye. Stall him by another day, then the Circinn might reach us in time." His uncle revealed a brief smile.

Chapter Four

True Valour

AD 564 Eildon Hills

The open road stretched into the hazy distance of a summer's day when Taran left Candida Casa. Around a distant hillock the way curved, beckoning him to explore what lay beyond. Hay fields were growing high and the purple-pink of the newly flowered willow herb lined the wayside. Taran felt free, released from his long studies, and the world felt bountiful, full of possibilities. Finally, he was heading north to resume pursuing his destiny, and he sang at the top of his voice, picking up a brisk pace, breaking on occasion into a skip. Reflecting over the past eight years, his head had been so stuffed with knowledge that it felt there was no further capacity, and yet he observed soberly that he was no more than an equal to the swine herder in God's eyes.

He headed into the hills north-eastwards, towards the lands of the Picts. How would it feel to speak his own language once more, to be with those of the same manner and customs, back in the heather hills and glens? But how, exactly, was he to reconnect with his destiny? Going north was the obvious direction. How would the High King make things clear to him? Or had he so deviated from what was planned that to reconnect would be a lengthy trial? He had in mind to visit Fillan and Colmcille, in that order, sensing that their spiritual insight might guide him. His big desire was to engage with the next quest to acquire another grace required for bearing fire to the north.

He overnighted in a village where he was not the only stranger passing through, and fell into conversation with a family looking in a pitiful state.

"Saxon riders came upon us as we were harvesting the hay," explained one young man. "They had drawn swords and spears and we had only scythes. Resistance was futile. They made their intent clear, for one caught my arm here with his spear." The man rolled up a torn and blood-stained sleeve to reveal a lengthy gash.

"Everything was abandoned for the taking by these thieves," sobbed a young woman with a child at her breast. "Some homesteads and fields were torched! We panicked and fled."

"Everywhere these Saxons ride, they plunder, taking with them any portable wealth," spoke another man, "and anything that cannot be carried off is mindlessly destroyed."

"That is only true of some," corrected the young man with the gash. "Some do not spoil the land when they intend to farm it for themselves."

As Taran journeyed on the next day, he encountered many more refugees. Women and children outnumbered the males, for husbands and fathers had fallen in defending what was rightfully theirs. Those spared the sword were a sorry sight, ragged and hungry. Grimy cheeks, partially smeared by tears, spoke of the suffering of muted children.

Taran was hailed by an older woman sitting outside her round hut. "Good sir, will you not rest here with us?"

Realising that he was being mistaken for a druid, he replied, "Thank you. I have not lost home nor loved ones though." Sighting a lone woman with a child approaching, he appealed, "Would you find it in your heart to take in these two? Their need is far greater than mine."

The woman glanced at the pair and turned away with a disdainful air.

Taran was angered by her dismissive attitude. "Have pity on these, not on me." His aggravation increased when the woman still refused to reply. He might not be a warlord whose orders would be acted upon out of fealty or fear, but was he not considered a druid? Did druids not hold authority too?

"Do you not fear judgement for turning away the likes of these?" he further challenged the older woman. "I tell you, the gods would have you show compassion and mercy, just as you have been shown to have lived a long life."

The woman looked piqued by his comment and glanced again at the mother and child.

Would she relent, thought Taran, will her hardened heart yield? The woman turned to him and scratched her head. Is she feeling embarrassed now? he wondered.

"Oh, come on, both of you!" she said almost reluctantly.

Despite the lack of grace, the mother was in such a wretched state that she turned in at the gate. As they started to converse, Taran moved on, glad to have some influence. He reflected on the woeful exodus before him and considered how their war songs were about boastful deeds of rampage and conquest, but none were sung about defeat; although maybe a fallen hero would be celebrated. He recalled, with remorse, his act of violence that had caused two innocent children to be orphaned. He had been no better than the Saxon raiders, bringing abject misery in his pursuit of ambition and personal gain.

Time to make amends, he thought. He need no longer feel the frustration of an impotent onlooker but could appeal to human decency by taking advantage of being taken for a druid.

"Will you not take pity upon this brother and sister?" Taran challenged a couple who stood guardedly beside their door. The girl and boy whom he had befriended along the way could not have been more than twelve and six years old and had become separated from their parents, unsure whether they were still alive. "Do consider how you will be judged at the end of your days! Will you turn a blind eye on these children?"

"But we are poor ourselves! We are just peasants!"

"And yet you are well-nourished. Surely you have enough to share, even if it means taking a little less for yourselves?"

Appearing stressed, the woman looked undecided until her disconcerted expression evaporated as she extended a hand to the young siblings.

Further along, he watched three refugees stray into the fields in search of food. They pulled at the unripe ears of grain and ate, trying to appease hunger pains. More followed their example, trampling down a portion of the field.

"Here! What are you doing? Get out of the field!" a farmer shouted.

A couple of wretched people close to the irate man looked up, and, deciding to ignore him, continued to gather the grain. It seemed to Taran that they could relate to his anger, but knowing that the farmer was outnumbered, took advantage of his impotence. More went trampling into the field to graze. The incensed farmer turned briskly down the road.

"This does not satisfy," complained one woman. "The ears are hard, even when they can be de-husked!"

Further up the road, a group of farmers standing defiantly by a gate to an enclosed field, brandishing pitch forks, hoes and axes in a menacing manner, caused the refugees to falter momentarily. No one spoke as the locals stood firm like a warband. The ones at the rear, growing impatient, started to push the crowd forward, causing those at the front to advance with an unruly surge. They kept to the road, not doubting that violence would ensue should anyone be tempted to enter the enclosed field.

As the day wore on into evening, Taran found himself sharing the plight of the refugees, without food or shelter. At least it was summer, he thought, and we do not have to contend with frosty nights. He walked on wearily with the subdued crowd.

"Come and rest here," one householder gestured to Taran, singling him out.

"If you fear your gods, then take in this man beside me."

"But he is injured! I can see his arm is no good – what good will he be to me?"

"Once, when I had a broken arm, I was taken in by a couple who thought the same. However, when my arm healed, I proved to be of great use, repaying their kindness many fold."

The local paused before gesturing the man to come to his house.

"Why did you do that?" Taran was asked by a man of similar age to himself. "You could have had shelter for the night."

"The man's need was greater. I have not suffered the trauma of losing home, livelihood and loved ones like you." He paused, correcting himself. "Well, I have, but that happened long ago. I can say that I have become used to not having a place to call home."

"How can that be?"

"What is home?"

"A place of shelter, I suppose, somewhere you belong and feel secure," replied the young man.

"You see, I have that and carry it with me."

The young man looked puzzled. He had an earnest face that Taran liked.

"My name is Adda."

Taran gave his name and continued. "My God looks over me and supplies my need. He is my shelter, stronger than any fortress."

"And who is your God?" Adda asked with interest.

Taran met the man's eyes. "The One who has made us and all things that you behold."

"I have been watching you for much of the day, and I have not seen you eat anything. You have only drunk water, so how can you say your God supplies your need?"

"My friend, I have learned to be content with little or with much." Taran cast him a friendly smile. "Fasting teaches the control of appetite. I do not doubt that my Father will supply what I need when necessary, as that has been my experience in all my wanderings."

They talked a good while upon this matter until the light was fading and the crowd they were part of started looking for somewhere to lie down for the night.

"Let us go into the woods and build ourselves a shelter," Taran said.

Taran was equipped with a weighty field knife that he used to prune branches and the two of them fashioned a shelter of sorts. He had his awning with him which he draped over a simple frame of branches.

"I am the last of my siblings who has not married," expanded Adda. Seeming intent to share his story, Taran was glad to listen.

"Our smallholding was doing well that even my older brother acquired more land where we farmed a portion of a fertile valley. All was as well as could be . . . until the Saxons came. With my eldest brother refusing to stand by and let the thieves pillage our place, my father stepped in to plead with him not to stand in their way, for what could we do against those armed with swords? The pigs just cut my father down . . ." He stopped, choked with grief. "My brother, trying to defend him, was brought down too. They were both killed by a filthy mob of those foreigners."

Taran felt appalled. "What became of the rest of your family?"

"I do not know. My mother ran away with one of my sisters and I have not seen them since – they must have taken a different direction. I have one other brother, but what became of him is anyone's guess. I wanted to stay, but a neighbour catching hold of my arm made me run with him."

Feeling the weight of Adda's grief, Taran patted him on the shoulder. "You have suffered much." He hung his head with his friend for a time and eventually brought himself to speak. "I have nothing to say that will lighten this burden that could make good your losses. There are no words that will reduce the effect of such terrible abuse."

Adda looked at him with tears falling freely from his eyes.

"But I will pray . . . come, Adda, let us pray." He saw the young man nod, although he looked slightly hesitant concerning what he should do. "You need do nothing but listen and share your thoughts with the One who holds ultimate power."

"I will," he replied.

After he had prayed, Adda seemed comforted. Taran was not surprised for he had felt the Presence with them, giving him the right words, but more importantly, bringing solace to the grieving man. They spoke at length; Adda asking many questions. Being in great need, he was keen to find help to endure his tribulations.

The next day, emboldened by his success of persuading some to take in a refugee or two, Taran appealed to the local folk and succeeded in thinning out their substantial number. Their reduced number, no longer perceived as great a threat, excited more sympathy and consequently more found quarter.

Arriving at one sizeable village, the refugees sat down in a large grassy space in the centre where a goat herd was grazing. The travellers expressed their hope with one another that a place of so many households would be able to help more than the usual ones and twos. They were joined by another group of refugees and, tired and hungry, all sat with a resolute air. Feeling threatened, the villagers presented themselves as a group, many with crossed arms.

One burly man, with a shock of red hair, raised his voice. "You must move on! How could we possibly care for so many?"

"But you have not cared for any of us," replied one woman, gesticulating with an outstretched arm.

"Why should we? We are only poor peasant farmers! Do you think we have food in abundance?" retorted the same man with beads of sweat now glistening upon his brow.

"You are not our blood and kin!" justified an elderly local woman.

"You are a bunch of thieves! You are not only intent on stealing, but destroying too!" shouted another man. Taran recognised him as the farmer who, on the previous day, had shouted at the crowd for trampling his field and then had gathered his neighbours in an armed stand-off.

An ugly exchange passed between the two sides, with oaths sworn as emotions increased. Some of the dispossessed rose to their feet to make their presence more forcibly felt. In the heart of the melee, two men grabbed hold of one another.

Taran stepped forward and pulled them apart. "My dear brothers, stop this at once!"

Whether it was his druid appearance or the imploring tone of reason – Taran was unsure – but they stopped jostling, and no one had to lose face. The assailants stepped back to their respective sides drawn up in this confrontation.

"I am not among the refugees," began Taran, raising his voice to address everyone, "but come as a man of peace, appealing for understanding." Realising that only those close to him could hear – for the talking and commotion continued beyond – he raised his voice. "Come on, will you be quiet and listen for a moment!"

Stepping on to a nearby boulder, he rose head and shoulders above the throng of people. "Good farmers, listen to me!" As there was still quite a hubbub, he cusped his hands about his mouth and bellowed, "Quiet!"

More of the crowd fell silent. He pointed demonstratively at a section that was still noisy. "You lot over there, be quiet!" Part of the crowd that was already compliant, told the noisy ones to be quiet. "I beg you local folk to listen to your conscience before making a rash judgement based on fear. And all who are seeking refuge, bear with me and keep quiet, for you do your cause much harm by shouting and fighting."

He breathed heavily, aware of his heart pounding so forcibly that his body seemed to sway. Surprised to have gained the crowd's attention, he muttered under his breath, "O Lord, help me."

"Good people, and I call you good because that is what you are in times of peace. I ask the people of this community to consider this. What if you were suddenly made homeless, as these people you see before you. Imagine being without silver or food, how are you going to eat? Picture the slaughter of loved ones – imagine how wretched and distraught you would feel. These people have been driven from their burnt homes and are now destitute. Consider that you are these people!"

"Well, we are not, and they are thieves, taking what we have laboured to produce!" retorted the burly man with the shock of red hair.

"Who are you to tell us what to do?" interjected the woman. "You are just a Pict from the sound of your accent – scum from the north!"

Not allowing himself to be flustered, Taran took heart that at least he had won their attention but also knew he had only moments to retain their willingness to listen. "Just think if you were in their place before you spirit them away. It is not hard to imagine . . ."

Again, he was interrupted by the audible sneer of the one who took it upon himself to oppose him, a skinny fellow with lank, greasy hair.

"Just be quiet, Wroid," demanded a broad-shouldered woman. "Give the druid a chance to speak!" She elbowed her way forward, looking as though she might clip the thin man about the ear.

"Thank you," Taran acknowledged the woman. "Imagine the Saxons pushing north and arriving here to seize your farms and spirit you and your families away. They come with swords and spears, battle-hardened – who among you could withstand them? You would be reduced to watching helplessly on – if you were not killed – to witness pillage and slaughter. You would be left with no choice other than to flee. Imagine how you would want others to consider your plight when you come to a new place seeking refuge?"

To his surprise, the crowd remained quiet. A man in his mid-forties who, judging by his well-groomed appearance and clean tunic, was not from among the refugees, nodded with a degree of understanding. His approval meant more than the spirited nods of the refugees who were glad of someone championing their cause.

Taran continued more confidently. "Life is so brief that death awaits each sooner or later, even more so in these days of great calamities. Everyone needs to face death with the certainty that we have lived worthy lives, that we can be commended as a courageous people guided by noble hearts. Where will our destiny lie in the after world? Will we be numbered among the unforgiven dead? Or will we be found worthy to be received into paradise?

Feeling constrained by the Spirit, he checked himself. "I have spoken as a druid would speak and I am thankful for your respect." He paused, wondering whether to reveal his identity and run the risk of losing their attention. "But I tell you that I am no druid, even though I might appear as one. I am a soldier of Christ . . ."

"Then why do you appear before us as a druid?" shouted someone from the crowd.

"A Christian priest that I have met did not pose as a druid!" remonstrated a large woman with an expressionless face.

"I come from the Celtic tradition and not the Roman. We Celts do not cut our hair short and shave about the crown." Taran turned away from the woman and spoke to the crowd. "Like druids, we are concerned with the unity between this world and the after world, of life and death, preparing and interceding for those who walk the perilous way between these two worlds. I speak with the authority of the One who created us, whose power to make all that is seen is at work even now, governing circumstances and events."

The well-groomed man in his mid-forties again nodded his approval and a woman to his right looked on with a smile. A young child pulling insistently at the hand of her mother was briefly scolded as she reverted her attention to Taran.

"The Creator Lord is full of compassion, who becoming a man lived with the poor. He healed and provided for many, showing the mercy of a God who will judge us by the standards he has demonstrated. We must be compassionate, my friends."

"The kind of deliverer we need is not someone to lick our wounds," retorted a ruddy-faced fellow with a booming voice. "Our need is for Arthur, ready to rise at the appointed hour. Arthur will come to our aid and vanquish the accursed oppressors."

"Well spoken," agreed another voice.

This gave Taran an idea for a fresh approach. "I tell you, there is a King far greater than Arthur who has already risen from the tomb with resurrection power. That same life power is at work in those who choose to believe. Christ, the King, promises to return, not as the humble, wandering teacher and healer that once he was, but as a valiant champion, infinitely more powerful than Arthur."

He could feel beads of perspiration breaking out on his forehead. "His very word alone, like a double-edged sword, will annihilate evil; every monstrous power raised to defy his rule of peace shall be crushed. His enemies, when they will look upon the sun-bright countenance of the noble King, will cry out for the mountains to crumble and cover them. He is the One in whom you should place your trust; One who is able to redeem your soul."

Words flowed with such rare fluency and articulation. Judging by the rapt faces of those listening, heavenly powers had captivated many ears and hearts. He reasoned, implored passionately. And in the end, someone interrupted with an agitated voice. "Therefore, what should we do?" Although spoken just by one, Taran wondered whether it was perhaps representative of what others were thinking.

"Be compassionate, be fair." Taran pivoted around surveying his entire audience. "It is clear your community cannot care for all the homeless here, for you are poor peasant farmers; but remember our proverb: *when food is scarce, it is generous to share it.* And for those seeking refuge, you are to consider those who are weakest, those in greatest need. Put their plight before your own." He surveyed the refugees, catching the eye of a few whose hope hung on his words. His eyes came to one beaming with approval – it was Adda.

"Again, I address this community. Whoever has space for one more to lie down in their hut, who can spare an extra portion to serve from the pot, even should it mean taking a little less for yourselves, this is what I say to you . . ."

"Who has given to us that we should give to others?" interrupted an old woman in an embittered tone.

"Charity begins with us; we lead by example. Even by the standards you respect from your own gods, do they not take note of your actions and judge accordingly? By your own beliefs, charity is approved, fairness is rewarded. It is on such things, along with the belief that Christ shall judge, that determines where we shall pass to in the afterlife."

He swallowed heavily, noting again the nodding of heads. Even from among those who were not demonstratively giving their assent, an unusual stillness characterised the whole assembly.

"Do not just estimate what the cost is to you now, but consider the practical gain! You will have an extra pair of hands to help in the home and in the fields. By showing charity, you will earn respect and loyalty if you do not lord yourselves over them. You may have to struggle for a short while, but in the long term, think on how you will gain."

The embittered old woman turned her back on him and elbowed her way through to the rear of the crowd. She was the only one who moved. Some, feeling shame at how they had first reacted, had eyes lustrous with remorse. Even the man with the shock of red hair, who had been belligerent at the start, had quietened down.

"The druid of Christ speaks well," said a voice from the crowd, which was met with other voices of assent.

"Thank you for your open hearts," Taran acknowledged them. "As for the remainder of refugees, you are to leave here with me. I give you my word that I shall walk with you and be your advocate, until the last has found sanctuary. Is that agreed?"

The refugees looked at him with a certain dismay. A brief silence followed, charged with uncertainty. Then Adda called out, "Aye, I will walk with you. Let the weakest among us remain here."

"Me too – I will walk on!" declared a young woman.

There was a slight pause before the well-groomed farmer responded. "I will take two people into my home."

This prompted others to make similar offers of ones and twos, but with too many speaking, Taran interjected again. He only needed to raise his arms for quiet to return. "All those who are offering sanctuary, stand over by that oak."

Several villagers moved in that direction, leaving a diminished number uncertain. This physical separation worked on the conscience of a few more villagers who joined the first group under the oak.

Taran appointed a couple of the refugees whom he knew were respected, to determine who were the neediest. By this process, those who were suffering most were paired with those offering sanctuary. Around thirty people were accommodated, which thinned the party to half its size.

Taran led the remainder, the less pitiful, out onto the open road, to continue their foot-sore trek.

"I wonder how much further you will have to go?" exclaimed Taran to those immediately around him.

"We need not fear – look at what happened back there!" replied the young woman who had been among the first to volunteer to walk on. "But what did happen? Those hard-hearted people were changed! How did you do that?"

"I do not think it was so much what our druid of Christ said," interjected Adda. "Did you not sense an extraordinary presence among us in the heat of those exchanges?"

"I was most certainly aware of the spirit of the High King present," spoke Taran. "Only he can speak to man's heart in that way." In his head, he was thankful for heavenly persuasion, hoping again to be an instrument to inspire compassion and to arbitrate justice.

At the next village, a similar consultation was held and more of their number were taken in. In this manner, every individual was eventually provided for, and Adda, who seemed loathe to part from him, was the last one to find a home.

Alone, Taran took to the upland glens and the hill passes, feeling exhausted from being caught up unexpectedly in the heady confusion of the refugee problem. In no hurry to proceed, he kept the same camp in the hills for two nights, sleeping long into the morning and lying down to rest early in the evening. He lived off what the land had scantily to offer: grubs, bulbs and boiled nettles. A rabbit and a fish were caught, but not having a bow, he had to resort to snares and a makeshift spear.

Refreshed and ready to move on, he left the wilder hill country and forest to rejoin the byways, free of refugees. He came to the banks of the River Tweed, with the Eildon Hills rising beyond, a view he had longed to see since hearing about Arthur. He recalled the popular belief concerning the hero, who, along with his warriors, lay sleeping within the hill, ready to be roused when the Britons were in critical need.

Passing the nearby ruins of the Roman Trimontium garrison, he considered this symbol of conquest and control over the local Britons. He noted how its engineering works, which at one time had exhibited the power and prestige of empire, had been reduced to naught. He remembered the abbot of Candida Casa commenting that the Antonine Wall had taken twenty years to complete, but had only been manned for a further twenty years before being abandoned. All that flexing of muscle, the moving of mountains of earth by thousands of slaves, which must have been truly monumental to witness, had so brief a use. And yet for those enslaved at that time, he reflected, what they were building must have seemed to be changing their world forever, affecting their identity. Feeling a tinge of pride that his people had resisted total Roman conquest, he acquiesced and remarked aloud, "The empires of men perish, but the heavenly kingdom prevails under a rule which does not kill nor enslave."

Gathering some straight branches into a bundle and securing these with a strip of vine wrapped about one end, he raised the bundle, splaying the free ends of the poles to form a circular footing. Upon this cone structure he secured his awning to provide some shelter from rain and wind.

Patiently, he endured the numbing chill of the Tweed as he crouched stock still on a submerged ledge above a deep pool and was eventually rewarded with the catch of a trout. He ate well. Reclining on his elbow, he dreamily watched his campfire flicker as the sun set.

Eildon's three peaks were gradually being enveloped in deepening shadows until they became a jet-black silhouette on a sky of dying embers. The light, which never wholly faded that night, just diminished, as the sun dipped below the horizon, leaving a luminosity behind the line of hills to the north. A deep afterglow suffused the sky with a flawlessly clear sapphire glimmer.

He reflected on the heady days of sharing the refugees' plight, of experiencing their hunger and rejection. Just as Romans had come and displaced, a new invader had appeared, all brazen, less organised than Rome's legions, but with that same unscrupulous hunger to seize what was not theirs. The one-time hired mercenaries of hefty axe-wielders and skilled swordsmen, tiring of their hireling status, had seized the initiative in an unstoppable onslaught of a servant rebellion.

The human strife sickened, making him consider the valour that warriors sought as a virtue. Where was the valour in being the oppressor? How could men, exhibiting their brutish nature, be lauded as heroes? They are nothing more than organised thugs. Valour, surely, had to be the virtue of the oppressed upholding justice and liberty and, therefore, Arthur had valour. If a war could be called "just", then Arthur's cause was a just one. And yet, he pondered, Arthur caused bloodshed, so could there be valour in killing and maiming? Could valour be a virtue for a man of peace such as himself? He thought of Colmcille's devastating pride and the error that had led three thousand to be slain. Had he shown valour, though, through repentance, accepting exile to free from the darkness as many as had been wiped out? There was a certain dignity, he mused, in confessing wrong and in bearing punishment. Maybe there was valour too in coming to a foreign land, beyond the support and identity of one's home. Would it not take humility to start a work from scratch? That took determination and a rugged character.

As he stared, mesmerised by the dancing flames of his campfire, he turned these thoughts into a prayer. "Father, forgive my sins, the blood-let that orphaned children, the haughty spirit that sought to be a warlord, to extort tribute by displays of supremacy. I was no better than these Saxon murderers. Deliver me from all such empty ambition, the vainglory of every kind of superiority, the desire for recognition and success. Even for the strong temptation to settle in one place, seeking comfort from the things of this world, forgive me, Lord."

He visualised the armour he once wore and of leaving it in a pile in an act of renunciation. "May evil and all that is unworthy, be frustrated and shattered, to liberate the good. May courage, the warrior spirit that once held sway in my former life, continue under your Lordship to serve your ends. Lead me in this quest, direct my steps to bear fire to the north, O, great High King."

He felt his own frailty, bowed under the weight of oppression.

"I know my limitations," he continued to pray. "I feel hunger upon the road; I am stretched as a lone individual to make a difference to the despairing. But with your Spirit, I have witnessed what can be accomplished. May I fulfil this charge to bring fire to the north. As I state this, it seems audacious; and yet, when I look to you, everything becomes possible because the whole earth is yours. You ordain the comings and goings of all mankind, bringing success against the odds and frustrating the might of kings and withering the sword arm of the warrior."

He opened his eyes and stared into the bright heart of the fire. Again, he bowed his head. "Thinking upon the cross where all futility seems expressed, that instrument of seeming defeat becomes the means of triumph. And so, if it please you, Father, take my inconsequential life and fashion it to achieve your purposes, through a demonstration of your excellency and utter supremacy over all things. So be it, Lord – I am your servant, a mere, roaming vagabond of the roads, but through you, the overcomer of anything that opposes your desire for mankind."

Staring once more at the fire, he perceived insubstantial forms taking wispy shape, emerging from its pulsing embers. Thinking his vision blurred, he rubbed his eyes. Wisps fused together to form what seemed to be a warrior's mail shirt, with overlapping iron platelets like the scales of a fish. For a moment it glowed with white-hot splendour.

As the shape dissolved, he observed wisps forming a war helmet with extensions on either side to protect ear and jaw, and an elongated section sweeping down the rear to shield the neck. He admired how the helmet was emblazoned with emblems of bears and bulls, with mysterious crescent moons interlaced with broken arrows invoking victory.

This too evaporated, and a shield appeared, highly worked, with raised bosses, engraved with intricate Celtic swirls running in never-ending, serpentine traceries to confuse the onlooker. He contemplated the Celtic knot that had no beginning nor end, said to even confound demons. He smiled that it also expressed everlasting life that took away the dread fear of death.

Then, he saw a sword materialise, splendidly crafted, with a decorative hilt, overlaid with gleaming bronze, with a large, polished gem placed into the hilt. He had never seen its like before. Its scabbard was of embossed leather, trimmed with burnished bronze, bearing the heads and bodies of semi-mythical creatures; a veritable heirloom to be passed down to succeeding generations. Then a leather belt appeared, which he only found notable for its plainness after such elaborately crafted armour, yet knowing how integral it was to secure the mail shirt and in providing buckles for sword and dagger. Finally, a pair of leather sandals, well-worn, muddied from miles run, made a brief and unspectacular appearance.

No further apparition came, despite his intense gaze to perceive more. Having renounced martial pursuits, this armour made one obvious connection. He understood it as the response to his question about the role of valour for the warrior of Christ. Knowing each piece was listed in scripture, he recalled that the mail shirt, which protected the vital organs, represented righteousness; the helmet symbolised salvation; a shield, the faith to fend off the attack of the evil one; the sword, the weapon of the Spirit; a belt for truth holding the parts together. Finally, the common sandals were as important as any other part, aiding the wearer to run with urgency, taking the heavenly message to the learned ones anticipating him in the north.

Is the King's mission not to be executed with military purpose and integrity? Am I not to bear the characteristics that the armour represents? I might be just a wandering pilgrim in the eyes of most, but underneath this identity, am I not truly a spiritual warrior? If I am to accomplish my ultimate quest, then it calls for those rugged, Pictish virtues of courage and strength, outspokenness and decisiveness.

It dawned upon him with great excitement that this must be the fourth revelation of his seven-fold quest. He marvelled at its occurrence, just at a time when he had wondered how he would receive a heavenly sign after four years of waiting since the previous sign at the waterfall.

Such valour, he surmised, suggests gritty determination and steadfastness. This too will be required to fulfil my quest, adding to the other graces revealed of mercy, surrender and love. Are these not crucial elements in making an effective pilgrim?

Chapter Five

The Wasting

AD 560 Rhynie

Oengus left Nechtan, encouraged by his uncle's cooperation. After selecting ten men to ride with him through to Drust's position at nightfall, he went to his hut to eat. He updated Alpia and Conchen about the fast-changing events, playing down the strength of the Fortriu. "Uncle Nechtan suggested that all able women are equipped with sword and spear to help defend our families."

Aunt Conchen stopped eating and gave him a lingering look. "Is it that bad?"

"I should be glad to bear a weapon," responded Alpia resolutely. "I felt vulnerable when the Fortriu broke through to mount our ramparts earlier. We only had kitchen knives to defend ourselves with!"

Oengus shook his head. "They would not be much use against a sword!"

"The Fortriu are more numerous although they lost more men than we did today."

"I shall be glad to fight for my people," returned Alpia. "I will go through the camp and muster all women willing to fight. I used to fight boys when I was young and beat the best of them!"

"Good. Uncle Nechtan will see that you and other women are equipped."

After eating, he left with his men on horseback, descending the hill over to the west to benefit from a cover of trees. There was no sign of the Fortriu. They turned south-west, continuing downhill on a gentler gradient, crossed a stream and rode the contour until reaching a valley with another stream to ford. They heard nothing all along their ride except the cascade of water and the wind blowing briskly in the treetops. Ahead was the hill where Drust's sentries were posted. Halfway up the ascent, they were halted by a voice in the darkness.

"Identify yourselves."

"It is I, your Lord Oengus."

"Welcome! Come on up."

They were led to the summit where five men were positioned.

"Lead me to Drust's camp."

One of the men untied his horse tethered to a tree nearby.

Safely led to the camp, Oengus and Drust greeted one another heartily, updating one another on the events of the past two days.

"We set Brude's camp on fire," Drust spoke with animation. "We easily overwhelmed the few men he had positioned there, mostly cooks who, with their soup ladles, were no match for us!"

"Brude will pass a cold night!" Oengus snorted.

"And a hungry one. We led their supply wagons away."

"Excellent. But you did not bring them here, did you?"

"Do you think I was born yesterday?" Drust passed him an affronted look before grinning.

"Without food or shelter, Brude will want to bring this campaign to a swift end."

"Do you think you can hold him off for another day?"

"No. That is why I have come to talk. I am thinking of luring them into an ambush tomorrow first thing, to strike a decisive blow. That way, we will either drive Brude home, or keep them at bay for another day. Then, hopefully, the Circinnians can swell our number."

They laid their plans in some detail and Oengus returned to the hillfort. Sleep was poor knowing he had to rise well before dawn with his contingent of men. His eyes felt dry and prickly from lack of sleep. The wind had risen during the night, so that when Oengus led a squad of some fifty horsemen across the stream down in the valley, they saw how the rising storm was turning back the leaves and even stripping some still green from the bough. He met up with a small group of Drust's men as was planned and advanced under the cover of trees towards a position above the valley that led to Rhynie. The Fortriu camp could be seen across the valley with many campfires flickering in the disturbed night. Oengus veered south with his men, riding to the edge of a high spur where the high ground was intersected by a narrow glen. This was their agreed place of ambush. They waited tensely, watching the stars fade as the darkness diminished. He wiped the condensation from his beard.

Oengus watched Drust's horsemen ride out to strike Brude's camp. Would the Fortriu be lured to give chase into the confines of a narrow glen? Oengus scanned the lie of the slope where he was to lead his contingent to attack Brude's rear, compressing them so tightly in the defile that the Fortriu would struggle to fight. It was a bold plan but a risky one, and he grew anxious about their families exposed in the hillfort, defended only by a small force under Nechtan. What if Brude ignored their incursion and instead launched an assault on the fort?

Oengus wrestled with doubts. *Has envy driven me, with Drust's exploits being the talk of the fort? Aye, that is maybe so, but it has not been the main consideration. We must take the initiative, otherwise Brude will overrun the hillfort this day. It is an audacious gamble, dependent upon Brude responding according to our expectations – but it is plausible, for Brude has not proved so adept a commander.*

In the half light, he could just make out Drust's men in their ambush position on the higher slopes. A cockerel was just audible, and only the brightest stars remained, pale, almost snuffed out as the pre-dawn brightening awoke a sleepy world. His hand wiped the dew from the shaft of his spear, and again he mentally plotted the line they would ride down the slope. The brae was steep close by, requiring care before it eased, allowing them to then gallop upon the Fortriu.

Hearing the thunder of horses' hooves, he could detect Drust's men swinging out of the main valley and up into this subsidiary glen. After a short pause, Brude's men appeared in hot pursuit, a goodly number, no doubt confident of dealing with Drust's contingent so that they would never ride again. He gleefully anticipated the charge to wreak havoc on the heads of these impertinent invaders. This could well be the turning point of the battle, he thought, and, at that moment, he was confident that Brude could be defeated.

Oengus led his men at a walking pace over the lip of the steep slope and paused. His nerves had made him move prematurely before all the Fortriu had passed below. At any moment, they could unleash their charge to cut off

Brude's means of retreat to Rhynie. It had to be carefully timed, not alerting the Fortriu until it would be too late for them to turn.

The pre-dawn light was now giving everything vague form, although shrouded in greyness. Brude's men halted, stopping before the narrows of the glen. They urgently wheeled about to regain the open ground behind them, where they regrouped in battle formation.

"Damn it!" Oengus cursed. "The bull has realised the ruse!" His horse was champing at the bit, expressing the mounting tension he felt himself. He looked over at Drust's position trusting they would not break cover. They held their ground. He wondered how much Drust could see from their lower position, which already, being in the forest, would not necessarily give sight of Brude's location.

"Look, my lord! They are returning to Rhynie." One of his men pointed at the left-hand flank peeling away at a canter.

"Should they continue to the hillfort, they might outride us!" Oengus said, anxiously turning his horse. "Come, let us make all haste. All are to ride with me, even those from Drust's camp. We need to defend our families."

In the gathering light, they swiftly traversed the foothills, over ground they knew well, riding an almost straight line towards the hillfort. But it was trackless terrain characterised by bog in the basins and rough ground on the hillslopes. Brude and his men had a defined track to ride along, where, in parts, horses could gallop unheeded – a route that would be faster for sure if it had led in a direct line to the Pap of the Bulàch. However, as the track followed the curving course of the stream, Oengus knew the enemy would be caused some delay. Could they outride the Fortriu?

Many questions went through Oengus's mind as they sped back to the hillfort. The Fortriu would know that at least part of the Ce force had been deployed for the pre-dawn strike, leaving the fort more vulnerable. If Brude were to strike first, before they reached the fort, the stronghold would soon fall.

Even if I and these fifty men and the thirty or so extras from Drust's band arrived first, it would only delay proceedings with the outcome being a foregone conclusion. Unless Drust could mount a counterattack. They had not discussed this, so eager had they been in talking through the execution of their ambush to perfection. Still, he could signal Drust with the carnyx to summon his troop to advance. Drust's contingent would not abandon their families at the fort.

They rode hard, galloping across the firm ground, but were reduced to a walk, or trot at best, through the stretches of bog. They passed a stone circle from where they could see Rhynie to their east. The sun rising over the horizon dazzled them. Even by screening their eyes, they could not tell what was happening on the lower ground, veiled as it was in shadow in contrast to the glare of the horizon. Ahead lay the hill they referred to as the Ord, whose wide bulk would obscure their view of the bull's progress.

Never mind bothering where Brude might have reached, he chastised himself; what is more crucial is to ride with all haste. Oengus took advantage of the drained slopes of the Ord, leading his riders over its shoulder. The deviation was only slight, avoiding the marshy basin immediately below, and they swiftly cantered along the edge of the thinning woods.

With Brude's tents burned, he thought, and provisions confiscated, the Fortriu would surely be seeking a swift end to the campaign. Nechtan would be keeping a keen lookout and would call every man and able woman to the ramparts once Brude was sighted.

The wind was coursing so violently on the crest of the woods that he could hear the distress of the trees above the thud of their horses' hooves. Veering away from the woods to resume a straight course, the hillfort rose above them bathed in dawn light, looking closer than it truly was. Half of the flanks of the Pap of the Bulàch were illuminated now as the sun rose above the hills; only the lowest ground remained in shadow where he anticipated Brude to be riding. He glanced over to his right eager to sight his adversary, but was unable to see them. Maybe they were already on the lower slopes of the sacred hill? He scanned the likely route Brude would take, up by the springs of Brigantia, along the route they had used the previous day. He could see no trace of them.

Aware that they would converge on the line that Brude would take if they maintained their current course, Oengus led his men over to the left, towards a hidden way he knew through the trees. That way would cut up towards the summit at an angle that would helpfully reduce the steepness of the gradient, enabling their horses to move with greater speed. Part way up, whilst crossing ground clear of trees, Oengus looked over to his right and for the first time saw Brude's men. The front of their long column, clearly seen in the bright sunlight, was approaching the springs of Brigantia. Surely, we are ahead of Brude, he thought to himself, for we are looking down on their lead riders. Have we done enough to reach the fort before them?

The walls of the fort loomed large ahead as he led his troop towards the portals on the south-east side. "Have your shields facing the fort!" he ordered. How close will we need to be before Nechtan could be sure of seeing the boar painted upon them and not mistake it for the bull? Would the portals be opened in time? Do we have enough of an advance for the portals to close should Brude be bearing down? Nechtan would see the approach of Brude's far greater force and surely realise that our own troop of eighty could be none other than ourselves. But some of Drust's men have been added to our number, and now more numerous, would Nechtan think our contingent was part of Brude's force attacking from a different direction?

It was with relief that Oengus reached the portals before Brude and that his own men, recognising them, welcomed them in, not with any jubilation, for they had seen the menacing advance of their superior adversary. The wind was blowing so strong upon the summit that they had to shout at close quarters to make themselves heard.

Oengus could see Brude had backed off, no doubt realising that he had lost the race. He watched the Fortriu regroup on the shoulder of the ridge where they had taken up position the previous day.

"Blow the carnyx to signal Drust to come to our aid," Oengus commanded immediately. Three times the horn emitted a rising whoop, repeated at intervals. If Drust was still in the vicinity of their hidden camp, Oengus thought, it would take time to reach them. Would the sound carry upwind through this stormy assault? It felt like things were conspiring against them this day. He shot up a prayer to the Bulàch, and on seeing Maelchon, instructed him to make urgent intercessions for their people.

"Look at the crows!" Oengus indicated the birds picking over the corpses below their walls.

"They are carrying off the fallen heroes to the skies!" observed Maelchon.

The women were out in force, wearing pieces of armour taken from the bodies of the dead. Their mood was heavy but fraught with strong feelings, seeking revenge for those who had fallen yesterday. Widows and mothers protecting their young would be fierce in their resolve to exact death, he thought. Alpia came and joined him, belted with a sword and brandishing a spear. She wore a helmet that hid much of her feminine nature. He thought that she could pass for a man at a glance,

"Caltram is with Aunt Conchen who is doing her best to distract the poor boy. He does not understand all that is going on, but knows his daddy is brave and shall yet win the day."

"I wish I had his confidence!" he uttered quietly into her ear lest any of his men should hear. "We will do what we can. The rest is with the gods. So far, we have defied the proud Fortriu."

After a lengthy pause of inactivity from both sides, Brude moved his entire force, keeping beyond arrow range around the northern flank of the summit, and took up position on the south-west side with the wind at his back. The troop manoeuvre caused some of the crows to follow to the rear of their column, struggling in their flight against the stormy wind.

"They have realised the advantage of shooting their arrows with the wind instead of against it," Oengus informed Alpia.

After a thoughtful pause, Alpia asked, "Is it not from that direction that we can expect Drust to advance?"

"It is. But seeing Brude's position will make him reconsider his move."

After a while, they saw a couple of bonfires being lit, and many of Brude's warriors bringing branches and brushwood from the woods. Groups of men kept on emerging from the trees with great bundles of firewood. How much wood do they need? Oengus asked himself, dismayed by the Fortriu returning time and again into the forest, plundering its resources, adding to huge piles. The fires soon burned fiercely in the raging wind with sparks flying towards the hillfort. After even more wood had been gathered, Oengus observed the Fortriu moving into formation, then advancing with deliberation towards their own position, with those at the rear bearing firebrands and faggots of brushwood. As the forward rank broke into a trot, Brude's archers fired a volley of arrows.

"Cover!" bellowed Nechtan in anticipation of the rain of arrows. The defenders made themselves small against the ramparts and behind shields as the cloud of grey terror whistled well overhead in the stormy conditions. By the third volley, having estimated the correct trajectory to reach their target, the missiles still had little effect other than to keep the Ce lying low – something which Oengus knew was the enemy's intent to provide cover for the advancing troop.

"Return fire!" ordered Oengus. He watched with satisfaction some attackers fall to the ground.

"Look over there!" Alpia pointed.

Oengus followed the line of her outstretched arm and saw mounted horsemen come towards the rear of Brude's force.

"Could they be Drust's men?" What could they do, he thought, being so outnumbered, with Brude holding the higher ground? "An advantage Drust has," Oengus spoke quietly to his wife, "is having the wind at their backs." No sooner had he said this than a volley of arrows came falling upon Brude's rear guard.

"Who knows, they might be able to hit Brude himself!" remarked Alpia hopefully.

"That would turn the tide," Oengus replied sanguinely. This is a welcome distraction, he thought. A mere flicker of wild hope rose in his breast, which was abruptly checked by the Fortriu's sword bearers breaking into a sprint, as they came en masse, fast approaching their ramparts.

Brude's archers sprinted forwards too, and, dropping to one knee, fired in quick succession at the defenders upon the ramparts, so close now as to avoid hitting their own. Their sheer numbers were overwhelming as ladders and grappling hooks made contact with the wall. The Ce fought back, hurling rocks down, with the weightier ones causing men to collapse behind their force. But as the Ce exposed themselves, the attackers' superior arrow power, aided by the forceful wind, started to exact a steady toll.

Ladders were dislodged, but many remained in place as the Fortriu reached the top of the ramparts. The sound of sword against sword rang through the air along with the roar of warriors as they wielded their weapons. Both men and women fell to the ground with shrieks. The Fortriu had managed to hold position at the intersection of the western and southern walls and seemed, to Oengus, to pause, only fighting to hold their exposed flanks.

"Shoot at them!" Oengus bellowed. The Ce archers fired into the packed mass of the attackers, easily finding their mark.

"Why are they not advancing?" Alpia asked.

"I do not know," Oengus replied. Just then, a thin wisp of smoke streaked behind the attackers, vanishing in the wind, soon followed by more smoke rising in thicker columns. "They are setting fire to that corner of the fort!" he remarked, realising that the Fortriu upon the ramparts were giving protection to their comrades at the base of the wall. Oengus moved swiftly to the western wall and, peering over, saw the Fortriu piling dry brushwood against the base. Briefly, it smouldered before the faggots combusted into a blaze, whipped into a fury by the wild wind. Vast numbers of men deposited more firewood that the fire grew so bold that tongues of flames leapt viciously up. The attackers quickly retreated, and the heat forced the Ce to withdraw from the south-western sector of the hillfort.

"Keep firing at them – they are vulnerable," Oengus ordered.

The Fortriu withdrew along with their archers to a position beyond the reduced range of the Ce archers firing into the wind.

"Fetch pails of water," shouted Nechtan, descending from the battlements to organise a human chain to pass the water drawn from the well. The flames scorched those at the front, who, unable to get close enough to douse the fire, despaired to see the water that was thrown swept aside by the assault of the wind. Meanwhile, the Fortriu did not let up with their rain of arrows upon the fort which were finding targets as women and men fell from the ramparts.

Nechtan came over to Oengus. "The timbers that interlace and undergird our walls are smouldering on our side of the wall!"

"Where are you going?"

"Onto the battlements to assess what can be done."

From where he stood, Oengus could feel the heat as he watched his uncle use his wooden shield to screen his face from the fire. Nechtan was struggling to move closer to the fire when, suddenly, he staggered back and fell from the battlements. He landed heavily within the fort with an arrow embedded in his chest. Oengus sent one of his aides to check on him whilst he monitored the battle.

Oengus noted that Drust had moved to the right of the Fortriu's rear guard, reaching ground that was level with the enemy. By now, the large contingent of the Fortriu who had retreated from the hillfort, had rejoined Brude's main force, and there appeared to be much commotion within their ranks.

The wind continued to blow with great power, causing sparks to fly into the midst of their dwellings. First one hut roof ignited, forcing the children within to break cover whilst a few people unsuccessfully attempted to quench the flames. Within moments, all the huts closest to the burning wall had combusted, adding to the growing number of children and elderly gathered at the fort's end furthest from the fire.

Why such wind? Oengus asked himself, as if we did not already have a powerful foe to contend with. He then noticed a mounted troop advance upon Drust's position, causing his commander to immediately mount a counter charge.

"Oh, what madness!" Oengus exclaimed aloud. "Drust is not one to be outdone, but what chance do so few have against so many Fortriu?" His immediate impulse was to order his own horsemen to mount an attack, but realising that the skirmish would be over well before they were able to reach the Fortriu, it would merely become their turn to be annihilated by Brude's superior numbers.

A sickening sense of doom engulfed him. Brave and valiant it might look, but Drust's charge was a gesture, ill-conceived, doomed to fail from the outset. He watched appalled as the Fortriu mowed down his own men, scattering the remainder to the north.

"Be ready at the gates to let the remnant in should they reach us," commanded Oengus to one of his aides.

Oengus watched the stragglers of his own riders come round the northern flank of the ridge, some fifty or so men making towards the gates. The Fortriu did not pursue but were regrouping in their safe position to the south-west, allowing Drust's contingent to enter the fort. Oengus scanned the grim faces of the riders, trying to identify their commander.

"Drust was hacked down from his saddle by an axe!" informed one of the newcomers, shaking his head gravely.

In the lull of the fighting, Oengus went over to see Nechtan, who lay mortally wounded, propped up by his aunt Drusticc. He recalled how his parents' household had once been so closely intertwined with Uncle Nechtan's that they had been like one family. That was until the Z-rod, together with his own father's machinations, had wreaked havoc upon their family unity. There was a time, and one that was quite recent, when he would have been glad to have seen his uncle dead. But Brude's aggression had forced them to put aside their considerable differences. His uncle had well-executed his duty, often at the forefront of the action, presenting an example of steadfastness before the younger men.

"Uncle," Oengus began uncertainly, "I regret what has passed between us!" He bent over Nechtan whose pallor indicated his uncle had little time left. "I would wish that Taran could be here now!" He surprised himself for saying this. But what did the past matter now as the shadows were cast over them, snuffing out their hopes. For once, he could speak words without any intrigue. He had seen his own father fade swiftly away, taken into the realm of the fallen heroes and felt that a son should be by his father's side at the end.

"No!" Nechtan slurred, the pupils of his eyes struggling to focus.

"You are not half the man Taran would have been," spoke Drusticc with hostility. "Leave your uncle and me in peace – you usurper! You are not welcome in the presence of my noble lord who fought – not for you – but for the Ce!"

Oengus rose and left them. How hopeless everything is, he thought. His thoughts turned to the precarious state of the siege. The fire was out of control, luridly illuminating the demoralised faces of his people gathered at the eastern wall. He felt sick. What option was left, trapped in a burning fort? Without Drust's force, he could no longer harry Brude.

"Lord, we have three arrows at the most for every man remaining," reported one of his aides.

Oengus acknowledged him with a nod. Spotting one of Drust's men, he asked, "Are there any of you left in your forest camp?"

"There are five."

"And then a further three will be on the hill with the carnyx," added another.

"And did Drust station men anywhere else?" Oengus pursued.

"Only the three that were sent to the Dee to meet with the Circinnians."

Would the Circinn arrive that day? he thought. If they had sent men on the day after their messenger had arrived, then they should be appearing that evening. Without Drust ready to receive them, what would they do? Seeing how Brude had the upper-hand and with the fort burning, the Circinn were unlikely to risk their men against the battle-hardened Fortriu, whose leader already held the status of king.

He watched Alpia take Caltram's hand and mingle among the women sheltering down near the gates. Looking over the battlements, he noted Brude's main force maintained their position beyond reach of their arrows, settling down around their fires as the day wore to a close. Brude had lost his tents, and Rhynie was a burnt-out settlement unfit for habitation. They too had suffered heavy losses.

A muffled noise, rather like a long and low rumble of thunder, made him look to the far side of the fort. He was appalled to see that the western wall had just collapsed.

What would Brude do now? He saw Fortriu approaching the campfires carrying three deer trussed to poles. So, they had foraged for provisions from the forest! The enemy appeared to be in no hurry, and could wait for the fallen wall to cool before attacking. Would it be in the night, or the next day?

As the fire was dying at the western end, Oengus inspected what remained. The wall was breached, and the fallen debris formed what was like a tilted platform for the enemy to easily penetrate. Some of the rocks had been so hot that they had fused together.

Later that evening, the Fortriu deliberately started heather fires on the windward side of the fort, which had been easy since no rain had fallen for days, and the heather, dried by the fierce wind, was like tinder. The fire drove towards them, filling the air with acrid smoke, which caused them to cough and their eyes to smart. It was more an inconvenience than a threat; a ploy, no doubt, to further demoralise – to remind that their situation was hopeless. Through the smoke, he could see the Fortriu being deployed to the south and to the east, forming a cordon of sentry clusters staged at every fifty paces or so. With the fires still smouldering over the scorched earth, the unmistakable reek of burning peat hung in the air. The Fortriu repositioned themselves wherever the smoke was not being driven, forming a swollen rank of men south-east of the gate. There, they drove sharpened stakes into the ground, set at a low-angle towards the fort, their points at a height to pierce a horse's chest. The whole ridge to the north-east was now smouldering, raising a thin column of smoke. He thought what the Circinn would make of the smoke should they be approaching.

Out of the smoke came a missile, lighter than a rock, spinning through the air trailing lengthy strands. It landed in their camp, and he noted how those closest to the object withdrew with revulsion. It was a human head. As he descended from the battlements, a man moved the head with his foot to reveal the unmistakeable face of Drust. He felt sickened, recalling their hesitant farewell outside Rhynie's gate. Had Drust known that he would fall? At the time, Oengus thought that nerves had made him uneasy. His commander had not shown those doubts when they had met the previous night when the ambush plans were hatched. They had been men of action at that moment, still with the ability to challenge Brude. What a loyal commander he had been, brave to the last, and so adept . . . except for that final and futile charge! Sensing that it was all over, had Drust chosen to die a warrior's death? Just then, the shrieks of Drust's widow haunted the air.

He watched the Fortriu light five smaller fires in sight of the hillfort gate. Parts of a deer carcass were distributed, and they were joined by others coming up the hill with pack horses laden with equipment. Cooking pots were unpacked, and meal preparations were underway.

Where have those come from? It would seem that we have not destroyed all their supplies! Perhaps reinforcements have come from Y Broch? The Fortriu looked settled, no longer inconvenienced by the blows they had endured over the past three days. All the remainder of that long day, the Fortriu went about their camp as though there were no battle to wage.

Before sunset, Oengus saw more warriors join the Fortriu ranks appearing from the springs of Brigantia. Gest joined him and the two looked down upon the swelling of the enemy's ranks, more numerous than when they had first appeared three days earlier. The air was blue with smoke from the smouldering peat, pungent in their nostrils and making their throats parched.

"What can be done?" his druid asked.

"Nothing!" he grimly replied.

"Are they going to mount an attack?" he gestured towards the gathering men about the fires beyond their gates.

"I do not think so. At least, not from there. If they will attack, I should think it will be through the breached wall."

"Then why are they there in such numbers?"

"To oppose us should we ride out."

"I see!" Gest hung his head. "I noticed that Brude has a similar number of men positioned out of reach of arrow shot beyond the breached wall."

"He seems to have an inexhaustible supply of men!" He was aware of a note of despair in his voice.

"How can that be? How many are in his army do you think?"

"Who knows. I would not have thought more than five hundred at the most."

"I thought that was the number reported to have crossed the Spey when he started this campaign!"

"It was – he has definitely gained more warriors! Having subjugated the Dal Riatans, Brude now has a contingent of Gaels, for we saw among their dead yesterday, untattooed bodies. The Cait are also a subordinate people, and just as Brude ordered us to send a force to oppose the Dal Riatans, so he must have required the Cait to send their three hundred, that is if they have three hundred warriors to field. Then there are the Fidach – and goodness knows how many they could muster."

"And all we have in reserve are the Circinnians!" Gest sighed unrestrainedly. That is, should they bother to come! They will only be one hundred and fifty at the most!"

Food was brought and Oengus ate with little appetite. He paced the battlements looking out on the enemy camp.

"They even have tents!" Oengus exclaimed, dismayed as he looked towards the enemy's main camp. He shuddered within.

Sleep came fitfully to him on that third night of the siege. The uneasy quiet had been broken periodically by the violent rattle of spears all around the hillfort throughout the watches of the night. The bulbous ends of the Fortriu spears, containing a hollow sphere filled with some iron ball bearings, clattered with an unsettling affect.

Feeling ragged when the new dawn broke, he looked with pity upon his sleeping boy who lay there with the innocence and oblivion of childhood. His hair had grown long and curled about his brows and ears. What was to become of him and the unborn that Alpia was carrying? Would any of them survive this day? He had no answer. His rising disturbed Alpia from her sleep.

"Ugh, is it morning already?"

Coming over to her without replying, he placed a hand on her shoulder as she sat up. Squeezing it, he left their hut, feeling like a frail shadow, with nothing substantial left to give. The fort was coming alive, not with the happy commotion of breakfast preparations, but rather, like him, all were wondering what fate awaited them that day?

Most of his diminished force were already in position when he mounted the ramparts. They were surrounded by their enemy on all sides, with large concentrations to their east and west. The morning light broke bright upon them and the forceful wind, dropping now to a fresh breeze, played with the ends of plaids, producing a shimmering effect that added extra vitality to the Fortriu warriors. The rising hills to the south looked majestic under the cover of forests, their pronounced undulations casting long shadows that gave texture to the land. It was one of those mornings full of promise that would normally make man feel bright; a day when he would enjoy a hunt.

The irony did not escape him: he, the hunted, the boar in his exposed lair, utterly surrounded and without chance to escape. His only hope was to die with honour, to spill enemy blood before his own was drawn from him. Seeing Maelchon across the way made him feel extremely frustrated. What good had it been to them to occupy the sacred heights of the Pap of the Bulàch? To what avail had been their offerings and prayers, together with the intercessions of his two druids? The Bulàch had abandoned them as though they were despised, to be given over to slaughter. Was this her intent all along, to devise a massive sacrifice of the best of the Ce to fall upon her Pap? Were her appetites so insatiable? Did she not already have her fill of valiant warriors? Maelchon had seen no visions, spoke no prophecies, and for all his devotion to the goddess, this was how she repaid them! Only Maevis had the eye, and what she saw had been so terrible that she shuffled away like an elderly one appalled by the revelation. No wonder she had not joined them.

The enemy raised their spears, brandishing them as though spoiling for the fight before pounding the base of the shaft five times upon the ground, keeping a rhythm that was chilling to hear. The sound from several hundred, acting in unison, was considerable.

"Sound our carnyx!" ordered Oengus. "Defy them with its roar!"

The player came to the edge of the rampart where it had collapsed, and sounded a long bass note that reverberated. The vibrating wooden tongue gave it a rasping voice, like the roar of a beast making its defiant stand.

He watched one of his men sharpen his sword on a whetstone. "They must take my blood before my family's!" he muttered, keen to be heard.

That summed up their position, Oengus thought. He arranged his orderlies and ensured that his warriors were positioned where necessary to make a bold defence. Although the falling of their fort was inevitable, he vowed it would be done at great cost, not just with their own supreme sacrifice, but paid for with the blood of their foes.

The Fortriu seemed in no hurry, maintaining their ritual spear-shaking with wearying frequency. What are they waiting for? he wondered. Strike and be done with it! The tension, mixed with the lack of sleep over four nights since Maevis's prediction, was keenly felt. Maybe they should be the ones to mount the attack? Had they not been valiant in the campaign, taking Brude unawares, twice spoiling his camp? He grimly smiled over the thrill of having got the better of his renowned adversary. Had their ambush succeeded, Brude would not have had the manpower to breach the fort on the previous day. It would have bought them time for the Circinn to arrive, and still with their own contingent intact, a very different scenario would now be facing them, even with Brude's reinforcements. An epic battle could have been fought with neither side assured of victory, both risking all for the honour of victory. But this was not fair sport. It seemed that the cat was playing with the mouse before a grizzly end.

Why not open the gates and mount a horse charge to their east, simultaneously with the foot soldiers attacking over the breached wall to the west? Better to die a heroic death than wait to be overwhelmed. He was being persuaded towards that decision when three horsemen rode slowly up to the breached wall. Oengus recognised one as the man who had come to the fort on the first day.

"Oengus!" he called.

"Lord Oengus to you," he replied, standing proud on the battlements.

"The king offers you peace."

What was this, some kind of ruse to take them off their guard?

"Your position is hopeless, and the outcome is sure," continued the enemy's spokesperson.

"If you believe that, then press home your assumed advantage and many of your warriors shall embrace death."

"Oh, we are quite prepared to do that knowing that victory shall be ours. But the king asks why should so many valiant men fall over a squabble between two households?"

"And who started that squabble? He should have thought about that before he crossed the flowing Spey."

"Do not speak ill of your overlord. He would have you know that he salutes the Ce for their valiant fight. He had not reckoned on meeting such fierce opposition and commends your fighting force!" The warrior lent forward and stroked the side of his horse's neck in an unhurried gesture. "King Brude wishes to speak with you out here on this scorched ground, face to face, to discuss terms of peace . . ." The warrior laid out the conditions of their meeting.

Was this a trick? Was Brude luring him out to take him captive? Maybe, though, it was worth hearing what terms were being offered. These could be refused, and they would then stand to fight to the end. Without an answer to whether this was a trick, the sight of the women and children within the hillfort made him agree to meet with Brude.

Oengus stepped over the rubble of the fallen wall accompanied by two warriors and came towards Brude, also flanked by two bodyguards as had been agreed. As Oengus neared his adversary, Brude shook his head, and, managing a slight smile, said, "All this fighting!" He gestured to imply the futility of it all and yet at the same time maintaining an easy smile, conveyed that he was not hard-pressed.

"We are prepared to fight to the last – even our womenfolk!" Oengus said defiantly.

Brude lifted his hand and waved it dismissively. "There is no need for that. The Ce have proved themselves to be mighty warriors. Why should I wish them dead? They are more use to me alive. I am prepared to give the order to depart from this hill and return over the Spey."

"In return for what?"

"Your homage!"

"You had that before you came with your army. Did you not click your fingers and I came with my warriors down the Great Glen, ready to fight your battle?"

"You were late!"

"We came as soon as it was possible to muster a campaign. The timing only appeared late due to the early strike from the Gaels."

"You do not speak like one who is vanquished!" Brude said, his smile disappearing from his lips.

"We are not vanquished and are ready to die as free men, hailed as heroes in the feasting halls of Fionn."

"That is fighting talk. I prefer the Ce alive rather than slain, which you shall surely be to a man and to a woman and even to a child if you refuse this peace offering."

"You already have our homage. I have not rescinded on that and have yielded due tribute."

"And that must continue," interjected Brude. "No late payments or half measures will be tolerated."

"That was only once, and did you not ensure I had learned my lesson!"

"And you will yield half of your warriors to me." King Brude looked at him stoically.

"You would emasculate me?"

"I intend to put an end to your military ambitions that seek to rival our reputation."

"You ask too much!"

"You are not in a position to bargain. These terms are to ensure your preservation. Half of your men, and the ones of my choosing, will leave here along with their families to make new homes at Y Broch and Craig Padrig."

Oengus considered the despicable terms that would, at least, ensure the preservation of the noble Ce. Warriors would live to fight another day and their womenfolk and children would not be slaughtered. The other choice was to face annihilation. He finally nodded his assent.

"And I have one final request." He cleared his throat. "It is a demand though, not a request."

"What is it?"

"That you yield your firstborn to me!"

"My lord!" he protested, astounded by his audacity.

"Do not fear, I shall not slaughter him to the Bulàch as a thank offering. I shall be like a foster father to him, just in the same manner that you and I were sent away from our families and raised under the roof of a famous warrior – is that not so?"

Oengus did not reply. If he refused, Caltram would perish along with everyone else, possibly meeting some slow ritualistic end before his very eyes to torment and shame him.

"His name is Caltram, is it not?" continued Brude in a gentler tone. "It is your father's name I believe, one who died a warrior's death fighting the Circinn. I will ensure that this young Caltram will be a pride to his grandfather. But, he will be raised a Fortriu warrior." The king raised his chin proudly in the air. He then adopted a compassionate tone that had a mocking inflexion to it. "Come now, do not look so deflated! I will permit you and his mother to visit him in my court."

Would it not be better to deny Brude all of this and make their final stand and die as free men? But on the other hand, not all was to be taken away. They would be left to rebuild their lives. Who knows that with the passing of time, and as fortunes invariably fluctuate, Brude might overreach himself? Then he could pronounce his own terms to Brude. Better to comply, surely, in the hope of rising another day, even if that day were to be ten or twenty years from now? Would not the humiliation of this day spur them to rise once more?

Yielding Caltram would be bitter, but he would surely come to despise this tyrant king. Caltram would not forget that he was born a son of the Ce, son to its warlord. Sparing his life could nurture Caltram to one day exact their revenge.

Grimly, Oengus extended his hand and agreed the terms.

The remnant of the Ce warriors was made to line up outside the fort. Brude passed along their line with a self-satisfied smirk, picking out the best of the men, leaving only those who were wounded. The Ce lived for another day along with their families.

"And now for Caltram," Brude said triumphantly.

Oengus turned aside and saw Alpia clutching his child to her side. She looked appalled, shaking her head with such reproach at him. He felt his gut spasm as he watched two Fortriu warriors prise Caltram from Alpia's arms. Alpia kicked the men violently, but to no avail. Caltram cried in great distress and the Fortriu laughed.

Chapter Six

After the Sacking

AD 560 Rhynie

The dawn broke brightly upon the ruins of Rhynie, inappropriately beaming cheerfully down upon the survivors following their defeat upon the Pap of the Bulàch. Having risen from their makeshift hovel of charred timbers, Oengus shook off the moisture gathered on his plaid. He felt dreadfully cold and stiff.

"How are we to rebuild Rhynie?" examined Alpia, seemingly holding him to account. "When will we have somewhere that does not let in the rain?"

"It will take time!" he retorted, defensively. "Over half our men who survived, have been taken. Brude left us with the wounded."

"He left us with our lives," Aunt Conchen commented flatly, gazing down at her feet.

"Some life!" complained Alpia as she placed a hand on her swollen abdomen. "And what kind of life to bring a child into the world."

He looked at her. She had turned her back on him and seemed to be wringing her hands.

"And they have taken my Caltram!" she complained further. She was slightly shaking and, judging from her quavering voice, she was gently sobbing.

"He is my son too!" He picked up a waterskin and stepped towards her. "Instead of complaining, do something useful and fetch some water." He held it out towards her. She was very slow at taking it.

"I will get a fire started," Aunt Conchen muttered as she rose with difficulty.

He noticed that she moved very slowly, as though each movement caused her pain. "Are you hurt?" he asked.

"No, just old. The dampness is unkind to aged bones. Once I get moving, it will be better. The fire will be soothing."

He acknowledged her weariness with a slight nod of his head as he set to removing part of the makeshift roof that had not kept the rain off them during the night. He needed to gather some thatch and at least make a good roof for them to sleep under. He thought of a place upstream where some reeds grew.

He looked for a suitable knife for the harvesting work ahead of him, bemoaning the fact that they had lost so much when a sickle would be hard to come by. It would be easier work with the proper tools, he thought, and his mind started to fill with all the hopeless images of destruction, wasting, the loss of life and limb of his people. The devastation of what lay about him had been his doing. Victory had once seemed within reach and the fact that it had seemed attainable made his defeat the more bitter to ponder and be appalled by.

"Oh, this is going to be frustratingly long before we return to some kind of normality," he muttered under his breath, impatient to find any knife, let alone choose the most suitable one. Just then, Maelchon made an appearance. Never had his chief druid looked so morose as he stepped towards the fire.

"Have some porridge," Aunt Conchen offered, rummaging about a pile of their belongings in search of a container of oats.

"No, I will not," he replied, absent-mindedly. "I have come to say goodbye."

"Oh! Where are you going?" Oengus asked curiously.

"I am going south," he returned vaguely. After a lengthy pause, he said resolutely, "I am leaving . . . leaving for good!"

"What do you mean?" His curiosity was now aroused by the finality of the druid's tone.

"There is nothing more for me to do here. What destruction . . . what a massacre! The flower of our youth has been plucked and trampled!" He drew in a lengthy breath and his eyes looked rheumy.

Oengus slowly shook his head with the gravity he felt.

Eventually, Maelchon spoke again, "The rites have been observed to commemorate the dead, marking the last of my official duties!"

"There will be other duties," encouraged Oengus.

"I have lived more than fifty winters and have served the Bulàch faithfully," the druid began, looking at him squarely in the eyes. "But what we have just endured is too much! Our youth were just hacked down, and many were taken into exile. What we are is a mere shadow of what once we were. Our valiant heroes did not even receive a burial."

Oengus examined him keenly, for he had never known Maelchon to speak with such emotion before. "There were just too many slain!" explained Oengus, feeling the need to justify the lack of funeral rites. "Our remaining men – the ones who are still able – were too few to perform burials along with the other pressing needs of making shelters. The dead are dead. Fire is still a fitting tribute to send their souls to the next world."

The druid massaged the corner of an eye next to his nose with a charcoal-stained finger. "The sight of their huge pyre shall haunt me all my days!" He shook his head with a sense of dismay and stared vacantly at the ground. "What is the purpose in serving the Bulàch when she fails to heed our supplications?" He half-raised his hands in an appeal and let them fall hopelessly back to his sides.

"Your service to the Bulàch is like no other!" remarked Aunt Conchen.

"What will you do?" Oengus asked with genuine interest.

"I need to leave this devastation . . . I am quite overwhelmed!" Again, he paused to poke the tip of his finger into the corner of his eye. "I am thinking to visit some of our druid fraternity. After that, I do not know where I shall go, or what I will do."

"Oh!" Oengus remarked, unsure what to say. "When will you come back?"

Maelchon looked at him with a strong degree of incredulity. "I am not coming back! As I said, I am leaving for good. I feel that I am quite out of my depth! I have been out of my depth since I was instructed to tattoo the Z-rod upon your cousin's back!"

"Taran!" he exclaimed with vehemence. He could feel his face turning red and an anger, from deep down, came shooting to the surface. "What does Taran have to do with this?" he shouted. He hurled the knife that he had in his hand into the turf at his feet. "Taran is dead – he is no more!"

"That is maybe so. The Z-rod presaged much menace, and what followed remains an enigma." He placed his palm against his brow as though he were ailing. "We see such mysteries darkly, and often do not understand until the fullness of time reveals their purpose. For all my learning and devotion, it has not been granted me to see the fullness of these signs."

Oengus's mind wondered, trying to figure out the significance of Taran receiving the Z-rod. There had been a time when he was forever looking over his shoulder, wondering if his cousin were lurking, ready to pounce. "What if Taran is behind Brude's attack – will Brude usurp my position and put Taran in my place?"

"I thought you just declared Taran was dead!" Aunt Conchen pointed out, much to his annoyance.

"Oh, I have given up divining the future," Maelchon grimaced, as though bothered with toothache.

It was Aunt Conchen who spoke up again. "If Taran was Brude's motivation, then why would Brude have spared your life?"

"I do not know! It seems the gods were idly playing with us." What is their purpose? he thought. They dangle us to prolong our suffering; amused to observe our misery."

Just then, Alpia appeared, wearied from carrying a wet waterskin which she placed on the forked end of a pole standing upright in the ground. She did not look at him. "What is this talk about Brude and Taran," she eventually asked rather matter-of-factly, as though to conceal her interest. He felt a stab of jealousy pierce his heart. Why was he so despised? As if it were not enough to fall in the dirt, it seemed all things conspired to rub his face in it. Unable to contain himself, he took a pace towards his wife and shouted, "Taran is dead!"

Maelchon seemed to become aware of the squalor of their hovel, for he remarked, "What a mess! Look . . . my hut is untouched. I suppose, due to it being situated apart from the community it was spared. Move into it – it is better than staying here!"

"What about Gest?" he queried, ignoring the offer, struggling to take in the enormity of what his chief druid was saying. Was his friend also of Maelchon's opinion?

"Oh! he will remain. I have passed on to him all the paraphernalia of my office. He is still young, has hope and has come of age – highly capable of taking my place. Maybe the Bulàch has a contention with me!" He shrugged his shoulders. "She is deaf to my entreaties and blind to our offerings. Perhaps my going might usher in a new era for the Ce. Lord Oengus, I bid you farewell. I doubt we shall meet again!"

"Wait! You cannot just leave like this!" Was all order going to fall apart, he wondered, frantically. Maelchon had been the mainstay of their community from Talorgen's time till the rise of the boar.

"As the gods do not speak to me, I am of no service."

Oengus felt crestfallen to be losing his chief advisor, even though he had struggled with the druid's gloomy predictions. Maelchon had brought legitimacy to his rule, guaranteeing that all due observances would be maintained with the Bulàch. Oh well, he thought, at least I have Gest and he has always been pleasanter to deal with. He came round to the idea of losing Maelchon as quickly as his chief druid could turn about.

Oengus spent the morning gathering reeds and more straight branches. He found the manual labour soothed his frazzled nerves. It then occurred to him that he need not be gathering these materials to improve their shelter since Maelchon had gifted them his hut. At first, he felt annoyed with his slowness of thought, until he acquiesced. His current errand had at least taken him away from Alpia's sharp tongue and withering looks. Besides, he rationalised, maybe Maelchon's roof needed some repairs and now he had the wherewithal to make it good.

Feeling exhausted, he sat down upon a grassy bank above a stream and stared onto the still surface of a pool, where the grandsires of oaks were reflected. A warlord should not be busy doing these menial tasks, he told himself, but should be recovering order to his community. Again, images of the days of battle replayed repeatedly in all their gory detail. The crackle of their fort burning along with the ominous beat of the spears of Brude's menacing force, replayed in his head. It had been followed by his humiliating surrender and the removal of his finest fighting men and his beloved Caltram. What was there left now except bleak servitude, and being bled dry by that leech who now deemed himself King of the Picts? Could there be a recovery? The overlord would be keeping a close eye to ensure he would be impoverished by crippling tribute payments to smother any hope of resurgence. How could he continue? All his vaulted dreams had come to naught; the men he had inspired now lay dead, maimed or deported. What kind of warlord was he? He felt sickened to his very core, as if some rot had consumed him.

He needed to move his people forward decisively and not allow discontent to breed insurrection. Recalling how Maelchon had left for good that morning, he realised how shaky a foundation he stood upon. "The sooner I can speak to Gest, the better!" he proclaimed aloud, rising to his feet.

Securing his bundles of reeds and straight branches to his horses' flanks, he quickly rode back down to Rhynie. The community lay below him like a bloodied bruise on the landscape, with the recriminating countenance of the Pap of the Bulàch, scorched by heather fires, looking scornfully down. He might be reeling, but he was not down, he told himself as he veered away from the main community and walked down to the stream crossing near to his friend's home.

"Gest, you are my one trusted ally!" he greeted him with what warmth he could muster under the circumstances.

His friend looked up from scraping some carrots he had in a shallow basin. He did not look exactly overjoyed to see him.

"Maelchon announced he was leaving," Oengus ventured, examining his friend closely.

"Aye, he has lost faith in everything." Gest tossed the carrot he was holding to the back of the basin, causing a splash of water over the side.

"And what about you – are you similarly persuaded?"

Gest held silence for quite a time before looking him in the eye. "It is hard to make sense of the world!" After another uncomfortable silence, his friend observed, "I believe I feel as devastated as you look!"

"We need to rebuild – restore some kind of order."

Gest leant forward. "We will need some insight into events. With Maelchon gone, it is hard to say."

"With or without Maelchon, it seemed hard to read the situation."

"The fulfilment of what the fallen star had come to convey has passed. Perhaps now we can hope for better days?" The young druid's tone did not sound convincing.

"I need another Drust to help rebuild our shattered community – to give some purpose and hope."

"And I need another with spiritual insight." He noticed that Gest's face looked brighter; seemingly, he already had someone in mind. "I have decided to look up Maevis!"

"That harbinger of doom! Surely, we are finished with predictors of calamity?"

"Has she not always spoken what is true?" his friend hotly defended, taking him a little by surprise. "When have her predictions ever been at fault? It is not for our fraternity to say what you want to hear, but to pass on what we hear in whispers and briefly glimpse from the other side."

"If I will ride with you to see Maevis, will you help me to requisition some workers to rebuild the stockade about Rhynie? We do not need high status men, just able foresters and carpenters – surely our realm is still full of them?"

"We can ride east together tomorrow," assented Gest with a vague smile. "If it be the will of the gods, I shall ride with you."

"And it seems that we shall be neighbours." Gest looked at him, enquiringly. "Maelchon has left us his home. My womenfolk will be very glad of a dry place to rest this night."

"How can you be leaving when I am about to birth a child?" protested Alpia later that day, looking him sharply in the eye.

He understood her plea, but her tone had made him defensive and had roused him. "I am not a midwife! Nola was spared the battle and she will deliver the baby. And you have Aunt Conchen, too."

"And what if the same fate befalls me as what happened to Eithni?"

"Why do you have to consider the worst outcome? Many bairns are born, and their mothers are spared!"

"Does our first child together mean so little to you?" Again, her tone was caustic, accompanied by a livid light flashing in her eyes.

Any residual feeling of pity for his wife expired. Naturally, he would have liked to be there at the birth of his newborn, but Alpia's hostility and overbearing manner drove him away. Was he not humiliated enough without being directed by his wife as to what he ought to do? Besides, other important matters were pressing, and this was not a time for biding at home, especially when it could still be days, even a week or two, before the baby would be born. He left the hut without further word, avoiding looking at his wife. He did catch a glimpse of Aunt Conchen, burying her chin into her neck, with compressed and elongated lips.

He walked his horse over to Gest's hut. The sun sparkled on the tumbling waters of the stream and lifted his spirits somewhat. He was glad to be on the move, about the business of reversing the ill-fortunes of his people.

It took the best part of the morning to reach the community of the priestesses of the Bulàch, bringing to mind that momentous journey made along that same way some five years previously, when he had determined to follow Aunt Conchen's advice and bring Eithni back to Rhynie as his wife. He reflected that it was never easy between him and women. Eithni, though, had been easier to handle than Alpia. Things would have been simpler had Eithni been spared. He reflected on how sober his wedding had been to a woman he had spurned, wishing back then that he were marrying Alpia instead! He felt intensely annoyed by the futile cycle of thoughts and the guilt they conferred. He reasoned to himself about his need to go away at the time of his wife giving birth, believing that Alpia would, in hindsight, come to understand that he had to attend to the more pressing matters of ruling his people and bring back a semblance of normality after the monumental upheavals.

On arriving at the community of the priestesses, he looked over to the place where he had helped fill the water skins with Eithni, and recalled how he had won her over, persuading her to return with him to Rhynie. What had seemed a challenging task back then was simple in comparison to the tasks facing him now.

They found Maevis at home. Immediately, the squalor of the hut struck him with its sole occupant sitting dejectedly in the shadows of a corner. She paid them only a cursory glance before reverting once more to looking into vacant space.

"Maevis! It is I, Gest." He stooped before her, trying to engage her with eye contact.

Although Maevis was an unusual and highly spirited woman, unlike any other he knew, there was now something withdrawn about her, something no longer connected that had come adrift. Her attitude was different from what he had seen when she was preparing to embark upon one of her spirit flights, or having just returned from roaming the distant places, perceiving hidden things.

Maevis eventually raised her face towards Gest and stared, appearing to wonder who he might be. Oengus noticed that her lips were slightly parted and were vaguely quivering with a sense of agitation. She leaned toward the light coming from the open door, revealing eyes that seemed to dance, unable to remain still, and yet were keen to fix their gaze upon his friend. She looked like a vulnerable animal in her lair, taken by surprise, unable to flee or to defend herself. Her bosom heaved in a voluptuous manner and even Oengus had to admit that there was something extraordinarily beautiful about her at that moment. Her signature high fringe revealed a white brow that was still youthful, setting off the dark enchantment of her large eyes to perfection. Again, he was struck by her air of mystery; an attractiveness that had previously escaped him. This enthrallment surprised him, knowing how he was usually the object of her scorn. The fact that something was broken within her, removing that haughty and bristly exterior, had revealed the woman in all her allurement. He felt his own heart beating faster and, with effort, he peeled his eyes away from her extraordinary, delicate loveliness.

How odd to think her lovely, he thought to himself. He then looked to Gest, aware of the gathering silence. It quickly became apparent that Oengus was the only one to come to his senses, observing how Gest remained entranced. These were highly unusual days, he reflected, where the semblance of normality had been stripped away to reveal something of the hiddenness of the soul of men and women. Reality had more of a dreamlike quality, where the details of day-to-day life were blurred on the periphery, and his raised senses were made more acute to perceive the heart of matter and being. He must have stopped breathing for he felt lightheaded and inhaled with a sharp and deep breath. greedily drinking in the vapid air within the gloom of the hut.

He watched Gest reach out his hand and take Maevis's hand within his. The two stared at one another as though he did not exist within the hut, and it seemed that he was witnessing this mysterious exchange as one who was detached, looking upon the scene as in a vision; or much like Maevis would have beheld upon one of her spirit flights, unobserved. Gest moved and sat down beside her, placing an arm protectively about her shoulders. Maevis reclined into his embrace as though she had been waiting this moment for an age, laying her head to rest upon his friend's chest. Her eyes were still open but unseeing the third person in the hut.

Oengus quietly withdrew, reversing slowly towards the door, engrossed by the tenderness of their togetherness.

He knew that Gest had to remain, and that he would have to proceed on his journey alone. He felt no anger or resentment; for what he had just witnessed seemed to be something that had been ordained from the beginning of time. He was not to meddle in it, for their union seemed sacred. Had he ever known such a thing? And he had to confess that he had not, and felt the bankruptcy of his own relationships with women. He envied his friend with an envy that held no resentment, even though it now meant that he had to continue about his business without his close companion.

The laceration of losing another long-time ally, was keenly felt. He had to rise even further in stature, if he were to make himself equal to the challenges he faced. Strangely spared from the vagaries of the flying arrows, he had not met his end. Why? It felt strange moving on without the sanction of his druids, but never one for being naturally religious, was it not more expedient to pursue matters without the delay of consulting the gods? Besides, he told himself, it seems that even the Bulàch herself was absent; having washed her hands of the Ce. How much had really been achieved by paying tribute to her? Had the rise of the boar been his own doing all along?

"We become what we want to be," he muttered as he mounted his horse and kicked it into a trot. He left the village and continued east to the fat farmlands of his people who had not endured the scourge of war, the wasting of fire, and the cruel end of the sword. He had extricated himself from the shadow of death and remained steadfast in the land of the living. Could he not rise again another day, without a druid's help, and prevail by sheer force of his will and ambition?

Chapter Seven

Summer Solstice on Munnir Esprid
AD 564

Taran had walked north, drawn to the summer solstice festival on Munnir Esprid. Druids, dressed in white garments, came to a ceremonial fire at the foot of the long, steep ridge of the mountain rising into the cloud. Their chief wore a garland of holly, and in his hand he held a withered circlet of oak. Scanning his audience, he began the address. "We celebrate the stalwart oak from which this crown was made at Yule. We praise the oak's longevity, which far outstripping our human span of years, endures through our harsh northern winters. The great oaks that stand today have witnessed the coming of the Roman and have watched their demise; their gnarly forms scorn man's brief pomp. We offer this symbol of nobility into the flames." Holding it aloft for a brief pause to be admired, he cast it into the fire.

He gestured the crowd to a nearby stone incised with cup marks.

"This cup honours Beli Mawr, celebrating his solstice fullness." Holding up a silver object, he spoke with renewed vigour. "Engraved upon this talisman is the double-disc, one larger than the other, representing the smaller and the larger suns of winter and summer. Intersecting the double disc is the Z-rod, the lightning bolt that leaps from heaven to earth, blessing the union between sun and earth, male and female. Note the Z-rod terminals," he held it aloft, a finger pointing at the tiny engraving which Taran nor anyone else could possibly see. "One shows a flower open to receive the sun's morning rays – the other, a closed flower furled up at night. In this potent symbol, there exists the equilibrium of heaven and earth: summer and winter, day and night."

A gust of wind blew some strands of hair across the druid's face. Pausing to brush these aside, he cleared his throat. "This occasion venerates Beli Mawr and his union with the Bulàch, who, discarding her ancient form when drinking from the sacred well, is resurrected as the youthful Brigantia in her mysterious cycle of renewal."

The druid rummaged through an inside pocket of his cloak, and produced a golden bracelet engraved with concentric rings. The lustre of the gold, along with the engraved designs, captivated the eyes of those nearby. "We celebrate the consummation of earth and sun, in expectation of fruit and grain to keep us through the leanness of winter. Reflect upon your work, of tilling and sowing, watering and weeding – from labours started at the crack of dawn, until the going down of the sun. We acknowledge before Brigantia and Beli Mawr, our dependence upon their favour, realising that our labours alone are insufficient to fill the barn. Not one of us – irrespective of strength, or knowledge, or from the sweat of his brow – can ensure fruitfulness. Warmth is required to germinate the seed; rain, at the right time, to swell the grain."

The druid scanned his audience as if to check whether anyone had the audacity to assume they possessed such power. He nodded to one side where two younger druids held a lamb which was slaughtered with a deft stroke of a knife – its lifeblood was captured in a bowl.

"We implore Brigantia and Beli Mawr to look with favour upon us, that storms will not spoil our crops. We offer up oblations of milk and bread, blood and gold."

Three druids came forward to lay the offerings at the foot of the stone to which the presiding druid added the gold bracelet, who waited, his eyes surveying the steeply rising line of Munnir Esprid. When the sun had touched the mountain's ridge, he sang a lengthy invocation to the sun, and to Brigantia. When all the verses had been completed, the sun had sunk from view, although its radiance still filled the whole sky.

The pilgrims returned to the bonfire, from which flaming brands were taken to light their cooking fires. Mead was poured, the smell of roasted meat on spits and skewers filled the air, and robust singing brought great cheer. Taran was eating with those he had travelled with from the previous day. Two druids approached, stopping a short distance off, seemingly hesitant to come closer.

"Will you join us," Taran beckoned.

The two came forward and sat down.

"We were wondering whether we knew you?" began one of the druids.

"I am Drostan of the Ce."

"The Ce! So, are you with Maelchon?"

"I am not a druid," he explained. "I respect your ways and once held your beliefs implicitly, fulfilling all the required observations."

"So why do you celebrate with us?" No note of antagonism was discernible in his voice.

"To be with my kindred – I have been away for four years. You venerate earth and sun, but I worship the One who created these."

"Ah, so you are a soldier of Christ," said one, pleased to define what he represented.

"Would you explain what your belief is?" asked the older druid rather drily.

Taran explained, from birth through to resurrection, the life of Christ, especially attesting to his authority over creation. They listened in silence, respecting his noble manner and reasoned explanation.

They questioned further until one of them said, "Let us fetch our companions, for what you speak of would be of interest to them."

They left and returned a short while later with four other druids, including the chief who had earlier presided over the ceremony. They pressed him to explain his beliefs. He felt excited, wondering whether this occasion was somehow connected with the anticipation of the learned ones to the north. "You live in the expectation that Beli Mawr will one day reveal himself in person upon the earth. He has already come! He was born in a distant land, and demonstrated great powers that brought healing and miracles over nature. He is the Christ, the Supreme One of heaven who bestows blessing and goodwill upon the earth."

The chief druid looked like he would interrupt, but Taran did not pause, for words flowed effortlessly from his lips. "The One for whom you await, identifies himself with words that might make your skin tingle at this Litha festival of supreme light: *I am the light of the world. Whoever follows me will never walk in darkness, but will have the light of life.*"

The chief druid, who a moment earlier had been keen to interrupt, now beckoned him to continue. Taran felt animated in the manner that had once overcome him previously when defending the plight of the refugees. "You spoke of the Bulàch's transformation from the old hag to the youthful Brigantia – the resurrection that comes with spring. The Son of God who died and was brought back to life declares: *I am the resurrection and the life. He who believes in me will live, even though he dies; and whoever lives and believes in me will never die...*"

With many other words, he shared more stories and teachings of Christ, and concluded, "Litha is a prayer ceremony, to vouchsafe a fine yield of harvest and livestock, is it not?" He noticed the chief druid nod. "Do we not anticipate bread from the bounty of harvest, and milk from the cow; offerings you made earlier at the stone? The Son, whom you are anticipating, says that we are not to just want the bread that moulders, but to desire the bread that satisfies the soul. Christ refers to himself as spiritual bread: *I am the bread of life. He who comes to me will never go hungry, and he who believes in me will never be thirsty.* Even the blood – another of the offerings you made to appease your gods – prefigures the sacrifice that God presents for us through the death of his Son."

He watched with some anticipation as the druids turned to one another to confer quietly. Finally, the chief druid spoke up. "It is curious what you are saying! But we expect Beli Mawr to reveal such things through our people and not by a revelation from foreigners."

"I am no foreigner," he mildly protested. Then, a new idea struck him. "You referred to the Z-rod earlier: the lightning of Beli Mawr bringing fertility to Brigantia . . ."

He paused, for what he had in mind seemed reckless. "To whom is given the Z-rod as a tattoo?"

"The warlord."

He stripped off his tunic, leaving him standing there in just his trousers. Every eye was fixed curiously upon him as he turned to reveal his back. He heard a woman gasp, followed by a couple of men muttering. Turning to face them, he said, "I received this Z-rod at my initiation, believing that I would be warlord. Our druid, Maelchon, was deeply perplexed; troubled that the Bulàch had instructed the tattooing of this symbol whilst the existing warlord, Talorgen, was still living."

"You are Taran!" announced one woman.

"I am," he replied fearlessly, for at that moment he felt untouchable.

"Then why do you call yourself Drostan?" objected another.

"To protect an identity that has blood money attached to it." Anxious to return to the matter of the revelation, he proceeded without pause. "Maelchon told me nine years ago: *To you is given this authority, but I doubt that it conveys all that we would have it mean to mortal minds.* Maelchon added that it was a mystery that not even druids could fathom."

The chief druid stroked his lengthy beard, deep in thought.

Taran proceeded with conviction, "But what was once an enigma has now been made clear!"

"Wait," said the woman who had identified him, "Maelchon is here. He can verify what you say."

"Send for him," ordered the chief druid. "Maybe he can prophesy concerning the meaning of this sign."

In a short while, Maelchon appeared. Taran was surprised how his former druid had aged, more than he would have believed in the years that had passed since he escaped from the crannog. His grey hair had mostly turned white, and his face was wizened. Of all the people he knew from home, here stood one he had no pleasure in meeting. He had to repress the hostility felt towards the man who had intended him to be sacrificed.

"You say that you are Taran," quizzed Maelchon, who eyed him without recognition.

"I am . . . do you not recognise me? I have obviously matured from the eighteen-year-old youth that you last saw at Wroid's crannog! Now I am full-bearded and with druidic haircut like yourself."

"Your voice is that of Taran's." Maelchon sounded somewhat intrigued. "It is true, too, that we were last together at Wroid's crannog."

"Show him the Z-rod," said the woman, impatiently, shaking her head incredulously as if to lament the slowness of these presumed intelligent men. Taran presented his back.

"Ah! It really is you!" exclaimed Maelchon, visibly stirred.

"I am the fugitive prince from Rhynie!" he declared, smiling.

"We thought you were dead!" said Maelchon. Turning to the others, he verified, "This is indeed Taran, and through the instruction from the Bulàch, this Z-rod was tattooed by my assistant."

After his own initial animosity had waned, Taran regained his composure. "Do not be afraid; you meant me harm, but God used it for good." He proceeded to talk about his own conversion, sharing the significant unfolding of the prophecies, hoping that his openness might prepare them to acknowledge Christ.

"This is a surprise!" declared Maelchon, with a slightly twisted smile. "I was perplexed that the Z-rod should be given when the Lord Talorgen, who bore the authoritative insignia, was still alive . . ." He struggled to finish his sentence. Taran noted how heavily the druid swallowed. "These things should not be, and much trouble followed." Maelchon looked away to avoid meeting his eye.

"Yes, it entailed giving me up as a sacrifice!" Taran was keen that the uncomfortable truth would not be glossed over.

Maelchon looked ill at ease and immediately came to his own defence. "What was to be done after the losses following the ill-fated cattle raid? Doing nothing was not an option since our enemies, knowing our whereabouts, surprised us with their ambush. Such events are more than earthly arbitrations – although others would have explained things away by naming you as the traitor."

Although detecting a note of sympathy in Maelchon's tone, Taran felt an intense flush of the old resentment rise into his cheeks. "Who stood in my defence? Only my father spoke up." He paused, keen to learn about his father. "Tell me, is he still alive?"

"You have not heard?"

"How could I hear! I have been exiled since my name has been singled out as a traitor."

"Nechtan is dead!"

The words rang with a dreadful finality to Taran's ears.

"He died nobly," continued the druid, "in defence of our people."

He remembered his father's surprising caress whilst Taran had been feigning sleep in the crannog on the night of his escape. From time to time, he had recalled his father's show of affection, a kiss that now had the poignancy of the final embrace. "How did he die?" he eventually asked.

"He died a true warrior, holding the hillfort from Brude." Maelchon looked as though he had more to say but cut himself short.

"Go on," Taran continued, wanting to tease out more information.

Maelchon shrugged his shoulders. "The warrior's life is always perilous . . . it was his time! Many fell with him, and half of those who remained alive Brude led into exile like spoils of war." Maelchon looked withdrawn as the light in the west slowly faded. The darkness seemed turgid, slow to gather pace.

"I do not think it takes much conjecture, for the facts speak for themselves!" Taran spoke boldly. If Maelchon was not going to expose what had likely happened, Taran felt it his duty to speak out for his father, as his father had done for him. "Oengus would want to be rid of the one who stood up for the truth! My father was brave and outspoken – he was the only one who dared speak up before Talorgen."

"No! You misunderstand my reticence to expand further!" Maelchon looked up from the ground. "We have suffered much and were nearly all annihilated. I would have you know that Oengus chose your father to be the commander of the fort."

"Nechtan was fearless and noble," spoke the woman who had first recognised him. "Do you know, he never gave up searching for you until his dying day?"

Taran was quiet, remembering the few times when he rode as a warrior alongside his father.

"And what about my mother?"

"What about getting back to our discussion of the Z-rod?" the chief druid said, a tad impatiently.

"No, let him hear," interjected the woman. "He has been cut off from his people all these years! It is only right that he should learn about his family."

Maelchon enlightened him. "She moved in with her sister Drusticc after your father died, both being widows. It was remarkable for they had fallen out following your disappearance. But grief brought them together."

"Tell her I am alive, and, God willing, one day we shall meet again." He paused, scratching the nape of his neck, wondering about others back at Rhynie he wanted to ask after, but decided that for the moment, news of them would have to wait.

"Now, concerning this revelation from heaven!" the chief druid re-introduced the matter foremost on everyone's minds.

"I should have been dead after all that has passed," interjected Taran with feeling, "especially with the bounty placed upon my head!"

"Some actively sought to track you down," revealed Maelchon. "But you are here now, and that beggars belief! As the Z-rod was not to confer lordship upon you, are you a messenger of the great Lord whom we do not know?"

"I do believe I am." Taran was surprised that his druid from home, known for his difficult manner, should have reckoned him as such a messenger. He argued Christ's cause long into the night. Some of the listeners, wearied from all the talk, left to either join the revelries around the main bonfire, or to ascend the mountain to the lit beacon upon its summit. Some, listening with curiosity, asked questions, whilst others argued, resistant, wishing to uphold the old order. Taran noted that Maelchon appeared the most curious, almost moved, even though his personality was the least likely to be persuaded. Even with the strongest opponents, the discussion came to an amicable conclusion and the group parted company.

Maelchon lingered, clearly wanting to speak more. "Well, well! – you are still alive!" he wondered aloud. "Oengus still fears you. He knew you were alive, in the year of your disappearance, for the high priestess of the Bulàch revealed as much. As Oengus grew in power as a warlord, I suspect he thought less of you, but now that he has been severely reduced to become a vassal to Brude, I suspect he fears someone taking control of the Ce." He paused before uttering with surprising concern, "Your being alive should remain a secret."

"I am no longer afraid. If you would have asked me earlier, I would have answered differently. I have renewed assurance that I am in the High King's hand and that nobody, nor anything, can touch me until his purposes for me are fulfilled. Tell my cousin that I am alive and that I have no design upon his person, or his position as warlord."

Maelchon raised an eyebrow, looking at him searchingly. "I will not be telling Oengus – I am no longer attached to his court."

As the druid continued to eye him with curiosity, no doubt struggling to comprehend the transformation from the youth he had been back in Rhynie with the soldier of Christ he had now become, Taran needed to respond. "You might look at me like that! I have changed. In some respects, I am no different, still unreconciled to certain things." He recalled that fateful day when the Z-rod was marked upon his back, and, unable to hold back his indignation, he said bluntly, and with some vehemence, "You caused me great harm! You turned my whole life about, forcing me to flee, to leave all that I loved, stripping me of my identity and my rights to be warlord. I have wandered as a vagabond through perilous places: been attacked by a bear, hounded by wolves, almost betrayed by the Fotla to be delivered into the treachery of the Circinn. I have endured horrific times on the high seas in a coracle and have nearly perished from cold in the wintry mountains." He looked him squarely in the face and pronounced, "Your actions set all of this in motion!"

"Taran!" the druid interrupted. "Do not speak like that – it was not my decree! I intended you no harm. I was only executing what the Bulàch had revealed." Maelchon stopped, making Taran wonder whether he was expecting another tirade from himself. "We must act according to what has been revealed. It was her mischief, not mine, that precipitated these things."

Maelchon had been looking at the ground whilst speaking and he now raised his eyes to meet Taran's. "Do you not remember what we believe? The Bulàch is mischievous in spring; for re-born as Brigantia, she desires an eminent young man, to become her consort, to enjoy him in her world. The druids say that from her comes success or failure – she is not one to easily predict or to placate. When it became clear that a curse was upon Talorgen's household – as one failure followed hard upon the heels of another – it called for drastic action. These were not my ways! You must have seen how awkward it was for me?"

Taran observed Maelchon's body had become taut with suspense.

"And I will add," announced Maelchon emphatically, "that I did not single you out for sacrifice! Talorgen had made up his mind, determining that since Oengus showed a ruthless element that appealed to the old warrior, you were then condemned for sacrifice."

He was unsurprised by this disclosure. Ruthlessness seemed to be the nature of all the warlords he had met.

Still, it shocked; for Talorgen was his kindred. So, Maelchon would have me believe that he was just as helplessly caught up in the tide of events as he had been himself? Catching the druid's eye, he raised his hand in a gesture of reconciliation and felt relieved of a burden.

"It was outrageous!" Taran eventually replied. "Human sacrifice – especially among one's kin – has been unheard of in our lifetime. I hated Oengus for his betrayal. We trained as comrades, depending upon one another – such bonds are sacred." Aware of how his brows were knitted tightly, he relaxed them, drew in a deep breath and felt a calmness to flow through him. He smiled with a warm generosity. "Maelchon, I have had my say and I accept that you, like me, were caught up in events bigger than ourselves."

"It is good to hear you say this," Maelchon faintly smiled and his hunched shoulders relaxed.

"But how can you continue to serve the Bulàch? She is so capricious!" Taran searched the druid. The other druids had left unconvinced, or so it seemed. Maybe the awakening would begin with the one druid who knew him. "What I have gained, through the loss of so many things, is immeasurable, and I do believe this will serve the salvation of our people. I would not trade it for all that Oengus has – or I should say, once had – not even for double the number of Brude's war horses, or five times his warriors, or even his lordship over the Picts! I would not wish to be other than what I am. Once I resented Oengus's devious success and would gladly have killed him, especially for seizing Alpia. Do you not see the peace and acceptance that has changed me? Christ is my King, and his companionship is sweeter than that of any woman and more steadfast than a father."

"You cannot say that Oengus seized Alpia," corrected Maelchon.

"How?"

"He married Eithni. Alpia remained disinterested in Oengus, and he knew that. Then, when Eithni died in childbirth, the gods determined to place Oengus and Alpia together. Even then, Alpia remained indifferent to him, even though she was like a mother to his child."

"But Ossian told me not long after my flight from the crannog that Oengus had married Alpia!" His head was now swimming.

"It is true that Oengus married within that time, but it was to Eithni, not Alpia."

Taran felt a slithering sensation pass from the back of his neck into his shoulders.

Maelchon expanded upon the details. Even after all those years, Taran resented that his one-time love should have married his usurper. At least the marriage was not so soon after he had disappeared from Rhynie! The abruptness he had formerly believed had once incensed him.

"And remember," continued the druid, "after no one had heard about you for so long – and with the Circinn swearing an oath at Derile's marriage that they were not giving you sanctuary – we all presumed you dead, including Alpia." Maelchon stroked the extensive bald patch on his shiny head. "Alpia has borne two children."

With the initial surprise over, Taran calmed down. Had he not moved on too? He wondered whether Ossian had lied, forcing him to focus on making a new life for himself? Then he recalled how the bard had been confused as to whom Oengus had married in the year of his flight, and, when pressed, suggested that it had been to Alpia.

"Have you seen Ossian, or heard anything as to his whereabouts?"

"No, nothing. The last we saw of him was when he celebrated Beltane after your initiation."

"I saw him four years ago – at his baptism."

"Ossian has become a pilgrim?" Maelchon's brows shot upwards.

"Tell me what happened at Rhynie? I heard of Rhynie's fall, something truly catastrophic, but I am ignorant of the details."

Maelchon put together a full picture, causing Taran to feel grieved over the plight of his people and especially over the loss of his father. The shock of that news still had not sunk in. They spoke at length and when Taran had satisfied his curiosity, he was about to excuse himself.

"Wait, do not depart just yet. This meeting with you was meant to be." The old druid looked at him with special significance. "I have continued with the old ways, but . . . I am weary."

Taran noted how the confession troubled the druid.

"But I have been a druid all my life and do not know what else I could do! I had hoped to end my days serving the needs of the people in the only way that I have been taught." He cleared his throat and looked like one who had been broken. "Taran, I do believe you have the answer to what I am searching!"

"Me? I am surprised to hear you, of all people, say that!"

"Ever since the Z-rod was tattooed upon you, I have been bewildered. It was obviously not given to indicate that you would be the warlord. It has caused much mischief and tragedy to befall the lives of many. The direction to bestow that sign upon you was truly the last time that I heard from the gods." He stopped, tugging at his beard, as though wondering whether to add something. "I do think that it is the only time that I have really heard something from beyond our seen world." He looked at him again with particular significance before proceeding rapidly. "Of course, I have played my part, discharging the duties of my office, performing the rites, delving into old lore. But the Bulàch has always been silent except for that one time."

Taran strongly felt that he should interrupt him. "If that was the only time you say that the Bulàch has communicated with you, then how do you know, for sure, it was her?"

"How do you mean?"

"I have understood enough that the great High King does sometimes communicate with people, seemingly in the context of their old ways – for they know no other – so that they will take note."

"Surely not?"

"Why not? The Z-rod was the means for setting me apart, and Ossian was likewise led unknowingly by the High King to prepare my escape. Being led eventually to Fillan's muintir, I learned about the High King. It strikes me that through the same sign, you have been left wondering until this day!"

He noted that Maelchon did not dismiss the suggestion.

"You mean that the Z-rod was intended as a revelation for me as well as it has been for you?"

"Precisely!"

"That there comes a blaze of light flashing through the darkness, pointing to a higher revelation of the one Creator who bestows blessing upon the earth."

Taran nodded, watching the druid's face carefully as it grew animated.

"You know, some of us old druids have pondered whether there is some great God who was here at the beginning of time, who transcending time and beginnings, created the earth and the heavens and all living things. However, such a supreme being has been concealed by our many lesser deities, and to such extent as to totally obscure and make that Creator unknowable. I have been much exercised since leaving Rhynie, about such a revelation, but have not found the truth. But now, I believe in my spirit to be upon the threshold of understanding the revelation you have brought to this mountain that has been rejected by the other druids. My fellow druids do not see beyond the sun and the earth, reluctant to acknowledge any other besides Beli Mawr and the Bulàch. Our finite minds struggle to make sense of what is seen and what causes the renewal of the earth and its fruition."

Taran smiled. "A fuller knowledge comes to you this night when the darkness is at its shortest. Even the night is not truly dark, for there is a twilight in which not even a star is visible."

Maelchon looked aside, raising his eyes into the night. "The Creator reveals himself at Litha when the light is at its utmost ascendancy. Well, I praise him that this light has penetrated my spirit."

Taran could see the druid smiling in a way that caused Maelchon's face to lose all its cold severity – a look he had never seen in Maelchon before. They parted company. The summer night sky shone with a luminous blue that lighted the ground sufficiently to be able to walk without a flaming brand. Taran lay down, exhausted, on a makeshift bed of slender pine branches, wrapped in his awning, too exhausted to make himself a shelter. He stared out west, observing how the face of the earth was wrapped in the benevolent embrace of a glowing twilight. How like the High King's blessing that had enveloped him through all the perilous dark times. The dawn was perceptibly brightening in the east, and, not feeling ready for the new day yet, he fell asleep. It seemed no time at all before he was aroused by spirited singing as the sun was mounting the skies. Their song was in praise of the sun's splendour and the words were familiar. Sitting up, he adjusted the words in praise of the One who had created the sun, the Giver of the true light of the world.

He crossed the rough ground whose hollows, filled with bogs, soaked his feet with their muddy wetness. Mounting Munnir Esprid's main ridge, grown thick with heather, he found a boulder to sit upon part way up. Rising above the tree line, the rounded hills swept along the horizon with what appeared to be a graceful fluidity, as though their once solid mass had become an animate thing. Down in the depths of glens, deep shadows remained, but on the higher slopes, a rippling play of morning light washed over the reborn land. A moorland lochan glimmered, encompassed by forests steaming under the new day's heat. He found the spectacle alluring, rather like glimpsing a world coming into being through the mists at the dawn of time.

Although much pleased by Maelchon's enlightenment the previous night, he still felt troubled by his inability to convince the other druids. He waited a long while, watching how the warmth, slowly but surely, evaporated the dew about him. Despite these lingering frustrations of not having yet borne the fire to the north, this new day still brought a sense of hope.

"Encircle me, Lord, with the light of your salvation,
to enable me to explain your extraordinary gift.
Encircle me, Father, with the radiance of your love
that I may be filled with compassion for my fellow man.
Encircle me, bright shining Son, to bring hope to the
heavily burdened.
All praise be to you, the Son of Man,
who alleviated the cares of the world from the
shoulders of the oppressed.
Encircle me, Spirit, with your heat that will dissolve
the heaviest dew of disbelief.
Cause me to shine with your radiance that blind eyes
may see."

As he deliberated further in prayer, the sense of frustrations lifted and doubts dispersed, just as the shadows grew less in proportion to the ascendancy of the glorious sun.

"So much for bearing fire to the north," he chided himself as the last spectre within himself expressed its reluctance to withdraw.

"Be at peace," came an inward voice, like a definitive response.

What rose as a suggestion within, became a bubbling spring of peace, welling up, lapping away at the vestige of disappointment until it was dissolved. The last resistance of disquiet dissipated, and an all-embracing warmth, channelling down his tingling spine, pervaded every fibre of his being. He felt some inexplicable sense of assurance that his time would come, just as the light grows from Yule to Litha, which nothing could prevent.

Chapter Eight

The Prophet

AD 564 Dindurn

The two-day walk to Dindurn passed quickly, for Taran's heart was burning within him to see his old anam cara and share all their experiences since they had last met four years previously. Would Fillan still be alive? he wondered. Surely, news of his death would somehow have filtered through, even to as far a place as Candida Casa. How would he find him? Fillan had already visibly aged when they had met at Dunadd, and so he quickened his pace, urging himself on as though every moment mattered before his dear old friend might pass from this world. The entire length of an immense loch weaving between the hills had to be walked, followed by a climb through the forest to reach the pass that would bring him to the familiar view of Strath Gunalon with its high peaks to the south.

As he looked upon the waters of the Loch Gunalon below, he recalled his heady flight from Domech's men, paddling a coracle. It felt a lifetime away. The descent was long and tedious; reaching the loch, he still had its entire length to walk before arriving at the woods at the far end, where he and Aniel had launched their coracles. The journey became arduous, and time seemed to pass slowly as the anticipation mounted of seeing his anam cara again. Beyond the woods, he caught his first glimpse of Dindurn hill, with its hall crowning the rocky crest, and its many huts covering its flanks. With the sun still high in the sky late in the afternoon, he saw the plain he knew so well and the muintir that had received him as a homeless vagabond. He looked upon it with fondness, which surprised him, recalling that it had not been an easy time. But memory had sieved out the difficulties, and these surroundings became the place associated with his nurture that later would lead to his awakening. It felt like coming home! Maybe it was rather like childbirth for a mother: a time of travail to be forgotten for the joy of what followed.

He found Fillan sat in a chair outside his cell, looking withered, rather like an apple that had not been gathered, still holding on to the bough, shrunken by the first frost. His hair had turned white.

Taran stood before him, smiling, until the old abbot eventually recognised him through squinting eyes.

"Ah! It is you, Drostan!" Fillan said with a tone as if he were expecting him.

"Fillan! How pleased I am to be here again." He felt his heart stir with great emotion.

"I had no word that you were coming – for visions are rare to me these days – but I sensed within my soul that I would see you once more before I went the way of all flesh." The old man's voice was thin, its pace slower than before. "My time is short. I have run the race and the High King has sustained me through eighty-one years." He smiled with great calm, his somewhat cloudy eyes lustrous in the late afternoon light. "Tell me, Drostan, how has it been with you?"

"You still call me Drostan?"

"That is the name you were known by for the two years you were here. As you assumed a new identity when you came here and eventually became a new person, it is fitting that the name of Drostan should be maintained. How did your studies go in Erin?"

Taran briefly scratched his head considering his named identity and then, remembering the question, he responded, "Oh, it seemed an eternity!" Recalling their dispute over this very issue before departing to Erin, Taran returned to the matter of his identity. "You have a point about maintaining the name of Drostan! I am a new person," he said with conviction, "and the old identity of prince has long been laid to rest. Maybe I should dispense with the old and truly become Drostan from now on."

"That is up to you – but as for me, Drostan is the name I pray for in my petitions to the High King." Fillan scratched behind his ear. "I recall our taut exchange back in Dunadd when you objected strongly to going to Erin. Anyway, I am no better . . . I knew the same impatience myself and how eager I was to leave Erin on my white martyrdom." He smiled fondly, moving a bee aside gently with a hand. "Youth cannot wait. And then, when I was here, I wanted back!" Fillan chuckled. "But studies prepare us, would you not say?"

"Indeed, they do. Just at this solstice, I held my own with the druids on Munnir Esprid. Had it not been for my studies, our discourse would have been much shorter."

"The druids respect learning," Fillan nodded. "They serve a lengthy apprenticeship under a master druid, thirsty for knowledge, keen to discern mysteries. Under the old order, they are the repository of wisdom." He looked up brightly. "And so, did you convince them?"

"Oh, I wish! For a time, they were understanding, seeming on the brink of being persuaded . . ."

"Do not be concerned – the High King will have succeeded in his purposes, you can be sure of that. I mind of the early days with Kessog when my knowledge was lacking. How I wanted back to Erin; to the island where men came flocking to worship the High King. Compared with back home, we seemed to be making such slow progress in what felt like an insignificant backwater." He shook his head and stared out across the fields beyond the muintir.

"But I was going to add that my former druid from Rhynie was there and he was persuaded. That was quite a surprise and the one I would have least expected to choose *the way*."

"There!" Fillan partly raised his hands in the air in a gesture of thankfulness. "I also mind coming to Dindurn, troubled by a sense of my own inadequacy. Kessog would pray and a person would be healed; Kessog could command an evil spirit to depart or mute a frenzied woman bent on frustrating the High King's purposes, and it would happen. Kessog spoke with authority, discerning dreams and interpreting them, while I felt as one making up the number in the group, without any special gift."

For a moment, he saw Fillan as he appeared outwardly: an old man in a chair outside his hut, before the image changed to the Fillan he knew – the great seer, the man of extraordinary prayer who poured out the molten silver of prophetic utterance.

"But, you know, Kessog was not like that for most of his life. Yes, he was always the older statesman, obviously of noble parentage, used to the diplomacy of the kingly courts, so he was never intimidated. He had that stature that came with being a prince that others recognised.

But as a soldier of Christ, although faithful, he was not especially remarkable. That is, until his final year. He did not speak about it, but I could discern his spirit longing for breakthrough. That drove him to night-long vigils standing in a freezing loch. Probably he sensed his time was reaching its culmination." He looked out into the distance with glazed eyes before finally exclaiming, "He impressed upon me the need to be fervent."

"I know," Taran affirmed warmly, recalling how he had left Aleine Brona and had fasted for three days prior to meeting the shining one.

"Then came the breakthrough of the missing axe incident . . . you have heard me speak about it before. It led to 'seeing' the very patch of ground where we were to dig to find the water source for Dindurn. Of course, you feel the disappointment when others fail to see the light. But know this: it is not our responsibility to bring conviction. Our part is to be faithful, to seek to speak in the Spirit, trusting that the King will be recognised."

Taran nodded his head.

The old man raised his face to the sun and seemed to enjoy its warming glow upon his tired face.

"Tell me – is Aniel about?" Taran asked.

"Aniel had the call to be a hermit and had my blessing to pursue that. Last time I visited him, I was surprised to find animals had gathered about him!"

"That does not surprise me!"

Fillan laughed gently. "When passing through the woods and into a clearing about his hut, there were dogs and geese, goats and even deer – all seemingly at one with each other, although mindful of a stranger coming in their midst." Fillan chuckled again with warm-hearted approval. "'There are many animals here,' I remarked to Aniel, to which he just smiled generously. Then he did that thing of his when he places the tips of his fingers together with an air of peace."

Fillan nodded his head fondly. Eventually he brought himself to pronounce, "The young man is doing well. Although he lives largely detached from the world, he does still converse with strangers when he goes down to the road and gets news of events and people for whom he continually prays. And, you know, people seek him out. They regard him a holy man to have the animals dwell in peace together about him. That is powerful, would you not say? I think it is, for people begin to see the King who rules over his creation."

Taran was pleased to hear about the one monk whose company he had particularly enjoyed during his difficult time at the muintir before his own inner transformation. It brought to mind his year at Elpin and Coblaith's place, away from the world; a domestic life pursued with the utmost simplicity and joy. He could not help comparing his own wandering state with another of his own age already established in his life's purpose.

After a lengthy silence, Fillan asked, "When we had our talk down by the River Add at Dunadd, how many of the quests had been completed? Was it not five?"

"There were three, were there not?"

"Only three when you consider the seven quests that the angelic apparition outlined. But remember, there are nine graces from the prophetic prayer – nine being the heavenly number for us Celts. Have there been others quests you are aware of that might have been fulfilled?"

Taran related the incidents on the road with the refugees followed by his vision of the heavenly armour in the campfire flames.

"The virtue of heavenly valour is significant," said Fillan approvingly, nodding his head.

"That would be my fourth . . ." Taran paused to correct himself, "I should say my sixth quest has now been completed."

"However, from what you have told me about meeting with the learned ones upon Munnir Esprid, that also sounds significant."

"Do you think so?"

"Discerning the King takes time. Consider Domech who, for so many years, stubbornly refused to know the High King. It took both a great travail for him, and persecution for us, before he finally acknowledged our Saviour. Do not doubt – your druid from back home believes!"

"Aye, Maelchon."

"Time and events need to pass – people do not just change instantly . . . and when they do it is very rare. Following the fall of your people, the one-time order of Maelchon's world had been turned upside down, causing him to question the Bulàch."

"I had hoped that the gathering of druids on Munnir Esprid was somehow connected with the *anticipation of the learned ones in the north*."

"That is at the climax of Ossian's prophecy, is it not? But the prophetic prayer, confirmed by your vision of the shining one, speaks of nine graces to acquire first. If the two prophecies are to be combined – and I think they are – then the learned ones would not be referring to the gathering at Litha since only six quests have been completed, leaving three yet to come. Furthermore, did the prophecy not state *far to the north* with reference to the learned ones? Munnir Esprid would not fit the description. Ossian shared this word with you at Rhynie, which probably suggests these learned ones live north of there."

He felt the abbot's insight giving him renewed orientation.

"And three more quests you say?" The abbot looked at him doubtfully.

What was he thinking now? he wondered.

"Although Munnir Esprid did not prove to be the ultimate quest," continued the abbot, "I do believe it to be one of the nine quests. Tell me, what have you gained from the experience?"

Taran thought for a while. "The following morning, as the new day was breaking, I felt an indescribable peace."

Fillan beamed. "Is this not a grace from the Lord himself to help you bide your time? You felt the disappointment of men stubbornly holding to their old ways. What you spoke, I am sure, will count for something in the long scheme of things, as it did significantly for Maelchon. But being young, you are impatient to see immediate change, as though it solely depends on your powers of persuasion!" The abbot shook his head, but the smile upon his lips conveyed that the admonishment was only making a point and was not intended as a reprimand.

Fillan cleared his throat and pulled himself more upright in the chair in which he had slipped down. "The High King has gifted peace. Your seventh quest is complete – I am certain of it."

Taran acknowledged with a perceptible nod, but did not feel convinced.

"When you were part of this muintir, did the words of the prophetic prayer not say that peace would be yours *when considering apparent failure*?"

"That is so. You wrote out that prophecy. I still have it here." He tapped his satchel indicating where the short scroll was kept. "Peace came as an extraordinary gift, right on the heels of a keenly felt disappointment."

"Mercy, surrender and love were the three you had acquired on your white martyrdom when we met at Dunadd," continued Fillan emphatically, "adding to the humility and perseverance you had already gained as a fugitive before arriving at Dindurn."

Taran interjected with conviction, "To which can be added *valour, to champion the oppressed; and peace when considering apparent failure.*"

"Leaving just two: *hope in the face of despair; and faithfulness to reach the very ends of the earth.*"

"I am encouraged. But as for the future . . ." Taran paused and pulled a face, "It sounds particularly grim!"

"It is best not to ponder, for we would flee like Jonah if we knew too much." Fillan smiled sympathetically. "Remember, though, has the High King not been sufficient in accomplishing each of your quests? Has he not been your strength and your wisdom? Have the ordeals not bestowed particular grace?"

"I do not deny it. When I look back, it is with extreme gratitude. But when forward I cast my eye, I fear."

"Look to the High King, not upon the trials. Your feelings are not unusual, or unholy." Fillan drew in a breath and his face softened. "Look at how Domech had persecuted our muintir . . . I was nearly crucified! Who would have thought that the mighty, upon the day of my execution, should be brought low! Who could have imagined how a crowd, gathering to be entertained by a gory execution, would voice support for me! Who could have foreseen how a muintir, scourged and destroyed by fire, would be rebuilt by Domech? These are wondrous things to contemplate! They demonstrate the Almighty's power made excellent when we, his people, are at our weakest and most vulnerable."

"And what of Domech, now?"

"He has gone to be with the High King he opposed for much of his life. He was a firebrand snatched from the fire at the end of his days and mercifully spared."

"Most would say he did not deserve it."

"Who of us, though, are deserving? Have we not all had our rebellion against the rule of the High King? But Domech proved true to the Lord for the final two years of his life. His heart gave way whilst he was singing the psalms with us here. Who would have believed that this one-time destroyer should be counted an heir to the promise!"

They sat in quiet contemplation, enjoying the benediction of the late afternoon sun as a breeze moved vigorously through the long, winnowing grasses shining all silvery on top of the vallum.

"And so, where do you go next?" Fillan asked.

"To Dunadd to hear word of one called Colmcille."

"Colmcille – I have heard of this pilgrim! Is he not the one whom blood and passion has marked? But he is committed to make good the losses. With such an intent, I am sure, the Lord will particularly bless."

"It is farewell again."

Fillan did not immediately respond as he stared into the distance. He thought the abbot had intended to ignore the remark. Finally, Fillan spoke and eyed him with a particular significance. "This is the last time we shall face one another upon the earth."

"Do not say such things," Taran admonished.

"No. It is well to speak plainly, to properly observe the occasion, rather than to pretend and miss the opportunity for fine words." Fillan had a twinkle in his eye. "My arrow's flight has made a huge arc and, for a long while now, has been on its downward course. The High King has indulged my wish to see you once more ... and now my soul is at rest for you are running the race and shall continue to persevere. My years are complete, and I depart with the satisfaction of seeing so much of the High King's purposes with my small life accomplished."

"Father ..."

"Do not call me father. There is only one true Father; the One who will never forsake you."

"You have been like a father to me," he insisted with feeling.

"Drostan – be patient. The High King's will shall prevail." His anam cara looked at him intently until that generous smile almost closed the abbot's eyes. "You have come far, my son. I can honestly declare that, for all the stubbornness you showed for a time as I tried to disciple you, it was worth it to see what you have now become. You bring peace to an old man – I do sense the succession."

"What succession?"

"The High King always has his emissaries. You know – I can trace the line as far back as Patrick! When he was a youth, bound in slavery, he discovered the Presence when alone in the hills. Patrick was the instrument used to persuade the king of Cashel to bow the knee before the King of kings. The king of Cashel yields a princely son, Kessog, who then adopted me, the illegitimate child of a princess, to make me a prince of a pilgrim here at Dindurn. Kessog prophesied that you would come and be difficult to disciple. Then it was given to me to reveal the nine graces, later verified by the shining one. Run the race marked out before you and run to win the prize."

The old man smiled with great satisfaction. "My years are spent and now you take up the baton. I applaud you as you set out, assuring you of my remaining prayers." Fillan raised his frail hand. "Ah! Before you go, I do believe I have a word of knowledge ..." He ran a frail hand over his face. "What is it now?" he added, screwing up his eyes. *"The beam of light shall penetrate the chamber and those who were dead, shall be made alive."* Fillan opened his eyes wide and coming to his senses, looked at him fondly. "It will make sense once you need to know it."

Taran repeated the prophecy, not understanding its meaning, yet assured it would become pertinent at the appointed time. He consigned it to memory, and bade farewell. Tears unashamedly coursed down his warrior cheeks. The interview with his anam cara had been memorable and as he walked along the track, he declared aloud to himself, "Drostan is good. Fillan says it is the name I had when I assumed a new identity and I am persuaded to leave the name of Taran behind with the past strife that I have renounced." He paused, before adding with determination, "From now on, I shall be known as Drostan; not out of fear to protect my true identity, but as a sign of my becoming an heir in that succession he just spoke of."

Chapter Nine

Out on the Edge

AD 564-565 Iona

In late summer, Drostan arrived at the wind-ruffled straits between the Ross of Muile and Iona's shore. Flailing his arms wildly about, he eventually attracted the attention of a monk on the far shore who set off in a coracle. Drostan watched his slow progress as the small boat bobbed on the strait's choppy waters.

Brought to Colmcille's cell, the older man recognised him instantly as Drostan stooped beneath the low threshold.

"I have been expecting you!"

"Here I am – you told me to come once I had finished my studies."

Ignoring his remark with disinterest, Colmcille spoke with animation, "I announced at prayers this morning that a pilgrim Pict would be arriving and that we would be breaking our fast to receive you with all the generosity that our poverty will permit."

"You do not need to do that. I can fast with you," he protested mildly.

"We will fast aplenty in the months that you will remain here," Colmcille said with a keen light in his eye. "Come – let us embrace." The two of them clasped one another. "We have much to talk about. Would you believe that at the beginning of last year, this place was without any construction, deserted except for myself and my twelve companions? Now we are numbering nearly fifty!"

"Tell me how you chose Iona?" Drostan asked with genuine interest.

"It all began with visiting King Conall – he is a distant cousin of mine – our great-grandfathers were brothers. Let us sit down first, for it is not a short story." Colmcille gestured to a stone bench which the two occupied. "The king of Dal Riata, unfortunately, was much impressed by my victory over the high king of Erin – a battle that ought not to have been fought!" remarked Colmcille in a repentant tone. It seemed to Drostan that the horror of the bloody battle still haunted him.

"King Conall insisted that heaven was on my side and that battles are not won by the size of a king's army, nor by the prowess of his warriors, nor the advantage of the ground held – but victory comes from the intercessions of saintly men! The king seemed to dismiss any moral judgement – upholding the right of kings to make war."

Colmcille elaborated at length on the moral justice of a cause.

"We went from King Conall's court in search of an island out of sight of my beloved Erin – a pledge I made when I accepted banishment from my homeland. After several landfalls, we came upon Iona and it suited us well with its low-lying, fertile valley, running from coast to coast, in addition to a fine swathe of machair stretching along the western shoreline. Iona was ideal for its distance from Erin and proximity to your people, Taran . . ."

"I have taken a new identity befitting my regeneration as a soldier of Christ. My name is now Drostan!"

Colmcille looked at him blankly, and proceeded to recount his story. "We needed King Conall's permission to settle on this island, which he granted, but he also added that this place was perhaps disputed territory following Brude's victory over Dal Riata. This was confirmed later when some officials came from Brude's court who asked, 'By whose authority have you settled here?' I explained by the authority of the great High King, at which their official insisted that it was Pictish territory and that we needed King Brude's consent. We were required to yield tribute to him from this land and livestock.

"I told them that we have something of far greater worth that does not perish like cattle, which they misunderstood to refer to gold or silver. Shaking my head they asked, 'What could be greater than gold?' I replied that I would explain this to the king after the coming winter has passed."

Colmcille leant back, looking pleased with these developments, owning a certain confidence concerning the pending meeting with the king of the Picts. "Let me show you to our guest room which shall be yours until you have a cell of your own. I will assign a couple of brothers to help you gather rock and turf to build your own cell." Colmcille raised his chin confidently. "By the end of the week, you will have your own place." Then he added, mysteriously, "Oh! I should tell you that another Pict is here – a brother you already know. Let me take you to his cell."

"Who is it – is it Ossian? I should very much wish to see my old friend."

Colmcille did not reply, but led him past some bee-hive cells. Coming to one, he stooped at the low entrance, and announced to one hidden from Drostan's view, "You have a visitor." The abbot walked away with the air of someone with other matters upon his mind.

Peering into the dim interior, Drostan's eyes took time to adjust. The one beckoning him to be seated looked familiar, but he could not place who he was. It was not Ossian.

"Taran! It is I, Maon or Munait, whichever is the easier for you to recall me by!" Unable to contain his joy, Munait rose to his feet, bumping his head on the low, corbelled ceiling. "Why, it is certainly good to see you, my brother – I had hoped that we might meet again."

"It is good to see you too. Now I no longer feel a total stranger here." Drostan felt relaxed. "Tell me, what has passed since we last met? Did you reach home? How is your mother?"

"My mother!" Munait's face clouded. "I had to go, to look upon her face and witness her joy to see me alive." Munait paused, too overwhelmed to proceed.

"Bide your time. I take it that she is no longer alive?" Drostan paused, feeling the shock of this news. "I am truly sorry. I feel the loss myself, more than you would perhaps appreciate, for she was like another mother to me." A fast succession of images passed through his mind, of Coblaith with her bow, the caring wife gathering herbs for Elpin; the foster mother gifting him with the very best of her possessions preparing him for the Minamoyn Goch; even parting with the faithful Garn. "Just the two of us kept an entire winter together," he mused aloud, rather distantly. "We shared our personal stories, and songs banished the bleakness of the long, dark nights."

"When I approached the house," began Munait, "I knew things were not right. The field was overgrown and the hut was dilapidated. None of the ways had been trodden and the vegetable patch in front of the house was high with weeds. I thought, at first, that perhaps my mother had abandoned the place and had taken up living with the folk down at the Dee. I opened the door to look inside one last time at the home where I had grown up. I tell you it was a sight that I cannot eradicate." Munait stopped, his lower lip vaguely quivering before he tightened his mouth. "Her skeleton lay on the bed, clothed in rotting rags. The blanket upon which she lay showed all the horror of decay. I tell you – there was such an oppressive fustiness in the air!"

"That is horrific," Drostan uttered under his breath.

"When I found the grave you prepared for my father, I dug a fresh hole alongside and laid her remains beside his."

Munait looked as though he had just filled in the grave. A silence ensued, which Drostan did not wish to break.

"How dreadful life can be!" continued Munait. "What a cursed day when I was taken by scoundrels and sold to the Gaels! The years of servitude, held against my will, were great to bear."

Drostan nodded his head sympathetically.

"And you know what is the hardest thing?" continued Munait.

Drostan shook his head and waited.

"Even the best thing – that of discovering the love of Christ . . ." Munait hesitated. "Well, I fear to say it, but it was that breakthrough that caused me to remain a further four years in Erin. If that had not happened and I had been granted my freedom, I could have come home and perhaps have found her still living."

Drostan remained quiet, until he recalled something Munait had told him back in Erin. "Were you not given your freedom on condition that you went to study before returning home?"

"That is true." He wiped a tear from his cheek. "But, I still wish I could have seen her one more time. Well, that was not to be." He sighed heavily, and then seeming to pull himself together, he stated, "I had rather be counted among the chosen of the Lord despite all the sorrows this life has thrown at me."

"And to know the balm from the Healer's hands that alone can restore your soul," added Drostan.

True to Colmcille's word, Drostan's cell was ready before the next Sabbath. Although the leader of a community that kept a strict regime of prayer and fasting, work and study, Colmcille made time for Drostan. "You have learned much, and I do not just refer to the knowledge gleaned from Clonard and Candida Casa." The abbot tapped the side of his head. "That is mere head knowledge. You are acquiring grace and wisdom unusual for your years." He coughed loudly, causing him to change his posture on the stone slab he sat upon. "Through adversity, you have made the High King your rock. Forsaken by tribe, and wandering as a true pilgrim, you know what it is to persevere and to become more aware of the Presence."

Leaning forward, Colmcille looked at him keenly from beneath his wiry brows. "I am much in favour of austerity, for comfort makes us careless. You know – I have decreed a rule of life here that declares: *The measure of our daily labour should be until the sweat runs liberally; the measure of our prayer should be until the tears run freely.*" Colmcille looked at him steadily as if appraising whether Drostan wholly embraced this rule. He found the abbot's stare disconcerting.

"Your seven quests have taken you where you would not choose to go," the abbot suddenly reverted to their former topic. "As a result, you have found the comfort of the High King's protection. Whilst you might not know the nature of the journey, the outcome – should you continue to be faithful – is in no doubt; although it will be in his own time."

He leant back, clasping his hands about a knee, and looked thoughtfully beyond Drostan's shoulder. "You will be with us for a time and shall be part of the delegation to visit Brude in his northern fortress once this coming winter passes."

"Do you think that my ultimate quest of bearing fire to the north is connected with this visit?"

"That will become clear," he said rather absent-mindedly, tugging at his baggy waistband. "Do not be concerned about missing the moment. God decrees it and it will happen if you continue to be compliant."

"I still have another quest before this final one of bearing fire to the north."

"Then be vigilant, mindful of your eighth quest. What is it?"

"Hope in the face of despair."

"That does not sound like a quest to go seeking!" the older man let slip with a rare expression of empathy.

Drostan bowed his head and sighed. "I have known so much despair that I would have thought I did not need a further lesson!"

A steady flow of visitors came to the island, those who came were more than those who left. News was brought from Dunadd and distant Erin, reporting on the fall of mighty men, the passing of warlords and the rising of new luminaries. Their island, out on the edge, which had a strong sense of detachment from the outer world, remained well informed.

After prayers one morning, Colmcille approached Drostan with a serious expression. "Before you go to the fields, you should know that Fillan has passed on before us. It was a peaceful death in Dindurn." Colmcille paused momentarily, before adding, "I should have liked to have met him ... but I shall yet do so in paradise."

So, my spiritual father has died, Drostan thought, struggling to think of the tools required to be loaded on the cart for the day's task.

On learning the news, Munait placed a comforting hand upon his shoulder.

Feeling the void, Drostan remained pensive on the walk across the island to the machair. A great soul had been taken, one far more worthy than his own. He owed so much to Fillan. What loving commitment the abbot had shown during his time of rebellion. How unassuming a man too, without boast, transparent in his struggles. And what a gift he had of divine insight.

If only I could be half the man, he thought, then I should be enabled to achieve much.

That day, the blustery wind grew into a gale. It felt to him that the Great Western Sea was making a demonstration of profound loss for a great man.

"It is hard just to stand up, let alone do anything of use," shouted Munait into his ear.

"I have quite a headache," remarked Drostan.

"Me too. This wind just sucks all moisture from eyes and nose."

"Drink some water – that is what the folk on Rùm told me when there was a storm."

They paused to share from a water skin.

"We need to expand this tillage," observed Munait. "Our community is growing so much that there is not enough food."

"At least the fish are plentiful, and birds too."

Placing their backs to the buffeting wind, they started to break up virgin land with spade and hoe. They worked hard until lunchtime. Finding a dune to shelter behind, they held their midday prayers, after which they ate a meagre ration.

"This wind can blow for days on end," said Munait. "We both come from far inland and are not accustomed to such raw forces."

"The wind seems to just turn the world inside out!" complained Drostan.

"Earlier this year, there was one storm that raged for days until all you wished for was a day of calm; to walk upright without effort. Such a wind makes you thankful for life's bare necessities."

They worked for half the afternoon, soaked by showers before loading the cart to start their return journey across the island. Drostan took one last look out to sea. "Look at those shafts of light bursting through the dark clouds! They light the sea with such brilliance!"

"Rather like the favour of the Lord breaking through our hardships."

"Aye. Even the most subdued light seems intensified upon the silvery sea, especially beneath these dark clouds."

Some days later, Colmcille made a strange request of Munait. "Go to the western shore and keep watch on the coast for a guest who will arrive from Erin around the ninth hour."

"But, master, guests do not land at the eastern bay!"

Colmcille smiled. "You will understand when this guest arrives. He will be so weary that he will not be able to continue. This pilgrim will not remain with us but will return on the fourth day!"

Munait watched the wild shore, scanning the horizon for a boat. Around the ninth hour, a heron, weary from its long sea flight, alighted close to him, exhausted.

This must be the visitor, said Munait to himself. Heeding the instruction given, he lifted the bird and carried it home where he cared for and fed it for three days. On the fourth day, in accordance with Colmcille's prophecy, no longer wishing to remain *as a pilgrim* among them, the heron returned southward back to Erin.

So many events, large and inconsequential, happened as Colmcille could foresee, punctuating the usual daily round of labour and devotion, through the harshness of the long winter. When the new year AD 565 dawned, prayer intensified concerning their visit later that spring up the Great Glen to Brude's fortress at Craig Padrig.

Chapter Ten

Opening the Gates

AD 565 Craig Padrig

One spring day, Drostan and Munait set sail from Iona as part of Colmcille's select group and then overland up the Great Glen to King Brude's seat at Craig Padrig. Drostan looked up to mountain ridges that were sculptured with great wintry cornices which, due to the accumulation of much snow had not totally thawed. Down in the valley, he observed that the birch was coming into leaf, and celandine spread upon the less-shady braes. Spring was exuberant as the lambs gambolled about the open spaces. At the top end of Loch Rihoh, the pilgrims camped on the less-boggy ground to the east of the river outflow. At the evening prayers, they prayed earnestly, nervous about how they would be received as holy men, associated as they were with Brude's adversary, Dal Riata. The old fears concerning the bounty upon his head, preyed upon Drostan's mind. It felt ironic that peace, the last grace he had acquired, should elude him during the long watches of that night.

In the morning, as the pilgrims were preparing to set off for Craig Padrig, a sullen crowd of Picts passed by their camp bearing shovels, a pick and the corpse of a young man. A little later, the pilgrims came upon the group, now digging a grave.

"Ask them how so young a man died?" Colmcille instructed.

He relayed the question and then translated. "A great water beast mauled the young man savagely whilst he was swimming in the river just earlier this morning. They tried to rescue him in a boat but were only able to retrieve the corpse. They say they have been troubled by this beast before, but evidently not for a while, hence their guard was down."

"What kind of water beast is it?" Munait asked the Picts.

"Like nothing that is natural in this world! Surely you have heard?" replied a young man, with hands dirtied from the digging. "Its appearance is incised on many a standing stone as a beast that is awesome in power, striking all with terror."

"Oh that! I have seen the image," Drostan replied, recalling the incised stone standing in the gateway at Rhynie.

"Well, we have the matter of crossing the river," Colmcille said resolutely. He ordered one of their own party to strip down to his under tunic and swim to fetch a small boat from the far side.

"I would not swim across," advised one of the Picts staring with astonishment at the pilgrim wading into the water. "The beast could still be about!"

When the swimmer had reached mid-stream, one of the Picts cried out, "Look! The water is stirred into a great commotion by the beast."

"Where?" Drostan asked.

"Can you not see? Look! Now the beast is coming to attack your companion." The funeral party all froze with terror on the bank, looking helplessly on. "Do you not hear its roar?"

Colmcille stepped assertively forward, making the sign of the cross. In a loud voice, he commanded, "In the name of the Lord Christ, go back at once!"

A sound of astonishment rose from the Picts, and some gazed open-mouthed, pointing at the water before turning to Colmcille with a look of wonder. They turned to Drostan for a word of explanation.

"Tell me, what did you see?" Drostan questioned.

"What, did you not see anything?" asked a young man.

"No. What you saw is from the world of darkness."

"What about your leader? He saw something! He ordered it to go away," added another youth.

After Drostan had translated, Colmcille smiled perceptibly. "You had better explain that what I did was for their benefit . . . and for the reputation of the High King."

Drostan turned to the funeral party and said, "Finish telling us what you saw and then I shall explain what has happened?"

"The beast was instantly seized with terror when your leader raised his hand in the air, making that secret sign and speaking I know not what! The beast fled with extraordinary speed as though grasped by some mighty hand that just hurled it back to the loch. It then disappeared beneath the waters."

"What you saw is demonic . . ." Drostan explained, tingling with excitement concerning the timing of this event, just as they were about to go to Brude's fortress.

"What we saw was plain to see with our own eyes!" objected one of the Picts.

"It physically mauled our friend to death!" remonstrated another.

"You saw it, whereas none of us did, therefore it is demonic. It cannot abide the name of Christ which our leader spoke." Still looking perplexed, he continued, "The demonic looks real and there are dire physical outcomes to those who live under the shadow of the powers of darkness."

"How come your leader saw it then?" asked the one with the soiled hands.

"He did not see it. But understanding what was happening, he looked in the same direction you were facing and commanded the beast to be gone. There is supreme power in the One we worship who can liberate you from your fears."

The funeral party stood aghast.

"Tell them to fear the One who is Lord over all creation, Master over every demon that sets itself against his rule," said Colmcille.

He translated.

"We should give thanks now," announced Colmcille.

Explaining they would pray, the Picts bowed their heads too, in imitation of the brothers.

"We will speak some more later; to you and to anyone curious about what you have witnessed," promised Drostan after the prayers.

As the monks ferried themselves across, one by one, in a coracle large enough for two people, Drostan noticed the young Picts hastily finishing burying their companion, having already dug the grave. As the monks walked downstream, Drostan looked back and saw that some of the youths had crossed the river in the coracle, and were now running to catch up with the pilgrims. Arriving at the foot of the steep Craig Padrig, Colmcille stopped their party again to pray.

So, he was not the only one to be feeling the tension of their upcoming meeting with the mighty Brude, thought Drostan. Noting Colmcille's disapproving frown that they had been followed, Drostan spoke to them again. "You need to leave us for a while as we have matters to discuss with your king." This seemed to discourage them from following further; but instead of returning upriver, they went on ahead up to the fortress. When the pilgrims had climbed the steep hill to the king's stronghold, they found the fortress gates closed.

"We come with a message of peace for King Brude," Colmcille had Munait shout up to the guard on the battlements.

"Wait there," came the reply.

They waited a good while, then were informed that Brude would not receive them. Colmcille went undeterred to the great gates and knocked loudly with his staff.

"Perhaps Brude is annoyed at our coming unbidden," remarked Munait.

"Pride is part of it," conceded Colmcille, "but Brude feels uneasy about the reports that will have been brought to his attention."

Realising their presence was being ignored, Colmcille made the sign of the cross and spoke in a voice loud enough for the guards to hear. "In the authority of the great High King, I invoke these gates to be opened!"

As Colmcille placed a hand upon the heavy portal, Drostan heard the bolts on the other side being drawn back with great haste. Colmcille stepped back as the gates were suddenly flung wide open, to the astonishment of the guards on the other side. Colmcille's party entered through the portal and were immediately barred by a line of warriors.

One of the guards ran ahead to the king's hall in the centre of the courtyard, no doubt, thought Drostan, to report on what had happened. In a short while, the soldier returned and announced, "King Brude will see you now." They were ushered to the wooden hall.

Drostan considered Brude to be around thirty years old. He noted how Brude's large, bent nose jutted haughtily out above brown moustaches and a firm jaw. The king wore a decorative torc of braided strands of gold like none other that he had seen. The torc had bulbous terminals that were ornately engraved, but he was not close enough to see exactly what embellished so lavish an ornament. Brude rose, and moving forward with a rigid step, his arm moved aside his scarlet cloak to reveal a shining mail shirt that bore a remarkable likeness to fish scales. A long sword hung from his belt in a jewelled scabbard, very like the one Drostan had seen in the vision he had seen materialise in the fire. Either side of the king stood grim-faced bodyguards, tall and broad, armed with spears, swords and axes. The king stopped a couple of paces short of Colmcille.

"Welcome, good people." Brude spoke with unexpected warmth as his heavily tattooed arm reached out from under the cloak, gesturing them to come closer. Colmcille stepped forward and clasped the king's hand.

Drostan, who stood beside him as interpreter, announced, "This is Colmcille, a soldier of Christ."

"Colm . . . what?" uttered Brude, bemused by the unusual name.

"Colmcille – prince of the Ui Neill dynasty of Erin, bearing a name that means 'dove of the church' – an emissary of the great High King of heaven."

"It seems that you were expecting us!" remarked Colmcille with a wry smile.

Drostan translated the comment.

"Excuse our lack of courtesy. You are men of peace we see, but . . ." The king stroked his nose, "We note that you are also men of extraordinary power." Brude gestured them over to a table, inviting Colmcille and Drostan to sit opposite. A bodyguard formed about the king opposite.

"Tell me, what matter brings you from Dal Riata?"

"We have come on a couple of accounts." Colmcille fixed him steadily with his grey eyes. "But first, we should explain who we are – and then the reason why we have come will become clear."

"Very good." Brude gestured to a nearby servant. "Bring us refreshments!" Once again, he gave them his whole attention. A servant poked at a fire nearby, which, bursting into life, cast its glow upon all manner of weaponry and animal skins that decorated the walls.

"We are soldiers of Christ. We do not bear the sword for it is futile compared with the weapons of God. We mean no harm to you and your people and come that you too might be fully blessed in knowing the power and grace of the great High King. He is above all, and to him we must give account at the end of our days."

Drostan proceeded to translate Colmcille's message about Christ's salvation, and how a heavenly covenant for Brude and his people could bring fulfilment and peace to the realms of the north. Brude listened to the man of God with taut eyebrows and great patience.

"What you propose is that we abandon our own gods, our ways, and put our faith in one in whom you speak of today?" Brude's half smile implied the absurdity of what was being proposed.

"Who can withstand the power of the Lord?" replied Colmcille unruffled. "You are undoubtedly a mighty king, victorious in battle against Dal Riata, and seemingly with power to hold hostage the royal offspring of other warlords of the north."

"What do you mean? Speak plainly," the king said, looking taken aback.

"Those three young men over there – are they not the sons of the king of Inis Ork?"

"Aye – you know them?" Brude looked surprised.

"No, I have never set eyes upon them before! I would not know of their identity, or their being held against their will, had the Lord not revealed it to me."

"So, you are a seer as well as a man of miracles!" Brude leant back, chewing the side of his finger.

Near to the three children of the king of Inis Ork, sat a boy of about four, who particularly caught Drostan's eye. There was something about the setting of his eyes and about his manner that reminded him of someone he could not quite recall. Several times, he looked at the boy, but hard as he tried to recollect his resemblance he was left bewildered. Having to translate between the king and Colmcille, he could give the matter no further thought.

"A mighty warrior of old declared," translated Drostan, *"'I do not trust in my bow, my sword does not bring me victory; but you,'* meaning the High King of heaven, *'give us victory over our enemies, you put our adversaries to shame.'* Colmcille was once a warrior himself, as too was I, of noble descent." Drostan felt uncomfortable about this early disclosure as to his own true identity, but felt compelled to translate what Colmcille spoke. Just as that feeling of unease rose, the recollection of what had taken place down at the river and then at the gates, reminded him of who held the real power.

"We were both in line to rule had we the will," continued Drostan. "But the High King called us to be warriors in an army that is invincible."

Colmcille leant towards the king across the table, which caused the guards to twitch nervously. He spoke in an undertone, which Drostan translated, "The power of the heavenly force is apparent at times when those who are mighty in the eyes of the world choose to resist, just like when you had your gates barred against us."

Colmcille leant back and, entwining his fingers together, continued to address the king. "I speak plainly, O king, lest my meaning be unclear, and you miss acknowledging the One who withdrew the bolts of your heavy gates. It is futile to resist."

"And who has power over the water beast," added the king. "I must confess, I am impressed. These are indisputable signs that beg for a judgement. But in this matter I will not be hasty, for I would consult with the wise of our realm before being persuaded further in this matter."

"Very well, O king. Permit me to mention the other matter that brings us to your court. We would seek permission to continue in our work on the small island of Iona."

"Granted!" returned the King instantly. This caused one of his courtiers to whisper into his ear.

"It would seem that a delegation came to you last year to ask by what right you settled upon the edge of our realm?"

"That is so," replied Colmcille, sitting upright and looking serene.

"By my decree, I grant you this island that you may continue in your work, and we shall not impede you."

"Thank you, my lord." Colmcille smiled broadly for the first time.

Conversation continued about other matters, especially the rising power of the Saxons far to the south that was causing a refugee crisis as witnessed and recounted by Drostan.

"Tell me," Brude addressed Drostan, "who are you? You are a man of great learning for one so young. You speak the language of the Gael and yet you are a Pict . . . and of noble birth, destined once to rule apparently, according to your master!"

Drostan hesitated momentarily, knowing how precarious his position was in the court opposed to the Ce. He had gone over this argument in his head the previous night, which had led to the decision to maintain his identity as Drostan. But at that moment, he recalled how fear had been cast aside on Munnir Esprid and he had boldly declared his royal identity. Was this not an occasion to express his trust in the supremacy of the High King, in keeping with their words earlier?

"My lord, maybe you already have your hunch as to who I am? In truth, you will know of me, although we have never met until this day."

"Come, do not speak in riddles, tell me plainly who you are and what manner of status you bear?" Brude spoke without annoyance, seemingly amused by the playful banter with someone he perceived to have been raised as a warrior noble.

"We are of an age, O king. In our youth, we will have done our military training at the same time. Your destiny was to become warlord of the Fortriu and overlord of a gathering Pictish federation. Your status has been considerably enhanced by crushing the Dal Riatan attack and in sacking Rhynie..."

"You are telling me who I am," interrupted Brude, without harshness, playing his part in the courtly etiquette. "But what of you, Drostan, if indeed that be your name!"

"Drostan or not! What is in a name?"

"There is much in a name; for then your kinship is revealed."

"And if I were to say that Elpin was my father and Coblaith my mother – would you be the wiser?"

"These names mean nothing!"

"They mean a great deal to me, although they are not my true father or mother – but they behaved as such."

"Then you are blessed to have had two sets of parents. But then do not nobles have foster parents? I can also claim to have two sets of parents!"

"Then I have three sets. I was removed from my true parents by the evil schemes of the Bulàch, druids and man; but God kept me, providing me with a couple who nurtured me until I was strong and ready to rise to take hold of my destiny."

"And so, tell me who are your parents? More importantly, reveal to me the royal line of women who gave you legitimacy to rule? That is the way we Picts trace our noble ancestry, is it not?" Brude smiled, seemingly noting that the preliminaries were concluding, and the matter of real substance was about to be revealed.

"Then you will have me made known. If I were merely a prince, and not a warrior of Christ, aware that my former power and influence has been stripped away, then I should not be inclined to tell you. Indeed, I would not be coming to your court. But I am not a man on his own, although at the time of leaving the household of my third parents, I acutely felt such a man! But I stand bold before you, that although I am stripped of all that once I had, I have been imbued with a new power and identity from on high . . ."

"Yes, yes, the High King of heaven," said Brude, a little impatiently. Then he smiled. "I do believe that I know who you are!"

"Go on, tell me and I will be straight with you – although mortal man would deem me a fool!"

"You are a close descendent of Mongfind of the Ce, Talorgen's sister. Am I not correct?"

"You are correct." He felt strangely liberated to reveal his former identity. "I am Taran, and if it were not for devious ploys, our alliance may have held."

Brude looked lost for words for a moment, although the smile never quite disappeared from his face. The king broke the tense silence. "Are you aware that I could have you arrested and turned over to your cousin, Oengus? There is a bounty on your head, which in the year of your disappearance, sent several adventurers in search of you."

Brude took a moment to smooth his bushy moustaches before continuing. "Then you passed into history, considered dead and of no consequence, and no one spoke of you anymore. How precarious a thing is life and power. The eminent ones of yesterday are supplanted – soon to be forgotten, their memory perishing with the few who truly cherished them."

"O king, I had such a view of things at the time," returned Drostan, aware of the Presence overshadowing him. "I was sorely afflicted by my great fall from the cusp of acquiring the lordship over the Ce. From that noble eminence, I plummeted to the depths of working the sod of the land. I became a nobody, with a pseudonym, in some forsaken backwater on the edge of the Minamoyn Goch. Later, I came close to being handed over by Lord Domech to the Lord Cynbel for a reward. Domech had all the power and connivance to make that possible. But you see," he looked at Brude in the eye, "however powerful we feel we are, which our station in life bestows upon us, we are nothing compared to the incomparable greatness of the High King. His will prevails. Because of an abbot who could hear his Sovereign's voice, an escape was made possible just before the grip of the Lord Domech closed about me."

He went on to explain something of his transformation during his white martyrdom. He came to sum up. "I am no longer afraid. A man is untouchable until God's will is done. Oengus and the Ce need not fear – I have renounced all political ambition and from exacting vengeance. I now have a far higher calling."

Looking impressed by his forwardness, and no doubt an admirer of courage, Brude seemed to put behind him the situation that existed ten years earlier. "Lord Nechtan, one of my predecessors, also studied the holy words in Erin. Those words were forgotten with his passing, when no one spoke of them anymore. But I do recall him as one counted as a pilgrim." He leant back in his seat, seemingly lost in thought. "Come back tomorrow, that I might hear more, and learn by what rule you live your lives and take huge risks to speak of your King. I should very much like that."

The pilgrims passed through Craig Padrig's mighty gates, and just a stone's throw beyond, Colmcille stopped. "Since it is the evening hour, let us worship the Lord here."

Drostan's heart was overflowing with thankfulness. To offer praise, just beyond the gates that could not withstand the Lord's injunction, made it highly appropriate.

Colmcille chanted a psalm, leading with a line on his own that the others then repeated in unison. His deep bass voice, reverberating clear like an immense brass bell – and an octave lower than all others – had the ability to swell from an undertone to an all-pervading pitch that arrested attention. The holy man's voice sounded of normal volume to those around him, but it carried afar most strangely. When Colmcille sang on Iona, all could detect his voice from a distance when all other voices ceased to be audible.

Whilst they were worshipping, some druids came from the hillfort, gesticulating to them as they approached. "Will you be quiet or go somewhere else!" one of them shouted.

"Your singing penetrates the walls of the fortress, like some terrible thunder, and disturbs the king," expanded another.

In response, Colmcille raised his voice until it boomed. On completion of the psalm, they returned to camp where many locals were waiting.

"We want to hear more about the name that has power to command the water beast," an older one said, with a look of awe in his eyes as though he had just witnessed the beast being flung back into the loch.

Colmcille explained patiently, answering their many questions. Drostan noted their attention was rapt, marked by an earnestness of a people living under fear.

A thin man in a frayed shirt spoke up in a state of agitation. "Brothers, I believe what you say. We have seen proof of the power when you overcame the beast. What must we do to be protected by this power?"

"Be baptised as a demonstration of choosing to live under the rule of a new Lord. His love will banish your fear."

"I should like to be baptised too," spoke a large woman.

"And who are you?" asked Colmcille.

"I am his wife."

Their children also stated their readiness to believe, prompting others to declare likewise.

"You shall be baptised now, here in the river," Colmcille responded.

At this, one or two shrank back, in fear of the waters that contained the beast.

"If you believe, the beast will neither appear, nor harm you." Drostan also added to what he was asked to translate, "Trust us, because we have to enter the water, too, to baptise you."

Without delay, those who had confessed faith in the One who could keep them from the beast, stepped forward. They hesitated momentarily at the river's edge, until two of the pilgrims waded in before them, signalling them to follow. With a sense of trepidation, overruled by their excitement, they were baptised; about ten in number.

The pilgrims were invited to the local homes. Drostan was aware again of the Presence, a most palpable manifestation, removing anxiety and concern, directing how they should speak or what they should do. That Presence was felt by all, enabling the sick to be healed, and stirred a tremendous desire amongst the locals to be instructed in *the way*. Such was the concern in the souls of the ordinary people that the pilgrims divided their days in half: spending the mornings at Brude's court, seeking to bring clarity and hoped-for acceptance, and their afternoons with the new believers who provided for their needs.

One day, a distressed man came to their camp, one who Drostan recognised as the first to have been baptised, along with his wife and children. "Will you come quickly? My son is burning with such a fever that we fear for his life."

"Why have you only come now?" asked Colmcille.

The man looked uneasy and was reluctant to reply. When the question was repeated, he explained: "The local druid had been sent for by my father. Having learned about the baptism of my whole household, the druid declared the sickness was retribution for turning from the Bulàch. He chided us severely for placing our faith elsewhere, exhorting us to reject Christ. We were forced to sacrifice to the Bulàch, being told that her power was far greater than the God of the Gaels."

Colmcille shook his head and, rising to his feet, said, "Why did you so easily doubt and turn aside? Let us go to your household."

When they arrived, they found the family in grief.

"Why did you come and lure us away from the Bulàch?" accused the mother. "You disarmed us so that you could kill our son?"

"Woman — do not be foolish!" Colmcille admonished. "Repent of your ways and put renewed faith in Christ. He is almighty — only, do not waiver."

"But the Bulàch had the power to take our son," protested the mother with a sarcastic tone. "It is too late to tell us to hold faith!" She let out a wail of grief and turned her back on the holy man.

The woman's father approached stony-faced. "Putting their trust in your Christ has brought this upon them!"

Drostan observed that the abbot seemed preoccupied and gave little attention to the insinuations levelled against them.

"Show me where the dead boy is lying," the man of God said calmly. The father beckoned him to a small store house next to their own. Quite a crowd was gathering on hearing the news.

"Drostan — come with me," Colmcille said with a note of decisiveness, seemingly with some particular purpose in mind.

Pushing through the crowd, the two men entered the hut and closed the door. The boy's body was laid out on a blanket upon the floor. The crowd could be heard noisily outside, contrasting with the deathly stillness within the room.

Colmcille dropped to his knees beside the corpse. Drostan recognised the son as one who had been involved in burying the young man killed by the water beast. The skin on his face seemed to have retracted somewhat and had pulled the young man's eyebrows higher upon his forehead, giving him the appearance of one taken by surprise at the moment of death. The pallor was the unmistakeable hue of death. Drostan also knelt, forming a prayer in his head, then waited for Colmcille to pray out loud.

Drostan, casting a sideways glance, saw the abbot frowning in an intense manner, whilst his lips moved inaudibly. Drostan started to pray and, after a while, looked aside once more to understand what might be required in this difficult situation. He had read of people being brought back to life in the scriptures, and had heard rare accounts, in their own times, but these were exceptional occasions. Colmcille was still praying, but now had prostrated himself in front of the corpse. Drostan continued to pray, believing in the impossible, but understanding that it depended upon the High King's will. He spent a considerable time interceding for the dead young man, stirring only when the holy man raised himself upright, whilst still resting on his knees. Colmcille's face, which previously had been slightly contorted in the earnestness of prayer, now appeared relaxed – but tears were rolling down his cheeks. This struck Drostan as being highly unusual for a man not given to expressing emotion. The two remained kneeling before the corpse, continuing in prayer, expectant in faith. Drostan considered the insinuations from the mother and grandfather and how this death could jeopardise what had been gained.

He became aware of the Presence beside them. At first, he experienced a sense of being thrilled down his spine. As the Presence became more apparent, an awareness of a holy otherworldliness filled the hut with an ineffable sense of glory. Drostan found his own cheeks now flowing with uncontrollable tears, and the words to his prayers dried up. His soul felt elevated beyond their impoverished surroundings, raised to a plane that was filled with exceptional radiance – not that it dazzled the eye, but rather brought an acute perception of being in the Presence of an extraordinary force. Amidst the wonder of that glow, he grew aware of a creative power, a sublime energy that enthralled and appalled, as his own finiteness and lack of virtue became more apparent. The power felt so frightful that it could either bring death, or bestow life – life as it was in the beginning of the world when substance, breath and spirit emerged from the void.

Whilst the Presence still remained evident, the intensity had diminished. Colmcille rose to his feet and stood resolute. Drostan was still kneeling when he watched the holy man take a couple of paces to come alongside the dead boy's head and announce, "In the name of the Lord Jesus, wake up!"

The corpse drew a sudden intake of breath and opened his eyes as though awakening from a deep and troubled sleep. His formerly waxen complexion was infused once more with the rosy hue of life. He sneezed a couple of times and then looked up at them, perplexed. Leaning forward, Colmcille took hold of the boy's hands and helped him to his feet. Drostan moved forward and, placing an arm about him, helped lead him outside into the waiting arms of his astonished parents. Amazement turned to perplexity, which, obviously too great for comprehension, gave way to sheer delight. The dismay of incredulous laughter from the parents was matched by exclamations of wonder and great joy from the crowd. The holy man exhorted them to turn their wonderment into praise to the Giver of life. So divine an act needed no explanation – words were totally inadequate and would have been profane in the midst of that aura of the Lord of Hosts. Drostan perceived the Presence begin to fade, retiring after meeting the pent-up need of his people. Some of the crowd began to celebrate, but the jubilation felt trite. One man stared at him with wonder and admiration – as though he had been the worker of the miracle. Drostan bowed his head and waved his hand to convey he was no one special. Drostan walked briskly away to ponder alone the marvel of what he had witnessed. A short while later he saw Colmcille do likewise. They caught one another's eye, but neither had anything to say, knowing that what had passed was too great for mere words.

Chapter Eleven

Estranged

AD 565 Rhynie and Craig Padrig

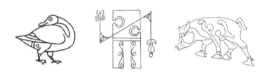

"Mummy, why are you going?" pleaded a three-year-old girl, clinging to her mother's skirts.

"Rowena, we must. But we will be back in a few days," replied Alpia.

"I want to come too," she said, pouting petulantly. "I do not want to stay here!"

"We will have a special time," interjected Drusticc. "You can help grandma about the house, and I will tell you stories. We can even have an adventure or two of our own in the woods."

Alpia watched her daughter seeming to consider this suggestion, for she looked vacantly to the woods, before renewing her pleas to accompany her. Alpia embraced her with a brave smile, and turned to join Oengus who was holding the reins of her horse. Rowena cried, unconsoled by her grandmother's efforts to comfort her. Breaking loose from her arms, she ran from the adults, screaming.

Alpia rode alongside Oengus, surrounded by ten bodyguards, trotting down the hill to pick up the trail northwards through the last of the hill country. She felt overwhelmed, triggered by Rowena's outburst, but mostly provoked by other matters. Struggling with her mounting indignation, she eventually spoke. "It is difficult to say goodbye! Thankfully, Rowena is a girl and can remain with us." She could detect the bitter note in her voice with its intended hint of insinuation.

"It is not my will that our sons are taken from us!" retorted Oengus, defensively.

"This came about because you are overambitious – started by your withholding part of the tribute!"

"Not that again! That was years ago!" As she glanced at him, he rolled his eyes. "We have been over this argument time and again." He shifted uneasily in his saddle.

"It took a fool to think Brude would not deal with you severely for that miscalculated shortfall, forever bringing your loyalty under question."

"And as for the rest of the events, I suppose you would have me held responsible too?"

She did not answer. She knew Brude was overbearing, not one for forgiving a wrong. She was in no mood, though, to exonerate her husband whose initial miscalculation had catapulted them into all the ensuing events.

"You can ride back to Rhynie now if that is going to be your attitude," he said hotly.

"No," she responded, passionately. "You will not deprive me of seeing my Drustan." Had she ever truly deferred to her husband? Did she not always speak out for truth? She recalled Aunt Conchen's challenge to be a force for reason and moderation as the wife of the warlord.

"He is my son as well."

She ignored the comment, choosing to home in on what was, to her, the crux of the matter. "You are responsible for bringing about our undoing! Not content with just getting on with life, you had those grandiose dreams of *the rise of the boar*. Creating a great force of warriors was bound to incite the mistrust of the Fortriu! You gambled on Brude being defeated by Dal Riata, to no longer defer to Brude and to cease those tribute payments. What were you going to do next? Cross the River Spey and seize their territory? Occupy Y Broch and have yourself crowned as overking of the Picts? Exalt your position over Cynbel so that he would be the one to pay? You would have done what Brude did to us: defeat, destroy and humiliate."

"Be quiet, woman!" shouted Oengus. Those riding with them looked round.

She kicked the sides of her mount, causing it to lurch forward. "I do not know why I married you!" she said over her shoulder.

He came up rapidly alongside, and she noticed how taut his body rose from the saddle.

"You are too puffed up, lacking intelligence to play your true position wisely," she continued with mounting vehemence.

"Oh, so you are my counsellor now, are you?" Oengus spat.

"When did you ever listen to anyone?" She had observed how stubborn he had become since he had been diminished by Brude. Obstinacy had been part of his nature before, but the wasting of Rhynie, the decapitation of his trusted right-hand man, the humiliating defeat at the hillfort, the considerable loss of life and the confiscation of half of his warriors had all taken a toll. The seizing of Caltram had been the final blow, one that she felt keenly too, even though the boy was not her own flesh and blood. Then Oengus had lost his two druid confidants. Her husband had been emasculated, but rather than accepting his losses, he compensated by becoming overbearing, still ambitious and ultimately deluded.

"That is ridiculous. Have I not listened to Maelchon and Gest? Did I not defer to Drust at times over military operations?"

"You live in a world of men bent on doing harm to others! You confer only to plot, and outdo a rival."

"That is not true, and you know it!" he retorted.

She saw how his face had reddened, glad that she had riled him. But then he went quiet, contrary to her expectation. Turning aside, he spat again on the ground, and, running his fingers through his long hair, he swept it back over his shoulders. When he spoke again, his former colic had dissipated in what she took as his effort to be reasonable. "I have listened to Aunt Conchen – she is wise."

"Only when it pleases you. Did you ask her opinion about delaying the tribute payment? You only confer with Aunt Conchen about domestic matters."

"Should a ruler be instructed by his aunt?"

She noted the old anger was back in his voice once more. How short his patience had become. "Yes," she retorted, "and by other counsellors too. You have isolated yourself; your close allies have been killed, or have abandoned you, and you have no one to consult. You are overbearing!" Her indignation was boiling over and she raised her voice even more. "These things do not just affect you – the whole community writhes in agony as a result."

"You are being ridiculous, woman! I am the warlord – it is mine to make decisions."

She decided to sidestep the main argument of her grievance to bring up something new. "And do not think that I do not know about your pleasure trips to the deer priestesses of the Bulàch!"

"Maevis has particular powers that serve our needs."

Flaring her nostrils, she was in no mood for reconciliation for she did not fear him. One for keeping her eyes open, she was able to discern what he was about, however hard he tried to conceal things. It was a relief to bring these pent-up resentments into the open. She thought of her dear Drustan, carried in her belly through the turmoil of those precarious few days upon the Pap of the Bulàch, surviving the siege, to then only be taken so cruelly from her arms by Brude's henchmen two years later, just in the same outrageous manner Fortriu's henchmen had cleared the costly platters into a sack at the end of a meal. Again, she held Oengus ultimately responsible. The image of Drustan being prised from her grip was something that haunted her daily; an image that distressed whenever she closed her eyes to rest.

With such reflections too painful to dwell upon, her mind went back to their early days, wondering why she had taken up with Oengus. She should have maintained her aversion that clearly appraised the kind of man he was before his reconciliation with Eithni. It had been clear then that he was headstrong and a hothead, driven by lusts for power and women. Was his lack of loyalty not evident when he turned upon his cousin?

Taran was infinitely the better man. She recalled their brief time of friendship, rueful of her own reserve when he had been so ardent. Perhaps things could have been different. But that was mere wishful thinking. Fate had taken Taran from Rhynie. But then, those who stood opposed to Taran – Talorgen, Maelchon and Oengus – none of them had power to prevent him from escaping! She had been powerless to do anything to spare her noble cousin.

"I feel deceived," she finally spoke up.

"How?" Oengus replied with hostility.

"You were not so foolish when I married you. You were different back then, putting your children first . . ."

"I still put them first!"

"You had been softened by Eithni's death . . ."

"More rounded, and less arrogant," he aped her voice.

They rode in silence for a short while before she pulled her horse to a stop. Turning in the saddle, she announced, "I do not want any more children! It would be too painful to bear if another son is taken from me."

"That is for the gods to decide whether we will have boys or girls."

"We have a choice too," she said, calculatingly.

"What do you mean?" Oengus sounded roused.

"That we cease to have relations!"

"That is absurd!" He reached over and pulled on the reins of Alpia's horse. Both came to a halt. He leaned towards her with his lips drawn back, rasping through his clenched teeth, "Do you not know how humiliated I already feel?"

She chose not to reply. Flicking the reins free from her husband's relaxed grasp, her horse bounded forward. This time, he did not pursue. She had nothing further to say, and it seemed that he was of the same opinion. They had no further exchange all the long road to Craig Padrig.

Arriving at the Fortriu court, Oengus was escorted to King Brude, who, not rising, looked at him stoically. Oengus knelt before him and kissed his hand. He offered the costly gifts of tribute and was made to feel nothing when Brude did not reach out to receive them. Confused, he looked about, wondering where to place the items, and, seeing the banquet table close by, placed them upon it.

An official indicated where he should sit – a place at the far end of the dais. Alpia, who had not accompanied him to greet the king, sat at the opposite end with her arm about Drustan. How content she looks, he observed, lost in her own world of her children. He looked about at the others seated around Brude and recognised Bargoit, his chief druid, and some of the officials. As for the others occupying the large space between himself and the king, there were men he did not recognise; minor officials, he thought, of little consequence. He felt the indignation of being placed below them, overwhelmed by his own impotence to suffer the king's contempt.

Choosing to ignore those he considered insignificant, he looked about the hall and his eyes fixed on the large shields, painted with the boar's head. His own emblemed shields adorning his enemy's hall as the spoils of war was sickening to look upon. His failed aspirations taunted him, reproaching him for daring to withstand his nemesis upon the Pap of the Bulàch. What was he now? All those ambitions had come to naught, and he was reduced to an object of scorn, made plain by his wife. Even a veiled allusion about his deferring to Brude had been sung by his own bard.

Matters had not gone well, he reflected. His agreement with Cynbel only lasted whilst the aged warchief remained alive. Had he not, though, so nearly succeeded in shaking off Brude's oppression? Cynbel had honoured their alliance, for the Circinnians had despatched the agreed number of warriors to aid him in the siege. But they had arrived a day too late. He often wondered what the outcome might have been had Brude not pressed his advantage home so soon and had delayed by a day. Drust's contingent, swelled by the Circinnian warriors, could have swung the balance of power to produce a different outcome. He believed that he had come close to overthrowing this tyrant's hegemony, coming a hair's breadth from at least gaining a stalemate in the clash of rivals. These necessary visits to Brude's court were humiliating affairs.

Derile had returned embittered to Rhynie, childless, dashing his hope that the royal lineage of the Ce that his sister represented, might possibly have intermingled with the Circinn. If a son had been born, then who knows – that boy might have been considered in the Circinnian succession! The new Circinnian warlord, wanting to prove himself and take advantage of the Ce's weakness, had resumed hostilities along the Dee boundary. Oengus had managed to contain the skirmishes with a guard patrolling the border lands, successfully intercepting some of the raiding parties. Oh, how senseless it had all become, he thought. This was a return to the futility that had characterised my great-uncle's rule.

Brude was currently holding court, listening to a dispute between two landowners. The king had been swift in coming to a judgement, disregarding the plaintiff's pleas. Was that not typical of his nemesis! Refreshments were brought. A party of foreigners then appeared, already known by the court. Their leader, a Gael, who did not speak their language, was reliant on a young man of similar age to himself. They had the appearance of druids, but when they spoke, they kept on referring to 'the High King' – and he recollected those two tedious soldiers of Christ, sent to Rhynie, who had vexed his ear.

". . . The young man was resurrected from the dead," explained their young spokesman, "not by any sort of druidry on our part, for we do not practise those dark arts, but according to the compassion and power of the High King."

"And can you confirm this?" Brude asked, turning to Bargoit, his own druid.

"It would appear to be so," Bargoit conceded with evident reluctance. "But perhaps the young boy was not dead!"

"Your own druids were present and had tried to heal the boy whilst he was still alive," the young spokesperson retorted, making his own defence without conferring with his leader. "It was they who pronounced him dead! We can also attest that the body had grown cold. Ask the family concerned, or anyone in the community – they will verify this."

Glancing over towards Brude, he noted how the king looked transfixed with a strange kind of wonder. The leader of the Gaels spoke to his interpreter, prompting him to recount a similar event that had occurred to one called Lazarus.

This curious report, he regarded with his usual scepticism. He recalled such claims made by Cynbel, a good while back, and he remained most dubious. The supernatural, unless it was serving some useful purpose to serve his own ends, he regarded as suspect. What was of most interest, to the extent that it was a major distraction to the matter being discussed, was the interpreter's identity. His voice and manner were most familiar.

". . . even Christ raised himself from the dead and appeared to many!" continued the interpreter.

It cannot be? Oengus said to himself. I am sure the voice is that of Taran! He even speaks with the accent of the Ce. He studied the interpreter's face in closer detail but could not be certain. A full growth of beard covered his lower face, and his forelocks had been shaved away to expose a high forehead, which would substantially change anyone's appearance. The wavy hair, he remembered, that fell across his cousin's brow, was a missing, distinguishing mark, which caused him to doubt. A couple of times he caught the man's eye. Did the interpreter not look slightly uneasy, keen to avoid eye contact?

During these observations, Caltram had come round the back of the dais.

"Father," the young boy said without warmth, standing at his side. He considered his son's appearance to be motivated more by duty than affection.

"Let me take a look at you," he said in a discreet undertone, holding Caltram at arm's length. "What are you – you must be eight years old now?"

"Nine!" corrected the boy, slightly irritated. They were silent for a moment. Caltram spoke again. "I can swim and know how to sail a curragh."

"And what about combat with sword . . . and how is your skill with arrows?"

"I won the archery competition from among all the lads of my age!" he beamed.

"You are my son!" he affirmed, proudly. "I was second to none with my accuracy in firing arrows."

"They say that I will make a fine warrior of the Fortriu."

"You mean the Ce," corrected Oengus.

Noting a sense of confusion, his son was unable to reply. The remark was a reminder of his own impotency. It rankled him beyond measure that he could not anticipate his own flesh and blood returning to Rhynie like he had done ten years earlier when completing his military training.

"Remember you are of the Ce, the son of the warlord. Do not ever forget that!"

The boy looked at him with a helpless expression, seemingly not knowing what answer to give. Caltram nestled into his side. Perhaps, he thought, my son does not wish to consider where his identity or loyalty lies.

Oengus reverted his attention to the interpreter, intrigued more than ever, concluding that it was Taran. What had become of him? How had he become a pilgrim? And why did these soldiers of Christ attract Brude's keen attention?

He noted how competently Taran spoke the language of the Gaels and how statesmanlike was his conduct. He felt a deepening unease, especially as this party enjoyed the overlord's favour in sharp contrast to his own diminished and sullied status. Had his cousin really embraced this foreign religion? Or was it just a cover, hiding some sinister purpose to claim the lordship over the Ce?

The felt threat unleashed all his former insecurities. If only one arrow fired from Wroid's crannog had found its mark, he would not have to be considering what was to be done now. What cruel turn of fate should have them both meet in a distant court at the same hour where he was held in such contempt?

Finally, lunch time came, giving him the opportunity to find Alpia.

"Who did the interpreter remind you of?" he asked as soon as he had her attention.

"Taran," she replied, rather matter-of-factly and without emotion.

"Yes, I thought so too. I needed, though, to hear it from someone else." He ran his fingers through his red hair, feeling flustered.

"You are not going to do anything stupid, are you?" warned Alpia.

Was she protecting Taran? he thought. Could he not even control his own wife? The old jealousy flared up within him. "What is that to you? Or should I be concerned that you once had a thing for Taran?"

Alpia turned abruptly away, leading Drustan to a place at the table that had room enough just for the two of them.

Chapter Twelve

Frustrated

AD 565 Craig Padrig

Drostan had recognised Oengus seated at the far end of the dais, noting that his cousin was made to know his place. He had also observed that the exchange between Oengus and his son had not been entirely easy, and how Alpia had sat at the side far from Oengus. She was with the young boy who had seemed familiar on previous visits, and the reason for that familiarity became obvious, for he looked like his mother.

Alpia had not been instantly recognisable. She was notably heavier than before, her thickset face burying her one-time engaging attitude. He noted how tired, drab and careworn she looked, lacking that enigmatic sparkle he had once admired in her eyes. This was surely the penalty of marrying Oengus. He felt sorry for her and wondered again why she had agreed to become Oengus's wife. He would not put it past his cousin to have used some foul play in gaining a woman. Or was she so fickle that she had settled for a man like his cousin, forgetting the treachery he had shown towards him?

How strange they should meet like this, ten years on from their last encounter in the crannog. The joy of life had been squeezed from her and she appeared full of anxieties that he could only imagine – a mere shadow of what she had been at Beltane when she had so captivated him. What if his wishes of their remaining together – after leaping through the Beltane fires – had come true, then how might things have transpired? He felt certain that she would not look, or behave, like she did now. What if Alpia was not a wife, or a mother – how would that impact him now? He dismissed his idle speculation, recognising that their lives had diverged dramatically from those heady days of youth.

The one-time vivid recollections he had of Alpia had been eroded by ten years of absence. Her kind words, and her image, had once sustained him through his lonely exile at Coblaith's homestead. Her absence had made his loneliness keener; her unattainability had sharpened his anger against his cousin. What he had been forced to forfeit had wounded him deeply, and though this old injury had healed, a scar yet remained, still sensitive to the touch.

He snapped out of these unhappy and futile thoughts, to focus once more on Oengus. If this was how it was to be warlord over the Ce, he did not envy him. He considered why Oengus's two young sons were there at Craig Padrig and not at Rhynie. Were they hostages, or being fostered? He had not touched upon this in his conversation with Maelchon back at Munnir Esprid. But the younger of the two was too young to be of fostering age.

What might he have achieved if he had been made warlord? What a journey I have made, to now reckon myself as the one who is blessed, he thought. Having forsaken everything, I have gained the pearl of great price.

After lunch, Brude requested the pilgrims to speak more about the resurrection. Drostan felt most conspicuous, unable to retire into the shadows as he would have liked. As a servant in the proceedings, he performed his part with humility, keen not to draw attention to himself, but naturally all eyes were fixed on the one who spoke Pictish, even if he were only the interpreter.

Would Oengus recognise him after all these years, especially with his appearance so altered? Surely he would be put off the scent by his knowing the tongue of the Gaels, of being numbered among the pilgrims. But the familiarity of his voice, his telling accent, would surely give him away? His discomfort grew and, at times, he sensed Oengus's eyes boring through to his core, even when he was not translating. He felt disarmed, no longer feeling the boldness he had known during his previous dialogues with Brude.

"You seemed uneasy at the court?" quizzed Colmcille, as they walked back to camp.

"The warlord of the Ce, my cousin – the usurper – was there," Drostan responded. He explained the events that had once made him the hunted fugitive.

"The one who is in you is greater than the one who is in the world," responded Colmcille. They reached camp and proceeded with their usual devotions of the hour, followed by the preparation of their simple supper. As Drostan lay to rest that night, he felt uneasy, and sleep was sporadic.

They appeared at Brude's court the following morning, as was their daily custom. Drostan translated a parable Colmcille was explaining, which was then followed by answering questions. Brude was engaged, enjoying the novelty of hearing unheard stories and histories from faraway places. However, it was not evident that the king yet believed, although all the signs he had seen, and the intriguing reports he had heard, had persuaded him to take particular note.

Colmcille closed proceedings with the chanting of a psalm. Drostan noted that the abbot's voice no longer disturbed, but rather fascinated, the king.

Before they left the hall, Brude beckoned Drostan over. "Is it not a strange coincidence that you two cousins should meet again!" he said smiling, now gesturing Oengus to join them.

What mischief is it that this overlord was brewing? thought Drostan. Perhaps Oengus had already guessed his identity and had spoken with the king? He made a quick prayer of appeal. Looking at King Brude, he could not detect anything malevolent, and then brought himself to look at his cousin. Oengus appeared uncertain and wary. Drostan then became aware of Colmcille coming to his side. So, my master has not left, he thought – and that knowledge brought some comfort.

"Taran – I never expected to see you again!" Oengus exclaimed, with dismay in his voice.

"Presumed dead?" Drostan responded coldly.

"No. I knew you had not died." Oengus ruffled the hair on the back of his head. "The high priestess of the Bulàch had seen you on her spirit flight, living with an elderly couple in the forest." Oengus fidgeted uncomfortably. "You look very different now!"

"You look much the same," and added, after a slight pause, "although much deflated."

"You have become a soldier of Christ and have learned the tongue of the Gaels. That is quite a change from what you had trained to be!" An uncertain smile formed around the corners of Oengus's mouth, which he held, awaiting a reply.

Drostan was in no hurry to speak.

"You must have quite a story to tell," Oengus goaded.

His cousin's smile particularly vexed him, as though they had parted on amicable terms. He thought of all the things he could remonstrate about.

"What is being said?" Colmcille asked. Drostan translated, glad of a diversion and an ally.

"On the contrary – a warrior's training is most apt in preparing a soldier of Christ," remarked Colmcille. "Courage is required for the two disciplines!"

Drostan translated the abbot's comment, before elaborating passionately, "Aye! Far greater courage is required of a man of peace. As soldiers of Christ, we can only trust in our heavenly King's protection when alliances are broken and family ties are dishonoured. The man of peace does not resort to firing arrows." He looked stonily at Oengus, detecting a slight twitch in his cousin's cheek.

All fell silent, and he noticed how Colmcille exchanged a glance with Brude. The king seemed to be on the point of saying something when Oengus started to quake. Had something profoundly moved his treacherous cousin? The bold warrior was now shaking uncontrollably.

"I have done you wrong!" Oengus confessed.

"And I have not hit back."

Oengus averted his gaze and wiped his eyes.

Drostan stood square on, fixing his cousin with a haughty stare. At that moment, Colmcille addressed him, not as an aside, but for all to hear. "Drostan – we do not need to fight the High King's battle. The day is won and the one defeated stands before you." Although the holy man's words were unintelligible to the others, his statesmanlike demeanour was noted by all.

It could not escape Drostan's attention how Brude looked contemptuously at Oengus. "By the Bulàch, you are a pitiful vassal!" the king uttered.

"Lord, be not hasty!" interjected Colmcille. Turning to Drostan, the holy man said, "Translate this proverb, *true greatness knows gentleness.* This shaking warlord demonstrates, unwittingly, the power of the High King, who *has scattered those who are proud . . . He has brought down rulers from their thrones but has lifted up the humble.* The example of this dishonoured lord serves our purpose more than the full sum of my words ever could."

Brude, though, maintained his demeaning gaze upon Oengus. "You are not worthy of your cousin. Talorgen was a fool to have chosen you over Taran. I could depose you and instate Taran in your place."

Oengus appeared to shrink. "It is the Z-rod that Taran bears!" he mumbled.

Perhaps only Drostan could comprehend his cousin's thoughts that had brought about this reference. He surprised himself by feeling an inkling of sympathy for Oengus who struck such a pathetic figure, upon the brink of being ruined. He decided to deflate the mounting pressure. "Years ago, I would have welcomed the king's suggestion, but not now. I bear the Z-rod, not as one chosen to be warlord, nor as a curse set upon me by the Bulàch, but as a sign from heaven to demonstrate its authority. My Z-rod indicates blessing, not ruin."

"Drostan – you need to forgive," appealed Colmcille.

He knew it too, but on this occasion, it was not something he could instantly pronounce. He felt righteously indignant concerning all the wrongs done. When he considered all his just complaints, and the severity of the experiences forced upon him, he envied the wholesome lives of others, and viewed the world through embittered eyes.

"Without reconciliation, all hell can break loose," continued Colmcille, addressing not only the two cousins, but Brude as well. Drostan dutifully felt bound to translate Colmcille's words for Brude's benefit. "Do I not know it. Due to my stubborn heart, I caused three thousand men to fall in battle. It was not a battle over territory, nor a defence of position, but for something so petty as a copied psalter. Pride had got the better of me, and pride gives birth to folly, which can lead to destruction. I have renounced violence. Instead, I make war against my own evil inclinations so as to put these to death, rather than my fellow man."

Colmcille had been clenching his fist so tightly that Drostan noticed that his knuckles were showing white. He then turned his hands, palm upward. "Drostan – your cousin confesses he has wronged you . . ."

"I know," he replied simply, knowing what had to be done. Again, he pitied Oengus standing there with his arms hanging limp, crestfallen – a powerless subordinate to the mighty Brude. He took a step towards him. "You meant me wrong, but God used it for the good. Come, cousin, let us embrace, for once we were as close as any brothers."

Oengus took an eager step forward and hugged him. Drostan felt a veritable burden fall from his shoulders. Warmth and light returned to his world, and he could look his cousin in the face without any smouldering hatred.

"Tell me," Drostan enquired, "how many children do you have?"

"I have three. The eldest is Caltram – Eithni is his mother who died bringing him into the world – and Alpia is the mother of the other two."

"I can see his mother's likeness," Drostan remarked, struggling again to consider how Alpia had become his cousin's wife. He moved hastily on, and asked, "Why are your sons here and not with you?"

"Have you forgotten? That is our way – we send our sons off to foster parents to be trained to become warriors."

"No, I have not forgotten. But why here, and not among our own people?"

Oengus hesitated momentarily. "That is part of forging a strong alliance between two tribes, is it not?"

"But not at so young an age . . . the younger cannot be more than four!"

"He is five, but he is timid and withdrawn, so looks younger."

In the uneasy quiet, Colmcille addressed the chief druid. "Broichan, I believe you have a slave girl in your household who comes from Erin. I request you to release her."

"What is she to you?" The druid squared his burly shoulders, looking back implacably. "I paid a good price for her, and she is useful."

"That may be so, but I am asking you to release her that she may return to where she hails from – to her family who needs her more."

"This is not a matter for you to meddle in," Broichan replied in a surly tone. "She is our servant. It took us a good while to make her understand our language, and it is only now that she is beginning to be useful."

Drostan noted how Colmcille fixed the druid with a steady gaze. Without any temper in his voice, Colmcille said to Drostan, "Make sure you translate all of this, word for word." His leader then addressed the druid boldly. "Know this, Broichan, if you will not free this captive before I leave Craig Padrig this day, the pangs of death shall come upon you."

On hearing the translation, the druid sent a defiant look back.

Colmcille turned nonchalantly and, bidding the king farewell, they left the fortress.

Colmcille picked up a white pebble from the river. "Mark this white stone," he said curiously, "through this, the Lord will bring about healing. Whilst I speak now, Broichan has suffered a heavy blow, struck down by an angel. A glass he was drinking from has shattered into fragments. He is now struggling to get his breath and the shadow of death is over him."

Colmcille folded his hand over the small white stone as though it were something precious, then led in singing a psalm. After their worship, Colmcille said, "We should wait here a while. Brude has sent two messengers urgently calling for our help, for Broichan is dying. This seizure has put such a fear upon him that now he is willing to release the slave girl."

Drostan noticed that the abbot's lips were moving in an inaudible prayer. A short while later, he heard horse hooves pounding the turf. On looking towards Craig Padraig he saw two riders advancing at full gallop. Pulling up their steaming steeds before them, the riders briefly related all the details exactly as Colmcille had foreseen, including the glass shattering in Broichan's hand whilst he was drinking from it.

"The king urges you to hurry back."

Colmcille handed the white pebble to him. "If Broichan will promise to release the girl, then and only then, dip this stone in some water and let him drink. He will be made well. But if he refuses, he will die there. Drostan – you accompany them."

Drostan rode behind one of the riders and arrived at the hillfort. Once he explained all that Colmcille had foreseen and had spoken about, the whole court – including Broichan and the king – were much afraid and in awe.

"Well, Broichan – are you prepared to release the slave girl?" asked Brude.

Broichan nodded, for he seemed incapable of speaking.

"Send for the slave girl at once," ordered the king.

"Bring a chalice of water," Drostan requested. One was presented quickly and, taking it, Drostan dropped in the white pebble. Strangely, the stone did not sink, but floated on the surface. This seemed very odd, for when he held it, the pebble had the normal weight of a stone of that size. He reasoned that oddness was the norm concerning many things that involved Colmcille. As Broichan eagerly drank the water, all eyes were upon him as some water ran down his beard, wetting a patch on his robe. Broichan's face brightened, and to everyone's amazement, he could breathe normally after previously labouring for air.

"The pain has gone!" Broichan testified, patting his side.

Once Drostan had returned to camp, he reported on all that had passed. Despite these interventions, he felt strangely unsettled and decided to confide to Colmcille. "Ever since meeting with Oengus, my spirit has been uneasy."

"Come, you have made your peace. Your cousin looked remorseful for what he had done."

"Even so, my spirit is greatly disturbed. I fear my cousin's treachery for he has lost much – even what dignity he may have once possessed has been stripped away. Did you not hear the king tell him that there was nothing to stop him from instating me in his place as warlord over the Ce? There is nothing that an injured and cornered boar would not stoop to do!"

He felt Colmcille perusing him thoughtfully, almost with an empathy, before he spoke. "You and Munait should walk the caim – the protective boundary of prayer –

about our camp. As you pace the circle, offer up prayer to remind ourselves of the shielding wall of the Lord about his servants."

Colmcille arose to attend to other matters, leaving the two to proceed sun-wise about the camp on foot. Munait began the prayer in a steady voice with Drostan discerning a certain gravity about his actions.

"We bind unto ourselves this night, the virtues of the starlit heaven,
light of sun, radiance of moon, splendour of fire, speed of lightning,
swiftness of wind, depth of sea, stability of earth, firmness of rock.
We bind unto ourselves this night,
the power of God to hold and lead,
his eye to watch, his might to stay,
his ear to hearken to our need.
The wisdom of our God to teach,
his hand to guide, his shield to ward.
the word of God to give me speech,
his heavenly host to be my guard . . .
against all Satan's spells and wiles,
against incantations of false prophets,
against the black laws of pagandom,
against false laws of heretics, against craft of idolatry,
against spells of women and smiths and wizards."

Taking a single step for each phrase uttered, Munait stopped part way round their camp. He looked to Drostan, who took up the remainder of the caim.

"Against the death wound and the burning,
the choking wave and poisoned shaft,
protect us, Christ, till thy returning.
Christ with us, Christ before us, Christ behind us,
Christ in us, Christ beneath us, Christ above us.
Christ in the heart of every man who thinks of us,
Christ in the mouth of everyone who speaks of us,
Christ in the eye of everyone that see us,
Christ in every ear that hears us.
We arise today through a mighty strength, the
invocation of the trinity,
through belief in the threeness,
through confession of the oneness
of the Creator of creation."

Arriving back at their starting point, Drostan felt a sense of peace. Munait squeezed his shoulder firmly as he parted. Drostan felt exhausted and went to bed. Although peace had been appropriated in his heart, it did not negate the sense of threat. Very soon, though, he fell into a deep slumber.

He awoke from disturbed dreams and remained sleepless awhile, prayer holding him on the twilight borderlands between slumber and wakefulness. Voices shouting, the thud of horses on turf and the jingle of swords clattering upon armour, prompted him to repeat snatches of the caim prayer. Now fully conscious, he felt his body drenched with sweat and questioned whether the sounds were part of reality. Emerging from his tent, he found other brothers outside.

"What is happening?"

His question was answered by one pointing downstream, where he could just make out a group of riders in the distance, not coming towards their camp, but fleeing.

"I saw riders," remarked Colmcille, "who on reaching the vallum of the prayers that you and Munait had paced out earlier, were routed in what can only be described as a panic."

Later the following day, Alpia went in search of the pilgrims' camp, and, finding nobody there, met with a boy fishing by the river.

"Do you know where the pilgrims are?"

"Aye — they are over at the village. They spend their afternoons there with my people — that is where I am from."

With it not being far, she wandered over with Drustan holding her hand, enjoying his chatter. Deep down she felt distracted about being drawn to meet Taran, nervous about how their exchange would go. As she neared the village she heard singing and, passing the outlying huts, she came upon a large group in the centre of this farming community. Young parents were lifting their voices with joyous abandon and older people sat and looked on with various degrees of engagement. The youngest children of Drustan's age were up to their usual antics, running around noisily in playful frolic. She observed, though, how the older children were singing with particular spirit; their expressions had a sincerity which surprised her. The singing went on for quite some time, led by their grey-eyed leader with a booming bass voice that sent a thrill down her spine.

A story followed, told by the Gael, looking upright and noble. She thought he looked rather out of place in this simple domestic setting, having first observed him in Brude's hall yesterday, looking every bit the statesman. How strange that one so evidently noble born should spend his time singing and telling stories with the common people every afternoon!

"... the woman was anxious, for she had lost a precious coin and was taking her hut apart, frantically trying to find the missing piece that made up her wedding jewellery. 'Oh, where could it be?' she asked. 'Has anyone seen my missing coin?'"

She enjoyed listening to Taran translating, not just relaying an account in Pictish, but telling the story with notable enthusiasm. He, too, seemed to be carried along in the same abandonment that had struck her about the older children, and the young couples when they were singing. He moved about before his audience as he told the story, stooping at times to gain their attention, amusingly intonating his voice when speaking the part of the woman. How at ease he looked, animated by the tale. And it surprised her that Taran, who was also of noble birth, was every bit as at home with the farmers as was his illustrious leader. The people were hanging on every word, so much so that when the younger children were making too much noise around the periphery, they were scolded by those listening.

"... when she eventually found the coin, she was so happy, eager to tell all her neighbours that the precious item had been found. 'Rejoice with me,' she said, 'for what was lost has now been found, what had been incomplete is now entire as on the day my beloved gave it me!' She cooked lots of food and invited them to eat with her."

She found the simple story intriguing, not only because the story was told with skill by her cousin, but because she had observed how the everyday nature of the tale had touched everyone, so that all could understand how frantic the woman had felt, and how overjoyed she was to have discovered the coin. The tale particularly moved her, for Drustan and Caltram were like two missing coins, without which, her life felt frantic and fallen apart. She relived the joy of being reunited with her beloved boys – a joy that was just as effervescent today as it had been yesterday, a euphoria that made her feel complete.

"*In the same way, I tell you, there is rejoicing in the presence of the angels of God over one sinner who repents,*" Taran pronounced, translating from a scroll that he held in his hand.

How far Taran has come, she thought. With his learning and ability to read and speak other languages, he is a sophisticated foreigner. And yet he remains that same humble man from the hill country of home! She felt proud of him . . . and also sad that their lives had diverged so far; lives that had been sundered apart at the very time their relationship was budding. She felt bitter, especially considering whom she had married.

As the pilgrims led the people in prayer, she withdrew with Drustan, stirred by what she had witnessed. Although she felt proud of her cousin, his life had taken a direction that was hard to comprehend. It was saturated with the talk of this heavenly King that still sounded alien and even a little disturbing. She tried to shake off the pilgrims' talk – for it was the thing that set them apart – and yet she became troubled, for the story shared sounded wholesome and true. She thought about returning to Craig Padrig, but dismissed the inclination, telling herself not to lose this opportunity to speak with Taran. Coming upon their camp beside the river, she sat down upon a boulder beyond the outlying tents and waited.

She did not have too long to wait, for soon she heard their approach, singing one of their strange psalms as they walked. Had she done right in coming, feeling again the many differences that set them apart? A notion to flee gripped her. But it was too late – Taran had seen her and was already approaching.

"I never dreamed that it would be like this when we met again!" she remarked.

"So, you did dream of meeting me again?" he said engagingly.

"Uh?" She felt dismayed. Recovering from his unexpected response, she remarked, "You have not changed totally then! Keen as always to attribute some special favour to my words."

He looked at her with a searching gaze. "I dreamed of meeting you," he returned simply, and let his arms hang limp.

She deliberately changed the subject. "What became of you?"

"That is too long a story to start. My destiny was not to be a warlord, and I am better for it. I mean, look at Oengus!"

She did not respond, for she did not wish to talk about her husband, but rather to refer to what better defined her life. "I am a mother now. This is my firstborn, Drustan. Caltram was not free to join me as he is undergoing his usual training at this hour."

"But Caltram is not your son?" he queried.

"He is like a son to me. It is true that he is Eithni's offspring, but I raised him. All in Rhynie would say that Caltram had life because I kept him alive when he was so frail, and there was little hope of him surviving."

"Drustan?" he pronounced strangely. "How odd!"

"Why?"

"I took on the name of Drostan after my escape – it is the name that I am known by now."

"You are still Cousin Taran to me and those of us from Rhynie." She reflected on his remark, thinking of the coincidence — but the heaviness of heart in not having Drustan and Caltram with her always, suddenly choked her with emotion.

"I have not seen you cry before!" he remarked, meaningfully.

What was he implying? How did his mind work? "You take pleasure in seeing what I am reduced to?"

"No pleasure, I assure you," he returned defensively. "I understand, though. It is clear that Brude holds Drustan and Caltram hostage."

She was silent for a moment, before she challenged, "Can you understand how a mother feels?"

He looked at the ground, not apologetically, she reckoned, but more as if he were dealing with a frustration that he wanted to pass.

"I do not know why I have come here . . ." She looked about with increasing agitation, willing herself to rise and walk away. Taran was changed and remote, seeming to want to punish her for not waiting for his return.

"Perhaps to apologise for your husband's treachery?"

"What do you mean? When he fired arrows at you from the crannog all those years ago?"

"He sent riders here last night to do us some mischief!" His voice sounded cold and hard.

"I had no idea!" she exclaimed, horrified. Checking herself, she cleared her throat. "So, that explains why he and his men were gone when I woke this morning!"

"No, it was in the middle of the night when he came riding furiously upon this camp."

"Maybe so — but he has gone from Craig Padrig." Had Oengus made for home? Where else might he go? Recovering herself, she remarked, "Well, I am not entirely surprised. Oengus has been haunted by you. Meeting you now, at this low ebb in his life . . . well, who knows what he is capable of!"

"Evidently. He broke down in shame and grief before me just yesterday, but obviously it was short-lived. He has meant me much harm, and despite his show of remorse, his old nature remains. He is a conniving opportunist." He paused, and, looking to the loch, he seemed to drink in its calm. He spoke with a measured slowness to give weight to his words. "You know – I have forgiven him."

"That is very magnanimous of you."

"We need to be merciful, just as we have received mercy from the High King. There was a time when I never imagined forgiving Oengus were possible. But, my ordeals have brought about a huge shift in my attitude."

"I understand something of what you are saying. We entertained a couple of pilgrims at Rhynie for two weeks and they spoke about this compassion and forgiveness. But it only seemed to be words with them, taken from some strange foreign teaching that did not quite connect with their practice. They were glad to leave us at the earliest opportunity."

"Alpia!" He spoke her name for the first time, and it had a hint of the way he used to say her name with affection. She recalled how he had waxed lyrical on that Beltane evening so long ago, declaring how fine a sound Alpia was to his ear, and how it became her and other such nonsense. She was warmed by the recollection. "What has become of you? How did you stoop so low as to marry Oengus? I could understand, and forgive you, for marrying any other man, but why him?"

"Oh!" she uttered despairingly. "That is a question I ask myself! It seems that I was truly fated to be his wife, quite contrary to my natural inclinations. If I were to tell you all, there would not be enough daylight remaining to finish telling you half of it!"

"You are distressed!" he uttered, seemingly surprised, and slow, in her opinion, to understand. "How unlike the calm and somewhat aloof Alpia I once knew!" He reached out and touched her shoulder.

"Just as you had not set out to become a saint, it would seem, so the Bulàch had decreed that I would marry the usurper of the only man I looked up to." Feeling tears gathering in her eyes, she closed her lids tightly and felt the saltwater course down her cheeks.

When she opened her eyes again, he was standing there in silence, looking detached. A lengthy moment of great awkwardness passed between them, which he broke with an exclamation, "It is too late!"

"Taran, I never told you this . . ." The words stuck in her throat, which her pride told her were better left unsaid. She struggled to continue, though, feeling the need to be candid. "I loved you. I only truly realised that once you were gone!" She wanted to say more, but those words, which had been a struggle to confess, conveyed everything she had come to say to him.

"You were forever careful about expressing any favour towards me!"

"Your ardour needed no feeding!"

"I remember saying at Beltane that if I were to become warlord, and did not have you by my side, there would be no gain."

"You got neither!"

He looked at the ground without responding. Had events crushed him? she was thinking. Then he suddenly spoke, looking at her with a serene smile, "And yet I have gained everything."

How strange he looked, not just physically with his forelocks shorn so bizarrely away from his head, but it was like he was living in a different world, disconnected from her reality. What had she hoped to achieve by coming to him? Things had been "too late" for far too long. Fate had cut her deeply with its swiping blade, leaving her life in pieces. Fate had slashed at Taran too, that had sundered him from a life in Rhynie and, although she did not doubt that it had been costly, he had somehow managed to overcome fate. She rose to go.

"Where are you going?"

"Back to Craig Padrig."

"It seems that you need to make a choice," he said, meaningfully.

She paused, unsettled by his strange ability to read into the depths of her soul. "I do not want to go back to the humiliation and shame of my position in Rhynie – to a life separated from Drustan and Caltram. I should be here and be a mother to them."

Taran looked at her boy and put his hand affectionately under his chin. "He is young to be separated from his mother!"

"He is only five. He was seized from my arms three years ago. I cannot abide it longer . . . it breaks my heart and takes away the will to live."

"Do not speak like that; it is the language of crisis with which I am so familiar. But you can use that to your advantage."

"How?" she replied, annoyed.

"We need not just endure. In this estrangement, seek the One who would turn your life about."

"You are speaking like a pilgrim with your strange sayings!" She felt the frustration mount.

"You have the choice. You can continue to hit your head against the wall or decide to walk around it and move on. If you want to be a mother to Drustan and Caltram, then act decisively."

They spoke longer and she took note. How different was their meeting from what she had anticipated. She had glimpsed the Taran of old, and just when she felt on familiar ground, Drostan the pilgrim intruded, strangely in control and detached from her world. Truly, their time was too late, not that she had ever intended anything rash. She had wanted to set things straight between them, to declare a love that had been kept hidden through denial all those years; a love she had not professed, but for which she had suffered, believing its silence added to her miseries. Taran had had to endure as a fugitive, alone in the world. She, too, knew loneliness, of being in a situation that felt beyond all hope, the isolation that had swooped down and carried her away from all that she held dear and sacred.

They said goodbye, which for Taran being a pilgrim was constrained, and even seeming understated as if they would meet later that day. She did not bother herself further concerning the lack of depth to their farewell, for their meeting had helped bring about a resolve that had been developing. She walked alongside the willows, billowing in the breeze that lined the banks of the Rihoh river, with her beloved Drustan at her side, holding firmly to her hand. The wind was light, shot with sunshine, and all that it touched, responded with gladness and abandon. How different from the wind that seemed to harrow her in Rhynie with its claw of ice that grazed her skin. In that moment, all was well, and she could perceive new possibilities. Her role back in Rhynie had become as derelict as the hillfort that had been breached by the conqueror and desecrated by fire. The influential role that Aunt Conchen had once envisaged for her as Oengus's wife lay shattered beyond redemption. Returning to Oengus felt pointless – they were at loggerheads, destroying one another. Oengus was a law unto himself and his outrageous attack on a camp of defenceless saints was the final straw. Oengus was so unhinged that she could see no recovery for him. He was beyond hope, making their union redundant.

She would appeal to Brude for permission to remain with her sons. He would probably accept, reckoning that it would humiliate Oengus, depriving him of his wife. If that did not work, then she would make her appeal through Taran, having observed how influential he and his fellow pilgrims had become with the king. She would make ready to leave for Rhynie the next day and bring Rowena with her to Craig Padrig.

When she returned to the citadel, she saw one of the bodyguards who had accompanied her and Oengus from Rhynie. "I had thought that you had all left this morning?"

"Everyone but me. Oengus ordered me to accompany you back."

"Why did the others leave in such a hurry that they did not even have time to bid farewell?"

The guard looked down at his feet, not finding the words to reply.

"You do not need to conceal things. I heard that you attacked the pilgrims' camp in the night!"

"That is so." He shook his head and looked pale.

"What happened? I know that the pilgrims emerged unscathed."

"Truly, powers protect them."

"What do you mean?"

"They had a large warforce surrounding their camp, which we did not see until we were close to their tents. They just appeared from nowhere out of the darkness. Those who were with them far exceeded our number, and we nearly ran into them. The horses first sensed their guard about the pilgrims' camp, for they reared and turned tail whilst we were becoming aware of what we were up against. The horses were terrified! I have never seen them behave like that, for they are trained for battle. I have ridden my mount these past seven years and not once did he behave like that, even when Brude came to sack Rhynie."

Some days later, when Colmcille and his companions were again attending the king's court, Broichan asked when they intended to leave for Iona.

"God willing, in three days' time."

"You will not be able to," replied Broichan, defiantly, "for I have the power to produce an adverse wind and to bring down a thick mist."

"The almighty power of God rules all things," replied the holy man calmly, "and all our comings and goings are directed by his will."

On the appointed day, Colmcille, his companions and some of the new Christians in the community, along with some druids from the king's court, gathered on the pebbly beach at the head of Loch Rihoh. As Broichan had spoken, a thick mist enveloped the water, driven by a steady wind blowing straight up the loch into their faces.

"It is just as Broichan has said," one of the druids uttered in a triumphal manner. "You will not be able to sail today due to the might of our gods."

"Nonsense," said Colmcille, with a dismissive motion of his arm. In the hearing of all assembled, he prayed aloud. "Almighty God, Ruler of the wind – enable us to sail and to make good haste, now that your purposes here are complete."

Turning to the sailors sitting on the shore beside their boat, Colmcille ordered them to make ready.

"Not in this wind – it is blowing straight to shore, and the visibility is too poor to navigate."

"Make ready, for we will surely depart." His tone was so steadfast that the sailors, looking at one another, shrugged their shoulders and prepared the boat to demonstrate the impossibility of sailing head into wind. As soon as they were in the boat and had pushed off, Colmcille ordered the sail to be hoisted into the wind. When this was reluctantly done, the boat moved miraculously forward at a great speed, to the utter dismay of the sailors and all those on the shore. In a very short while, the wind that had been blowing full force up the loch, turned completely about and bore them down the loch in a south-westerly direction, towards their beloved isle, where now they had the king's permission to remain.

Chapter Thirteen

In Question

AD 565 The Western Sea

Once they had reached the sea at Loch Abar on their return to Iona, Drostan sat alone in the boat's prow, turning over his many thoughts. The past weeks had been momentous: the gaining of a king's support from a position of hostility; winning the favour of the common people; and witnessing the impotence of the druid's power in thwarting the High King's purposes. Another attempt on his life had been made by Oengus, followed by the muted encounter with his one-time love, Alpia. Truly, so much had taken place in so brief a time that he felt entangled in a mesh of people and events and needing to make better sense of what had passed.

How strange, he thought, that I seem fated to be offered the things that I once eagerly wanted, but for which I no longer yearn! Carvorst had brokered the peace between us by offering to bring me back to Aleine Brona on my own terms; Brude moots that he could instate me in Oengus's place; and then Alpia declares her love for me! I am enabled to deny the things I once craved, satisfied by something greater, which previously I had not thought possible.

He considered Alpia, and how once he had so wished her to be his woman. That Beltane evening was still vivid in his memory and the love it provoked could be felt afresh. He could still recall some of their dialogue and her pledge of friendship that, at the time, he had taken to mean more. Had her admission of love for him, just days earlier at the camp, been the true revelation of how she had felt all along? He might not have enjoyed the heady joys of reciprocated love with Alpia as he had experienced with Aleine Brona, but he had most certainly been buoyed up by her solidarity while he was portrayed as the traitor in Talorgen's camp.

What was to become of Alpia? he thought. She who once had been in control to the point of appearing aloof, now seemed crushed. He prayed for her deliverance from the unpredictable hand of that serpent, Oengus. His cousin had been sincerely contrite before him, but once his back was turned, the old treachery remained unchanged. He recalled his sense of deepening despair after their unexpected meeting, and the impending doom that he could not shrug off, until he had paced out the caim.

Could it be that my eighth quest has been accomplished? he considered. Fillan's prophetic prayer, had been read so many times that he could repeat it to the word: *hope to prove firm in the face of despair.* The despair had most certainly been great, and for good reason, as events proved. Hope had overcome that all-pervading fear, the knowledge that he was not alone, that things were not what they seemed. How the angelic host had encamped about their camp!

Hope had been exercised and appropriated. Surely that quest has been fulfilled? He grew excited with the sense of completion of another quest, along with the acquisition of the eighth grace of demonstrating and attaining *hope*.

His thoughts returned once more to Oengus. A hand of reconciliation had been offered, but Oengus chose to ignore it. Had his cousin not been offered the opportunity to turn from his scheming treachery to walk in *the way*? There had been that moment of hope, but then the old nature trampled on it as something despised. Where would this lead for his cousin? He found it odd, on the one hand, to wish that Oengus would renounce his old ways, and then on the other, to vehemently desire his abrupt end, with all his old animosity. That troubled him. He struggled long in the prow, as it bumped along the crested waves, wrestling with his natural emotions, turning over the many wrongs Oengus had committed, until his head became hot, seething with indignation.

"I cannot hate another and say that I love my Lord," he admitted to himself.

In the simplicity of his statement, he prayed in his soul, "Father, take away my hatred, so that in forgiving I might wish my cousin well." He recalled how Fillan had dealt with his arch nemesis, the Lord Domech, and was strengthened by that example to harbour no ill, amazed by the outcome that had seemed so unlikely.

The one overriding impression that repeatedly occupied his thoughts was the sea of animated faces as they raised their voices in worshipping the High King — their rapt expressions when carefully listening to the explanation of the scriptures. Truly, that had been exceptional, for it was not just one or two people, but a whole community that had embraced faith. Fillan had foreseen it when he said that his time in Erin marked out the interval between two phases. Before going to the land of the Gaels, he had wandered among small communities, touching the lives of a few individuals; whereas after he had completed his studies, he would be among throngs of people, engaging with their lives. He thought of walking with the refugees, fleeing the Saxon hordes; the discussion with the eminent druids and the mass of worshippers gathered on the slopes of Munnir Esprid. And now, beneath Craig Padrig, so many people had turned from their fears, and had formed a rudimentary muintir close to the River Rihoh. Munait had been appointed its abbot.

Could it be, he wondered, that even the ninth quest had been fulfilled – *faithfulness to lead to the very ends of the earth*? Craig Padrig was far to the north where he was to bear fire. I have been so swept up in the tide of events that I have not properly had time to consider the enormity of all that has taken place. His heart pounded that he could hear its rhythm beat in his head as though trying to bring in line his racing thoughts. Well, it was not our doing, was it? The High King had shown specific signs to persuade the hardened warrior king to take note. He thought of the subjugation of the water beast. How like the events he had read of Christ subduing the demons, freeing men from their oppression! then of how Brude's stronghold was barred, and how those bolts had been retracted. The resurrection of the young man, though, was what truly turned the people, and caused the druids to oppose them. What days followed . . . and again, the multitude of exuberant faces filled his mind with inexpressible joy. It has been the High King's faithfulness that has brought these things to pass, a faithfulness that becomes more and more evident that it starts to shape my life – that I can press on in faithfulness because he is faithful.

Time seemed to stand still as we sang and enjoyed the favour of the people. How different from the perfunctory prayers that sometimes occurred back at Clonard. What a sense of oneness we all felt that negated our identities as Gael or Pict; a unity that overcame the divisions between the Ce and the Fortriu, when only two years previously there had been slaughter.

Lost in the wonder of these recollections, Colmcille joined him. Judging from the gravity of his expression, the holy man had something of substance to say.

"Your destiny is not to remain on Iona," he announced abruptly, and without any preamble. "The Spirit has revealed that the task of bearing fire to the north has not been fulfilled at Brude's court."

"How strange you should say that! I was thinking the very opposite!" and he elaborated on all his recent thoughts.

"Indeed, the gates truly have been flung wide for the Fortriu to acknowledge the High King."

"What happened was surely a fulfilment in the far north of which the prophecy speaks?"

"Oh, I do not think so. You have a eighth quest before that final one."

"The eighth quest is characterised by despair. Several times we felt that, like when the son of the newly baptised died and the whole community wavered under the influence of their druid. Or, personally, after Brude had revealed my identity to Oengus, there followed such a mounting despair that led Munait and me to pace the caim about our tents!"

He was disappointed to note that the holy man's expression remained unchanged. "The prophecy indicates that the learned ones will be anticipating the coming of one who bears news of a Saviour. Broichan and his kind adamantly opposed our message, obstructing us with their dark arts."

Drostan was thoughtful, and, looking intently at his feet, he noticed Colmcille unhurriedly scan the horizon with his usual nonchalance. "Will you not come north with me?" Drostan eventually burst out, believing that the outcome would most certainly be successful if the holy man were to accompany him.

"No. My commission is clear: to prepare others to be sent out – you are part of this mandate. Now that you have a fuller understanding of the supremacy of the Spirit against all adversaries, you are ready for the final part of the quest. Undoubtedly, the hardest is yet to come; but remember, *through one you will conquer the world.*"

"Ah! Ossian's prophecy. I wonder where he is, or if he is still in this world?"

Ignoring his aside, the holy man continued with careful deliberation. "The High King is a vallum about you. You are outspoken in championing the cause of the powerless, and possess that warrior-like valour to bear fire to the north. Keep these things in mind whenever your own spirit wavers."

He received this with a sinking feeling that, however, was buoyed up by the encouragement of the saint's words. After a lengthy pause, Colmcille asked with a searching intonation, "What part of your adventures have you found most challenging?"

"Certainly, the ordeal of passing through the Minamoyn Goch was difficult." He felt sceptical as to the direction their conversation was taking. "But worse was being adrift on the open seas in a flimsy coracle! When on land, I have knowledge to draw upon to survive; but at sea, amidst all these elemental forces, I am at the mercy of God."

"Our Lord, though, calmed the storm by a word of command." Looking as if to continue, Colmcille unexpectedly fell silent. With the wind picking up, the boat's prow rose before falling with a thud, raising spume into the air. He flinched to receive this cold wetting, though the holy man seemed oblivious to the discomfort.

Finally, the older statesman broke the silence. "You will have heard how the men of Erin liked to emulate the desert fathers! In seeking a 'desert' place, our people ventured out in coracles in search of desolate shores to wholly commit their lives to the Lord."

Drostan nodded, feeling a tense, sinking sensation.

"They do not contrive where they should go. Some make it to land, or to islands way over the horizon, some drift for days to discover a distant land, whilst others discover their place of resurrection. We are to heroically seek our High King and to ultimately discover that our security rests in being intimate with him, that our safety is resting in the shelter of the Presence."

"I do not like where this conversation is going," he admitted, aloud.

"You are to be courageous, not to doubt, nor to turn back," the older man replied solemnly. "When you despair, seek within you the knowledge of the Presence. He is your anchor in the storm, the distant fire on the shore guiding to safe harbour. *He who watches over you will not slumber.*"

Colmcille could have expounded, with bold certitude, how fortress gates were opened and how the dead were raised. But this language of survival troubled Drostan.

"When we attain to the full measure of faith, fear no longer has mastery over us; for his goodness will lead us home, though ten thousand dangers oppose. You are that warrior, Drostan. Your entire life's training has been to make you robust and resolute to achieve the goal. We are a warrior people, noble of birth, fit to be kings, yet humble enough to be mere soldiers." The intensity in his gaze was disquieting. "You will leave the day after you have set foot on Iona."

"So soon?"

"The tide in the war has turned, and we must pursue our advantage. Brude, and much of his court – and certainly the community around Craig Padrig – acknowledge the supremacy of the High King. Remember how it was with Patrick in the beginning. Once he had lit the pascal fire on the Hill of Slane in defiance of the druidic rules, the chief druid prophesied that the flame of faith could not be suppressed. That same fire has lit a beacon upon Craig Padrig and its sparks shall kindle many hearths among the Fortriu and beyond. Move on in this momentum, as the fire-bearer to the far north."

"I do not feel as ready as you seem to think!" he confessed, believing the truths spoken, but finding them hard to appropriate.

"If it depends upon our feeling competent to do something, we will never deem ourselves ready! Would you rather pass your days concocting all kinds of plausible excuses and grow fat and dull?"

Reluctantly conceding to the inevitability of the quest, he wondered how much further north he was to go. How much more land could there be? The further north he had ventured, the more extreme the environment became.

"I keep thinking about Fillan and his talk about the succession. It is like he has left me his sword and shield to take up, to advance into the forefront of the battle. I feel so alone!"

"If there were others with you, could you truly depend upon any one of them?"

"I feel bolder when part of a group. The challenges at Craig Padrig were made lighter for being shouldered by many."

Colmcille pursed his lips. "Certainly. However, man is fallible."

"I know that I am fallible." Again, he pictured himself alone, adrift upon the Great Western Ocean bound for goodness knows where.

"Our Father will not forsake you. In the hour of calamity, when the ordeals seem too great, and you confront insuperable odds, his power will be made perfect in your weakness."

They reached their small island out on the edge, gathered under a dark, overcast sky that made the sea an unsettled mass of heaving grey. The outline of the low-lying land was all blurred, smudging out its familiar details. After prayers, Drostan retired to his cell and, to take his mind off the quest, he finished copying a psalm left incomplete before setting out for Brude's court. He looked fondly about his basic cell, whose low-arched roof seemed to breathe in the guttering light of his candle; thankful for shelter from the northern climate to which he was soon to be exposed.

He had misgivings as to what lay ahead, so big that he hoped he might reach some natural end there that night, in this place of resurrection, to pass quietly in the dark of night from this uncertain world to the place of no further strife. He bemoaned the fact that such passing was normally the reward of the elderly, and that for him, he would have to endure the ordeal that loomed ominously ahead. He wondered whether Colmcille had really been correct in saying that the *bearing fire to the north* had not been fulfilled. The rise of the rebel within, kicking against authority, was keenly felt and he flinched at the assumed superior knowledge of his elders. But, had he not felt like this when Fillan had sent him off to Erin? Even going in obedience to study there had not alleviated his concerns that he had been sent in the wrong direction to what had been prophetically revealed. He envied Munait, left behind at Craig Padrig to strengthen the people and to properly establish a muintir; and he remembered Aniel's contentment as a hermit in his place where all kinds of animals found sanctuary. He craved both the more settled existence, and the excitement of a community that had been awakened.

With difficulty he slipped into a light slumber, and it seemed only moments had passed when the bell was rung for their middle-of-the-night prayer vigil. Rising, he went through the routine half asleep, returning to bed exhausted. He slept soundly until the bell summoned again to the morning prayers. A meagre breakfast followed, before he picked up his coracle and a few necessities and was swept along by the community down to the bay. He felt weary and sick within – one condemned to never enjoy for long, the simple lot that made up the lives of his fellow men. On reaching the beach, the brethren filed past him, each placing a hand briefly upon his shoulder in a sign of solidarity.

Colmcille took up a psalm which the whole muintir heartily sang – the praise rose and fell like the ebb and flow of the sea.

"They mounted up to the heavens and went
down to the depths;
in their peril their courage melted away.
They reeled and staggered like drunken men;
they were at their wits' end.
Then they cried out to the Lord in their trouble,
and he brought them out of their distress.

He stilled the storm to a whisper;
the waves of the sea were hushed.
They were glad when it grew calm,
and he guided them to their desired haven.
Let them give thanks to the Lord for his
unfailing love
and his wonderful deeds for men."

Drostan paddled out into the sound where a flowing tide helped bear his coracle north. Looking back at the sixty or more brethren lining the shore, still singing in a gesture of supplication, he resolutely dug his paddle into the waves. When the wind eased between gusts, he could just detect a faint utterance of their singing. When the wind was all that he could hear, he looked back and saw the whole muintir still standing where he had left them, presumably still singing. This surprised him, for Colmcille was a stickler for punctuality, and their continued presence upon the margins of the sea was a departure from the way he conducted the life of the muintir.

His eyes ran over the familiar outline of the low hills, the rocky extrusions that erupted from the green machair that the previous day he had seen dense with buttercups, daisies and orchids, nodding briskly as they were combed by the Atlantic wind. He could make out the vallum's tidy arc about their colony of heaven; hemming in a tight cluster of poor hovels within – a transient abode for those who disdained the opulence of the world. At its heart rose the simple oratory, appearing like a humble shed, but something he knew to be a fortress of praise, where heaven was moved to look upon their prayers with favour. The sea encompassed their island fastness like a girdle, setting it apart as a consecrated thing.

This had been the shortest of sojourns. His was truly a pilgrim's life, a stranger in the world, whose home was not one of familiar walls, but rather of an awareness of the Presence abiding with him. He sang aloud the psalm that his brothers had sent him away with, feeling this connected him with them and, more importantly, with the One to whom he sang. He sang it over and over, finding great solace tempering his fears.

The huge bulk of Muile rose mountainous to his right, riven with the vast inlet of a sea loch whose head wended inland way out of sight. The land rose dark and dramatic under a storm cloud. The occasional shaft of vivid light pierced through the turbulent smudge of a curtain of rain, infusing a shot of radiance that penetrated through to the grey blue of the sea. The water gurgled under the leather hull, which as a living thing, breathed like an abdomen with its slight movement caressing his bare feet. Dominating Muile was what they simply called Ben More – the "big hill" – looking particularly immense that day when deep gloom and sweeping light wrestled. It struck him how the fingers of God were caressing his creation with great fondness, infusing him with courage, inciting a renewed spirit for adventure.

Later, small islands came into view along with rocky outcrops and skerries that the surf swelled about in a deliriously menacing fashion. These summits of subterranean peaks provided lone haunts for seals and birds. He passed close to an island, bristling with a vast array of regular columns, set in serried ranks. Some were broken stumps, eroded by the heavy sea swell, but others rose to support a roof over a sea cavern. He marvelled at this mysterious construction, way out at sea – far from the gaze of common man. It struck him how like his own life it appeared, played out on the margins of the world, contending with the vagaries of ocean and at the mercy of his King.

Truly, I am being shown strange marvels that remind me not only of the excellence of their Creator, but also that he accomplishes whatsoever he desires.

A good way further, beyond the scatterings of small isles, a low but long, rocky isle came into view which became his goal to reach by the close of day. As the sea swell rose, he was reminded of how frail his efforts were and how truly he was at the mercy of a benevolent God. The wind, rising from the south-west, provided good steerage and he made landfall before dark.

As he lay on a beach, he looked out onto the blue of the sea, ruffled into white crenulations by the keen wind. Where wave crests broke, the air was filled with spume infused with rainbow hues by the light of the westering sun. A few skerries offshore presented the last remnant of land that sank beneath the vastness of the Great Western Sea. A low bank of greyish cloud had formed on the horizon, and, mesmerised, he watched the sun sink behind it. Gradually, violet and red streaked through the misty vapours, and its edges were burnished with molten gold.

The night was cold, even for the northern summer. Later, rain fell intermittently but heavily, making sleep fitful as he lay curled up under the upturned coracle. The sandy machair that seemed soft at first, grew surprisingly unyielding as the night wore on.

Chapter Fourteen

Transition

AD 565 Rhynie

As Alpia rode back with her single bodyguard and entered the hill country just north of Rhynie, it seemed to her that more than a week had passed. As she had surmised, King Brude had approved, with a calculating smile, of her moving to Craig Padrig to be with her children, warning her, though, of "dire consequences" should she attempt to remove them. She looked along the trail ahead with the familiar lie of the hills and the steep rise of the Pap of the Bulàch on her right, thinking this was likely to be the last time she would be returning home. How extreme life had become. Ten years ago, she reflected, I was a maiden, bored by the changelessness of my situation in the stagnant backwaters of the hill country. How swiftly events changed my circumstances, with Eithni taking a liking to Oengus. She rued the hand of fate that could exact so heavy a penalty, through no indiscretion of her own but that of her friend. And yet these circumstances had provided beloved children whom she would not be without.

She considered how to take Rowena without being suspected. It would be easier if Oengus were not present, and if he were, she would just have to bide her time until he was away. She really did not want to face him whose recent treachery made him more despicable. What of Aunt Conchen, though? She was like a mother and her closest kin. She would miss her. Could she be open with her about her intentions? No, better to keep her in the dark, for Aunt Conchen was also close to Oengus and had been the instigator of their union. It saddened her that she could not take her into her confidence, and the fact that she had to bear the enormity of her decision on her own made it feel weightier. She would have to act with nonchalance and, to avoid arousing suspicion, she would not gather all their belongings, only what was required for their journey.

As she neared Rhynie, she looked over to the foot of the steep slope rising to the Pap of the Bulàch, recalling that heady Beltane evening when she was free, enamoured by Taran's intense attentions. Had she flung caution to the winds, like Eithni had done, she could have orchestrated her own fate rather than becoming the victim of another's choices. She thought of what life with Taran could have been like, living in exile. How less heavy would separation be from her place of belonging when sharing that exile with the one you loved. Was there still opportunity to rewrite her life? She thought about her encounter with Taran – the pilgrim – and could discern something of the old bond, although he had mostly been detached in their conversation. What was to be expected other than some confusion after ten years of separation and monumental life changes for them both!

She dismounted from her horse, which was led away by her bodyguard, and went close to the threshold of her home . . . and paused. She could not hear voices from within. Her heart pounded and she bit her lip with determination as she crossed the threshold. Oengus was within, lying heavily asleep on the bedding, looking florid and bloated. He is probably the worse for wear from some drinking bout, she thought; such sprees had become common ever since the burning of the hillfort. Where was Aunt Conchen and her own daughter?

Never mind, I will use the time to gather a few things. She quietly went through a cabinet and gathered her jewellery that she determined to barter for her immediate needs in starting a new life near Craig Padrig. She came across the costly dress of purple, recalling how it had turned her head with its exquisite finery. It was an item associated with her ill-fated marriage and she pushed it to one side, cautious not to make a noise and disturb Oengus. She found a much more practical dress that she tightly rolled up and placed inside her shoulder bag along with a few other necessities, including clothing for Rowena. About to close the cabinet, she had a sudden change of mind and reached for the costly dress. It would fetch a good price at Brude's court, furnishing her immediate needs, and she could be rid of its unpleasant associations. No one's suspicions must be aroused by seeing that dress in her shoulder bag – so she concealed it at the very bottom. She placed her bag behind some firewood near the door and searched for food. I will have everything we need for our journey, but I must appear to be travelling lightly, as though going on an outing in the woods.

She could hear Aunt Conchen and Rowena approaching, chatting amiably. Rowena was animated about deer they had seen. Fearing her daughter's childish spirits might arouse Oengus, she decided to intercept them outside to minimise the noise of what she anticipated would be a happy reunion. She took some brisk paces towards them and noted that they were coming from the stream for they were carrying full waterskins.

"Mummy!" cried Rowena, dropping her small waterskin as she came running to her. Aunt Conchen shook her head and bent with difficulty to retrieve the abandoned container. Alpia felt her daughter's arms clasp around her back as she stooped to embrace her before lifting Rowena off her feet, revolving her round on the spot.

"Alpia!" Aunt Conchen pronounced her name with affection. "It is good to have you back, but what made you tarry a further day among the Fortriu and not return with Oengus?"

They entered the hut and their voices disturbed Oengus for he shifted position on the bed.

"Oh, I wanted more time with my boys." She tried to sound convincing.

Aunt Conchen seemed to weigh her words. "I thought as much. Oengus could not be drawn on the subject. He came back in a strange mood yesterday and drank himself stupid last night. I take it that things did not go too well at Craig Padrig?"

She shrugged her shoulders dismissively. "You know, the usual humiliation of the one coming to pay tribute." She looked over at Oengus, wondering whether he was awakening, but he had only turned his back on them.

Aunt Conchen shook her head and hung the waterskins from a beam near to the firepit.

"So, what has been happening here?" she enquired of her aunt.

"Och! Very little. Drusticc kindly came here to sleep the nights with me . . ."

It seemed to Alpia that Aunt Conchen had stopped mid-sentence. "Go on," she encouraged, "it seems you had something more to say."

Aunt Conchen came closer and, lowering her voice, said meaningfully, "Talorc, Nechtan's son, has been rousing discontent – at least that is what it seems to me!"

"How do you mean?"

"Ever since you have been away in Craig Padrig, he has been gathering his friends and their numbers increase. They do not consume much wine, preferring to talk. I do not like it. Ever since Talorc returned from his military training shortly after the burning of the hillfort, it looks like he has an axe to grind on account of his father's death and the disappearance of his big brother Taran. He assumes, like everyone else, that Taran is dead, and is probably holding Oengus responsible."

Alpia felt a slight colour rise in her cheeks, recalling her time with Taran two days back. So Oengus had not told Aunt Conchen that they had encountered him.

"As Talorc did not meet with his friends last night when Oengus returned seems significant. Keen not to arouse suspicion, I would say! Do you think I should mention it to Oengus?"

"Oh, it is probably nothing. Besides, what would Oengus make of it? Would he not act rashly and Talorc might become another innocent victim?"

"Oengus does seem particularly out of sorts," agreed her aunt, passing a meaningful look.

"Did he speak about his visit to Craig Padrig?" Alpia explored, keen to exact what her aunt might know.

"No, not a word, and it seemed odd that he was dismissive about why you had not returned with him. Is everything alright between you? I know how things are . . . strained!"

"Oh, you know! Same old thing – we muster on through!"

Rowena, who had been tugging at her skirt, had become more demonstrative to gain her attention. "Aunt, I am going to take Rowena out. I have missed her and would like some time with her, particularly whilst Oengus sleeps."

"I understand."

The gravity of what she was about to do made her go over to Aunt Conchen and kiss her cheek and put her arm around her.

"What is that for?" she quizzed.

"I am glad to see you again, that is all!"

Aunt Conchen did not look altogether convinced but let the remark pass.

She took Rowena by the hand and at the door took her shoulder bag.

"Why are you taking your bag?" Aunt Conchen asked.

"I have prepared some food. I had planned to take Rowena on an outing once she had returned to the house." She looked at her aunt who, raising no further objection, did appear to regard her plan as slightly unusual. Why would she not take Rowena out? Was it not a normal thing for a mother to do after an absence? But perhaps the haste of her departure, so shortly after they had drawn water from the stream, had seemed unnecessarily fast. She walked to the threshold and cast a final glance over at her husband lying dishevelled in a heap on the bedding, sweating. He disgusted her and she moved decisively outside, greedily taking in the fresh breeze after the air that smelt of drink and stale sweat.

"Come on," she tugged at Rowena's hand to make her move faster. "I promised you an adventure when I came home, and we are going to have one!"

At that, Rowena seemed to rouse herself from her dreamy state and skipped alongside. Alpia knew her aunt was not altogether convinced about their short outing and regarded her embrace as odd. Would her aunt alert Oengus concerning her suspicions? Not wishing to linger, she went straight for her horse and headed north. When out of sight of Rhynie, she doubled back through the woods parallel to the trail where another way went west through the hill country, skirting the southern slopes of the Pap of the Bulàch. As far as she could tell, no one had spotted her turning about and should anyone who had seen her leave be asked, they would reply that she had gone north.

Her horse was weary from their earlier journey and moved without haste. She would overnight with a relative who lived near the Deveron, whose confidentiality she trusted. It was not that far, and they would easily reach there before nightfall. She then began to feel anxious, for this route was not well used, and although better for her purpose of leaving Rhynie undetected, it carried the threat of robbers. She had all her wealth in her bag, and she worried for their safety.

She cast a look back. Rhynie was already far out of sight, but the top of the Pap of the Bulàch, sculptured by the outline of the hillfort, brought painful memories of the siege; most notably, Drust's head hurled over the ramparts and all the carnage that brought a cloud of carrion crows to hover overhead. Again, she pictured that horrendous moment when Caltram had been prised from her arms and that had undone her world.

There were no regrets in leaving, other than parting from dear Aunt Conchen. Again, she wondered whether her aunt would alert Oengus . . . The enormity of what she was about began to sink in: abandoning home, leaving her roots and her people. Life had dealt her a whole series of disappointments, along with all the perceived securities proving insubstantial. The Bulàch had been incapable of defending their community, the sacred hill was impotent, lying desecrated. With the former things sliding into insignificance, the time had been ripe to leave for quite some time now. Glad to find the conviction and the courage to move on, she felt more settled about circumstances.

A new life beckoned among a people who had triumphed over her own, and she would become part of a community where people were turning to the one God of the Gaels. Their strange beliefs aroused her curiosity. Would there be any future with Taran? Would his interest in her be rekindled? Admonishing herself for her idle thoughts, she felt in her guts that she was doing the right thing to remake a life into one that she would not regret. For once, she would be the one taking control of her own circumstances instead of events dictating what she should do. She also felt assured of a welcome among the pilgrims and, moreover, had obtained Brude's permission to settle. As she picked up her weary pace, the proverb came to her mind, *Your feet will bring you to where your heart is*. Yes, she was heading where she most wanted to go.

"Where did you say they had gone?" asked Oengus.

"They said they were going for a short outing. I expected them back before now – it is nearly nightfall!" replied Aunt Conchen. "I do hope no misadventure has befallen them!"

He looked at her, wondering if she knew more than what she was revealing. He did not believe some accident had occurred, for lurking at the back of his mind was the shadow of Taran now looming large, threatening his world. Alpia had tried to remain nonplussed by his cousin's presence, but he knew how close they had once been, and this reappearance must have rekindled feelings for one she had presumed lost. After losing his power, and lacking the means to rein in his wife, it felt like the final straw.

His thoughts turned to Taran. What force preserved his cousin? Was it something to do with the Z-rod? He had been sure of finally wiping Taran out when he attacked the pilgrims' camp. He had believed the camp to be defenceless, only to then encounter some extraordinary force far greater than their own. He shivered at the recollection of how their horses had reared, refusing to advance before their riders had become fully aware of what supernatural force they were up against.

I have had all the presumed advantages that come with being warlord: a fighting force to carry out my will, and alliances that had placed a rich reward upon Taran's head. And yet, he, who had been made homeless, powerless, without influence, has survived against all the odds, and has become such a force to be reckoned with. He has even turned the head of my arch-nemesis. What strange powers accompany him? What a different route Taran's life has taken: becoming a man of learning, speaker of other tongues, who has fully embraced a faith I despise for all its foolish talk.

Should he pursue his wife? It would not be out of love for her. But Alpia had taken his one remaining child. Rowena brought him joy in a world that had fallen apart. Her childish ways distracted him from the stark realities that confronted him daily and he deeply resented being robbed of the pleasure she brought him.

"She has deliberately gone from here," he uttered finally, examining Aunt Conchen's face. She did not respond. Was even his aunt against him? Did he have no one he could trust? "Woman, you should speak if you hold any affection for me!"

He noticed Aunt Conchen's head slightly tremble, and though her eyes met his, he detected a void within their depths, as though she no longer possessed those faculties which had once made her impressively wise.

"Alpia said she was taking Rowena out for time together – that is all!" Her statement seemed unfinished to his mind, for her intonation suggested her thoughts had been left hanging. What was she concealing?

He stepped closer. "There is more that you know which you are keeping from me!"

Again, her haunted eyes met his briefly. She did not look frightened; just timid. Finally, she said as one in deep reflection, "She embraced me."

"So? What is unusual about that?" Again, he searched her face, unable to fathom what she meant. Aunt Conchen turned away as if to say that was the end of the matter, and he decided that it was pointless pursuing further. What was he to do? Dusk had descended and it would be difficult to go searching for his runaway wife.

Needing fresh air, he picked up his plaid and a sword, and went out, wanting to be alone with his thoughts. He went through the citadel's gates, past the salmon and beast stone that he had often touched for luck. What was the point in touching it anymore, he thought, for what good had the Bulàch ever done for him or others? The sky had turned a deep blue upon which the treeline was etched in deep silhouette. He welcomed the gathering darkness consuming all the details of the open ground before him, so much so that he occasionally stumbled as he walked down the brae to the stream. It was even darker down there under the shade of the alders and the willows, but his eyes had by now grown accustomed to the gathering night. As he progressed upstream a good while, the land lay enveloped in darkness, and yet some faint light played upon the flowing waters of the stream. The gurgle of the waters soothed his recent bad humour, alleviating some of his cares.

"Alpia can go . . . good riddance to her!" he said aloud to the stream.

There, under the cover of darkness, his life felt hidden from mankind as he wandered further, far from the observation of others. In the encompassing darkness, he was his own man once more, freed from a bickering wife keen to remind him of his shortcomings. He came upon a pool that was dark, overhung with alder, which caught none of the faint illumination from above.

Was this not the pool where Eithni washed me? he wondered. She had been much more fun to live with – a person like myself, without hidden depths, or superior knowledge; a woman who had been open, easy to get along with, had it not been for my jilting her. I will not dwell on that, though – it was rectified and we made our peace and could have made a go of things had we been given the chance.

He sat down upon the rock where he had laid his clothes all those years back whilst Eithni had splashed him with water. "O, for those carefree days," he whispered sonorously with the sound of the breeze stirring the leaves overhead. Well, they were not so carefree either, for did I not have to suffer Talorgen's heavy-handed ways! But by comparison, my burdens are much greater now. He remained a long time. At first, the traffic of his thoughts was brisk, then he started to imbibe the calm from his surroundings and the thoughts subsided. Eventually, a stillness enveloped him, a calmness like the placidness of the pool which lay at his feet. An owl hooted some distance off with a melodious call that seemed to emerge through a thick cover of moss.

The sky was overcast but not so solid as to shut out the moonlight, for the undersides of the clouds gleamed with a significant radiance. Occasionally, the clouds parted, allowing a stray beam to illumine a patch of forest below, as though probing, but unable to alight upon the forest floor. Later, he heard the rusty creaking rhythm of approaching geese. At first, they were just a distant suggestion that had him half-wondering whether he had truly heard them. The sound grew and became unmistakeable, yet the flock remained out of sight. In the low level of light, he unsuccessfully searched for their skein and yet was able to follow their course from their honking. Then, there they were! His keen eye could just detect their formation overhead, in silhouette against the moonlit clouds, seemingly following the stream's course for guidance. His eyes focused upon their formation, which struck him, for a brief moment, with its resemblance to a boar's head! He was filled with wonder, thrilled by this unexpected sign; but before he could question its meaning, the geese, forever shifting in their formation, caused the image to vanish as quickly as the suggestion had come.

The goose was Alpia's sign, and, like the flock, she had flown from him. Again, his thoughts turned towards her. Did he want to retrieve her? Why would he? Was he not tired of all the recriminations? "Why bring her back to torment me?" he spoke aloud. "Can I not swallow what remains of my pride and feel no distress in losing her?"

Once more, he considered the brief semblance of the boar's head made by the geese. He thought it a sign to say their marriage was over, the union of goose and boar was no more. The geese also reminded him of the huge staging that had appeared to the south of Rhynie when his power was at its zenith. He had taken comfort from their three-day presence that replicated the three years taken to build his fighting force. Had it not been an impressive achievement? No one could say that he had not realised his ambition. He had made good and had almost prevailed. Did he not harry Brude's army, coming close to winning the day? If only they had been lured into the defile, what a different outcome there would have been, and then Brude would have been the one paying tribute! He thought of Drust and considered no one ever had as good a right-hand man as he had had. Had they not coordinated their efforts superbly well as he recalled the agreed signals made with the carnyx? He smiled. What vagaries of fate had made Brude's commander heed the approaching defile? Destiny, hinged on the alertness of that one man in that moment! How bizarre fortune outworks itself; how by a mere thread hang the destinies of warlords and their kingdoms.

The boulder he sat upon had grown so unbearably hard that he moved on. He wondered where to next? Thoughts of retiring home for the night were far from a mind grown fertile with reflection. Conscious that all his thoughts were retrospective, he urged himself to look forward to contemplating what was next. How could he extricate himself from the shackles of Brude's hegemony? What could he do, with Caltram and Drustan held hostage? The Ce might have made some recovery after the shocking blow, but they were a shadow of what they had been.

I know, I should look up my old friend Gest. I have not seen him for an age. I might have lost Drust and my chief druid, and he felt the grief and the lost status for a moment, but I still have my druid friend. *Better one good thing that is, than two things that were*, he recalled the proverb. I wonder how he is getting on with Maevis?

He walked with purpose back to Rhynie, where he took his horse from its stall. He met no one and had no intention of telling anyone of his plan. This was his business, and the rest could guess. The thought empowered him.

The way to the priestesses of the Bulàch was well familiar, the road taken when undoing the wrong when he had retrieved Eithni. Now, it appeared as the way of coming to terms with realities, and of new possibilities.

He arrived just as the eastern sky was brightening after the passage of the night. A woman was gathering water down by the stream, reminding him brightly that it was at that moment of drawing water together with Eithni that she had come to accept returning with him to Rhynie. He could even recall how the waterskin that had spilled over the pebbles beside the stream had washed the dust off their unremarkable forms to reveal their distinctive colours, striking him as an image of resurrection of what could have been had Eithni been spared.

He knocked on Maevis's door, hoping that Gest was still there, not relishing meeting with the high priestess. As there was no response, he knocked louder and was relieved to hear his old friend call out, "Who is it?"

Ignoring that the question had been asked in a grumpy manner, he replied, "It is I, the bearer of the boar!"

Gest opened the door, looking very much half asleep.

He did not receive the welcome he had hoped, but passed it off due to the unusually early time of his unannounced arrival.

"What brings you here at night?"

"It is morning," he returned brightly.

Gest rubbed his eyes and yawned. Maevis's head emerged from a heap of blankets as she propped herself groggily up on an elbow.

"Come, my friend – is this the way to greet your warlord?"

As he smoothed his unruly hair, Gest began to look more alert. "Why do you visit us?"

He had hoped for a welcome, and the question was stark for its absence of warmth. Had it been such a good idea to have come after all? he thought. Ignoring the coldness of the reception, he ventured on, preparing to give Gest the benefit of the doubt. "If for nothing else, then I visit you for old time's sake!"

Still there was no indication of reciprocal friendship. He felt disturbed and was of a mind to depart from so frosty a reception. But he had ridden all through the night with hopes of some clarity as to the future direction his life should take.

"The old times have passed!" announced Gest drily.

"What do you mean? Can a warlord not expect some guidance from his druid?"

"I am no longer your druid." There was something final in the way Gest delivered his words that took him aback. He felt a slight tightening of his stomach and he licked his lips that had become dry.

"How is that?" he asked, dropping any semblance of warmth, keen to get to the heart of this rebuff. He became aware of Maevis staring at him with her pale face framed by that short-cropped fringe.

"The goose has flown," she uttered softly, as if it were an involuntary exclamation.

It sent a chill down his spine and, at that moment, he keenly regretted coming to this home. However, he said to himself, I cannot deny that Maevis has a remarkable ability of second sight. Was it not better that I am aware of reality and can act accordingly rather than guess and blunder my way forward? No, I am here, and I should hear them out, unpleasant though it may be.

"We parted company some time back at this very door. I have retired and found solace with this woman after the ruination that overtook us all. You, on the other hand, went on riding, optimistic, tireless to rebuild your reputation."

He did not care for the unveiled contempt in Gest's words. "Maybe that is the difference between us. I do not give up!" He slightly raised his chin.

"And what do you hope to achieve? Can you not see, man, that the old dreams lie shattered?"

He did not reply.

"All that formerly supported you as warlord has been removed. Your best men were taken, leaving you with the slain and the maimed. Wake up! Maelchon has abandoned you, and . . ." Gest stopped and turned quizzically to Maevis to exchange words in a whisper that he could not quite make out. "Even Alpia has abandoned you, it would seem!"

"Well, what good was Maelchon anyway?" he said, deliberately passing over a reference to a wife from whom he was relieved to be parted.

"Maelchon has become a pilgrim of the one the Gaels follow. His old world was shattered, just as it was for everyone, but I do not agree with what he has become!"

"And you — what have you become?" he asked without malice, curious to know how Gest had dealt with the misfortunes that all had endured.

"Me?" he repeated, perhaps wondering why it mattered. "I have given up faith in the Bulàch."

"You do not believe she exists?"

"No, she exists of sorts in her shadowy world as a malevolent force. She is out to ensnare mankind, give a few good outcomes that her worshippers entreat from her in order to ensnare. Her intent, ultimately, is to do harm, to bring us down into the shades of her underworld!"

"If you believe that, then why do you not follow Maelchon's example?"

"I have given up heeding the gods for they cannot do any lasting good. Better to ignore them and find a woman to love and live a quiet life, not bothered about things too big for us to alter. Mark my words, if you respect the gods, they take notice and you become marked."

It struck him how Gest had not only lost his former faith, but also the kind nature that had made him once affable about all manner of things. Truly, he seemed to have withdrawn from the world and he wondered how responsible Maevis was for this? "And what about Maevis? Has she abandoned her faith?"

"As much as she would like to be free, she is plagued by all kinds of images that horrify her. Truly, I cannot begin to tell you how she suffers!"

He noted this was really the first show of any tenderness expressed by his former druid friend, the sharing of which gave him hope that Gest's hostility would soon evaporate. He looked over at the high priestess, curious to know how she was reacting to being talked about openly. Her fingers were running along the ragged edge of a blanket as though anxious to repair its frayed hem, and she seemed either oblivious to, or disinterested in, their conversation.

Gest went over to her and, kneeling, placed his arm about her. His hardness dissolved as he soothed her, and he did not appear to object anymore to the intrusion into their lives.

They were quiet for some time. It was Maevis who unexpectedly broke it by suddenly leaning forward. "The boar who once bristled with haughty pride is now a shadow, disappearing with the passage of the geese."

The words that came unpleasantly to his ears, seemed to drain her of energy. She looked appalled, with that same haunted look he could recall when she had burst into their council with the premonition of Brude's marching army.

What was it she had said back then? he thought. "The bull snorts and scrapes his paw", or something like that! And now the equally ominous message from beyond this world, sent a shudder down his spine. Deciding to leave before the curse of their household took hold of him in its grip of dark despair, he turned to the door. He momentarily hesitated, thinking to bid them farewell, but he thought better of it — to leave them alone whilst Gest comforted Maevis who was now trembling uncontrollably and sobbing.

As he mounted his horse and turned back to Rhynie, he tried hard to ignore Maevis's words by concentrating on the easily intelligible exchange with Gest. "What do you hope to achieve?" had been his former druid's question. A proverb came to mind with sobering effect: *A friend's eye is a good mirror.* But could he still consider Gest his friend? Maybe not, but his question was pertinent, one that he had been attempting to answer without success, in an effort to move beyond the stark reality of the subservience of the Ce to the Fortriu. Yes, he was the optimist, not one for quitting, for whilst he had breath, he believed there was hope. The Ce just needed time to recover, as it had been with the warriors whose open wounds had taken months to heal after the siege.

Mind you, that had been for the more fortunate, he considered, for others had succumbed to fever and disease and were no more. Did not the proverb ring true, though, that *however long the day, the evening will come*? Do I have the strength, though, to reach the end of the day? I cannot achieve what is required on my own. He gloomily wondered who would help him, a concern that had made him turn to Gest. If only I had Drust by my side, then just maybe there would be some hope.

By the time he had reached Rhynie, he was famished and in need of drink to banish his sullen thoughts. Aunt Conchen greeted him indifferently, not even enquiring where he had been all night, but she had cooked up a tasty venison stew which he washed down with copious amounts of wine, eager to escape his depressing outlook.

When he awoke later in the day, he was thirsty, and his head ached.

"Talorc came by earlier!" Aunt Conchen remarked as he ran a wetted hand over his burning face.

"Uh! What did he want?"

"He wants an audience with you, he and his friends at sundown in the hall."

His curiosity was slightly aroused.

"I am not sure of that young man!" his aunt continued, after what had been a lengthy pause.

He ignored her comment, for she had grown sullen in her old age and aired her misgivings as one who had lost hope. He busied himself, sharpening a blade on a whetstone, thinking how a new generation of young men with ambition could perhaps help rebuild their fortunes. Maybe Talorc has some suggestion? Although he thought he should be wary of Taran's brother, the two brothers had grown up apart and he reckoned there was not much love between them, just as it was between himself and his own younger brother. Well, he would take a couple of bodyguards just to be safe; no, better double that . . . or even double again to be sure. He could be magnanimous and move on from the past and make new allies from unlikely people. Had he not done that with Cynbel, and even repeated with Nechtan, Taran's own father? But recalling Nechtan's dying words gave him forebodings and he became somewhat agitated. Better to have my full guard there for this meeting, just as if it were a delegation sent from Brude himself!

At sundown he became aware of men gathering in the hall, glad that the waiting was over, and he could learn the business and hopefully put his nervous unrest aside. His trusted guard came to his home saying that all was ready. He accompanied him and they emerged through the rear door of the hall, surprised to see about fifteen men with Talorc. It was just as well he had taken the precaution of bringing his full guard that outnumbered those who were seeking the audience by two to one. His eyes quickly ran over the group, and he was relieved that none were armed with swords – his guards will have seen to that. Talorc rose to meet him with a friendly smile and came forward to embrace him. Talorc's left hand was open in a friendly gesture, but his right hand was bent back as though it was disfigured.

That is odd! – I did not know Talorc was maimed, he thought as he stepped to meet the young man. Was Talorc somewhat nervous for his smiling eyes struck him as being rather too contrived?

At the moment of embrace, Talorc straightened the contorted hand, revealing a dagger that had been concealed up his wide sleeve.

He instinctively stepped back. "Guards!" he shouted, but they did not move. His hand found the hilt of his sword and, as he was drawing it, with its grating sound of iron upon the iron lip of his scabbard, Talorc's blade came thrusting up. The knife pierced his flesh from under his ribs and he fell to the ground, aware of a grievous wound and yet not feeling the full force of its pain. The image of the boar's head that the geese had formed, flickered in his mind, dematerialising as the flock shifted shape.

Chapter Fifteen

Walking Inis Gemaich's Waters

AD 565 The Western Sea

Drostan was glad to rise at first light. His spirits picked up on finding a good-sized crab caught in a small net he had secured among the rocks the previous evening. Before long, a fire crackled in a sheltered hollow, upon which he baked the crab in its shell.

The brisk, prevailing wind sped his coracle along and the sea swell, breaking menacingly against the hard contour of the rocky isle, ensured he kept his distance from shore. He vigilantly scanned the water for any difference in surface texture, indicative of a submerged skerry. Rounding the point, a vast tract of sea opened before him with the Aird nam Murchan peninsula on his right showing grey in the murkiness of the distance. The menace of the troubled sea's vastness tempted him to return to shore. He recalled Colmcille's stories of white martyrdom adventurers, whose quests, however absurd they might appear, were strengthened by the desire to press on to know their Lord more intimately.

With that sinking feeling of powerlessness out on the swell of the open sea, he prayed almost continually, achieving the seldom realised desire of pilgrims to pray without ceasing. Far from any reference point on shore to gauge progress, he was left clueless. He kept paddling, despite the seeming futility, believing it made some small difference. Stroke by stroke, surely, he was getting closer, quite contrary to what his eye was conveying.

Out of the misty haze, a couple of islands came into view. They looked familiar and he reckoned them to be the mountainous Rùm with the neighbouring Inis Y Copa Peer to its right, where some years previously he had made landfall. He could not be certain, though, viewing them from this angle, for Inis Y Copa Peer lacked its distinctive great tower of rock hanging in the sky over the green fields above its sandy bay. A third island later came into view, low-lying, like an enormous sinking vessel. A strong current dragged him westward, which he countered with powerful strokes, afraid of being drawn into that void of an ocean without land. He struggled, desperate to maintain control, to keep land in sight and steer northwards, towards the fulfilment of the prophecy, to the learned men who would be anticipating his arrival.

The current became too strong to oppose, and, exhausted from the futility of his efforts, he gave up paddling against the tide, abandoning himself to God. What if he were to find his place of resurrection out at sea? Then the quest would be unfulfilled. How would that glorify God? he asked himself. He rebuked himself for such thinking. Had the prophecy not been given specifically to him? Had it not sustained him over ten years to give him direction and purpose? Later, after feeling forlorn, he noted the ebbing flow slackening, replaced by a rising tide. When the current started to bear him towards a bay on the southern coast of Rùm, he broke into song. With a grateful heart, the surf carried his coracle the final yards, sweeping it with considerable speed up onto a shingle shore. It was a desolate place, without habitation, but nevertheless presented a haven at which to overnight.

On the third day, he waited for the ebb tide to slacken before putting out to sea and was able to steer a passage parallel to the rugged, mountainous coast of Rùm. He had not seen a single soul since leaving Iona and the bleakness of this rough terrain suggested another day would pass without meeting anyone. Navigating beneath the last peak of Rùm on his right, the much lower Inis Gemaich came into view to the north-west. It was not so far off. Clearing Rùm's land mass, the distant view to the north-east revealed a rank of spiked peaks. "That must be Inis Niwl," he said aloud, recalling the wonder of sailing into one of its big sea lochs on his quest to find the conical hill.

Nearing the east end of Inis Gemaich, the tide seemed to ebb, drawing him westwards into the open ocean despite his best efforts to make for shore. Surrendering to the tide, he rested as the ocean inexorably dragged him where he feared to go. Watching the passing coastline, he noted the decaying structure of an old fort on the rising headland. Westward contained no sight of land, just an endless ocean into which, he imagined, previous pilgrims had found their place of resurrection. With renewed strength rising out of apprehension, he took up his paddle, hoping still to reach the shore of Inis Gemaich. Drifting beyond the western cliffs of Gemaich's extremity, distant smudges of islands appeared far out west, on the very rim of the world.

"More islands!" he exclaimed, surprised to see land so remote. The far-reaching sky seemed immense, dwarfing his person and miniscule efforts, making him profoundly aware of being helplessly adrift upon the emptiness of ocean.

"Perhaps that distant rim is my destination. I should abandon my own effort," he said as he placed his paddle on the floor of his coracle.

As the sun descended, he drifted west of Inis Gemaich.

Then progress was halted, far sooner than expected. It was as if a rising tide countered the former ebb, so that when he paddled again, the water felt slack. With renewed hope, he turned back for Inis Gemaich. Scanning the high headland, he noticed a thin trail of smoke rise against the green of the land. Would there be a friendly reception? This, too, he prayed about, for the illusion that he had any control over his life had been removed. Even the most basic needs of food, shelter, safe passage, of navigating in the right direction, were not taken for granted.

Stepping ashore raised an immense gratitude within him. He climbed an arduous brae, struggling initially to find his land legs, directed towards the smoke spiralling up from the ruined fort. Clambering over the broken ramparts, he saw a small hovel built against a wall where an elderly figure sat beside a fire, stirring a cooking pot.

"Hello!" he greeted. The fellow looked up. "Ossian!" he cried in disbelief.

Ossian did not appear at all surprised and, smiling good-naturedly, remarked, "You will be ready for something to eat!"

"I thought that perhaps you too had passed away, just as Fillan has. I have been asking after you wherever I have been – in Dal Riata, at Dindurn, and even asked King Brude himself, and no one knew."

"It was revealed that I would see you one more time," smiled the old man, looking a good deal frailer than before, more translucent as though the heavenly light was already infusing him.

"When making for here, the ebb tide swept me westward."

"I know," the old man said without surprise. Drostan looked at him searchingly. "I was watching your difficult progress and prayed. As soon as I was done praying, your coracle made headway back here to Inis Gemaich."

Drostan moved close to the fire and crouched down on his haunches in the shelter of the broken wall to avoid the wind.

"It was never to be that you would speed on past and miss this encounter." The old man smiled generously, looking up from the fire.

Ossian turned the fillets of fish skewered on sticks. "These were caught this afternoon, a double amount anticipating your arrival. Make yourself at home. It is only a poor hovel, but it is out of the wind and rain, with room enough for two."

Compared to being adrift on the high seas, this "hovel" was a haven. A place secure from the might of the ocean and the vagaries of its currents; shelter from the wetting of waves and the sting of salt in sore hands was so welcome. To be beside a fire, resting weary limbs, felt luxurious.

Drostan shook his head. "It is hard to believe that I should find you in so outlandish a place! It is as surprising as meeting you under the Stone of Refuge."

"There are no coincidences, are there! Coincidence is just how unbelieving folk label providence. I have prayed for a final opportunity to perhaps be of service in the fulfilment of your long quest."

They ate and spoke a good deal, filling in the substantial gaps since they last parted almost six years previously.

Drostan looked beyond the crumbling ramparts to the bare moor and to a sky of tattered cloud where a few fulmars wheeled and cried mournfully above the vastness of the Western Sea. "What led you here, though?"

Ossian chewed on something, in no hurry to answer. "I wanted to experience the white martyrdom that you and others have sought. My legs no longer have the strength to bear me down long roads to the courts of the land, telling my tales and singing my songs." He stopped to rub a calf muscle. "After I was baptised, I joined Fillan in Dindurn and benefitted much from his instruction. After a long while, I became restless and made up my mind to fast, to perceive what was at the root of this unrest. A place of exile appealed, novel for one who has spent a life revolving around festivals." Ossian smiled as one at peace with the whole universe. "And so, the desire to seek God in a desolate place grew, to cultivate my relationship in my twilight years, making up for all those years lived in ignorance."

"You seem calmer about your white martyrdom than I was with mine!"

"You were starting out on your own, young in your knowledge of the High King. Is it surprising that you found it hard? You also had to battle with your feelings for Aleine Brona."

"Do you not miss company, since your whole life has been spent in society?"

"There have been times, I cannot deny. But wandering from court to court also meant many days on my own. I have no desires anymore . . . well, that is not entirely true." He looked wistfully up at the clouds. "I do have the ardent wish to grow a great intimacy with our High King. As that desire heightens, the need for company lessens. He is all sufficient, would you not say? Once we find ourselves centred in him, the distractions and lesser affections fall away. He is the supreme One – our very great desire and reward."

At that moment, Drostan thought Ossian looked almost weightless, made buoyant by a great peace. An aura of huge acceptances wrapped him in something akin to a glow. They talked at length. Both enjoyed singing the King's praise, offering up prayers, unhurriedly, feeling the presence of One to whom they had yielded in a great seeking that had led to their full surrender.

"You will be in no great hurry to move on yet awhile?" asked Ossian.

"It would be good to rest some days here," agreed Drostan, who as an afterthought added, "I sense this will probably be our last time together!"

As he lay there in the dark with the murmur of the sea in the distance, he was thrilled by the unmistakable hand of God.

The next day, Ossian led him down a steep way between the cliffs to a small beach from where a rocky shelf jutted out. Their fishing tackle was fashioned from a well-seasoned branch foraged from the seashore.

"I came equipped to Inis Gemaich," elucidated Ossian, "with twine, fish-hooks, knives, a couple of pots, my container for tinder and other sorts of useful things." He chuckled as one content to have reduced life's necessities to these few basics.

Settling themselves on a ledge at the end of the shelf, they baited a hook with a worm, and cast. Although the day was overcast, the great expanse of sea filled their eyes with light. The rhythm of lapping waves lulled them to a deep rest.

"Tell me," Ossian began, his tone invoking a question, "what became of your dog? I mind he was a rather special kind – like half-wolf, able to keep those marauding fiends at bay at the Stone of Refuge."

"Ah, Garn," Drostan began rather distantly, recalling with enormous fondness the bond that had been theirs. "The day when we two parted after that meeting in the Minamoyn Goch, was the day of his demise."

"How?" Ossian asked with genuine surprise.

Drostan recounted the details of their encounter with the enchanted Gwid that led to the firing of the deadly shaft that was either poisoned or bewitched. "I took his loss badly, as you might expect, alone as I was in this world with all the odds stacked against me of moving beyond my misfortune: made a fugitive from my people and an exile in lands I did not know. My one faithful companion was cruelly taken from me. Garn's loss brought a great emptiness; his murder seemed to underscore the futility of life. Often, I have considered how that noble dog had defended me; accompanied me on every hunt; walked the desolate ways through that great wilderness; slept by my side." He ran his fingers across the stubble of his shaved forehead and then through the lengthy mane of hair. "Such bonds are immeasurable. With Garn, I did not feel so alone."

"I can feel your loss," Ossian spoke with unexpected tenderness.

A sudden surge of emotion overwhelmed Drostan at that moment, taking him by surprise. Wiping his eyes, he continued, "But, I took strength from Garn. Stirred by his indomitable example, I vowed to move forward with the same courage and determination; not to concede defeat, nor believe the lie of the purposelessness of life."

"You remind me of that fellow back at Dindurn – the one who has the special relationship with animals?"

"Aniel?"

"Aye, that is the one. He has a wonderful rapport with all animals, showing them special regard."

"Aniel has a particular gift that is rare to find. Garn was my one ally – always true, forever at my side, quick to defend, eager for adventure. Who could want for a better companion? I tell you, that dog was the trusted comrade that once I believed Oengus had been. Garn did not fail me, though, and for that, I am forever indebted to that noble hound's example that I choose to emulate."

The two men fell quiet, allowing the great expanse of ocean to carry each away, alone in the diminishing of their thoughts, until they were caught up in the great calmness.

Ossian broke their lengthy silence rather ponderously. "The prophecy states that it is for *your fulfilment and the anticipation of the learned ones to the north*. Who, would you say, are the learned ones?"

"The wise who do not yet know the King, must be the druids."

"After the notion was given to me that you would pass this way, I have been thinking about this matter. I recall a place they call Meini Heyon y Pentir whose standing stones have drawn pilgrims from as far away as Gaul." Ossian tugged on his line. A fish had taken the bait and the old bard began to roll up the line. "Oh! It got away! As I was saying, Meini Heyon y Pentir is like no other place of druid worship apparently. There was once quite a cult based there and what Meini Heyon y Pentir had to say about matters, and concerning oracles spoken there, were second to none and reported to all kinds of distant places. I wonder whether they are the learned ones?"

He listened thoughtfully, absorbing the information. "Where is Meini Heyon y Pentir?"

"You may have noticed, on the clear afternoon when you arrived, a chain of islands far out to sea. You can only see their hill tops from here. Meini Heyon y Pentir is out there, an apt location for the north in the prophecy, would you not say?" Ossian looked at him brightly.

"It seems I have quite an expedition ahead of me!" Drostan spoke unenthusiastically.

Ossian was quiet, looking as though he would let this remark pass. "You know our longings are often expressed as lying beyond the horizon, in some distant haven many days sail away that can only be reached after enduring many ordeals. It is the habit of us bards to sing about our legendary heroes making epic journeys to destinations like the land of Tír na nÓg where the blessed ones depart after death that allegedly lies way out west."

Drostan caught a slightly mischievous twinkle in the corner of the bard's eye.

"You look anxious! Let me regale you with a tale from a distant age." Clearing his throat, he stretched his neck in readiness to tell his tale.

"Oisín was a handsome warrior from Erin who fell in love with Niamh, a beautiful blonde-haired woman, of exceptional grace and comely of form. She had the most endearing wit that charmed the days and nights away in one unending bliss. Niamh hailed from the otherworld and could tell all manner of fantastic tales. She spoke of a land of joy, where a plain provided abundantly, found by following the honey path of the setting sun over the ocean wave. All who set foot upon its shores were transformed and remained eternally youthful.

"Oisín accompanied Niamh on a magical horse that could gallop across the seas, and they arrived at Tír na nÓg. They passed what seemed like three years there, and although everything was perfect, Oisín became homesick for the folk and land he had left behind. Disappointed that her love in this paradise was not enough, Niamh reluctantly agreed to their returning on the magical horse to his land, but warned that he was not to put a foot upon his home soil. When they arrived in Erin, Oisín found three hundred years had elapsed, and all whom he once knew, were no more. As the couple roamed through the old country in search of something recognisable, Oisín fell from the horse. Within moments, he grew excessively weary. Staggering over to a clear pool, he peered into the face of a very old man, bald and virtually toothless, his skin wrinkled and flaccid. All the years he had been away had overtaken him and he suddenly died."

"You have not lost your ability to tell a good story," Drostan congratulated.

"Let me speak to you concerning a new wonder," continued the old bard with greater enthusiasm. "On the Garvellachs, I met with Brendan, whom they call 'the Navigator', who spoke of his voyages far out west, going from one empty horizon to the next, fearless of coming to the edge of the world." Placing his fishing rod down and securing it under his foot, he leant towards Drostan and spoke in the voice of one who has seen incredible things. "Brendan encountered mountains that spewed fire, shot blazing missiles into the sea, and spoke of crystal halls adrift in the northern sea that rose with an alluring beauty like nothing he had seen before. He saw strange lights that danced with changing colours in the night sky." Ossian chuckled with delight. "He even had an astonishing encounter with an immense whale that came up under their craft, lifting them proud of the waves and remained long enough for them to celebrate the sacraments on Easter morning!"

Ossian picked up the fishing line and re-cast it. "I have also heard these same journeys told by others. As incredible as they are, they have been embellished by storytellers seeking to make ears tingle. I know their craft – it was my own way once. They speak of Brendan reaching the isle of eternal youth – Tír nan nÓg – where they were refused permission to go ashore."

Ossian shook his head with disappointment. "They say that Brendan's journey went in search of Eden! Be that as it may, Brendan did tell me, though, of coming to an uninhabited land of fair climate and plentiful growth at the furthest extremity of his voyage. What seemed of greatest importance to the 'Navigator', was that in seeking to fulfil his own spiritual yearnings, he discovered the Lord's guidance and grace, revealing the wonders of his creation. In a sense, we cannot know the High King better, but rather are more filled with wonder of the mysteries that surround him."

Drostan nodded before quickly interjecting. "I have one question. Why does the High King not call someone experienced, like Brendan, to bear fire to the north?"

Ossian took his time, recasting his line into the water, before answering. "Each are called to be faithful to their own calling. Not all are to pursue a course to the earth's extremities. However, I do believe strange divine stirrings come to many, inciting us towards a heroic quest. After the first flush of excitement passes, many soberly step down to concern themselves with the mundane and the easily achievable. What separates the heroic from the pedestrian is the courage and conviction to take hold of what allures us forward, to the exclusion of all else. It takes faith, trusting that the High King will enable us."

After finishing their evening prayers on another occasion, they remained seated on roughly dressed stones that had tumbled from the walls of the fortress. Drostan opened a subject that he had often considered.

"Tell me about those magic words you spoke to the advancing wolves at the great Stone of Refuge – how did you come by those?"

"What is there to tell?" Ossian said with a shrug of his shoulders. "That was before I knew the King!"

"Well, yes," he said awkwardly. "But I am intrigued. How did you come by those powers?"

"They came from the dark side. At my baptism, I renounced such powers, cast off the wizard's mantle and became a man under the authority of the King." His tone implied an end to the matter.

Drostan remarked by way of conclusion, "Well, I was glad of the powers that you had on that night."

"They were put to good use that night," agreed Ossian. "But those powers are easily used for our own glorification. The more you use them, the greater a control they exert, and you become less of your own person and more the slave to some malevolent power."

Ossian rose to place a pot of water on the fire, bringing the fading embers back to life with some dried heather, and peat from the wind-dried stack.

"I remember the first time I set eyes upon you," recalled Ossian with a smile. "You were so love-struck that you seemed ignorant of what was going on around you!"

"Ah, well – that is the nature of these things." Drostan shifted a little uncomfortably.

"I am not intending to embarrass you. Who has not been in love and loses sense of what is happening around them? It is because I could identify with you, at a critical time in determining the succession, that I took the outcome to heart. I could see that your spirit was upright, that you were the worthier of the two."

Drostan stared, mesmerised by the flames licking at the underside of the cooking pot. Although those events happened a long time ago, he felt ashamed of his distraction. "I knew our initiation was momentous, but I had no idea about the significance of the Z-rod."

"Just as well," remarked Ossian, feeding more dead heather sprigs onto the fire. "Who could stand under such a burden! It is well that the King does not reveal too much concerning the things that lie ahead. If he did, we would run for our lives. Rather, he leads gradually and the experience of overcoming one challenge better prepares for the next. That way, we learn to trust."

Drostan sidled closer to the fire for the wind was harsh. Ossian spoke again. "I had come from the Fortriu (where the warlordship had just been conferred from Galam to Brude) and arrived among the Ce, to find another succession taking place. Those were unsettled times with Dal Riata flexing their muscle, and Angles and Saxons displacing Britons to the south. In that turmoil and great uncertainty, people were seeking a new order to lead them from the brink of chaos."

After a pause, Ossian added significantly. "There was astir, in the souls of some, a spiritual search. We Picts, who are on the extremity, began to feel that the old order was unable to offer a way forward. My meeting with Fillan had been a turning point. Although I was hostile, his compassion challenged my obstinate nature and deflated my proud spirit. The spiritual power and beauty of meekness disarmed the dark forces that accompanied me. The faith he represented may have been on the fringe back in those early days, but it had virtue through his strange humility. The brave gentleness of the soldiers of Christ – even under threat of losing their lives – was something that seized my attention."

"Yes, Fillan was distinctive. His gentle persuasion was rarely assertive," agreed Drostan.

A wisp of steam spiralled briefly up from the lid of the pot, before evaporating in the cold air. The light was fading, and with the shadows deepening over the island, the sea looked cold, more hostile.

"The giving of the Z-rod struck me as hugely significant," continued the old man. "I wonder if the Bulàch, sensing perhaps that you were to be the bearer of liberating power of the true King, had set this mark upon you, as someone to exterminate? She imagined that your sacrifice might put a halt on the King's rule spreading among us."

Drostan found Ossian's thoughts illuminated this disturbing period. "For a long time, I resented the Z-rod. Then when we met under the Stone of Refuge, you reckoned that I would never be the warlord, foreseeing my role as the fire-bearer."

Ossian interrupted him. "I mind we spoke of the gift of fire, rightly revered by man as a gift of God. Druids revere fire – an element used in some sacrifices. What we did not appreciate then was that fire is also the symbol of the Holy Spirit. You are the fire-bearer, the faithful witness who druids will recognise. Go with boldness – be assured that the One who goes with you is far greater than any powers arrayed against you."

After they had eaten, a deep satisfaction came upon them. Drostan remarked, "I saw Alpia at Craig Padrig, and Oengus too!"

"Oh," Ossian muttered but with a tone that implied that he was only mildly interested. Nevertheless, Drostan proceeded to relate the incident of his cousin's final treachery at the pilgrims' camp and of the High King's deliverance; and then Alpia's visit the following day. "She has been sorely afflicted by the whole situation surrounding the Z-rod!" He enumerated the many ways that this was so.

"I detect that love for her has not entirely expired, despite the passing of ten years!"

He shrugged his shoulders, feeling the disappointment and numbness that followed. Eventually, he exclaimed, "She is another man's wife!"

Ossian poked the fire with a stick, and his pensive face clouded over some private reflection.

When Drostan awoke in the morning, he seemed to recall waking in the middle of the night to discover Ossian was no longer beside him in their tiny hovel. A storm had been gathering, and Drostan had left the shelter to observe its extent; thoughts of leaving Inis Gemaich were on his mind, but not in such conditions. The moon, nearly full-orbed, cast a mysterious radiance upon a sea flecked white – its darker portions looking perilous like rippled metal. He scanned for Ossian's presence about the ruins, but saw no trace of him.

Surveying the sea, he recalled seeing a boat struggling in the clutches of the storm, slowly but inexorably drawn towards Inis Gemaich's rocks. Concerned for those sailing, he had prayed for their deliverance. When he had opened his eyes, he thought he had seen a gaunt figure walking on top of the sea, making little of the waves as though walking a firm path. When he reached the stricken vessel, the man took hold of probably a line – something he could not see from that distance – and turning about, the boat followed him beyond the island's point. Drostan had the impression of getting cold, and of returning to the shelter, still to find Ossian absent.

Had it been a dream? He felt his plaid – it was quite damp. The whole night, though, had been punctuated by dreams, leaving him quite confused as to what had been real.

Well, maybe my plaid just got wet in the storm, he thought, when I went out, and these other things had just been part of a dream.

After Ossian woke up, they spoke about the storm that was now blowing over.

"I thought I saw a boat in distress in the middle of the night," remarked Drostan, closely studying the old man's features. "It was close to being dashed upon the rocks."

It seemed to Drostan that Ossian looked disinterested, but nevertheless he decided to continue. "Then, I thought I saw someone walk across the waves to rescue the boat and lead it safely beyond the western cape."

"Oh!" responded Ossian, idly.

Did he perceive Ossian had been taken off his guard?

"Sounds like a dream to me!" Ossian said dismissively as he rose and walked over to the crumbling wall of the fort to look down upon the sea. "It looks like the sea is calming down."

Had he been dreaming? That would be the natural explanation. But Ossian's moment of seeming disquiet, followed by a quick dismissal of the incident, made him wonder.

After another day, the sea grew calmer, and they remarked that this was as good an occasion as any for Drostan to depart for Meini Heyon y Pentir. He was loath, though, to part, knowing that he would not see Ossian again. "Times are passing quickly," he remarked, "and with them, the people of consequence are taken from my life. Fillan has gone before us. My own father, and Coblaith, who was like a mother to me, have given up the ghost. Then there is Colmcille, who though not dead, I am parted from, at a time when I would value his guiding presence."

"You must put into practice what has been learned, and aspire to become what you are destined for."

Drostan nodded his head, but thoughts on life's transience preoccupied him.

"This is the briefest of encounters. You have given me a sense of hope when I felt overwhelmed, and provided guidance when I was unsure of the way. You have strengthened my hand, although I still question why this task has fallen on me."

"It is not for us to question the appointment." Ossian straightened himself after folding a blanket. "Men of faith pass away and leave an inspiring trail, as it were, of brief radiance through the heavens. They did not start as giants – they only became great in proportion to how courage fashioned their faith. But you are not just starting out," smiled Ossian, encouragingly. "Your star is rising, reaching towards its zenith."

Drostan gathered his few possessions and accepted some smoked fish Ossian had hung. They walked without talking, down to the beach where the coracle lay upturned, weighted down by three large stones. Drostan stood immobile, feeling awkward.

Stepping forward, Ossian placed his hands on Drostan's shoulders and held him firm. "This is your time, Drostan – it has been your time ever since you set out from Rhynie. It is not great abilities that God uses, but our surrender to him that he will honour."

Ossian looked him steadily in the eye. "Now let me pray for you." He began a lengthy prayer, full of thanksgiving for this providential encounter, bursting with praise of the King's character. Then, he came to the heart of the prayer. "May Drostan be of steadfast heart, be warrior brave whilst crossing the seas, wise in knowing when the time is ripe to speak boldly. May he be resolute in action when you rouse him."

The old man paused, before recommencing with a more fluent delivery as though he were transmitting words given to him. "Drostan, you are about to receive a most particular hope. Hope that will remain steadfast in the clutch of danger; hope to bear the ordeal and fulfil the quest to a prepared people. Hope shall never perish, for it is not determined by human feelings, but on the assurance that our Lord determines events to their conclusion."

"Thank you, Ossian," he replied, sobered by what lay ahead. "I will take those words to heart."

"You do that. You are not likely to disappoint, but even if you do," Ossian added with a twinkle in his eye, "the High King's purposes are not frustrated by our mistakes – he will work a way around them."

Drostan looked with great fondness on one who had looked out for him since his days at Rhynie, and he held Ossian's benevolent image with fondness and gratitude, as he paddled out to sea. Ossian's ancient features started to dim in his mind, behind which a greater radiance gathered. The brilliance reached an intensity, before finally fading. Emerging from the fog, the purple flower of a thistle appeared, before wilting with the passing of all things. It struck him that Ossian's fading was like the story told about Oisín, and how the fateful falling from a horse suddenly projected Oisín three hundred years forward into abrupt decay. The image of Ossian, though, did not end in decay. Replacing the flower was a clustered bundle of thistle down ready to detach itself from its shaggy crown in a new resurrection.

Chapter Sixteen

Sanctuary

AD 565 Craig Padrig

"Where is Taran?" Alpia asked of the pilgrim who had been leading a meeting in the community, close to the River Rihoh where she had last seen her cousin.

"Do you mean Drostan?"

"Aye, you call him Drostan."

"He left for Iona."

She thought she must have looked crestfallen, to have then been questioned with mild concern, "Do you know him?"

"I once knew him," she found herself uttering rather absent-mindedly. Then, coming to her senses, she added, "We had met again just some days ago, when I came to one of your gatherings."

"Well, you are welcome."

Recognising his accent, she went on to ask, "You are one of the Ce, are you not?"

"Indeed. I am a good friend of Drostan's."

"But . . . you are not from Rhynie, for I do not recognise you. Maybe you had trained with Taran . . ." She paused and corrected herself, "with Drostan, I mean, during his military preparation?"

"No." The man smiled enigmatically, mysteriously adding, "We shared the same mother – at least for a time!"

"What kind of riddle is this? I know Taran's brothers, and you are no son of Domelch!"

"Forgive me, for I am presenting you with a riddle. Let me be straightforward."

She did not reply, but keenly observed the pilgrim's face as it grew serious.

"Drostan stayed with my people after escaping from his cousin."

"Who are your people?"

"You will not know them – they were ordinary, farming folk who lived in the hills beyond the Dee. Elphin and Coblaith were their names; noble in character – as Drostan would attest to – but peasant by birth." He paused, and, angling his head slightly to one side, he seemed to search her.

"And you – the son of peasants – have fared well in life, it would seem!"

He smiled. "My life is a weave of colours – both dark and bright!"

"And whose life is not! Tell me, what is your name?"

"Maon."

"Maon," she repeated confused. "That is no name for a Pict!"

"That is true," he smiled again. "My real name is Munait."

"More riddles?"

"No. It is simple. The Gaels call me Maon." Again, he inclined his head to one side as his grey eyes scanned her once more. "And I am wondering who you might be? A woman of Drostan's age from Rhynie. Drostan was not that long in Rhynie when he was forced to flee. There is only one woman's name whom Drostan mentioned when we used to reminisce about the old country, back on Iona. Would you be Alpia?"

She felt her cheeks flush. So, Taran had spoken about her! A warm sensation welled up from her stomach. She noticed Munait's demeanour had grown grave.

"And that would make you the Lord Oengus's wife?"

She detected a guarded tone in his voice. "Yes, I am." As her husband's attack on the pilgrims' camp had obviously caused consternation, she added, "But you need not fear, I come in peace, I assure you . . . and I hold no malice towards you and your community."

"Then, what brings you here, if I may be so bold as to ask?"

It was her turn now to feel slightly agitated. How was she to represent her circumstances? "I . . . I have no further part with my husband," she confessed with difficulty. How would she be judged? "His attack on your camp was the final straw!"

"Oh! And what do you intend to do?"

"To make a new life here." Recovering from her consternation, she quickly proceeded, "I have Brude's consent to remain where my children are."

She noted the pilgrim's face had softened before a perceptible smile broadened his face. "As I am sure that Drostan would insist, you are to make your home with us."

"Will Drostan be coming back?"

"If the High King wills it."

There was the pilgrims' talk again that sounded strange to her ears. "But as far as you know, did he mention that he hoped to return?" She regretted asking her question the moment it had been asked, for she was being unguarded, and it felt unseemly for a wife — newly separated from her husband — to be asking, with such interest, after another man. She need not feel distraught that Taran was gone. Had he not said it was too late? She composed herself, remembering that her main reason for being there was to be with her children.

Munait gave a perceptible shrug of his shoulders by way of responding to her enquiry, and then, seeming to acquiesce, he inhaled noisily, and added in an expansive manner, "Drostan has been entrusted with a mission of *bearing fire to the north*. As to where exactly that is, he does not know – nor does any man! It weighs heavily upon him, keeping him much in prayer."

"Noble Taran!" she found herself exclaiming involuntarily. "He always had that air of a man set apart for some special destiny! Do you know he bears the Z-rod?"

"Aye, and that puzzled him for a long time. Now, he is much clearer as to what it means."

She waited impatiently for an elaboration that never was presented. "Well, are you going to tell me, or are you leaving me to guess?" She heard her voice sounding a little irritated.

"As you know, it is the sign of lightning – the gift of God that can bring both fire and fruitfulness to the earth. Fire purges, burning and consuming what is destined to perish, preparing the cleared ground for planting and for harvest. As Drostan would attest, *through one you will overcome the world.*"

"You speak of strange things!"

"Indeed. These are not idle words, but prophetic. And the wonder is that some of the prophecies were not all uttered by pilgrims, but were entrusted to a wandering bard."

"Oh . . . you mean Ossian?"

"I believe that is his name. Ossian was a chosen wanderer, entrusted with a heavenly message."

"Drostan spoke about strange things uttered to him on a hillside above Rhynie years back, which he could not recall at the time, other than to be cunning, brave and . . . what was it? Something that did not make sense at the time, about his need to be *humble*!" She paused, as her mind wandered back more than a decade. "I witnessed that part of the prophecy being worked out, when he was being held, against his wishes, in a crannog. Drostan was cunning and brave, outwitting Oengus." She felt her former admiration rising again, a signal emotion that most emphatically accompanied thoughts of the cousin she had always most respected.

"It is not all about Drostan's skill and ability to survive against the odds. Yes, Drostan is warrior-brave, but no way could he have prevailed if it were not for the High King – and the help of others. My parents cared for him . . ."

"So, from the crannog, Drostan found your parents?"

"Yes, and they nurtured him, for he had broken his arm."

"He broke his arm?"

"Aye – when escaping from the crannog, he fell from his horse, deep into a ravine."

"Oh, poor man!"

"Anyway," she noticed how keen he seemed to move on, "the High King preserved him through the Minamoyn Goch where he had a mysterious encounter with Ossian under what he called the Stone of Refuge. I should not say 'mysterious', because in hindsight, it is apparent that this was a divine appointment. The bard strengthened his resolve, directing him on his destiny to be nurtured again, this time spiritually, under Fillan's care."

"It seems that Drostan has had many adventures!"

"Yes, and they are not over."

She felt him surveying her keenly for a moment.

"And what about you?" he pursued, before continuing with his speech. "You appear to have undergone a series of adventures that have led you here?"

"I do not know if I have been led here!" Was this pilgrim going to suggest that she was there because of the hand of his High King?

"Whatever way you may look at it, our journeys are not driven by blind chance, nor by the fickle ways of the gods of the Ce . . ."

She interrupted him effusively. "I do not hold faith in the Bulàch anymore! What good has she or all the others of her kind done during our dire need at Rhynie?"

She felt him observe her closely, before he spoke once more. "Maybe you are ready to be reconciled with the One who holds all power – who reaches out in compassion?"

"You would have me be a pilgrim?" She felt her heart beating with indignation. No one was going to force that upon her.

"It is not for me to coerce, only to indicate the futility of the old ways. Although we can seem to stumble blindly on, there is One – maybe hidden to you at this time – who is directing your ways, offering salvation from out of the destruction you have experienced."

Thoughts of Oengus came to mind, the self-made man bent on supremacy through all his wily scheming. Where had that brought him? He had been on the brink of destruction for some time. She detested his ways. But what about herself? Was she not walking the same self-made way, in denial of higher powers? There was a time when she thought that the goose could exact an influence that would lead to good outcomes; a notion planted there by her aunt. But that which was to no avail, had led her into a hapless marriage. It seemed the only power in this world was the brute force of man's will, like the rise of the boar, which proved no match for the supremacy of the bull. In her estimation of things, the High King did not rule over all. Man's ambition appeared to be the driving force that shaped events, determining whether one would be spared, another maimed, and the more fortunate in her eyes laid to the dust. She had been spared and was now reunited with her beloved children. They were all that mattered; they were her world for whom she willed to live.

"It has been interesting meeting you, Munait . . ." She paused with deliberation. "I should call you Maon, though, for you have turned your back on the ways of the Picts." She paused, considering that she was perhaps too quick to condemn. "Truly, I appreciated learning about my cousin. I often wondered what became of him after his escape and how he would fare."

"I am still a Pict, and proud to be one."

So, I had ruffled him, she observed.

"I am a Pict who acknowledges the true King, one who can stand firm in the knowledge that my Lord is closer to me than a sword is to a warrior."

"If you are a Pict, then you should abide by your name of Munait."

"That may be so," he conceded.

She turned to leave, aware of her own haughtiness. However, she wanted to depart giving no impression of wanting to embrace an ideology that particularly sounded so foreign to the world she knew.

"Wait! Do you have a place to stay?"

"I do at Craig Padrig," she replied, half-turning to face him. She was somewhat anxious about how arrangements would work out. "My boys are both in the service of the king."

"You would be welcome to make your home here."

Had he detected the concern she felt?

"Mind you," elaborated Munait, "our life is simple here, without the finery of Brude's court, and our fare is most ordinary."

"Oh that! That is the least of my concerns. Our ways are not . . ." She stopped to correct herself, "were not so grand at Rhynie. We were always the poor relative to the Fortriu – particularly since we were humbled into submission."

"You are among friends here!" Munait added, with genuine warmth. "In our community, there is no distinction between Fortriu and Ce, Pict or Gael. Come, let me introduce you to a family who would be glad to take you in. You can remain with them until such time a home can be built for you and your wee girl. We are not far from Craig Padrig, so it will be easy for you to come and go to see your sons."

"Well . . . I am not sure."

"Unsure of our ways and our motives?"

She noted how perceptive he was. He was also humble, not to have taken offence at her words intended to ruffle his patience. This humility thing is quite foreign, she considered. "Be humble" was the injunction that had puzzled Taran all those years back, and she could recall how it had exercised her mind too. And yet it had served Taran! He might be a pilgrim she did not understand, but had he not oddly risen in the world with a nobility that Oengus never possessed, despite all the vestments of power that her husband liked to clothe himself with? And yet, Taran and Colmcille – for all their nobility – had that common touch, winsome with the ordinary folk, which she so admired. Why was she so antagonised, though, in the presence of these pilgrims?

"That is most kind," she responded finally to Munait's invitation. "It would be easier to be here than be regarded as some kind of chattel in Brude's court. I am well acquainted with humiliation, but I do not go courting it."

When Alpia went up to Craig Padrig three days later, King Brude greeted her, which struck her as odd for he did not usually pay her any attention. She noted that more people than usual were seated in the hall. "It would seem that your husband has been slain along with many others!" His face was dead pan awaiting her reaction.

"Slain, my lord?" She felt confused, but not cut to the core. "What has happened?"

"It seems some bloody insurrection is taking place. Talorc, and other discontents, are on a killing rampage, eager to rid themselves of Oengus's household! It seems you managed to escape."

"Talorc! He is a mere youth," she remarked involuntarily. "Why is he bent on doing this?"

"Youth does not mind where it sets its foot," the king replied.

Just then, she recognised Aunt Conchen and Derile at a small table below the King's dais. Her aunt looked diminished.

"Go – join your fellow Ce," he gestured graciously with an arm extended towards her people. His manner surprised and she did not delay, keen to learn about the turmoil she had escaped.

Aunt Conchen half-rose on recognising her, but Alpia had moved so swiftly that she forced her aunt to be seated. They hugged and were silent. She felt her aunt's body shaking and became aware of her sobbing. She kept her eyes closed, caught up in her own maelstrom of emotions difficult to fully comprehend, and languished in that embrace that was like a place of sanctuary. When she opened her eyes, they met with Derile looking on, who by this time had risen and was holding her arm. Derile's face was red, her eyes swollen from crying. Wiping her eyes with her sleeve, Derile managed to utter, "Alpia, I thought you had been slain with the rest!"

"Who else, apart from Oengus, has been killed?"

"Talorc killed my mother . . ." A new wave of grief broke over Derile.

Aunt Conchen, who had recovered sufficiently by this time, took up the story. "I had warned Oengus that I did not like the look of Talorc and his companions." After this brief comment, her eyes hardened, "Did you know about their plot?"

"Plot! No, of course not. How could I?" Alpia was aghast by the suggestion.

"Everything happened immediately after you had returned to Rhynie. You suddenly disappeared with Rowena as soon as you had emerged in our midst, and I could not help noticing that you had acted strangely."

Alpia could understand how it might have looked, but the insinuation shocked her that for a moment, she was at a loss of what to say. "Aunt! My mysterious behaviour was because I had decided to leave Oengus and bring Rowena with me to be with my boys. I had no idea what was about to take place!"

Her aunt examined her closely, with a stern expression. Alpia was relieved when her aunt's face relaxed into the merest suggestion of a smile. "That is what I thought after you had gone. But then the killings started, making me wonder whether you were in the know. It is well that you left when you did . . ." She paused, seeming, to Alpia, to be catching up with her racing thoughts. "You and Rowena would not have been spared the slaughter."

"How did you both escape?"

Derile was the one who answered. "I was returning home after drawing water from the stream. It was just going dark. Normally, I would have been cooking after sunset. However, we had run out of water – the gods spared me through this inconsequential need!" She stopped to wipe her eyes which had suddenly filled with tears. "I heard my mother's dreadful screams. I saw her run out of the house with Talorc's men in pursuit . . ." She wiped her nose with the back of her hand. "I saw her hacked down and I turned and ran."

"That was when you ran into me," Aunt Conchen took up the story. "I was on my way home after visiting Domelch when the shrieking started. It felt like the air itself was astir with all the murderous commotion taking place. How terrible to see such things happen done by our own people! Derile took me by the hand, and I ran as fast as my old legs would take me, which is not fast. But we hastened, as best we could, and soon were in the darkness of the forest, delivered from all the carnage."

"How amazing that you both escaped!" Alpia added with particular emphasis, "Certainly, neither of you would have been spared with your close associations with Oengus."

"We did not know where to go!" Derile continued to relate the events, "but remaining near Rhynie was not a choice. I had thought about returning to Migdele, but there is a change in warlord there and, as you know, the old hostilities have resurfaced."

"I said, let us go to the Fortriu," her aunt interjected, "for many of our finest men were brought here – men we know, who would show mercy towards us. Besides, since the tribute payments are still being made, King Brude has a commitment to protect us. So, we found shelter and succour among our own kin this side of the Spey. They were the ones who urged us to come to the king and they brought us here this day."

"What has the king said?" asked Alpia.

"Not much." Derile shrugged her shoulders. "It seems he will let the murders run their course until all that spleen is spent!"

"He will want to bring order again, for an impoverished people will be unable to pay him the same tribute."

Alpia noticed that her aunt had recovered her sharp insight. Just then, Drustan joined their group and held her hand.

"Is this . . ." Aunt Conchen hesitated in a sense of wonderment. "Is this Drustan?"

"It is," Alpia confirmed and, turning to her boy, encouraged, "Go and greet Aunt Conchen."

"You are becoming quite the young man!" Aunt Conchen said admiringly. "I hardly recognised you – you have grown since I last saw you."

It struck Alpia how fortunate her boys had been taken into exile; something she would never have deemed a positive. With the dawning realisation of being spared the horror of the blood-let, she felt immense relief; and especially thankful to be reunited with her beloved aunt.

But what of Oengus? she considered. Despite the animosity and contempt that characterised their relationship, she would not have wished him such an end. However, his rule was bound to be contested, sooner or later.

"Where will you stay?" she asked her aunt.

"I do not know. We are appealing to the king's clemency."

"You should join me at the muintir."

"What is that?"

"The community of pilgrims."

"You have not become one, have you?" A trace of disdain was discernible in her aunt's voice.

"No, I am not a pilgrim. But they are a peaceful people, hospitable and kind. You will find a welcome among them, as I have found."

"Do you mind those two miserable fellows we had to endure that the Lord Cynbel had sent to Rhynie? Who would ever want to be a pilgrim after their example!"

"Well, I think you might be pleasantly surprised by the pilgrims who live here. Gael and Pict live in harmony – even the animosity between the Fortriu and the Ce is not evident amongst them. Muintir is their word for family – that is what they are to one another."

Aunt Conchen did not look convinced, but desisted from her objections. She changed the subject. "Where is Caltram?"

"He will not be here until the evening meal. He is busy with his military training."

"Oh, I long to see him. It has been too long!"

Chapter Seventeen

The Cross of Stones

AD 565-566AD Meini Heyon y Pentir

The seas, never truly quietening after the storm, caused Drostan's coracle to spin, buck and dip. Waves splashed into the craft, making for frantic baling and causing him to wonder whether he could remain afloat. Wet through, the cold gnawed through to the bone and impeded his movements, and his clothes chafed his skin.

Recalling the psalm sung from Iona's shore, one line stood out which he began to repeat with increasing fervency: *They cried out to the Lord in their trouble, and he brought them out of their distress.*

Huge seas raised him to the heights of great crests then dragged him powerfully down into the troughs in a sickening sensation. Numbed by chill, his knuckles closed around the paddle that helped maintain some balance, and his ankles became bruised against the coracle's willow frame. Although his stomach experienced great hunger, it was the sense of impending doom that made him most sick. Twice, he saw the huge bulk of basking sharks run close by, their jaws wide open, sifting the sea for small feed. He envied their ability to glide effortlessly through what was, for him, a turbulent upheaval.

Then night fell, fiendishly dark, and he despaired of ever surviving this wild sea. The blackness was full of unanticipated waves that swamped his craft time and again, keeping him baling more often than paddling.

He repeated his single line from the psalm, *They cried out to the Lord in their trouble, and he delivered them out of their distress,* clinging to the hope that he was in God's hands and that his King, not only knowing of his whereabouts, had also purposed him to be there. Confessions of faith kept him mentally alert through the dreadful dark – a night that seemed unending like no other. The undiminishing perils assailed, slowly crushing his spirit, as wave upon wave buffeted him into unknown darkness and turmoil.

He considered how many men of Erin, going about their white martyrdom, had been swamped and spun in the same helpless manner? How many did reach land? Did they despise life so much as to be so recklessly abandoned? Or were the thoughts of being with their Lord of such supreme consideration that they readied themselves to depart from this world? What was the mettle of his own faith, if he were not ready to embrace this death and consider it only a portal through which to enter the courts of the High King?

By now he was thoroughly chilled, convulsed by uncontrollable shivering.

Tiring of the futility of his own thinking, he chanted aloud, "*They cried out to the Lord in their trouble, and he brought them out of their distress.*" The repetition of this one-liner was not sung as a charm, but as a faithfilled plea to focus his mind from being wholly overwhelmed.

The occasional star, seen between the wind-driven clouds, began to pale and look uncertain. Was his vision impaired? Certainly, his weariness was like none other he had ever known. Could he trust his senses to perceive things correctly, in all the commotion of the Great Western Sea? He stared at the shadowy forms of the clouds sweeping past, wondering whether these were paling to presage the coming of a new day.

"*Hope in the face of despair,*" he spoke aloud, reminding himself of the eighth grace of the prophecy.

Most decidedly, daylight had begun the slow process of diluting the night. Forms reappeared, at first spectral, then more substantial, gladdening his heart. He laughed out loud having been preserved through what surely had been the worst of the storm.

Then a wave came, unanticipated, that flipped the whole craft, pitching him into freezing water. He flailed about in the panic of being immersed into such cold water, and, with horror, saw his upturned coracle move away from him. Taking control of his shallow breathing that had quickened, he purposefully trod water and more slowly moved his arms for buoyancy, consciously opposing the frantic thoughts that would have him already defeated in the catastrophe. Summoning all his efforts, he flexed his muscles in the numbing inertia of the freezing water and swam towards the swamped coracle. Not being a strong swimmer, he wondered whether he could reach his craft that continued to drift away, realising that he had to reach the coracle within the next few moments whilst some strength remained in his limbs. His arms felt heavy, ineffectual in their quest. He paused to tread water and to master his breathing that had again become shallow, unable to satisfy his lungs.

Be calm, he told himself, recalling the instruction in his military training when facing a foe. Once again, he repeated the line – this time in his head, because the effort to give it voice was too great – *They cried out to the Lord in their trouble, and he delivered them out of their distress.*

He swam in a deliberately slower manner, more measured, applying greater strength to his strokes. Repeating Fillan's prophetic prayer – *hope in the face of despair* – countered the inner panic that would have him believe he was doomed. Not doubting that his one-time anam cara had been inspired to utter that line for this very moment, he clung to its significance, gathering faith to emerge from this ordeal and to fulfil his destiny as the fire-bearer. The coracle seemed closer, almost seemingly held in the turbulence, permitting him to approach. Not being taken by surprise, his Lord had mysteriously and inexplicably ordained such a crisis. Drostan looked into the face of death and, defying it, declared that this was a necessary rite of passage through which he would emerge to fulfil his purpose.

On taking hold of the coracle, an elation broke through him like a burst of hot energy. "Thank you, thank you, thank you!" he repeated, offering praise to his Saviour. Clinging to the upturned craft, he rested his aching limbs, grateful to have this floating aid amidst the unruly waves.

Marvellously preserved through one disaster, he became acutely aware that his whole body was facing the threat of becoming inert. How much longer can I withstand this chill? he thought. He called out to the Lord in his great distress and moved his legs and free arm, not with hope of propelling himself towards land, but to create a flicker of warmth through his tiring muscles. He would yet defy death.

I need not fear death, for Christ has mastery over it. Death was nothing more than a portal through which every human had to pass. Resurrection had swallowed fear, deposing a dreadful ogre. The thought of casting off the shackles of an ailing body, to rise with scintillating newness before the presence of the King himself, became a wondrous thought.

Do not think of death, he told himself, for surely it is not yet for I have not accomplished what I have been called to do. What was to be made of the providences of God should I perish here? Then an insidious thought slithered into his thinking from nowhere. Have I been hugely mistaken by the call? Have the prophecies just been a coincidence of man's own making? If that were so, then what of my faith – have I lived for a lie?

He recalled that during the days of his military preparation, he had pictured death as the valiant warrior. After overwhelming many foes, he would finally be run through by a sword; and whilst dying, he would be raised by comrades praising his feats. His escapades would be immortalised in the halls of warlords, by bards who knew how to elaborate a hero's tale and make it even more splendid. Perishing alone at sea, though, seemingly to no avail, appeared futile.

An enormous protest arose against these questions and doubts. He determined to believe, for there were many evidences of the High King's deliverance over the past years, preserving him through the strife, readying him for a greater quest. To choose not to believe would seem to take greater faith. He recalled Ossian's words at their parting, concerning hope that would remain steadfast in the clutch of danger – a hope that would never perish; hope that was not based on human feelings, but on the High King's character and will to bring about all that had been prophesied.

Coming to mind was that image of Alpia at Beltane in all her beguiling loveliness, looking upon him with her slightly enigmatic smile. The picture changed into the person he had recently encountered, broken by his cousin. If only fate had not intervened, she would have been my wife. Had she not declared her love for me from the time I had been ousted? If only I had known, I would have been comforted in my lone distress. But then, such love appearing unattainable, might have deepened my despair! Although I might be unable to undo any of her misfortune, the High King could. Feeling life ebbing away from him, he prayed for Alpia and the tender-faced Drustan.

As the pale white orb of the sun peered blearily through the massed clouds upon the horizon, he knew this was the moment for matins. He pictured his brothers back on Iona, kneeling on the rough stone floor within the oratory. Colmcille would be there, who, gifted with second sight, might possibly be aware of his great distress.

Daylight was gathering apace. On riding the crest of a wave, he caught a glimpse of land. It was not just the mountain tops he could see, but the entirety of an island. However, it was still far off that to hope to drift there and remain alive, seemed most unlikely – even if the tides were favourable. Although swimming that distance seemed impossible, he nevertheless made small strokes in that direction, stealing a little time from the dying process. Again, he whispered his one-liner, and taking great comfort from it, willed his voice to be louder, until he succeeded in repeating the chant as a demonstration of his resilient spirit. He recalled Colmcille's deep, resounding bass, strangely throbbing with its ponderous, unearthly reverberation that disturbed the pagan ear; and though he could not imitate such a compelling voice, he sensed

Colmcille singing with him there. He would blend his song with the chanted psalms that his brothers were singing back on Iona. He would use his dying breath to praise the majesty of the King with all that his unvanquished spirit could muster. He would go down to the depths with praise spluttering from his lips.

They cried out to the Lord in their trouble, and he brought them out of their distress, once again became the defiant, rallying call, channelling every vestige of willpower to remain afloat. His chanting took on a rhythm, taking its beat from the water lapping the hull of his coracle.

What was that? Thinking he had heard a voice, he looked about, but saw nothing. Had he imagined the sound?

"Hello there!" sounded a human voice, not far off.

Drostan managed to slowly rotate the sunken coracle towards the direction from where the sound had come. To his amazement, a large boat, with its sail flapping to reduce its speed, was approaching.

"Help! Over here!" he called.

After nearly coming to a halt, the sail was pulled in slightly to give the vessel some headway. Picking up speed, the boat passed him, then went about and very slowly drifted directly towards him, head into wind.

"Thank you, Lord!" he cried out. He started to laugh.

When the boat came alongside, his arm was securely taken hold of. How extraordinary they should be there, he thought. How comforting to be held, despite the hurt, knowing that his ordeal was over.

Lowering the sail, the crew detached the halyard from the top of the sail and fastened a rope at its end. "Pass the loop over your head and arms," instructed one of the sailors. His arms were so numb and unresponsive that he felt hands assisting him. Then the halyard, taking up the strain, lifted him out of the depths. Safely aboard, many explanations followed. With his replies only being monosyllabic, the sailors suggested answers that he could either agree with or dismiss, and soon they began to piece together his story.

"But you, how . . ." Drostan was unable to finish.

"How did we outrun the storm?" someone suggested. It was not the question he had uppermost in his mind, but he nodded, thinking it would help explain how they had found him.

"We were caught in the storm and driven off course last night, whilst trying to make for home," began a broad-shouldered man in his mid-forties, who seemed in charge of the vessel. "Unable to make it back to land, we kept ourselves on a course to keep us out in the open seas during the dark, in fear of running on to skerries. At daybreak, we started to make for home. No sooner had we trimmed the sail to take us westward, we heard your strange singing carried downwind."

"You are ever so lucky!" remarked another sailor, shaking his head in disbelief.

"I am so very thankful . . ."

"Thankful that we happened to come by at this moment and in your location?" volunteered the skipper.

"Aye. But I am thankful . . ." Still the effort to marshal his thoughts and master his tongue seemed too much. Later, he was able to comment, "I believe I was chanting my last. Truly, I am thankful for the King sending you to these waters at this prescribed time!"

"The timing and the coincidence are exceptional! Surely your God heard you," the skipper observed.

"Are these not exceptional days though!" remarked another. "We heard, only the other day, of a currach being driven by a storm towards the rocky cliffs of Inis Gemaich. The sailors swore they were on a collision course, and nothing could prevent them from being dashed against the rocks. Then a strange figure emerged, an old man they said, walking the waters as though it were firm ground. Extraordinarily, he took hold of their line and pulled them safely around the point. I mean, who can believe such a thing happening?"

"Well, I can," responded another. "The sea is a place where miracles happen – and have we not just witnessed another?"

Drostan smiled.

After making landfall and resting for five days in the home of one of the sailors, he continued his journey north towards Meini Heyon y Pentir, which was "just four islands away". Fresh supplies were given along with a replacement paddle. Still recovering from his ordeal, he took his time along the leeward reach of the eastern coast. Beyond the hills, featureless ground sprawled, semi-submerged, with extensive tidal flats, appearing like a raft of land floating upon the sea. Pitching camp there, he discovered an interior without habitation, pockmarked by a vast profusion of lochans. At the end of the second day, at the extremity of the third island, he looked out across a broad sound. Meini Heyon y Pentir lay beyond on the great isle to the north, whose lofty peaks rose in charcoal hues into the brooding cloud across the shallow sea of sunken reefs and protruding rocks.

Calm weather on the third day enabled him to navigate through the skerry-strewn sound, where barely submerged reefs threatened to tear his leather hull with their serrated edges. Glad of fine weather, he reached the fourth island without issue, and now was forced to voyage along its western coast exposed to the full force of the Great Western Sea. Sweeps of extensive bays, bright with white sands and backed by dunes bristling with marram grass, with the lush machair beyond, presented a kind aspect of the land. But the hills beyond appeared to his imagination to have boiled over, out of the cauldron of creation, into an enormous outpouring of rock. Great whorls of rocky extrusions, rising under a blue sky, knitted together a rugged landscape by which he plotted his progress. He followed beneath a range of hills that ran a long way westward, undulating in diminishing sweeps until the ridge finally plunged under the sea. A long tongue of white sand ran beneath a strait of turquoise-coloured shallows, to rise once more in one final hill to form the nearby island. Making landfall on a beach, he surveyed the desolate coast beyond whilst the brisk wind combed the daisies, buttercups and tiny orchids in endless waves of motion that were mesmerising to the eye. Overjoyed by the pristine beauty that lay at the edge of such monumental ruggedness, he decided to camp there.

The frail life of the machair existing between the ocean's breakers and the harsh upheavals of rock struck him as representative of his own life, surviving despite the huge odds opposing him. Heaven's hand had preserved him in extreme and extenuating circumstances. His heartfelt praise to his Saviour overflowing with relief and thankfulness, picked up the refrain: *They cried out to the Lord in their trouble, and he delivered them out of their distress.* Hope founded on the High King's promise, rising out of his greatest ordeal, had resulted in great peace. That hope brought assurance that all would be well, despite appearances and his feelings of utter vulnerability. With such a Champion on his side, who or what need he fear? It had been a hard lesson, though, the trauma of which he had to share with the household who had cared for him as he repeatedly spoke about his near-death experience. He came back, time and again, to the hand that spared him.

He thought of Alpia again, and of their strained meeting and the sad eyes of the boy that oddly shared his own pseudonym. He felt compassion for them and recalled how he had prayed for their preservation when his own was most at stake. Would Alpia take his counsel and leave Oengus to be with her children?

The sun sank behind a bank of cloud upon the ocean's horizon, and it grew cooler. Amidst the perils of his journey, the High King's constancy remained a reassuring light infusing the clouds with golden benevolence at the day's end. Although the needs to make a campfire and to find food beckoned, the moment of gratitude and assurance lingered so long that the hour became hallowed; too holy to be disturbed by attending to mundane chores.

On his fourth day, he passed a coast indented by lengthy sea lochs; and for once, he was glad to be travelling by coracle, for walking would have entailed extensive detours inland. Nevertheless, encountering the capricious draw of tidal currents drained him.

"Where are you going?" called out a fisherman.

"Meini Heyon y Pentir! Is it far away?" he replied, hollering across the water. He paddled closer to the man who likewise leisurely brought his own coracle towards him.

The stranger had a benevolent grin and an easy air. "You are going to the stones?" he asked, not concealing his surprise. "It is quite a distance!"

Drostan fatalistically shrugged his shoulders, took note of the directions, then parted. Rounding a headland, he made camp for another night, eating the last of his provisions.

"I will fish tomorrow," he determined aloud, as he lay down under his coracle. Soon, the sleep of the weary engulfed him.

By the time a fish took his line the following morning it was near midday. Still, I am in no hurry, he reminded himself, appeasing the sense that he should really be on his way. He was content to have an easier day of paddling which brought him eventually to a narrow strait. Two fish, caught on a trailing line, provided for an evening meal and a breakfast. That afternoon, he saw the great stones of Meini Heyon y Pentir bristling the low skyline close to shore. Have I reached the end of my quest? he thought, as he climbed the rise to the stones. Eight quests had been fulfilled and here I am at *the very ends of the earth.* He came to a substantial monument, far more elaborate than the stone circle on the hill above Rhynie. The stones rose high and sparkled in the sunshine with an alluring sheen.

As he wandered about, he was struck by two things. Firstly, the stones had been surprisingly arranged in a cross formation, encircled about the intersection by more stones. Secondly, he was surprised by the absence of human activity in that sacred space, for the grass was long, untrodden by the feet of worshippers. A short distance from the stones were some round houses, where he found an old woman knitting in the doorway of her hut.

"No one bothers worshipping at the stones anymore," she responded to his question.

Can I have come to the right place? he thought. Had Ossian been mistaken and spoken of their reputation from a bygone era when the stones attracted people from as far as Gaul?

The old woman showed a surprising indifference to the magnificence of these colossal structures that must have taken past communities a monumental effort to erect.

"Is there a druid in these parts?" he enquired.

"There is Fotel. He is regarded as something of a druid, I suppose." The old woman yawned, revealing a toothless mouth.

"What do you mean by 'something of a druid'?"

"Fotel is the one we consult about the times to sow – or if, for example, there is some dispute, then the matter is taken to Fotel."

"And does he treat sick people? Is he able to cure?"

"Aye, right enough, sick people go to Fotel, too."

"It sounds like he is a druid!"

When the farming folk started returning from their day's labour, a short and stout man, with a preoccupied air, came over to him. "I hear you have been asking for me?"

"Are you Fotel?" Drostan asked uncertainly, for the man had not shaved his hair in druid fashion.

"I am. You are not from these parts, then?"

"No. I have travelled a long way and almost lost my life at sea . . ."

"Uh?" he uttered, idly curious.

Drostan gave him the details.

"Seems like you have been preserved for a purpose," he uttered meaningfully.

"Those are my own thoughts. Such things do not happen by chance, do they? I mean, consider a vast sea and how small a human head appears between the breaking wave tops. Then comes the wonder of a vessel, precisely where I was, hearing my chanting above the sounds of the ocean. It is wondrous, is it not?"

"So, why have you come?" Fotel asked with aroused interest.

"I will tell you. But first, let me ask whether you are a druid?"

"Well, I used to be. I was brought up in the tradition . . ." He hesitated, before adding, "Times are changing, would you not say?"

"How do you mean?"

"There is less regard for the old ways. People are intent on making their living, and . . . well I think that is their right to choose. They still look to me for advice, or to act as judge in community matters." Fotel paused, before asking, "Which druid master did you study under?"

"I am a druid of Christ," he said, pausing to collect his thoughts. "Let me explain. I come in fulfilment of a prophecy of bearing fire to the north which will be for the fulfilment of the learned ones anticipating the dawn of a new era." Drostan studied his face. Fotel looked attentive, but not surprised.

"Who is this Christ?" enquired the druid with mild interest.

Drostan expanded, and was frequently interrupted by questions, although Fotel kept gesturing impatiently with his hand not to stop. At least he is getting more interested, thought Drostan.

"I should like to hear more – but tomorrow. This could be important for the whole community . . . but first, I need to understand properly."

"Very well," Drostan replied, sensing that perhaps the long, hazardous journey had not been in vain. And yet, he observed, Fotel's interest was not that of a learned one anticipating his arrival. About to part company, he asked, "Are there other druids near Meini Heyon y Pentir?"

"No, I am the only one in these parts. There are others, but they are far away."

The prophecy did allude to going to the learned *ones*. But then, he reasoned with himself, would this message not find a more ready acceptance with a druid who had already sensed the passing of the old order? If Fotel acknowledged the High King, then he might lead other druids into this knowledge.

"Have you a place to stay?" asked Fotel.

"No, I know no one in these parts."

"Then, you had better stay with me," he said without much enthusiasm.

Over the coming days, they discussed much. He was puzzled by Fotel, for he could not decide whether the druid was either slow to understand, or more reluctant to believe. He appeared interested, but was dull in the uptake – bringing encouragement and despair in the same breath. He found others in the community indifferent, preoccupied about their daily industry of fishing and farming than interested in the powers that governed the seasons and the tides; although they did indicate that they might take note if he could first convince Fotel.

Days turned into weeks, and this passing of time did not escape his host's attention. "Are you planning on staying the winter?"

"Most definitely," he replied, not relishing the thought of winter travel.

"Then, it would be well if we were to help you build your own hut. That way, you will become more of a permanent part of the community."

The village gathered stone and turf, and his small shelter was soon complete. He was glad of their help, yet troubled by their apathy. Perhaps with patient explanation, together with demonstrating his faithfulness to the High King, they would take note.

Many a start, though, was punctuated by a whole series of disappointments. "Look at the cross formation of the stones," he remarked one day, having many times walked up the central avenue, flanked by the colonnade of stone monoliths. "Surely this cross has significance, a sign that will have remained a mystery for generations, that now I can explain. Is there another standing stone arrangement like it in all the land?" He turned to Fotel, hoping to witness that conviction he himself felt.

"Well, yes . . . I would have to concede that it does seem significant!"

Was he on the cusp of accepting, thought Drostan, just needing some other evidence to corroborate this testimony? He thought of all that had passed at Craig Padrig: the attending miracles demonstrating God's power and compassion; the raising of a dead boy; subduing the demonic beast; being preserved from Oengus's mounted charge . . . If the High King would only demonstrate his supremacy in such a way to these apathetic people, then surely they would believe? He prayed for a sign that would usher in the dawn.

With the passing of time, and nothing miraculous happening, he doubted himself. He struggled with the idea that if he were Colmcille, this community would have been convinced long ago. To counteract his mounting sense of inadequacy, he recalled that many at Craig Padrig remained stoic in their old beliefs, despite the contrary evidence. Had the druids not tried to frustrate their departure with the opposing wind? Although he would not claim to have the gift of healing, the High King had used him with Aleine Brona and could do so again here, should he so choose.

Winter passed into spring. Grain had been sown and the lambing season was upon them. He took the opportunity to celebrate Easter at the intersection of the avenue of stones, where a burial chamber was situated. He was encouraged by a good number of people responding to his invitation to join him.

"Those buried in this tomb, according to your beliefs, have passed through this earth portal to the isles of the blessed way out west. That is their hope, but who can be sure of being righteous enough in this life to be granted passage to the place of eternal youth? No one has come back to life and emerged from this cairn, have they? Death has had mastery over each." He scanned the faces, and noting their interest, felt encouraged to make his point.

"Christ rose from a tomb. Two days he had been dead and then, on the third day, he was raised to life!"

The crowd stood still, and he thought them attentive; but maybe their interest was nothing more than fascination in a tale from a faraway land?

"Who has shown mastery over death and removed the guilt of mankind? Has any one of your gods done such a thing? Has any heavenly power assured a certain passage to paradise?"

They looked engaged, and no one raised a word of objection. However, conviction was missing. After praying, they went homeward, talking about crops and livestock, a new baby and a dying man.

Beltane followed soon after Easter, when the village again gathered at the ancient stones where Fotel presided over a ceremony that Drostan was familiar with. He noted how impassive the druid went through the rituals, an indifference echoed by those attending. They departed, much in the same mood as after the Easter celebration, satisfied that a ritual had been observed lest ill-fortune occur should they have been absent. The occasion provided an excuse, too, for merriment to alleviate the weariness of their toil.

He recalled the word of knowledge Fillan had spoken: *The beam of light shall penetrate into the chamber of the dead and those who were dead shall be made alive,* and tried to apply this to the burial cairn at the intersection of stones. It did not make sense there at Meini Heyon y Pentir, where the light from the rising or the setting of the two solstice celebrations did not shine through the portal of the tomb. He considered that maybe the meaning was more metaphorical than actual?

He had been loaned a strip of land which kept him busy with the sowing of oats and the cultivation of a few vegetables, none of which were ready to gather. He depended upon bartering the fish he caught for other commodities like milk, cheese and eggs. The occasional goodwill of his neighbours also provided for other needs.

As days lengthened into summer, Fotel's mood changed. What had started as a promising attitude had become one of scepticism. "Trusting in a God of some faraway nation does not seem so relevant for us here . . ." he paused, before adding in a slightly mocking mimicry, "at *the ends of the earth*!"

"He is not just the God of one nation. All of Erin has become Christian, along with Dal Riata, and many in Alt Clud. Even amongst us Picts, communities worship Christ."

"Then I stand corrected, for these peoples are neighbouring us," Fotel acquiesced after briefly laughing dismissively over his own doubts.

Had it not been for the prophetic words Drostan had received, for the certainty of men like Colmcille, and the hunch of Ossian in directing him here, he would have given up. Ten years had taught him to be patient, to persevere in his teaching and try new approaches. He recalled the broken arrow sign up on that high wintry pass, indicating that the battle was the Lord's, that the victory was his if he remained assured in that hope. Had the High King not also given peace in the quest fulfilled on Munnir Esprid, a peace that could withstand discouragements, acknowledging that man could not produce seasons of enlightenment? The gift of hope had been acquired during his shipwreck, a gift to be exercised, choosing hope over despair. As for valour and zeal, was he not demonstrating that every day, like a ready-warrior utilising every skill, fastening on the heavenly armour through daily prayer? Maybe he was lacking in love? He recollected the time at the foot of the great waterfall, when, overwhelmed by the Father's love, he had been affirmed in the servant-hearted love demonstrated towards Carvorst. Surely, though, was he not demonstrating that same loving patience here with the slow-understanding Fotel and the apathy of this community?

Fotel never showed hostility. He was always ready to debate, encouraging him to labour on, unlike other people who only expressed a passing interest in what he had to share before dismissing it. Visitors came, wise men and druids and healers, all of whom listened, fascinated by the parables and the histories of the patriarchs and the prophets. He concluded, though, that they were more entertained rather than felt a need to consider the Creator God.

Again, he thought that he was the barrier, that if a servant like Colmcille had come, people would be convinced. He again prayed, many times, for some sign to cause wonder that would break through their indifference – but nothing happened. His sense of inadequacy was appeased when he remembered Fillan's account of their early days on Loch Lumon. These men, commended for their faithfulness, did not see great breakthroughs. Nevertheless, they had seen ones and twos coming to faith.

This inability to stir interest deeply troubled him. Maybe he just was not an evangelist – a thought that had occurred at the time of the summer solstice on Munnir Esprid. Lack of instruction that had once prevented him from convincing others, was no longer the case. For all his learning, his knowledge seemed to lack the ability to persuade. This self-doubting plunged him into a state of depression.

Ossian's instruction to persevere in adversity, and not to lose hope, led to the decision to fast. A whole week passed without eating food. Hunger had been overcome and he retired into a routine of prayer. Another week followed with some people mildly mocking this austerity whilst others tried to persuade him to eat, concerned for his health with his inability to get warm. Still, no one was inclined to express any spiritual interest beyond asking him to repeat the stories of the prophets – more by way of passing the long evenings rather than out of felt need. Darkness was lengthening as daylight diminished earlier each day.

Again, he thought of Ossian's reckoning that this was probably the place. Ossian had always been perceptive and, in his experience, had never been wrong. Could it be that Ossian had been mistaken on this occasion? But then, he argued, contrarily with himself, about the huge significance of finding the holy man on Inis Gemaich, and that his hunch had been divinely inspired.

Chapter Eighteen

An Unexpected Pilgrim

AD 565 Craig Padrig

When the rowans were hanging heavy with their red fruit, and the bracken had turned yellow and the shimmering birch had become golden, Alpia was drawn to listen attentively to one she knew well speaking at the muintir.

". . . the Christ I once despised has become the foundation of my life. I know there are people of the Ce here, for not only had I heard report that some had taken refuge in this place, but I recognise the faces of those I used to dwell with. It fills my heart with thankfulness that the High King has spared some of you from the killings."

Alpia studied the speaker intently: his druid hairstyle was well-familiar. But what had changed – which made him appear quite different – was the loss of his morose manner. Maelchon visibly reflected the change that he had been speaking about.

"I tell you good folk, not to place your hope in the Bulàch, for she is a shadow compared to the unsurpassable brilliance of the Creator of all things. She, and her kind, are among those who have rebelled against his rule. She has power over you, to only serve her own ends, and that is to keep man from seeing the true light. For years I had served her, and those who knew me back then would attest that I never lacked zeal in observing all the rites, and in according her reverence."

He raised his pilgrim's staff, as though to announce a new thought. "Today, we celebrate Mabon, a time when the light diminishes and the darkness takes hold. But, we need not fear, for these are natural cycles that the Creator has ordained, making us mortals mindful of the brevity of life and prompting us to act wisely, with kindness towards one another, sharing the bounty of the harvest with those less fortunate. Today, we give thanks and praise to the Faithful One who produces such fruitfulness, whose mercies are always new, who gives good gifts, both to those who acknowledge him as well as to those who choose not to. Regard your time as fleeting, my friends, for soon all shall face our Maker, without foreknowledge of when this shall be. Consider how uncertain life is, not only a warrior's life, but those hapless bystanders who are in the way of violent men."

After the meeting, Maelchon came immediately over to where Alpia stood with Aunt Conchen and Derile, her sister-in-law. "It is you!" he greeted them with uncharacteristic warmth, taking each by the hand. "Praise God that you have been spared!"

"What has become of you?" asked Aunt Conchen.

"That, my dear woman, is a long story! Is there somewhere we can sit down?"

"We three all stay together in one hut," replied Alpia. "It is just over there – come!" Her head was spinning with the many questions she wanted to ask.

Once they were seated and a drink was in the hand of their former druid, Maelchon proceeded. "After the ruin of the hillfort, I struggled immensely with all that I had once believed that had tried to make sense of the world. Wroid, my druid mentor, had passed on and I felt bereft of finding any solace, even though I kept the company of the most enlightened druids. Then, at Litha, last year, I went with some fellows to observe the rites on the holy mountain in the south they call Munnir Esprid. Can you imagine whom I should meet there?"

Alpia watched him search their faces, as though expecting someone should know.

"Taran!" he exclaimed with an air of incredulity. Maelchon's mouth broadened into a slight grin that Alpia still found a most unusual expression. Taran again, thought Alpia – he does seem to get about and be a man of influence.

"It was not an easy meeting; at least, not at first, holding me to account for naming him as the intended sacrifice. We druids, though, were the human face of it – although, in truth, it was Talorgen's decision. Beyond the human arena, the malevolence of the Bulàch was at work, desiring his young blood. It is not without reason that she is depicted with the teeth of a bear, or the tusks of a boar. Rapacious is her nature."

How strange to hear him speak like this, thought Alpia.

Maelchon paused, taking a draught of a cold, herbal infusion she had served. "Taran talked about the Z-rod, giving clarity to me for the first time, concerning why he bore the warlord's insignia. As I said back at the time, it was quite a mystery. Taran spoke of the power of the Creator bestowing blessing upon the people of the earth through the lightning symbol, and that as the particular bearer of this sign, Taran had been set aside as a warrior of Christ for the task of 'bearing fire to the north', as he is wont to declare. The breakthrough for me was this revelation of the Creator who is before all others in time and eminence, who has been obscured by the likes of the Bulàch."

How strange to hear Maelchon denounce the Bulàch, considered Alpia, and that this revelation should come about from her cousin.

"This brought light to my eyes," continued their former druid, who briefly framed the side of his face with his hands for added emphasis, "for my eyes had grown dim in the twilight of my troubled faith. This is not some new god brought by the Gael, but one who has always been."

Again, he paused – was it for effect, Alpia mused, to make his point?

"I do believe this God was the one who spoke to me on the day of Taran's initiation!" Maelchon announced with the utmost conviction that his voice could muster, so different from the levelled strains Alpia was used to hearing, that once teetered on the dull. "As I said to Taran, it was the only time in my long life as a druid, that I truly believed a revelation had been given to me, although, at the time, I thought it was a communication from the Bulàch. Taran indicated that God often speaks in the context of our beliefs, of what we understand. That was the turning point, the end of a long search, revealed through one I had nearly put to death!"

"Whatever is the world coming to!" exclaimed Aunt Conchen. "I cannot believe I am hearing this, Maelchon! You were always meticulous in observing all the old ways. To hear you say you have abandoned them is hard to comprehend, and, moreover, it is extraordinary that you should become, of all things, a pilgrim!"

"I know! But I was lost in the old ways!" He held out his arms in a helpless gesture. "I had reached a dead end, broken by all the destruction that the Bulàch was either incapable of delivering us from, or which she had maliciously brought upon us as a destroyer."

"You do look visibly changed," Alpia eventually brought herself to remark. "You have been softened. It is like spring has vanquished winter!"

"That is exactly how it feels!" Maelchon exclaimed, again with another smile that previously seemed so alien to his nature.

"And yet," added Aunt Conchen, "you have not totally abandoned the old ways!"

"How do you mean?" Maelchon looked at her quizzically.

"Well, did you not celebrate Mabon with us just earlier?"

"Oh, that! There is much that is commendable from our old lore, but celebrating the old festivals should be in praise of the Overseer of the seasons, acknowledging our dependence upon his munificence. Think about it – those observances are more ancient than what we had previously believed, before the Bulàch cast her shadow over our perception of the world and brought it under her thrall." Alpia watched him lick his dry lips. "The most learned of the pilgrims will tell you that much of our former teachings are a legacy from a primary revelation of the Creator, even though the originator of that lore had become forgotten. Our festivals are marked by the sun and moon. But, who placed these orbs of light in the skies? Who decreed the transitioning of time and the passing of seasons? These are the workings of the Creator for which he should be praised. Are they not reminders, too, of the transience of all things and of our own seasons of life? Should we not heed the gathering of darkness, the descent into winter as reminders of our own journey and destination?"

Maelchon cast them a searching look, as if to judge whether they had understood. Seeming satisfied that he had adequately answered the question, he continued with a note of curiosity in his voice. "Tell me, how did you escape the killings?"

Each of the women told their story. Aunt Conchen was the last, and upon concluding, said, "I have been old for so long that I am weary."

"Do not say such things!" Maelchon objected. "Recall what our proverb says, *Do not resent growing old, for many are denied the privilege.*"

"Oh, we have missed you!" declared Aunt Conchen in a brighter fashion. "You are right – I am here for a purpose, but exactly what that is, I have no idea!"

Maelchon studied her with his chin slightly raised, as if to say he knew but chose not to speak further upon the matter – at least not for the time being. Instead, he turned to Alpia. "So, you left Oengus before he was killed! It is not for me to judge, but you will have had your reasons . . ."

"Yes, I did! If I were to tell you half the story, sleep would overcome you!"

"What an end for Oengus!" he mused, tugging at his beard and shaking his head. "I suppose a warlord cannot relinquish power, for if he did, the new warlord, seeing the former one as a potential threat, would have him murdered, would he not?"

"He could not admit defeat," declared Alpia. "Even after the fall of Rhynie, he was still scheming to rebuild his reputation and to somehow contest Brude's overlordship."

"Oengus was ever the optimist!" pronounced Aunt Conchen, wiping a tear from the corner of her eye.

"My brother was pig-headed," declared Derile, whose voice showed no sign of remorse.

"Pig-headed, eh?" considered Maelchon. "Well, I suppose that is apt for did he not adopt the boar as his inspiration? You know, it did seem that he came close to succeeding in his ambitions, for Brude was most hard-pressed initially to gain his victory. I must admit that I was taken in by his rule and vision and remained on his side right up until the time of our downfall."

"We all were," declared Aunt Conchen. Alpia noted how more tears welled up in her aunt's eyes.

"It seems that our story is written by ambitious men!" Alpia voiced aloud thoughts that were fermenting within her. "Violent men are like a huge wave that drag everything along in their course. It is not for us to choose our way, for the person of peace is unable to sit to one side and hope not to be affected. I had foolishly imagined that I might be able to change the course of events by marrying Oengus . . . but I failed!"

"There, there!" Aunt Conchen said, putting a comforting arm around her. "You did what you could and probably preserved us for longer through your counsel. There comes a time when such men choose not to listen, bent on carrying out their destructive ways."

"They are of a kind – Talorgen and Oengus, I mean," observed Maelchon. "In the sayings of Christ, he observed that *all who draw the sword will die by the sword*."

"All this death and destruction!" began Derile. "I have lost everything. I feel no sadness for my brother. He used me as an object to barter with when marrying me off to the ancient Cynbel in exchange for a fragile peace. What is to become of us? We are uprooted, living as exiles in the land of our conqueror." The tears coursed bitterly down her cheeks.

"You have reached your lowest point," uttered Maelchon meaningfully and with surprising empathy. "Such grief can lead us to consider a way beyond it."

"What do you mean?" Derile wiped away her tears and looked up at him.

"You can choose to either wallow in grief in your dismantled world, remaining there utterly lost and in despair; or you can do the courageous thing and let grief prompt you to move on!" Maelchon looked as if he might continue, but must have decided to leave his counsel short, perhaps in the hope that it would be better remembered and have its desired impact. He cleared his throat and straightened his tunic. "All of what you say about Oengus is true. But is a man wholly evil? For all his faults, Oengus had some noble desires. Did he not bring Eithni back to Rhynie as his wife after he had abandoned her? Did he not heed the caution of us druids? Did he not receive the instruction of the pilgrims?"

"He was either forced or persuaded to do all of those things!" protested Alpia.

"That is maybe so . . . but he could have chosen not to," returned Maelchon. "Imagine if different pilgrims had come to Rhynie, he might have responded well to their instruction and changed his ways!"

"You surprise me, to speak like that," interjected Aunt Conchen. "Did you not maintain that our fate is decreed, and we walk in the path assigned to us?"

"That is what I used to think. Now, I am not so sure. It seems to me, from what little I know about the Creator, that he is not some distant being who has established all the future course of events, but rather is one who invites us to respond, amidst those circumstances, to choose well to avoid taking the wrong direction." He looked at Derile and, gaining her attention, continued. "That is why I say choose to either remain in bitter grief, or to rise from the ashes and move on. Going back to Oengus, he had his opportunities to choose wisely, but burning ambition had taken hold of him and led, not only himself, but others, too, to destruction."

"Is it not said," responded Aunt Conchen, "that *a man may live after losing his life, but not after losing his honour?*"

Chapter Nineteen

Chambered Cairn

AD 566 Inis Ork

Starting the third week of his fast, Drostan walked down the long avenue of the stones late afternoon as the sun was fast descending. A rosy glow flowed over the neglected monument. It struck him afresh how abandoned these stones had become, indicative of the spiritual indifference of the community and the slow wit of their druid. Had he not sensed, from the outset, that this was not likely to be the chosen place of the learned ones despite it being the most northerly isle in the chain and at *the ends of the earth*? Fotel could never be described as one of the learned ones anticipating some revelation. The words of the High King came to mind that if a village does not receive your word, then you were to shake the dust from your feet and move on to those who would listen.

Basking in the last of the sun's rays, he lent against the colossal centre stone of the monument, feeling its deathly cold and unyielding hardness against his back.

"I must move on!" he uttered aloud with conviction.

The setting sun suffused his tired eyelids in a red glow, like a benediction. It brought rest and he was in no hurry to break from this rare peace after months of emotional turmoil and frustration. The High King's words, *Well done, good and faithful servant,* came involuntarily to mind.

Shadows from the standing stones lengthened then faded as the last of the light dipped beyond the horizon. The shade deepened with a cold grip on a land that felt forsaken. The thought struck him that the High King was removing his light from this community who had not heeded its illumination during the day. It proved to be no passing thought, for it gathered pace, bringing the sense of something perceived within his spirit. Was this awareness not highly significant, at the end of his two-week fast?

"Faithfulness is a godly grace," he thought aloud, seeking resolution as to what he should do. "It is the ninth grace mentioned in Fillan's prophetic prayer and confirmed by the shining one: *faithfulness to reach the very ends of the earth.*"

After months of self-doubt, he felt affirmed in having remained true to his calling. So, was this it then – the last of the quests completed with such an immense anti-climax and sheer frustration?

Be ever hearing, but never understanding; be ever seeing, but never perceiving, came to mind. If people had been given many opportunities to hear, but had refused to receive, had he not fulfilled his part? The outcome was not his responsibility, he decided as he walked slowly down the avenue of stones towards the huts. Maybe the ninefold quest was to prepare him for something yet to come at another destination. He went resolutely to Fotel's home.

"My fast is over!" he announced.

"Ah, good. And what has been revealed to you? Anything for our benefit?" Fotel asked with mild curiosity, but also with a hint of a sardonic tone.

Drostan felt annoyed. "I am moving on. I realise that I have not reached the place anticipating my arrival."

He felt Fotel's stare as cold as the shadows that earlier had fallen from the stones. It moved him to declare, "I have explained all that I can; but unless the Spirit brings life, and the people have ears to hear, then all teaching is useless."

"We have listened – you cannot say we have not!" defended Fotel, obviously piqued by the implication. Then with a slightly roguish grin, he added, "Perhaps the problem is with your way of instruction!"

"I have been wasting my breath," he replied calmly. He turned and left. Fotel's attitude confirmed the decision to move on.

Drostan broke his fast and the next day took the cross-island trail. It was a long and weary way, not that the terrain was challenging other than peat bog, but he had been weakened by so long a fast. He reached a peninsula on the east coast from where he could see the mainland, small on the distant horizon. He went over to a fisherman cleaning his nets.

"How far north does the mainland go?" he asked, pointing at the distant shore.

"That coast goes to a windswept cape where two seas meet. From there the coast turns abruptly eastward."

"Is there an island beyond the cape?"

"No. But if you were to travel to the far east from the cape, there are islands to the north."

"Truly?" he responded, both excited by a new possibility and daunted by the prospect of more perilous times on the ocean.

"The islands support many people," added the man. "It is quite a centre which still attracts pilgrims to its stone circles and burial cairns."

They talked some more. As it was growing dark, the fisherman invited him back to his hut. Due to unsettled weather, he stayed there for the next three days. He made himself useful by mending nets and gathering kelp from the shore and digging this into a large patch of ground beside the fisherman's hut. He was thankful for this stay for he regained strength after his lengthy fast and hasty departure.

Fair weather allowed him to set out on the fourth day towards the mainland that appeared smudged on the far horizon. His heart that had been heavy with the thought of enduring yet another perilous adventure, was relieved to experience calm seas and a favourable wind and current to steer him over Y Kilmor Mawr – the great strait. Dusk descended part way through the afternoon in mid-winter and he prepared himself mentally for an extremely lengthy period of darkness, twice as long as the day. With sinking heart at the prospect, he bemoaned his fate to be making this voyage at such a time of year. Images of that tempestuous night after leaving Inis Gemaich briefly haunted him, until he remembered God had intervened, sending a boat to pluck him from the jaws of death. Was he not indestructible whilst this last quest remained? he thought. The High King maintains his steady watch over me . . . still, I would do almost anything to avoid repeating that experience.

The sea was surprisingly calm which, gladdening his heart, produced an overflow of thankfulness to his High King. Y Kilmor Mawr was extensive, and the night hid the hills of the mainland to the east that had been clear to see from the peninsula. The pole star stood bright, and he kept this to his left, paddling with measured strokes and resting when his arms ached. He sang psalms to keep his spirits up, grateful that being afloat in a coracle through a long night was nothing of the ordeal he had anticipated. The worst he had to endure was the perishing cold, but even this served the purpose of paddling on with renewed determination to cross Y Kilmor Mawr.

Morning broke crisp and clear on the second day of this new voyage, revealing a line of hills rising individually out of a stark landscape. One rose distinctively, like an immense tower with sheer sides, and he set his course upon this, paddling in a straight line. As he eventually neared the peak after an arduous day of paddling, he made for a promontory, around which he ran ashore on a bay of sand. Exhausted, he lay down on the sand, covering himself with his upturned coracle and slept like the dead. The cold awakened him. The sun was setting out west from where he had come. Feeling very thirsty, he went in search of fresh water.

After quenching his thirst, he urged himself, "I must make a fire." He gathered well-seasoned driftwood from the high-tide line and soon was cooking three of the five mackerel caught on a trailing fishing line when crossing the strait, setting two aside for breakfast.

The next day, he followed a desolate coast with stark hills accentuating the wildness of a storm-beaten land, absent of trees. The mournful wail of sea birds and the sound of distant surf breaking upon the rugged shore kept him vigilant. Still tired from crossing Y Kilmor Mawr, he did not reach far that day and camped, out of the wind, in the shelter of sand dunes. When the rain fell heavily, he curled up tighter under his upturned boat, thankful for shelter as he listened to the patter on the skin of the coracle. On the fourth day, he rounded the high cliffs of the cape where the two seas met in quite an agitation. Progress was arduously slow, and fear was heightened by the dread of past ordeals. The passage beyond the cape became easier, beyond the turmoil of crashing seas, with a wind at his back. The shoreline eastwards was deeply indented with inlets reaching far inland, making travel across the mouths of sea lochs much swifter.

On the fifth day, with the weather still unseasonably fair, he glimpsed on the far horizon, a ridge standing separate from the lie of the coast. Unsure whether this was a promontory joined to the mainland by an unsighted neck of land, or if these were the islands of the north, he made for them. On the sixth day, with the weather still relatively calm, although grey and drizzly, he clearly sighted the islands across a sound.

Noticing how turbulent the waters had become again, he put into a bay where wisps of smoke trailed from some huts behind the dunes. He paddled over to some men spreading a net between their coracles, and called out, "How is the fishing?"

"No bad!" said one, without emotion. "Where are you coming from?"

"From around the cape," he said dismissively. "Tell me, what are those islands over there?"

"Inis Ork. Are you heading there?"

"Probably!"

His reply received a puzzled stare.

"Tell me – does one of the islands have a large stone circle?"

"It does," confirmed the same man. "It is quite a centre, attracting people from our parts and even beyond at certain times."

"Today, is the winter solstice," remarked an older man, slowly plying out the net. "Already several pilgrims have crossed to gather at the big stone circle they call the Ring of Brodgar."

"You should not delay, for the tide is rising," continued the first man. "It is best to cross the straits on rising water. The sea will look like it is boiling and full of menace. If you cross at the wrong time – and mind you, most of the time, it is wrong – it can be disastrous. Many have perished and many more will come to an untimely end. Steer towards an imaginary point, two hand widths of an outstretched arm to the west of the islands to reach target. Trust me, it is the only way of reaching Inis Ork."

"The ebb tide is the one to avoid, for it will drag you eastwards into open sea as it slackens," added the old man.

He thanked them and paddled out into the sound where he encountered a huge force forming small whirlpools and waves to break into one another. It felt like the turbulence from some mysterious beast beneath the surface going about a malicious purpose. Taking the fishermen's advice, he made for the prescribed, imaginary point west of Inis Ork and soon felt the tidal flow eastwards. At around midway point, the tide slackened, and the passage became easier. Realising the tide was reaching high water, he applied skill and strength with the paddle in the hope of reaching the islands before the ebb tide would take effect. This section of the crossing proved far easier, and, passing through the narrows between two islands, he emerged into an immense inland sea appearing as though it were encircled by land in all directions. It felt like he had completed some rite of passage, overcoming mysterious forces beneath the surface, passing from one world to a place of separation and difference.

The fishermen's directions led him to the north-westerly part of the "inland sea" where he discovered another opening to the greater sea beyond and also to the shallows of a shore that formed a tidal marsh. Beyond, lay a brackish loch which he paddled across towards the standing stones bristling the low skyline. He went to explore the ancient stone ring, said to be the precursor of other circles throughout the land of the Britons and the Gaels.

The circle was immense, and he inspected the raised stones comprising of various forms and colours, seemingly not quarried from the same place. He was impressed by how the ring was sited between two lochs, filling basins upon either side of the narrow isthmus where the stone circle had been erected. Encompassing the horizon was a low-lying ridge, forming what was like an additional ring, with breaks in its perimeter. The sky appeared immense, and it impressed him how the elements of earth, air and water conjoining in this place, to make him feel miniscule in such spatial magnitude. It seemed like a stage upon which to mark solstices and equinoxes and the phases of the moon. There, ritual was enacted, enhanced by the splendour of the natural amphitheatre and the mystery of place, placating the sun god with offerings that expressed their fundamental dependency upon his consistency for fruitfulness to spring from man's labours through the seasonal cycles.

Already mid-afternoon, people had gathered in family and community groups, exchanging easily with one another, sharing food and drink. Drostan approached two druids preparing elements. "Do you lead the ceremony from within the ring?"

"No. The ceremony proper is at Twmpath Dôl."

"What is Twmpath Dôl?"

"It is the chambered cairn beyond the isthmus – across the fields over there," he indicated the location with an outstretched arm.

Fillan's final prophetic words came to mind: *The beam of light shall penetrate into the chamber of the dead and those who were dead shall be made alive.* "I must go there," he declared aloud, realising that he was at the wrong place; the chambered cairn is the chamber of the dead.

"You would probably be too late to reach there before sundown!"

Girding up the long hem of his garment, Drostan sprinted off, noting how the sun was already setting. The slope down from the stone ring propelled him towards the isthmus which was almost consumed by the lochs on either side.

The *beam of light*, he reckoned, must refer to the winter solstice; that is why they are gathering to celebrate the setting of the sun at its most southerly point. Light would diminish no more beyond this point, but rather, passing beyond its most downward point, would regain momentum to begin its ascendancy. This had always been quite an occasion, in the lean of the season, at the lowest ebb of the year's cycle. The druids had made a marker for this turning point, stating, as it were, "no further" to the sun. From this marker, people could look ahead to days of growing light and gathering warmth, to germination and the rebirth of the earth.

The sun was turning the clouds golden, and he wondered whether he could reach the cairn before the sun dipped behind the horizon? He maintained his sprint, crossing the boggy narrows of the isthmus, then past two giant standing stones, standing like a portal on the far side. In a short distance, he came to a much smaller stone ring whose truly gigantic stones dwarfed him. These rose vertically, some with angled tops, to the sky as though pointing to the place from which hope and life emanated.

"Where is the cairn called Twmpath Dôl?" he gasped whilst approaching a group whose leisurely pace shared none of his own urgency.

A couple pointed ahead, "Make for the tall marker stone over there. From that stone, you will see the cairn."

Dismayed with himself for failing to enquire earlier about their ceremonial procedures, he had passed the time of day, uselessly marvelling over its location. How could I be careless of prophecy? It was like I was asleep! He remembered how he had chastised himself years before on his poor ability to recall prophecies specifically entrusted to him. Why had I assumed the main events and the most distinguished druids would be officiating within the Ring of Brodgar itself, for it clearly contained no chamber of the dead mentioned in Fillan's vision?

Stretching across the field like some athletic colossus before him, his elongated shadow urged him swiftly on. He prayed that he would be enabled to arrive before the sun had finished setting and hoped that he would intuitively know what to say and how to act. This was the culminating point of his destiny, the conclusion of the nine quests. Had he not been set aside to be a channel of blessing by revealing the true source of light and life to the druids anticipating this illumination?

"May these be the wise and learned ones – not like Fotel – who you have prepared for this coming!" he uttered audibly under his breath.

He flew past the marker stone and, looking back, saw the sun almost settling on the summit of a hill on the neighbouring island to the south-west. The clouds were now turning golden, making the west glorious, and his shadow, stretching even longer, seemed to be urging him to the finish line. His energetic outline darkening the ground before him, pointed precisely to the cairn he was fast approaching, a man-made mound that rose to quite a height above the druids assembled around its entrance. Dressed in white linen, they were already interceding before the chamber of the dead, mediating with the unseen powers of their ancestors to direct blessing upon their community.

Forming an arc on either side of the chief druid, the crowd had left an aperture fanning out towards the setting sun, permitting its rays to enter the low passageway into the chamber. Towards this humanly formed arena he ran, into which his massively elongated shadow had already entered. Many of the onlookers shaded their eyes with a hand, squinting, trying to determine who he was. I must appear as a mysterious silhouette to these onlookers, he thought.

"Cast away, O man, whatever impedes the appearance of light!" spoke the chief druid raising his staff, acknowledging the departing sun. Upon this cue, the gathered assembly cast garments to the ground as symbolic of their dark deeds.

He noted how the low corridor into the tomb, aligned with utmost precision with this solstice, was aglow, as the dying sun poured a blood-red light down its passageway. The setting radiance illuminated immense stone flags lining the walls, penetrating the chamber with its ruddy luminosity of a sacrificial hue. That obscure, shadowy place was now a stage where the living desired communion with the spirits of the departed.

"This is the moment spoken of in Fillan's prophecy: *The beam of light shall penetrate into the chamber of the dead and those who were dead shall be made alive.* I have arrived neither a moment too soon, nor too late!"

The chief druid, who had paused in his proceedings, faced him.

Suddenly, there came to Drostan's lips, words memorised from his studies in Erin:

"Arise, shine, for your light has come,
and the glory of the Lord rises upon you.
See darkness covers the earth
and thick darkness is over the peoples,
but the Lord rises upon you
and his glory appears over you.
Nations will come to your light,
and kings to the brightness of your dawn . . .
Then you will look and be radiant,
your heart will throb and swell with joy."

The translated text flowed from his lips with a flamboyance quite uncommon to him, delivered with a conviction that he owned.

"What manner of man is this who brings such tidings?" asked the chief druid, turning to one of his companions.

Drostan realised that the chief druid was blind. How ironic, he thought, that their most senior one, to whom the community looked to for direction, should be blind. He felt a strong urge to reach out and touch the man's blind eyes.

"He has the appearance of a druid," informed one, without hostility. "But he is not one from our fraternity . . . and we do not recognise what he says."

"This might be the low-ebb of the sun that you venerate," began Drostan, tentatively, "but I come to announce one whose radiance never fades. *God is light; in him there is no darkness at all . . .*"

They listened in astonishment, and as he perceived, with interest too. Then one of the leaders, stepping forward between Drostan and the chief druid, said, "Our forebears spoke about a prophecy handed down from one generation to the next." At this the man stumbled. Drostan wondered whether the man was finding it hard to recall the prophetic words.

"Tell me," encouraged Drostan, "what do the words of the prophecy proclaim?"

The blind druid then spoke with a hopeful intonation. "Our forebears spoke of *one, who having been destined to rule, would bear fire to the north – a fire searing the soul like a bolt of lightning.* It was determined that this fire would come at the darkest time that no one could resist or extinguish."

"Could these spoken tidings herald that light?" spoke the one who stood between the chief druid and Drostan.

"Wait!" spoke one with a commanding voice who stepped forward, not dressed in the raiment of the priestly caste, but garbed as someone eminent in the community. A bodyguard flanked him. "It was said that the revelation would be accompanied by a sign!"

Hearing this, quickened Drostan's urge to touch the blind man's eyes. Stepping up to the chief druid, he placed a hand kindly upon his shoulder. "Would you permit me to pray for your sight?"

The old man hesitated as he turned to face him. The chief druid gazed with a sense of wonder, with eyes that did not squint like everyone else's into the sunlight. He nodded.

Drostan placed his palm across the man's eyes. "So that you might put your faith in the One who gives light to see, I pray in the name of the High King of heaven – the mighty Christ – to bring light to these eyes."

When he removed his palm, the blind druid blinked several times, looking around him startled, not as a blind man, but with all the wonderment of one able to see again. In contrast to his previous sombre manner, he laughed, seemingly recognising faces he had formerly known. Tears began to flow, and he looked away to the distance where the last of the sun's rays disappeared, his eyes drinking in the lustre of the waters upon the inland sea.

Wanting to reveal the Z-rod upon his back to prove he had been *destined to rule*, he recalled how previously, at the base of Munnir Esprid, it had not produced the desired effect. He hesitated, saying to himself, I do not want to appear foolish. At the same time, an insistent urge, not his own, demanded it be shown. "Concerning your prophecy," he continued, "I am one who was destined to rule." Again, an even stronger impulse gripped him to reveal the Z-rod, which to ignore would have been outrageous disobedience And yet the natural voice within again protested that this was mere folly. Untying his smock, he slipped it from his shoulders, declaring, "I am the one, of whom it is prophesied, would *bear fire to the learned ones far to the north.*"

There was a bemused look from those he was addressing.

"And, you say, this fire would sear your souls like a bolt of lightning?" Devested of his smock, he presented his back to his audience.

A cry of dismay went up.

"The lightning fork of the Z-rod!" said the warlord of Inis Ork.

"Here, let me see," spoke the chief druid, turning Drostan, to better view the tattoo in the fading light. "It is the warlord's mark!" Turning to his companions, he said, "This confirms the prophecy," before adding to Drostan,

"Tell us of the One who not only brings life to eyes that were dead, but illumination as well to our souls."

As careful instruction began, someone built a fire to the side of the tomb, around which they sat. They questioned the fire-bearer concerning things they were keen to comprehend. Others joined them from across the isthmus, confused, enquiring why the druidic procession had not come to perform the usual rites at the Ring of Brodgar.

Drostan heard a bystander remark, "Our chief druid can see again!"

"Then why the delay?"

"The chief professes that the light we have been long awaiting, has finally come!" and went on to report how a strange runner had come with unexpected tidings, who bore the insignia of a warlord.

"What light?" asked one of the men.

"You know – the light the druids have been anticipating – surely you have heard talk about this?"

"Yes, of course he knows that," said a woman. "Who has not heard the prophecy!"

"It is the light that no one can extinguish," continued one, looking at them wide-eyed. "They say it is the light that brings life in all its fullness."

"Is this some new religion?" queried the woman.

"The strange druid and warlord, whom no one knows, speaks about the One called Christ whom we have heard reports of. You know, other Picts have already believed in this foreign God."

"Aye! Mind, we heard accounts of one of Christ's druids raising a dead boy back to life near Craig Padrig!" said the wide-eyed man.

"And other such strange things," picked up a young woman, "such as how the water beast had been constrained merely by a command from their leader. Apparently, with just a word of authority, Brude's barred gates had been flung open, unable to withstand the power of these men!"

"They were even able to sail head on into wind!" said an old man incredulously.

There was no argument, no resistance, no impeding misunderstanding that had so hindered his task at Meini Heyon y Pentir. Drostan wondered at that delay, all those months apparently wasted by Fotel, who seemed to have deliberately obstructed him. That delay had led to his arriving on the day of the winter solstice when the learned ones, waiting in anticipation, would be receptive to the proclamation of the light. Even in the apparent frustrations and the dark setbacks, the High King's purpose had not been thwarted, and all that Drostan needed to do was to respond in faithfulness to the prompting of circumstances

Although the High King had done it all, he was filled with wonder at having been chosen and prepared as the human instrument that the Giver of light had used. He recalled Ossian's prophecy years before on a hillside in Rhynie, that, to fulfil the quest, there would *come much strife, like a blight threatening to consume*; that *heartache and anguish* lay before him, with journeys *full of ordeals*. Adventures he would consider his *undoing*, would become *rites of passage* for his preparation. Had the heavenly utterance not said that he would be *the doer of mighty deeds, and the acts will be the making of the man*; that he was to *take heart*, for, *through one you will overcome the world*?

Through the godly Fillan, confirmed by the Shining One, accomplishing these quests would be the means of acquiring nine graces. Or was it, he wondered, that the graces had enabled him to achieve the quests? Many of those graces had been incomprehensible at the outset, with his warrior's upbringing placing little value on such things. The injunction *to be humble* had confounded. But with hindsight, humility had signalled a key shift in his outlook, a readiness to learn, preparing him to obey and to fulfil the prophecy. All the delays, the frustrations and disappointments, even the catastrophe of being shipwrecked, all had prepared him to fulfil this ultimate quest.

The occasion was like no other solstice, and the chief druid, understanding that, said, "I have been reborn, and there is no longer the need to climb the death mound for my customary night-vigil. Truly, I tell you, the former era has passed. That rite of passage, of dying to the old has been fulfilled. There is no need for me to strike a new flame from a flint, for we have received the true light that lights the soul of man and disperses the shadows. Let us all hail the dawning of a new era."

Chapter Twenty

Tensions

AD 567 Craig Padrig

Drostan passed the remainder of the winter and the fickle days of early spring on Inis Ork, strengthening this new community whose druid fraternity were eager to learn.

"So, where are you bound for next?" asked the warlord.

"Craig Padrig. It is a destination where I am known and where I have a good friend."

"Is King Brude your friend?" the warlord responded with evident concern.

Understanding his apprehension – knowing Brude held hostage this warlord's children – Drostan replied, "I am known by him. You may be surprised to know that King Brude is a friend to us pilgrims!"

He left for the mainland, not precariously contending with capricious rip tides of the Pentland alone in a coracle, for a curragh was offered by the nobles as a token of their appreciation. He watched the high cliffs, wreathed in mist, recede beyond the peaks of the waves, thrilled by the revelation that had accompanied his coming in faithfulness to the call of Christ.

The euphoria of what had occurred on Inis Ork held him in such buoyant mood that he found it difficult to give much concentrated thought as to what lay ahead. Concerning his future, the one overriding thought was to arrive at a known place to catch his breath. East of Craig Padrig were the lands of his own people, but going there appeared out of the question with Oengus's murderous intents. The end of the prophecy puzzled him, for it directed him east where he would find *great peace*.

I should not concern myself too much about how things will work out, he thought. Prophecies have the tendency to be fulfilled when we are willing to be guided and make the effort to move forward in trust.

He reached Craig Padrig some days later, with a sense of mounting anticipation and gladness. It had been two years since he had first arrived as part of Colmcille's mission, which felt longer after all that had passed. And yet, the very familiarity of the place made it seem only weeks since he had been leading meetings with Colmcille. He made directly for the community which had received the pilgrims well, where faith had blossomed among the people after the boy had been raised from the dead.

"Why, it is Drostan!" exclaimed one with evident delight.

Drostan smiled, knowing the man by sight. "Is Munait still here?"

"He is leading the meeting. Come, I am going myself"

Arriving in the centre of the community where they used to meet, Drostan was surprised to find no one there.

"The muintir is a short distance from here," explained the man, sensing his confusion.

"I will just leave my coracle here, then."

Beyond the huts, a well-trodden path led across open ground to the muintir. Prayers had already commenced. Hearing Munait's familiar voice recite the liturgy, gave him a sense of homecoming. Before long, heads were turning in his direction, and since the twilight was deepening, he found it difficult to recognise many faces.

Suddenly, he felt overwhelmed. How many perils have I been delivered from? he considered. Upon the brink of death, I was rescued by those sailors who my Saviour sent at the crucial moment in all the empty sprawl of the ocean! His heart offered up praise to the High King. Feeling tears well up in his eyes, he bowed his head and let a couple of drops fall surreptitiously to the ground, like a precious thank offering. Pulling himself together, he focused on the proceedings.

On completing the liturgy, Munait said, "I believe our brother Drostan is with us." He craned his head, scanning the many faces now shrouded in shadows.

Drostan arose and, rather self-consciously, walked to the front. The two men embraced.

"Ah, it is so good to see you again, my friend!" exclaimed Munait.

Drostan responded with warmth but lacked the same effusiveness, feeling sobered by recent ordeals.

"Tell us about what has passed with you?" Munait continued, loud enough for those who had gathered to hear.

Clearing his throat, Drostan recounted the basic facts from the time of being misled by Fotel, which, causing a delay, had meant arriving at Inis Ork at the exact time for celebrating Yule. "The people on those islands had received a prophecy which had produced a great anticipation. I had little to do – no arguments to present . . ." He passed over the details of the blind druid receiving back his sight, sensing that it was too hallowed a thing to mention at that moment, anxious to avoid any misinterpretation less anyone misconstrue that it had been, in any way, his doing. "I passed the winter on those islands, teaching and guiding them in *the way*. With the druids and the warlord gladly bowing the knee to the High King, the rest of the community followed their example." He paused to take in a deep breath. "I have never known such wholehearted acceptance without the usual hostility. Truly, the Spirit of the High King brought conviction to the hearts of men and women, and even among many children."

After the meeting, he was surrounded by folk and, becoming aware of two people pressing in towards him, he looked towards them. "Ah, Alpia! And is this . . ." He stopped, not trusting his eyes, "Aunt Conchen?"

The frail, old woman opened her arms and hugged him. She wept. Seeing Alpia looking on fondly, he reached out an arm, inviting her to join their embrace. Alpia did not hesitate. How restorative it was to be in the embrace of his own people, he thought; and they too must have felt the healing balm, as neither woman wanted to let this moment pass too quickly.

"Were you part of the gathering?" Drostan asked the two women with curiosity.

"Does it surprise you that we are pilgrims?" asked Alpia.

"Why, yes, of course! There is usually resistance and objection. People need time, and some pass on by, eager to follow their own inclinations."

"I never thought I would become a pilgrim," confessed Aunt Conchen, "not after that miserable pair who came to Rhynie. But, you know, it was seeing Maelchon abandon the old ways that made me take note . . ."

"Maelchon is a follower of *the way*?" he asked, careful to clarify.

"I know!" responded Aunt Conchen with an enthusiasm surprising for her great age. "He was such a stickler for proper observance of all the rites to placate the Bulàch."

"I am not dismayed," he returned, recalling their previous meeting on Munnir Esprid. Still, it felt novel that his former druid should have become a pilgrim.

"And you, too?" he asked Alpia, with a tenderness that surprised him.

She smiled with that characteristic economy of expression that gave her an enigmatic air. Why does that look so appealing? he asked himself.

She nodded her head and informed, "You should know that your mother is here."

"Where?"

"She does not attend the meetings," explained Aunt Conchen, somewhat under her breath. "She has only recently arrived following Talorc's murder."

"Talorc ... my brother?"

"Aye!" Aunt Conchen remarked, as though he was dim-witted.

"Aunt! – perhaps Taran does not know what has been happening."

"I am called Drostan now," he corrected.

"You are forever Taran to us," insisted Aunt Conchen. "Anyway, I thought everyone knew that Talorc was killed," she defended herself.

Alpia enlightened him about the insurrection.

"So, Oengus, too, is dead!" The news shocked him. He was not quite sure why, but he felt a veritable wrench in his guts. He knew how he would have been glad to hear the news formerly.

"You look shaken," observed Alpia.

"Why should I not be? We were once as close as brothers!" A sense of regret for what should have been swept over him, with all the poignancy of missed opportunity. "It seems from what you say that Oengus chose his way and played his part, casting himself with all the ruthlessness that characterises all the warlords that I have encountered. I comprehend his ambitious choices and can perceive the things that threatened him. I also understand how he was led to make extreme decisions. However, I choose not to dwell upon all that came to pass . . ." He paused, overtaken by unexpected emotion, "I prefer to remember Oengus at the time when we were comrades before our returning to Rhynie; with our pledge to defend one another, when we ran as though we were truly a pair, Oengus with his brawn and me with my . . ." He groped for the word.

"Openness to being taught," Alpia offered.

"But was that not true of Oengus too, in the early days of his rule?" Aunt Conchen contested. "Oengus responded to my suggestion to bring Eithni back; he made peace with the Circinn; he tried to build up the honour and renown of the Ce . . ."

"It is clear that he worked towards creating some good for the Ce," Drostan professed with a certain conviction. He could tell that his words were having a certain effect upon Alpia, for she looked lost in thought for a moment and then became eager to share what was on her mind.

"You are magnanimous!" Alpia exclaimed, slightly under her breath, in an utterance of admiration. Again, she paused, although it was clear that she had more to comment. "I am convicted . . . and rightly so, for I believe that I have not been entirely fair in my estimation of Oengus!"

Drostan observed that her contrite manner made those around her wait patiently, eager to hear what more she had to say.

"If you can forgive a cousin and comrade who betrayed and twice tried to murder you," she began, looking at

Drostan, "then I feel constrained to be more generous towards my late husband."

"Oh, Alpia . . ." remarked Aunt Conchen with affection.

"Oengus was a good father. He did truly love his children, and I admired that about him." She paused to wipe away a tear from her eye. "He also had moments of being kind and generous . . . I should not deny those things, especially when it is so easy to list all his faults!"

"And he rebuilt the confidence of his people . . ." added Aunt Conchen.

"Yes, that too – but he was over ambitious and exceeded his reach."

"It is easy for us to say that now in hindsight," defended Aunt Conchen, "but at the time, he inspired his people towards greatness, rescuing us from the petty skirmishes of my own husband's choosing, lifting cattle from the Circinn. No, Oengus had a grand vision, and all of us were for it . . ."

"But look where it led us?" protested Alpia.

"Almost to success, my dear. How close we were to outwitting the Fortriu. Oengus could have led us to greatness, were it not for one greater – Brude!"

"But it did not lead to greatness – only devastation, killing, uprooting and humiliation."

Drostan could see how upset Alpia had become, that despite the attempts to be fairer towards her late husband's memory, the bitterness remained. It led him to remark, "The fact that you have tried to be more charitable in your estimation of Oengus has revealed the beginnings of a huge reconciliation with all that troubles you."

She looked at him with some surprise and then, what seemed to him, to be a slight flush of wonder.

"Taran," Alpia began, "you are a good man! You respond to what is right."

Feeling his face flush, he sought to change the subject. At that moment, Maelchon appeared. Although Drostan had learned that the former druid was now a follower of *the way*, he was struck by the lightness of expression that had transformed that one-time sullen face.

"This is a happy meeting!" observed Drostan.

"Not just another coincidence like on Munnir Esprid!" observed the old man with a smile. "I am much encouraged by what you shared concerning the events on Inis Ork. How privileged to be part of such divine happenings!"

"Both a privilege and an ordeal," clarified Drostan.

"Anything that is worth achieving usually has a price! The greater its importance, the more arduous the path," observed Maelchon. "The demonstration of the Z-rod's power has truly been revealed on Inis Ork. What was once concealed in mystery, has now been made manifest!" Drostan observed that Maelchon's brow knitted, seemingly by a new thought. "It is said that *'experience is the comb that life gives a bald man!'* Well, I may be old and have lost much of my hair . . . but I feel like my life's experience can still be put to good use." He cleared his throat, and asked with an uncharacteristic eagerness, "Tell me, where are you off to next? I should very much wish to accompany you!"

Drostan hesitated before replying. "I had wondered about going home, but did not think it would be possible, presuming Oengus was still alive. But I see that events have moved swiftly on and now, it appears, my home has moved here!" He looked around the faces who were dear to him and was warmed.

"You should bide with us a while," interjected Munait, "we have much to talk about."

"Do not speak about going when you have only just arrived!" protested Alpia, with unexpected fervour.

"No, you should stay with us for a time," agreed Munait, who suddenly looked distracted. "Colmcille sent word that he would be arriving by the next full moon."

Drostan felt ambivalent about the news of the abbot's imminent arrival. Last time, he sent me off on a desperate voyage! He felt the inner rebellion, protesting against those who held such authority over his life, consigning him to dangerous situations. He recalled his reaction towards Fillan when, against his own wishes and directional inclinations concerning Ossian's prophecy, he was packed off to Erin, in the opposite direction to where he believed he should venture. He still struggled with that decision, for the delay it had felt, especially the additional year at Candida Casa. Was the whole process to begin all over again? Were *strife*, *heartache* and *anguish* to accompany him in his endeavours as Ossian's prophecy indicated? And how was he to cope with his former druid accompanying him? Although Maelchon appeared a changed man, memories of his taciturn nature still prevailed, bound up with the former druid's complicity in the intention to make him a sacrifice. And, moreover, was he to be separated so soon from Alpia? Were their paths never to be the same?

"Come, you must meet your mother," entreated Alpia.

Did she sense my inner turmoil? he wondered. Is Alpia perceptive enough to come to my rescue? He replied, "I should like that very much. Let us go and not delay another moment."

Alpia led him back to the village centre and spoke quietly to him along the way. "I should explain that your mother is much changed! She, like all of us, has been through much, leaving her like a garment that is frayed and torn in places. We all share a house: Aunt Conchen, your mother and me.

Derile was with us too, but now she is married to the king's brother and is already with child!"

"At least this time, she has not been forced to marry an old man!" remarked Aunt Conchen, whose slow progress made Drostan feel impatient, full of longing to see his mother. Alpia led them down a side way and entered a hut.

"Aunt Domelch – meet your son!" announced Alpia, with evident satisfaction.

His mother looked at him without recognition it seemed. She had aged – her hair was all grey and her eyes appeared dull above leadened eye sockets. She looked uncertain, even confused, unsure of the world in which she had found herself, unfamiliar with its prompts and expectations. But he could still recognise that she was his mother. After an initial hesitation, which passed when she smiled, he crossed the floor swiftly and embraced her in his arms. They remained in their clinch for quite a while without an exchange, and when they did release one another, both were lost for words.

Alpia came to the rescue, explaining a summary of events that had eventually brought Drostan back.

"Taran – I never expected to see you again!" she remarked with emotion.

"It has been a long time – twelve years by my estimation," he replied.

"Oh, what times we have been through!" Domelch shook her head so slowly that it seemed to him that the tragedies of his father's death, the insurrection of his brother that led to his death, very much overshadowed her life.

"I thought you were dead! It has been hard to understand that you were alive when I have not been able to see you!"

"I was prevented from returning to Rhynie," he explained.

"I had expected you to return and stake your claim to the lordship. That is what your father had expected!"

Did she really expect me to depose Oengus? Well, that is what I once thought back at Dindurn, when it seemed that opportunity had presented itself through Domech's intervention. That was a long time ago and it struck him then how much he had changed − enabled to lay aside all that resentment and ambition. About to reply, his mother continued.

"Talorc did the right thing in deposing Oengus. I was proud of him, for was he not just as much an heir to the promise, being a descendant of Mongfind? I had hoped Talorc would settle down and become a ruler. But he was young."

"He liked the idea of riding with his reckless friends as a law unto themselves," commented Aunt Conchen, shaking her head.

"He was a leader though, for others followed," Domelch persisted.

"Aunt Domelch! What kind of leader goes around murdering and pillaging his own people?" Alpia protested.

"You were not there!" she glowered at Alpia.

Everyone fell silent. Drostan had not expected his mother to justify his brother's wild rampage of terror.

"And look at you!" his mother continued with unexpected vehemence. "You have shaved away your hair in that ridiculous fashion and become a pilgrim!"

"Yes, I am changed, a different man to the one sent into exile." He spoke soberly, "I did think about becoming the man you would have had me become . . . but my life took a different path."

"Your father would have been ashamed of you!" Her look of disappointment, bordering on contempt, cut him unawares.

An uneasy quiet pervaded the hut. Aunt Conchen busied herself with food preparation, but seemed to be challenged by the task, forgetful of the procedure. Alpia came to her aid.

"I am going to speak with Munait," Drostan excused himself, eager to escape the unexpected hostility. The cool and darkness of the night felt kind. He could wander beyond the recognition of others, away from their applause and their reproach. He decided that he did not even want to see his old friend just then, finding the anonymity of the gentle night soothed him to his core. He had never really envisaged his homecoming, but if he had, he would not have expected his mother's rejection. Time changes people, he reflected, and the appalling events that had befallen his people had certainly taken their toll. And yet, he reflected, the chaos that broke people, also awakened some to their need for true security. He was surprised, though, that Talorc – for all his despicable actions – was held in higher esteem by his mother than himself. Then he considered Christ's words that the world would despise you on account of him.

He sighed. How bitter-sweet is this life!

The following day, Munait called on him.

"Join me and Maelchon to the king's court." He placed an arm about Drostan's shoulders.

Drostan was keen to leave the hut where his mother obstinately continued to rebuff him. As they set out, he asked, "Do you often go to the hillfort?"

"Every day! Just like we did in the past. Only now, it is better! Bargoit and those other druids who continued to oppose us, have been sent away. Brude has chosen us as his spiritual advisors."

"The king is a pilgrim too?"

"Yes. But in some ways, he is unchanged; still the strong man, keen to uphold his rule over his neighbours."

"It seems that our tribes are all turning to *the way* . . . with the exception of our own people!"

"That, I feel, is about to change," added Maelchon, significantly.

"And maybe your arrival heralds a change!" suggested Munait. "I am curious what Colmcille will say when he finds you here."

Drostan avoided airing his own thoughts on the matter. The three men did not exchange words on the stiff but short climb up the final part to the hillfort.

"So, it is Taran!" King Brude greeted him, rising from his seat in a show of respect which surprised Drostan. The king extended his arm, they shook hands and Brude sat down, exchanging pleasantries. Shifting to one side, the king leant heavily upon an elbow resting on the arm of his throne chair and looked at Drostan thoughtfully. "Perhaps you are the man to bring peace and order among your people!"

"How do you mean, my lord?" Drostan asked with interest.

"Did I not once say, when Oengus was here, that I could put you in his place?"

Drostan did not respond.

"Are you not a legitimate heir to the lordship over the Ce?"

"I was," Drostan reluctantly conceded, bowing his head.

"What do you mean, 'was'? You are still alive . . . therefore you remain an heir!"

"Long ago, I renounced any such claim, my lord."

"That was while Oengus was still alive. I can understand that being a soldier of Christ, you did not seek conflict, nor would resort to murder. But you are a rightful heir and a learned man – you could restore peace to your people."

"My lord, although I have such an ambition to bring peace, it is not as a warlord," he expanded.

"Consider this – you could purge the sins of your brother for the atrocities he perpetrated amongst his own people!"

He felt the king's eyes keenly scrutinise him. "If I felt I had to expiate the sins of my brother, it would not be through this way."

"Come, you were destined to rule. Answer me this: is the Z-rod not tattooed upon your back, just as it is upon mine: the sign of the true warlord?"

"How would you know that?"

"News came to me of your actions upon Inis Ork and how you revealed this sign to the people there."

"That, my lord, was for the purpose of fulfilling a prophetic expectation that the bearer of the High King's peace would come from one who had been marked to rule."

"There you have it – you are destined to rule!"

"That, my lord," interjected Maelchon, "is the earthly view of things. I was the presiding druid at Taran's initiation, and now, with the benefit of hindsight, I see that the sign was conferred upon him, not as one who was to become the warlord, but as the bearer of heavenly blessing and power. What has passed upon Inis Ork, testifies to such a view."

Drostan was struck by the irony concerning his destiny which had changed over the years. He recalled being "wooed" by Domech, until he could not help himself from declaring that he was the rightful heir. How badly he had wanted to be the warlord back then; but now, he wanted none of it! Added to these strange developments was the still unaccustomed support of Maelchon.

"You are unusual! Many a man would rejoice to become the warlord and be given it by one who has the power to confer it upon him."

"Tell me, who is ruling over the Ce?" Drostan asked, eager to move on from being the focus.

"Gartnait. He is appointed the task of restoring law and order so that the Ce may recover."

"Gartnait, son of Lutrin?"

"That same one. Do you know him?"

"I do. We sometimes trained together on military exercises. Gartnait is a good man. However, he is not descended from Mongfind."

"He is not," agreed the king, "but he is appointed as guardian until such time a true heir can be appointed. There is possibly another heir, should my sister-in-law, Derile, give birth to a son. Unfortunately, the heirs are much too young, for Talorc ensured he killed all the older ones alive on the far side of the Spey, making himself the sole heir."

It seemed to Drostan that the king finally accepted the fact that he could not perform this office, but was disappointed when the king finally responded, "Maybe yet, you will reconsider!"

Chapter Twenty-One

With Great Peace

AD 567 Craig Padrig

Some days later, Colmcille arrived up Loch Rihoh.

"Drostan, your task has finally been fulfilled," the abbot greeted him. "News of what happened reached Iona, but I would be pleased to hear things from your own mouth."

Drostan gave an account, made lengthy by Colmcille's questions and comments. Eventually, the abbot moved on from what had recently taken place to the reason that had brought him to Craig Padrig. "You are to accompany me east to your own people. They are the one tribe which has not yet acknowledged the High King. Given the harrowing reports of recent events, your people need Christ's comfort."

"I am of the same opinion. It is also fitting that it follows the final direction given through Ossian's prophecy."

Colmcille eyed him thoughtfully with a lingering look that made Drostan feel uncomfortable. "And you would not go were it not for the prophecy? Would you not obey your abbot's orders?"

"Abbot! I am of the same mind. I am not objecting – merely adding that your will is in line with the prophecy and my own inclination."

"Your own inclination should not come into it," Colmcille replied dryly.

Drostan smarted from this unexpected reprimand. To have been congratulated for remaining faithful and being an instrument to all that had happened would have been Fillan's way. At that moment, he keenly missed the empathy of his former anam cara.

"There is another who would gladly join you," suggested Munait.

"Who might that be?" asked Colmcille.

"Maelchon – the former druid at Rhynie and now a most loyal brother." He hesitated and Drostan noticed that his friend licked his dry lips before continuing. "I should like to go too."

"No, you are to remain and continue in your work of building up the believers here. You are the one in whom the king confides and turns to for counsel – therefore, you are not easily replaced." The abbot cleared his throat and announced, "We will depart the day after tomorrow. But first, let us seek King Brude's protection over this venture."

With the overking's approval, and his acceptance that Drostan still rejected the lordship over the Ce, the three made ready to ride after the morning worship. A good number gathered to bid them farewell; among them, Aunt Conchen, Alpia – holding the halter to someone's horse – and Maelchon already on horseback, his face fixed eastward with a keen and hopeful look. His mother was noticeably absent, whose rejection Drostan accepted with a certain inevitability. Drostan embraced his old friend, Munait, with all the warmth of having shared a common destiny, whose paths had overlapped at times which brought each a sense of mutual accord.

Aunt Conchen was in tears. "I always had a special fondness for you," she began, wiping her cheeks. "You know, I tried to convince Talorgen of your suitability to be his successor, conscious of your noble spirit. But with the course of events favouring Oengus, I lent my support to him, to steer your cousin from his impulsive ways. But now, with the passing of time and momentous events, I can see that my hopes were not to be . . . and yet they served the purpose of a much higher calling. Taran – I am proud of you. I know the High King is with you, whose Spirit has been guiding, steeling you to be his warrior. His peace go with you as you bring that peace to our people, so sorely tried in these times."

"Thank you," Drostan said under his breath as he clasped her in an embrace that did not wish to quickly yield. He wondered whether they would meet again, given the frailty of his aunt? He turned to Alpia, whom he had consciously reserved till last. She did not look ready to say goodbye – not exhibiting the manner of one who dreads farewells – for she looked indifferent. He felt puzzled. Why would that be? An unspoken communication passed between them.

"I am coming with you!" she said finally, with quiet determination.

"Come on – it is time we departed," announced Colmcille, a tad impatiently.

"Alpia! Have you the consent of the abbot?" Drostan asked, fearing that her hopes were about to be dashed.

"No one will prevent my leaving. Our paths have been sundered apart all these years, and now it is time we journeyed in the same direction."

"What is this talk?" Colmcille questioned, more impatiently.

"I am joining your party," Alpia replied, resolutely.

"No. There will be no women among us!" he announced in that peremptory manner of one used to being obeyed.

Alpia looked at the abbot dispassionately, seemingly unmoved by his injunction. She turned to Drostan with a great calmness. "No one and nothing will stop me from walking in your footsteps!" She moved her long hair aside from her face and flicked it with an air of defiance over her shoulder. "Once, I allowed opportunity to pass through my fingers . . . but I will not allow that to happen again. My life has been led by the expectations of others; but from now on, I shall follow my own instincts. Life is too short and precarious to drift along in resignation."

"Woman, you cannot be part of our party – I will not permit it," repeated Colmcille.

"You cannot prevent one from returning to her people and to her calling," she replied with a calm defiance, but with dignity and respect in her voice.

"I do not impede you from returning to your people, but not as part of our group. Where women are present, there is distraction to man."

"Master!" Drostan interrupted, sensing that it rested with him to find some reconciliation. "Alpia is a fellow pilgrim and noble in character . . ."

Colmcille interrupted, looking him steadily in the eye. "This woman is a hinderance to you, Drostan. You have a choice to make – think carefully whom you will follow."

"I am a servant of the High King, and my allegiance is without question," he hotly declared, feeling unjustly piqued to have to make this declaration.

"Master," spoke Alpia, "I am as Drostan, choosing to follow the High King's call, to serve his purposes."

As Colmcille looked at her with mild surprise, Drostan wondered whether their leader was about to acquiesce and concede to her wish. Colmcille mounted his horse and, once seated in his saddle, turned again to Alpia. "It is well that you are a pilgrim and choose to return to your people. You have my blessing – but not as part of our group." He looked to either side of him, and raising his chin in the air, announced, "Come, make haste – too long we have tarried."

How he resented the abbot's authority. Yet, at that moment, he recognised from deep within, that he ought to defer, knowing that his own selfish inclinations could stand in the way of the purposes of the High King. He cast a look of resignation towards Alpia, loathing himself for not acting more gallantly towards her noble aim. All was in turmoil in his heart, and he felt sickened by this death to self. Would she not hate him for this? He found it difficult to look her again in the eye, but when he finally did, there was no reproach there. Instead, there seemed to be understanding, but it struck him that she did not look like she was about to defer to the abbot's authority, confirmed when she rose into her saddle. Aunt Conchen tried to help Rowena up on to the horse but, lacking the strength, Munait came to assist – an intervention that surprised Drostan, but pleased him greatly, for the action expressed the solidarity of a friend. Alpia's youngest boy took his mother's hand and rose with alacrity behind her.

"Is Drustan free to leave?" Drostan found himself asking, in need of something to say.

"Why, yes," she smiled. "Now that Oengus is no more, he is no longer held as a hostage."

"And what about the oldest boy?"

"Caltram?" Her face clouded momentarily. "His destiny lies here among the Fortriu – he has been groomed to be a warrior in the king's court. Last night he told me he belongs here."

Colmcille moved off with Maelchon. and Drostan knew the moment had come to bid farewell. "Alpia, I had no idea that it was your wish to join us!" He felt his heart racing, and overcoming his hesitation, he added, "It seemed that longings lying dormant were about to be fulfilled."

"They shall yet be," she returned calmly.

"I must leave, although it is with great travail, believe me!"

"Go on your way as you must . . . and go in peace!"

How could she be so calm? Was Alpia not an enigma to him – this expression of affection and commitment followed by that detachment! He recalled those heady feelings all those years back at Beltane when they leapt together through the flames, pledging some youthful fidelity to one another, and then of visiting her the following day when she was in denial of what had passed. He mastered his feelings and bowed towards her, turned his horse, then followed his abbot, both despising the subservience, and yet trusting in the High King to work things out. Why his master's obstinate resistance? I have had to renounce my own natural will, time and again. Am I never to spend time with Alpia? Are we destined to be always apart? Further heated objections surged through his head to the point he felt overwhelmed and exhausted. Eventually, reason returned as he acknowledged that the High King continually blessed him. Although I appear to lose, he observed, I actually gain. Can I not trust the King to work things out? Has the prophecy not declared that I shall go *east with great peace*? But I did not anticipate Alpia's wish to join me as a pilgrim! Could it be that she is part of my destiny? Circumstances have always put her far from reach that I have not dared dream of such a possibility.

Had he not been promised peace? Not just peace, but *great peace*? He dared not look back at the one he had loved in the beginning, but instead, kicked his horse to catch up with Colmcille and Maelchon. How the matters of the heart cloud things, he told himself, bringing himself to pray. He struggled in his prayers, but found a breakthrough when words flowed from his spirit and a strange peace oddly held him – one that he could not have deemed possible moments earlier.

Turning back in his saddle, Colmcille remarked, "That woman and her children are following us."

"That woman has a name – Alpia!" Drostan found himself interjecting in the heat of the moment.

"She has been born for greatness," spoke Maelchon, calmly. "A nobler woman would be hard to find."

Good on Maelchon, thought Drostan, the morose Maelchon, for standing up for Alpia. To think I was resistant to journeying back home with him! Drostan looked round and saw Alpia trailing them at a distance, pleased by her obstinacy, following what she believed was right. He wondered, though, where this would lead, knowing Colmcille was not a man to yield, especially to a woman.

Before sundown, they reached the Spey. Across the waters rose a raised bank capped with pine trees whose trunks shone with a ruddy hue in the rich light of the evening. Beyond, the land rose in gentle undulations. Home at last, thought Drostan, as he watched the ferryman cross the river to meet his passengers.

"I will take the horses across the river," Drostan said, removing his plaid and giving it to Maelchon. He mounted his horse and led the other two mares into the waters. Hesitating, the horses needed to be encouraged to launch out on to the flood bearing the thaw from the Minamoyn Goch. As the strong current swept them downstream, the horses objected, wilful to turn back to the Fortriu shore.

With difficulty, he managed them across to the far side, back to his homeland after years of absence. He looked back to Alpia, pausing on the far bank.

"You are not to return to help her," ordered Colmcille, coldly.

He expected as much; but again, he felt torn, desiring to assist her and her children.

"The flood will test her resolve as a pilgrim," Colmcille stated further, with some interest.

"But she has bairns with her, and the river is in spate!" Drostan protested, but knowing that his words would fall on deaf ears.

Drostan watched Alpia kick the flanks of her horse as they entered the water. She gathered up her cloak, wrapping it around her shoulders to keep it clear of the water. He watched her with mounting admiration as she surged forward into the deeper waters, undeterred by the swiftness that began to lead them downstream. He could see Rowena lean further forward, gripping the horse's mane, whilst Drustan placed an arm around his mother's waist. She rides like a true warrior of the Ce, he thought, like the spirited girl she used to be when she kicked me hard for pulling her hair when we were once bairns. However, he was concerned for them, for his own crossing had been difficult – the horse he had been lent, proving jittery when swept along in the current, had taken mastery to control. Moreover, Alpia had young children to bear in mind and, with nothing else to do, he prayed for their safe deliverance.

"Do not fear for them," spoke Colmcille, as though reading his thoughts; "they will arrive on this side."

His abbot's gift of foresight was both a comfort and an annoyance. As a result of this gift, Colmcille could be detached, not empathising with the struggles of those who were uncertain about the outcome of events.

With admiration, Drostan watched Alpia control her horse through the worst of the flood and come into the slacker waters of their side. As the horse emerged onto the bank downstream to where they had been waiting, Drostan watched its flanks shed its water and noticed how Rowena shook the water from her legs. Unfurling her cloak, Alpia wrapped it about her girl with enough length remaining as to secure it in her own waistband. How noble she looked; how adept at handling a horse in such challenging conditions. What resolve she shows, and he admired her.

"Let us go," Colmcille announced. "It is good how she masters a horse, but I wonder, though, how she can master herself?"

"Alpia is very rare among womankind," defended Maelchon. "She can show up many a man!"

Ignoring the comment, Colmcille asked Maelchon, "As this is your country, tell me where can we lodge this night?"

"I know folk here at the ferry who will welcome us . . . if they have been spared Talorc's scourge."

"Then lead us – but I would have you both know that Alpia and her bairns shall have no quarter with us."

True to Maelchon's word, they received a warm welcome and were the subject of much curiosity as to the purpose of their passing into the lands that outsiders had avoided these past months. Drostan wondered whether Alpia had found lodgings for the night, again silently riling against his abbot's stubbornness at putting her to the test. In his spirit, though, he felt at peace concerning the welfare of the noble lady with her children.

Next morning, they set out on the trail as the sun rose above the pine forest. Drostan glanced back to see whether Alpia was following, but could not see her. Several times, he looked back wondering whether she would lose their trail, since she did not know exactly where they were heading. After many backward glances, he grew despondent. Perhaps she has overslept, he thought, or had been delayed in some way. Knowing there were crossroads ahead, he considered how she would know which way to take if she were not following?

On approaching the trail intersection, he was delighted to see Alpia already there. She greeted them with a slight rise of her chin, but otherwise ignored their presence, as though they were strangers. Drostan greeted her with a broad grin and a nod of the head, to which she returned a slight smile in her customary, economic manner. They rode on and it became apparent that they were heading towards Rhynie. By noontime, the Pap of the Bulàch came into view and Drostan noted how the trail was unusually quiet. On reaching Rhynie, its devastation appalled him. Only a few huts had been rebuilt since the wasting and an air of abandonment hung over the community, as though still mourning its own demise and the many who had fallen in defending the community. All those he held dear had either fallen, or were in exile, and all that remained was a broken place, a mutilated community. A charred shield lay on the ground nearby, one that was larger than what a warrior would bear; and he stared at it, bewildered by its fierce portrayal of a boar.

"You will be wondering what this is." Maelchon spoke, strangely attuned to his thoughts. "This was one of several shields that Oengus had ordered to be erected on the raised ramparts of the new Rhynie. It does not look anything now . . . but it had been a symbol of hope of the resurgent Ce."

"I have indeed missed much!" Drostan observed, sensing the pride and the suffering that this charred remain represented.

"It would have been better that these things had not come to pass," observed Maelchon, mournfully. "But then, had it not been for this destruction, I and others might still have been following the Bulàch!"

"The High King moves in mysterious ways," observed Colmcille. "Out of the ashes rises new growth, stronger than before."

"Come down the brae," invited Maelchon. "My old home was across the stream and had been spared the wasting."

They descended into the shade of the valley bottom and found the hut still standing, now occupied by Nola and her family. They passed the time of day asking after mutual acquaintances and, having their enquiries satisfied, they prepared to move on.

"Have you seen Caltram?" enquired Nola.

"Why do you ask?" asked Maelchon.

"I continue to be amazed how one so small could ever have survived! Never have I delivered one so wretchedly small and see him survive. It makes me wonder what the gods have purposed for him."

"You should ask Alpia. She is not far off and will tell you how the young man fares in King Brude's court," added Drostan.

The midwife looked at him curiously, no doubt wondering, Drostan considered, why Alpia was not riding with them.

"Where is Gest?" enquired Maelchon. "Is he still staying in his hut over there?"

"Have you not heard? Gest left here, not that long after your own departure. He now stays with Maevis, at the community of the priestesses of the Bulàch."

"Does he perform the services of a druid?"

"We do not see him! What is Rhynie now, compared to what we formerly were? Why should anyone bother to come here?" She shook her head in dismay at what a bywater this once thriving community had become.

"Colmcille – I should very much wish to see my former assistant, not for the sake of times past, but because . . . I believe, we are being summoned there."

"We are emissaries of hope to those who have lost faith in the old ways," Colmcille said, with a significance which Drostan recognised as his trademark. "We should start with those we know. We need others to join us in announcing the coming kingdom of the Lord Christ. How far is it to ride there?"

"If we leave now, we shall reach there by sundown," replied Maelchon.

"Then let us make straight there without delay."

Drostan recalled Gest as the young man freshly arrived from his abode by the sea – a wonder worker of tattoos, full of lively banter. He had been such a contrast to the master druid, and Drostan wondered how events might have shaped him. As they left Nola's home, he caught sight of Alpia riding down the brae towards them, glad that she was shadowing them successfully, seemingly keen not to become too close so as to raise the hackles of the abbot. Colmcille had ceased to remark about her presence.

They reached the community of the priestesses of the Bulàch before sunset and came to Maevis's hut.

"Will you permit your former druid to bide here this night with two companions?" he asked before the door was opened. They waited for a response. The door was moved ajar by Gest looking somewhat dishevelled. This surprised Drostan for he remembered how this young man took care of his appearance. There was a momentary blankness in Gest's look before recognition sank in. Gest was hospitable but expressed no delight at receiving them.

"This is the bearer of the Z-rod!" a woman's voice exclaimed suddenly and peculiarly from the shadows. "I have seen you once before, residing in the forests with an elderly couple."

"How can that be? No one came that way!"

As Maevis did not respond, Gest illuminated. "She saw you on a spirit flight."

With his eyes adjusting to the dim interior, Drostan began to make out Maevis's form huddled in the corner with her knees drawn up under her chin and her hands clasping her shins in an anxious manner.

Maelchon introduced Colmcille, and Drostan noticed that the presence of a Gael made Gest uneasy.

"What has become of you?" Gest asked of Maelchon. "You left Rhynie broken and disillusioned. But now, it seems that you have become spiritual once more!" Gest's tone communicated his mistrust, and with the older man not responding immediately, it led him to demand, "Why?"

"It is due to Taran here. Do you mind how confounded we were that the Z-rod was tattooed upon his back? That symbol led to our defeat and humiliation. Well, it was not the Bulàch who spoke to me up at the stone circle, but the true Creator. He is the One, druids say, had dimly passed into the distance, but in truth has been overshadowed by the gods of our own making." He went on to reveal Taran's quest finding its ultimate fulfilment upon Inis Ork, speaking of Christ who restored sight and liberated them from their fears.

Maevis started to shake in the corner, occasionally squealing pitifully, though at times emitting a disturbing growling noise.

"No more of this talk if you want shelter here this night!" warned Gest, so uncharacteristic of the man Drostan once knew.

"She is possessed," remarked Colmcille, a comment that was not understood since it was spoken in the Gaelic. "See how she started to quake when we spoke of the Lord. Malevolent spirits cannot abide his name." Colmcille changed his tone to that used by one offering a solution to a problem. "Tell our host that she can be freed."

Drostan translated.

"She would not thank you for robbing her of her powers – and for what? In exchange for a foreign way?" Gest's tone was so hostile that they dropped the subject. "I do not want further talk about religion – I am finished with all of that! What Maevis possesses, though, is undeniably real and insightful."

"Do you not mean what possesses her?" Drostan corrected. "It is clear that she is a slave to this power, so surrendered that she has lost her own will and freedom!"

"I will have no further talk!" Gest replied sharply. After an uncomfortable silence, Gest went on to observe, in a slightly mistrustful tone, "It is strange how the fugitive prince should return upon the demise of the Lord Oengus!"

Maelchon changed the subject, and before long they stretched themselves out wearily on the floor. Gest rummaged around, putting in a few leftover vegetables to a broth pot before adding much water to cater for the increased number of mouths. With the atmosphere decidedly subdued, the pilgrims prayed before sleeping that night. Drostan observed how their prayers, which were said apart from their hosts, distressed Maevis. She became unusually agitated, shifting her position deeper into the shadows furthest away from the guttering flame in the centre of the hut.

"Maevis ought to be delivered!" observed Colmcille. "I fear that many demons have made their home within her."

"Ought we not to pray for her?" Maelchon asked.

"The Spirit tells me that now is not the occasion. Leave it for the morning, and meanwhile let us take our rest and be thankful that we have shelter, even though the welcome is cool."

As the dawn splintered through every crack and crevice of their hut, Drostan noted that Maevis was the first to rise. She looked so distraught that she was incapable of controlling her limbs that involuntarily made sudden movements. she muttered in a deep and gravelly voice that unsettled them as she questioned herself where the waterskins had been placed. When she found one, she went quickly to the door, anxious to exit.

Drostan was not the only one to have noticed her perturbed manner, for Colmcille shook his head, provoking Gest to exclaim with agitation, "It would be best if you leave immediately after breakfast."

The pilgrims talked about where they would travel next and agreed to continue east, out of the hill country to the good lands. "I have some friends that way," Maelchon announced brightly, "at a place called Deer. I feel a sense of conviction that we should go that way – a place where I believe we would be received warmly."

Drostan idly went over to the threshold, looking to the sky to gauge what the weather might bring that day. Grey clouds scudded across the sky in an unsettled manner, although the sun was shining, and he predicted heavy showers would soon fall. Aware that Maevis had now been gone quite a while for someone drawing water, his eyes scanned the stream's course in the centre of this small community and saw her chatting to Alpia. He decided to wander nearby, hoping to catch something of their conversation, and, walking along the line of a stone wall, made himself small behind it, nearest to where they spoke. As he peered through a crack, he could see Maevis looking animated, but without the fear and timidity of the previous night.

"...the goose comes like one who has migrated from her old land!" he heard Maevis remark.

"I bear the goose, it is true," replied Alpia. "Do you recall that was how you addressed me at Lughnasa some years back and I received it as a sign to wed Oengus?"

"But this goose before me now is different from the one I met back then. This goose celebrates being wild and free. She has great ability to guide, and has power in her wings to go wherever she chooses; beyond mountains and even over great seas. Such power I have not encountered before." Maevis looked timid again, reluctant to speak further, and yet she remained, even though her waterskin was full.

Alpia looked at her significantly, and Drostan watched her reach out her hand and place it upon Maevis's shoulder. "The goose is our symbol of the Spirit of the Creator God, able to range far and free."

He noticed that Maevis was beginning to tremble again.

"This goose is mindful of others," continued Alpia, "calling them to join the flock. He is also powerful, capable to protect the weaker ones in the flock."

"I am afraid to yield to the goose. I feel a great revulsion within, and yet, at the same time, I want to be embraced by you."

"I understand," Alpia replied simply, and without further ado, she prayed. "Lord, release Maevis entrapped by those who cannot withstand the radiance of your Son."

Maevis's body briefly contorted, and even from where he was concealed, Drostan could hear a sudden exhalation of breath. He saw her taut body relax, and noticed that she looked exhausted, standing there motionless, as though she might collapse.

"I am free," Maevis finally uttered. She wiped her face repeatedly, like one would do when removing a cobweb. She smiled, and looking about her, seemed to stare in wonder at her surroundings. Eventually, she spoke with a normal voice, "I choose to fly with the geese!"

Alpia embraced her in her arms and the two women shook with emotion.

"Come," Maevis invited Alpia, "come to my hut and grace us with your lovely presence."

Alpia looked uncertain. Was it on account of Colmcille's injunction? he wondered. He emerged from behind the wall and approached them. "Join us," he said simply and with great calmness. "I sense that what has taken place will make all the difference."

As they entered the hut, Drostan observed how the holy man immediately recognised Maevis's changed state. As Alpia stepped across the threshold, Colmcille seemed not to mind and even had a faint smile of approval.

Gest looked up, also aware of Maevis's transformation, and his own sullen countenance looked quizzical.

Colmcille held Alpia keenly in his gaze, and remarked, "You have shown your true motivation. I had to first observe to make sure you were coming as a true pilgrim, and not because you wanted to follow Drostan."

"I am a true pilgrim!" she said with a slight haughtiness. "However, your rebuff made me journey closer with my

Lord. From the crossing of the swollen Spey, to arriving here, I have been much in prayer, and I do believe I have been led by the goose. I have known Maevis for some years, noting how disturbed she has been in spirit, and I rejoice that the High King should free her so simply, and even through my prayer!"

"We felt restrained last night from praying to free her" replied Colmcille. "It is clear now why this was so. From now on, you are to join us as a fellow pilgrim."

"Alpia," Maelchon beckoned her attention with a look that Drostan noted came near to being tender. "I sense that there will be a new home for us at Deer – a sanctuary to tend to the ailments of many and bring healing to the Ce."

"I have a presentiment that Deer will be a place of *great peace*," uttered Drostan, perceiving in his spirit the dawning of a new era, enticing with all its possibilities. He longed for a settled existence, to prepare and to sow, to remain to see growth and fruit, and witness all the seasonal changes that excite and challenge. He longed to be part of a community, to see outcomes emerge from unpromising beginnings. But would Alpia be there working at his side? That seemed something beyond his wildest imaginings.

Colmcille leaned towards him. "Ask our hosts whether they will travel with us to Deer?"

After Drostan had translated, Gest looked slightly perturbed. "I do not know!"

"Why not?" Drostan kindly challenged.

"Why should you want us? Did you not know that I actively worked with Oengus, doing what I could to ensure you would not return to the Ce?"

"That is past. Besides, you were merely discharging the duties of your position."

"I still do not feel comfortable to embrace a religion that I have been opposed to, especially after rejecting all religious observance."

"But what you have seen happen to Maevis – surely that changes everything? What further proof do you need to acknowledge the Creator – the One who liberates?"

Gest shrugged his shoulders and finally commented, "It might take time to accept all of this – it has happened abruptly. Besides, I never envisaged working alongside Maelchon again."

"And is that such a bad thing? Once, you worked well together. You can see that Maelchon is changed. His vast store of wisdom has been imbued with new meaning, along with new revelations previously hidden from sight."

"It is true that Maelchon is a vast depository of wisdom," Gest ruminated with a hint of readiness to reconsider the invitation; "but it seemed that it was to no avail when Rhynie fell."

"You do both know that I am here before you?" exclaimed Maelchon. "Am I that much changed? Is it so obvious?"

"Yes!" chorused Drostan and Gest together.

"I feel a great change, from the time of grovelling about in the twilight, compared to now when I am walking in broad daylight."

Drostan expanded, wanting to pay his former druid a compliment, but continued addressing himself to Gest. "Maelchon is like a man who, wandering among the foothills for years, finds a previously hidden way, and is led up a great glen into the heart of mighty peaks rising before him in all their magnificence. These peaks he had glimpsed tantalisingly from afar during his wanderings, their snow-capped tops merging with the clouds, making it hard to distinguish between what were sublime heights from what was insubstantial vapour. Now, he is enthralled by the pristine brilliance of those summits rising towards the dark blue of the heavens."

"I can see such a change in him," Gest conceded with a perceptible smile. "Often, he used to be lost in his own world of meditation. Now, he appears communicative . . . and not just when discharging his duties!"

"Will you not join us then – both you and Maevis?"

"Well, I do not know . . . "

"What holds you back?" asked Maelchon.

Gest looked physically uncomfortable. Finally, he repeated emphatically, "I have been so opposed to any further religion."

"This is not a religion," replied Drostan. "It is not the following of a set of rules, nor the observance of rites and repetition of prayers. Although it does contain those elements, it is much more a response to an invitation to walk with the Presence in *the way*."

"I am surprised that you bear me no malice!" remarked Gest, scratching his head.

Drostan found himself replying with just a smile rising with great warmth from within.

"Gest," Maelchon spoke with a ponderous note in his voice, "join us and see. You can always return here if you find *the way* is not for you – although I would be surprised if you decided to turn back." The older man scratched his beard, striving for something more to say that would convince him. "You know how together we meticulously observed all the old rites, and made our supplications to the Bulàch. It was to no avail and that broke us both. The goddess ignored our pleas, because if real, she was no more than a counterfeit; one from the dark side, intent on obscuring the true Creator. The realisation of our ineffectual commitment to her caused me to turn away, just as the whole futility has undone your life."

"You understand me well," agreed Gest.

Drostan observed that the young man was responding with warmth.

"And yet," Maelchon elaborated, "there are the gifts of the Creator that have been clear all along, which we celebrated with our festivals. We continue to recognise that he is the Giver of all good things: the growing warmth that manifests itself in spring; the fertility of soil and cattle; the fruitfulness that he yields – all these blessings the Creator gifts. Losing sight of these truths, our ancestors subsequently attributed such manifestations to the Bulàch. In Christ, we have lost our fear. There is no uncertainty of his affections as there was with the Bulàch. We do not need to placate him, only to follow."

"Gest, my dear, what have we to lose?" Maevis enjoined. "Consider what we might gain!"

"You, too?" Gest spoke as one being persuaded amidst his ongoing doubt.

"I have lost my spirit guides," Maevis expanded. "Their presence, which would at times suffocate me, are no more. I no longer feel their presence lurking within and I can breathe freely. And yet, because I have been so used to their presence – the insights they gave and the spirit flights they enabled – I fear what life will become without them!" For a moment, Drostan noted that she looked forlorn. She shook her head and proceeded, "I should like to join Alpia and her people to understand what could lie ahead along *the way*."

"If that is so, then I shall accompany you. I cannot envisage life without you!"

The pilgrim group received a warm welcome at Deer, where Maelchon was held in such high esteem that they found an openness among the people. Moreover, they were intrigued by the change that had come over their former druid.

After two days, Colmcille drew Drostan aside. "The Spirit affirms this is the place to establish a muintir for the Ce and you shall be its abbot. The High King has provided you companions to help establish this place. Even Gest and Maevis shall remain here and shall become your helpmates. As for Alpia, she has proven herself and has challenged me." He paused and Drostan observed that the holy man's eyes were smiling with particular benevolence. "She is an exceptional woman, one chosen by the High King, for did we not all feel constrained not to deliver Maevis from her demons? That liberating task was reserved for Alpia, revealing that she is attested by the Spirit, and a sign for me to acknowledge. This deliverance will yet fully persuade Gest."

Colmcille paused and gently scratched the edge of his ear, before continuing, "I have not been in favour of women being part of our muintir on Iona, and I think it is right for that to remain so for our community there. But here, Alpia will be useful in creating a muintir of both men and women, along with their children, and I believe it is right for you to follow that practice here."

Drostan received this news with gladness, unable to contain his smile.

"As for me," the abbot continued in a concluding manner, "I shall return to my calling of preparing others to reveal *the way,* and in establishing new muintirs, like Munait has done at Craig Padrig. My mission has been accomplished and I rejoice that the Ce now has a light to be drawn towards in their great darkness."

Colmcille departed that day, accompanied by a fellow from Deer to guide him back to Craig Padrig.

"How kind of the High King to eventually lead our ways along the same path," Alpia remarked to Drostan that evening.

"It seems beyond my wildest dreams."

"There was a time when I hoped for your return."

Drostan noticed that her eyes appeared larger than usual.

She confessed with uncharacteristic feeling, "Eventually, I lost hope, and had to find my life's direction without you."

"And my destiny led me further and further from Rhynie. I lost hope of ever seeing you again. And then when we did meet, you were already married, and to my rival, too, who once again tried to kill me!"

"That was not an easy encounter," she reflected with sadness clouding her eyes. "You were so changed too – it was not just me who was unavailable; you were committed to a way that I did not understand, one that appeared so foreign."

"Such is the natural apprehension of *the way*!"

"I felt so lost and hopeless at that time. I had only my children to live for and they were held hostage – I felt utterly powerless!"

"All of that is past!" He reached out and held her hand. "We have a new start. You are now without husband and I, as always, am without wife. This is our opportunity, not only to work together in this place, but to be man and wife together."

"You are asking for my hand?"

"I am!"

"Where is the poet that I admired on that Beltane evening?" she coaxed, with a smiling reprimand.

"That poet was shunned!" he reminded with a mischievous smile. "The excitement is there, coursing through my veins, giving me a hope that has eluded for so long. I only lack the words because I could not imagine this would ever be possible! But now that the reality of us being together is becoming apparent, I own those same feelings of extreme joy that had me take your hand back then to leap together through the Beltane flames. Now that your hand is once again within mine, I ask whether your hand will truly remain holding mine always, without doubts, when tomorrow may dawn all overcast, and the sun is blotted out?"

"Not only my hand shall remain, but all of me. Do not fear, Taran – only you have ever captivated my heart, for I never gave it to Oengus. I only yielded to him to play my part."

"We have both journeyed ways fraught with extreme difficulties," he reflected. "It seems we have both had to put aside personal preferences to achieve a particular end."

"I was thinking the same."

"And there will undoubtedly be fresh challenges here at Deer."

"But we have one another to face these together."

"And the High King!"

"The High King too . . . and those with us from Rhynie."

"And your children – Drustan and Rowena – whom I embrace together with you."

He noted that Alpia paused, and he wondered what she would say. "I have observed these past days that they give you their respect, even affection."

"You know, I do not mind them being Oengus's offspring . . ."

"They are mine too!" corrected Alpia.

"I was about to say that. I want you to know how the High King has given me acceptance of all that has passed. Without him, I do not imagine for one moment, that it would have been possible to come to terms with the brutal betrayal of a cousin and a comrade."

He fell silent for a short while, lost in difficult recollections. Then coming back to the present, and to the prospect of a new life there at Deer, together with Alpia, he spoke with great warmth. "I was thinking of Aunt Conchen, should we not send for her?"

"Yes! And what about your mother?"

He was silent for a moment. "Her too. She cannot be left unless she chooses to remain among the Fortriu."

"She may come round to reconsider everything!"

"Whether she does or not, she is my mother, my only close relative. I should like to care for her even though it be costly!"

Alpia responded warmly with a smile that exceeded her usual economy.

At that moment, Maelchon approached and when he came close, he hesitated. "I feel that I might be intruding upon a significant moment!"

"It is significant, but you are not intruding," returned Drostan.

Maelchon looked at them quizzically.

"We are to be married! Just one moment, Maelchon." Drostan leaned forward to whisper in Alpia's ear. "Shall we ask him to marry us?"

Alpia nodded enthusiastically and Drostan conveyed their request.

"You do not surprise me!" confessed Maelchon with a slight smile. "It seems you were destined for one another from a long time ago. Of course, I will marry you. Only this time," he looked significantly at Alpia, "you will be making your vows to the High King, not to the fickle Bulàch."

"Only, let us wait for Aunt Conchen to join us, and your mother if she is willing to come."

"Agreed!" Drostan responded warmly.

"And I should like Maevis to be my companion at the ceremony, for we are now like sisters."

"That being so, then I choose Gest to be my attendant so that he knows there is no animosity felt towards him. I choose to regard him as family."

"This is all quite providential, I feel," observed Maelchon.

"How do you mean?" quizzed Drostan.

"We have all encountered great losses. All our securities have been severely shaken, and now we have been given a new beginning. Who would ever have thought that we three standing here now would be pilgrims along *the way*, working together a long distance from Rhynie!"

"Far from Rhynie?" protested Drostan. "If you had journeyed where I have been, you would have a different idea of distance."

"Perhaps," Maelchon replied with a certain thoughtfulness, "I do not refer to distance as stages walked; rather that we have come far from our pagan origins, from our particular factions and allegiances. We have been forged together, against all probabilities, to become a people of hope; broken and yet remade, more resilient to the challenges, because we have One who lives and listens, who empowers."

Drostan nodded thoughtfully, reviewing his arduous journey before being led east *with great peace*.

"That is our experience, is it not?" agreed Alpia.

The End

Glossary

Place Names

With many of the original Brittonic/Pictish place names forgotten, educated guesses have been made using the Brittonic (Old Welsh) equivalent of current Gaelic and Norse names in areas beyond the influence of Dal Riata in the mid-6th century. Although little is currently known about Pictish language, it did have its linguistic variations from the rest of ancient Britain, and these differences, when known, have been used. The pronunciation has been phonetically transliterated (at the expense of correct spellings that are complicated to pronounce for non-Welsh speakers) to help with the flow and enjoyment of the drama.

Aird nam Murchan – Ardnamurchan, the lengthy peninsula jutting out westwards, forming the natural divide and marking the boundary in the era of this story between Pict and Gael.

Alt Clud – Brittonic for "rock on the Clyde" which is how the inhabitants of the rock referred to Din Brython, modern-day Dumbarton.

Y Broch – major seat of power of the Fortriu warlords; modern-day Burghead.

Candida Casa – monastery, founded by Ninian, in modern-day Whithorn, Galloway.

Cartray – "the town of the fort" in recognition of the Roman garrison at modern-day Callander that lay in ruins at the time of our story. Callander is an anglicisation derived from Gaelic, Calasraid, with different possible meanings.

Craig Padrig – Craig Phadrig in Gaelic, stronghold of the Fortriu at the top of the Great Glen, standing above modern-day Inverness.

Dal Riata – Scots Kingdom in modern-day Argyll.

Dindurn – hillfort of the Fotla Picts, near St Fillans, Perthshire.

Dinottar – Dunottar fort, a Pictish stronghold upon the cliffs near modern-day Stonehaven.

Dunadd – hillfort capital of Dal Riata, near modern-day Kilmartin.

Erin – (Ireland) divided into sub kingdoms, e.g. Munster, Connacht, Leinster, etc.

Inis Gemaich – Brittonic for "twin island" is the Isle of Canna, connected at low tide with its neighbouring Isle of Sanday.

Inis Kayru – modern-day Raasay, a name derived from the Norse, meaning "roe deer island". Kayru is phonetically spelt from Welsh, a generic word for deer.

Inis Niwl – Brittonic rendering of "isle of mist", referring to the Isle of Skye. It is unknown what Skye was called pre-dating the Gaelicisation of the Northern Hebrides. At the time our drama is set, the influence of the Gaels did not extend north of Ardnamurchan.

Inis Ork – modern-day Orkney. "Ork" possibly deriving from the name of a Pictish tribe.

Inis Y Copa Peer – Isle of Eigg, one of the Small Isles.

Loch Abar – considered by some to be a Pictish name meaning "Loch at the mouth of the river". Modern day it is known by its Gaelic name, Loch Linnhe.

Loch Gunalon – Loch Earn, derived from the Gaelic: Eireann, simplified as "Erin" (Ireland), associating this watery route with the passage of the Irish monks.

Loch Lumon – Loch Lomond.

Meini Heyon y Pentir – meaning "the standing stones of the promontory", modern-day Callanish on the Isle of Lewis.

Migdele – modern-day Meigle, Angus.

Minamoyn Goch – the Cairngorm Mountains are known in Gaelic as Am Monadh Ruadh, "the red hills". "Minamoyn Goch" is a Brittonic rendering of "the red hills".

Mounth – Grampian Mountains, dividing northern and southern Picts.

Muile – Gaelic for modern-day Isle of Mull.

Munnir Esprid – literally, "Spirit Mountain" – modern-day, Schiehallion – a pointed peak in Perthshire.

Pap of the Bulàch – the hill above Rhynie now known as "Tap O' Noth".

Pictish Tribes (7): Fortriu, Fotla, Fib, Fidach, Cait, Ce, Circinn (see map).

Rhynie – seat of the Ce warlords.

Rihoh – translates as "roaring", perhaps the original meaning of the River Ness. "Ness" is also a Norse word, denoting a headland. Loch Ness is perhaps named after its river that flows out from it.

Rùm – Isle of Rum, one of the Small Isles.

Tír na nÓg – the isles of paradise for the Celts.

Twmpath Dôl – meaning "meadow mound", the likely meaning of Maeshowe, chambered cairn on Orkney.

Western Sea – the Atlantic.

Y Kilmor Mawr – the great strait, modern-day "The Minch".

Definition of other words

Anam Cara – soul mate, denoting a mentor.

Angle – Saxon – Jute – Germanic tribes who established themselves in current-day England.

Bairns – children.

Beli Mawr – Celtic sun god.

Beltane – early summer pagan festival.

Brae – a slope.

Brigantia – the transformation of the Bulàch (mother-earth goddess) from the old hag into the young maiden at springtime.

Briton – the indigenous Celtic peoples of Britain before the arrivals of Angles, Saxons and Jutes.

Bulàch – probably Brittonic/Pictish for "old hag" or "witch", the mother-earth goddess known by the Gaels as the Cailleach, and in 20th-century Scotland as "Beira". The Bulàch transforms herself into the youthful goddess "Brigantia" come spring, when the Bulàch drinks from the well of eternal youth.

Caim – a prayerfully marked-out clockwise circle about something by means of pacing, or indicating with an outstretched right arm, to incite heaven's protection.

Carnyx – a lengthy battle horn whose moveable jaw and wooden tongue gave it a range of tones from a deep drone to a high shrill note, textured by a rasping, growling or rattling drone.

Coracle – a light craft for one person made of stitched and pitched animal hides stretched over a wooden frame.

Currach – a leather craft, larger than the coracle, powered by rowers and a sail.

Din – dun, an Iron Age hillfort.

Gael – refers to a speaker of Gaelic, the language of the Irish and of Dal Riata.

Litha – the summer solstice festival.

Lughnasa – the early harvest festival celebrated on 2nd August, following the reaping of the hay and in anticipation of the growing grain that was maturing and would be gathered in the following month.

Muintir – Christian community – colony of heaven, also known as a monastery, a term avoided as it gives an unhelpful impression of a medieval equivalent far removed from the basic-building structure used in this early time.

Oratory – the simple chapel in the centre of the monastic community.

Pict – the indigenous peoples north of the Forth-Clyde divide.

Pictish Tribes (7): Fortriu, Fotla, Fib, Fidach, Cait, Ce, Circinn (see map).

Red Martyrdom – the ultimate sacrifice of giving one's life whilst in pursuit of following God.

Saint – an early biblical term for a Christian pilgrim, not referring to the special holy status conferred on an individual by papal decree.

Samhainn – Halloween festival.

Strath – a long, wide valley.

Torc – a neck ring adornment worn by high-status warriors.

Vallum – an earth mound about a settlement.

Vellum – parchment.

White Martyrdom – the deliberate leaving of the protection and identity of one's tribe and country to seek to know God better.

Yule – end of year pagan festival.

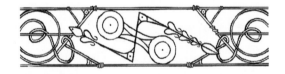